The Heart Goes On

BOOKS BY KATE HEWITT

The
Heart
Goes On

KATE HEWITT

bookouture

Published by Bookouture in 2020

An imprint of Storyfire Ltd.
Carmelite House
50 Victoria Embankment
London EC4Y 0DZ

www.bookouture.com

Originally published as *Far Horizons*

Kate Hewitt has asserted her right to be identified
as the author of this work.

ISBN: 978-1-80019-108-2
eBook ISBN: 978-1-80019-107-5

Dedicated to my dear mother, Margot Berry, who gave me a love of both history and reading. I love you, Mom!

CHAPTER ONE

Isle of Mull, 1819

The sea was calm tonight. Harriet Campbell stared across its flat gray surface and wondered how far *The Economy of Aberdeen* had travelled in one day. There wasn't much wind. Perhaps it was still close to shore, nestled among the green curves of the Inner Hebrides, waiting for the wind to pick up and take her to the New World, the New Scotland.

Only that morning, *The Economy* had set sail from Tobermory, on Harriet's home island of Mull, and it had taken her heart with it.

She sighed, and a slight breeze ruffled the ribbons of her bonnet. It wasn't as if the voyage had come as a surprise. The MacDougalls had been planning to emigrate for several years now. Harriet had known this day would come. What she hadn't known was what Allan would ask of her the day before he sailed.

"Care for one last stroll?" he'd said as he poked his head round the door of the Campbells' kitchen late yesterday morning. Harriet had been in the midst of the weekly ironing, and the kitchen was full of drying sheets, flapping like the sails of the ship Allan would be travelling on the very next day.

"Allan!" A rush of sweet sorrow swept over her at the sight of his dear face. Whenever Allan had business on Mull, he made sure to stop at Achlic Farm, and that usually meant staying for tea as well as taking a walk with Harriet. She loved the times when they simply walked together in easy companionship, needing no words between them.

Since they were tiny children, she and Allan had been close. Kindred spirits, her mother used to say, formed at the cradle. The Campbell and MacDougall families had always enjoyed a close friendship, ever since Harriet's grandmother had married Allan's great-uncle. That made them kin, no matter how distant, yet a bond far dearer than that existed between Allan and Harriet.

She couldn't really remember a time without him. One of her first memories was when she was four years old, and lost out in the rain. They'd gone to a kirk meeting up on the hillside, since the first Riddell baronet wouldn't build them a church, even though he owned nearly all the land from here to Fort William. The service had been long, and she had wandered away. It had started to drizzle and she'd felt cold and frightened until Allan had found her, huddled among the rocks at Duart Castle. How she'd managed at that age to walk all that way, Harriet had no idea, but she could still recall the relief of seeing seven-year-old Allan coming to fetch her, mixed with a childish pique that it had taken him so long. She also remembered the reassuring warmth of his hand as he'd led her back home.

Although the MacDougalls lived on the mainland, they managed to visit Mull at least once a month, and each time Allan and Harriet remained by the other's side, as if they'd been stitched together.

"I'd think it strange," Betty MacDougall, Allan's mother, had once said, "if it didn't seem so right."

And it did feel right… they'd never run out of things to talk about, even when they were silent. They'd delighted in the same books and ideas, laughed at the same private jokes, shared the same dreams.

Over the years they'd exchanged letters, full of ideas and laughter, of faint and distant hopes as yet unrealized, never making mention of what Harriet now burned to know.

Did Allan love her? Love her, not as a cousin or friend, but as a woman he wanted to spend his life with? She knew him like the back of her own hand or even her own heart, but she still didn't know the answer to that question.

"Can you free yourself from all these sheets?" he asked, lifting up his hands in wry defense from the flapping linen.

Harriet laughed, even though she could not quite rid herself of a certain wariness. She didn't know if she could face a final farewell, not when all that she'd hoped for had been left unsaid, at this late date.

"Get away with you." Eleanor, Harriet's eleven-year-old sister, smiled and shook her head. "There's nothing here that can't wait. I'll make the pastry for tonight's pie, and you can have all the time in the world." Her hazel eyes sparkled with kind mischief. "Or as much of it as you can before tomorrow's sailing."

Harriet nodded in grateful acceptance. It would be rude and foolish to refuse Allan now, and she knew she didn't really want to. She wondered if she could refuse him anything.

Besides, farewells had to be said at some point, whether at the kitchen door or somewhere more private. "Thank you, Eleanor. You're a good lass, and a help to me." Harriet patted her sister's shoulder before taking Allan's arm and walking out into the summery sunshine.

It was a perfect July morning, breezy yet with the sun still warm on her face, a few cottony clouds scudding along the horizon. The air was scented with peat and heather and sunshine, and Harriet wondered if Allan would miss it when he left. The smell of home; the only home either of them had known.

Neither of them spoke for a few minutes as they walked along the rolling hills and meadows that stretched out from the Campbells' farm in the center of Mull all the way to the eastern shore. David Campbell was one of the last small landowners in this part of Western Scotland; he owned two hundred acres and he clung to them with tenacious pride.

Allan and Harriet followed the tumbled rocks of an old dry stone wall until they reached the old ruins of Duart Castle. Over a hundred years ago the castle had been the magnificent stronghold of the clan Maclean, and then afterwards an army garrison. Now it lay abandoned, grass growing in the main hall, the roof gaping with holes and the walls crumbled to broken stones.

With a pang of dread, Harriet wondered if her own dreams were likely to follow a similar path. At this moment, with Allan having never said a word to her about his intentions, it seemed far too likely. She'd tried to reconcile herself to such knowledge over the months, but now, the stark reality of it was impossible to ignore. He was leaving tomorrow, with no declaration of his intentions. The only reason for that could be because he didn't have any.

She glanced at Allan, his expression preoccupied, a frown line etched faintly between his brows. His dark hair was ruffled by the wind, and the brown eyes Harriet knew so well were now shadowed with concern. He caught her glance and smiled ruefully, but there seemed little cause now for real joy or even the easy companionship of former days. All there was really left to say, Harriet thought with another cold pang, was farewell and Godspeed.

"Remember when I found you here?" Allan asked, interrupting her dark thoughts. "You were curled up among the rocks, looking for all the world as if you were just waiting for someone to come along."

"So I was." Harriet turned to him, smiling in memory. "It seems a long time ago, now." Allan nodded, and she ventured, "everything's ready, I suppose."

Allan nodded. "We'll spend the night at the inn in Tobermory before boarding ship. One hundred and eighty-five passengers… you've never seen so many people there."

Harriet nodded. A sailing to America was always a major event in this remote corner of Scotland. Tobermory itself was no more than a few fishing cottages huddled against a rocky shore; it had been formed only thirty years ago as a planned settlement in order to encourage the herring trade, but few farmers had the knack for fishing. They wanted land of their own to sow and reap, and too much of it already was being taken over by grazing pasture for the far more profitable sheep.

Harriet swallowed past the lump in her throat as she imagined all of the MacDougalls' worldly belongings on board that boat, and Allan and his family with them. Foolishly, it felt sudden. It wasn't as if his departure had caught her by surprise. They'd both known it would happen. Allan's father, Alexander MacDougall, had talked of nothing else since the clearances had begun.

"Land for the taking… fish fair jump into your hand. And you can be your own man there, no dancing to another's tune." Sandy MacDougall's face would harden at this point, for the only reason his family lived at Mingarry Farm was because his wife's distant kin said it could be so.

Sir James Miles Riddell, the Second Baronet of Ardnamurchan, owned forty miles of land on the western shores of Scotland and the isle of Mull. He'd appointed Alexander as one of his tacksmen, to collect his tenants' rents and hand them over, which was as unpopular a job as one could ever imagine, made even more so by Riddell's recent intent to turn farmland into grazing pasture—and tenants out of their crofts and cottages.

"No more than a jumped-up tradesman," Sandy had said on more than one occasion, for the Riddells came from merchants in Edinburgh and had only bought the baronetcy a generation ago. They spent most of their time in Berwick, although they lined their pockets with farmers' rents all year long. "Asks me to do his dirty work while he scuttles out of the way," Sandy would say with a shake of his head. So far, the Enclosure Acts hadn't affected this remote part of Scotland as badly as other parts of the Highlands, but Harriet knew it was only a matter of time. Sandy did too, which was why he'd been so eager to emigrate.

"Everyone is his own man in the New Scotland," he'd announce at nearly every family gathering. "Imagine such a thing!"

Harriet had heard these fervent proclamations for years. At one point, Sandy had tried to convince Harriet's father, David, to emigrate with them, but he wouldn't budge. "The Campbells have lived on this farm for fifty years," David said grimly. "My father bought the deed free and clear, when there was still land for the taking. And we won't be moved out by a bunch of sheep, I can tell you that."

"It might not be that simple," Sandy warned, but Harriet's father had just shaken his head. Harriet suspected her family did not have the resources to emigrate, certainly not in the style the MacDougalls anticipated. The MacDougalls had already picked out their parcel of land on the Platte River on Prince Edward Island, five hundred acres they could call their own.

Three months ago, Allan had taken her aside, on a walk much like this one except a hard frost covered the ground and the sky was pewter gray. He'd held her hands lightly in his and told her they were emigrating.

"July, I expect. Father's arranging the passage."

"And what will you do?" Harriet had struggled between an even, practical tone and giving into the terrible numbness that threatened to overwhelm her. Allan… gone. An ocean and a lifetime away.

Allan had been silent for a moment. He kicked at the stony ground with the toe of his boot. "Help Father with the farm, I suppose," he said after a moment. "Although like him, I have dreams."

"Do you?" Harriet lifted her chin, but did not dare ask what kind of dreams he had, and whether she was included in them, despite the unspoken hope that still kindled her heart.

"Ah, Harriet." He opened his mouth to speak, then closed it. Yet there was a look of longing and even hunger in his eyes that Harriet instinctively responded to. She took a step forward, their hands still clasped.

She did not have the courage then to ask him what he wanted to say. If Allan were to propose, surely now was the time, and yet when she raised her eyebrows in expectation and more than a little hope, he simply shook his head and looked away.

Harriet had slid her cold hands from his. The moment had passed, and in desolation she wondered if she would ever know if Allan thought of her as just a friend, or if, like her, he saw their friendship as something sweeter and deeper.

In the long, dark months since then, Allan had not given her one word of encouragement. Not one word of hope that she might be included one day in these far-off plans and dreams.

Even though they had continued to exchange letters and visit, their conversations always skirted the subject of the MacDougalls' departure, or any deeper feelings either of them might possess. Harriet began to wonder if she'd imagined the years of tenderness and affection between them. The easy companionship that she had always felt with Allan, that she had always depended on, began to feel strained and awkward, their conversations littered with all that remained unspoken, and that loss grieved her as much as his actual departure.

Now, knowing this would be the last time she'd see him in who knew how long—perhaps, her heart whispered, forever—she longed for at least that familiar friendship to be restored. If she couldn't be Allan's wife, then she still wished to be his friend.

"It's a grand thing you're facing," she said as they stood by the bluff, looking out to a placid, slate-colored sea. She plucked a sprig of heather and held it to her cheek. "All that adventure." She inhaled the clean scent of the heather. If she closed her eyes, she didn't have to look at Allan's face, see the uncertainty reflected there.

"Ah, Harriet." Harriet opened her eyes and Allan gave her a smile twisted with bittersweet hope and regret. "You know adventure isn't my calling, not like it is Archie's."

Harriet knew Allan's younger brother as a lovable scamp, someone who managed to get in and out of scrapes with ease, always insouciant, even in his recklessness. "Still, I imagine you'll enjoy it," she said a bit stiffly. "You've wanted to be your own man, same as your father, Allan. You'll welcome the change, I'm sure."

"Aye, I will." Allan gazed out at the sea, his eyes as dark and fathomless as its calm surface. "I hope I'll have the chance to make my way in the new world."

"So you should."

There was a moment of silence, as awkward and tense as had ever been between them. Allan forced a smile that didn't reach his eyes. "Father had been talking about emigrating for so long. I wouldn't wonder if half of Kilchoan thought we'd never leave."

"They'll believe it now," Harriet replied. "What with Mingarry Farm let out and all of you gone, there won't be a single Mac-Dougall on the mainland." Her voice was brittle, and she fought a rising sense of despair. How could they talk as if this leaving wasn't rending at least one of them in two?

She turned away, wrapping her arms around herself to ward off the chilly breeze from the sea.

"Harriet…" Allan began, but she spoke over him, afraid of the note of apology in his tone.

"I think Rupert and Margaret will get on at Achlic," she said with false brightness. "I'm sure I'll appreciate the company."

Allan's younger brother and sister were staying in Scotland, at Achlic; Rupert to finish his education and Margaret to keep him company and help Harriet. Rupert would take lessons with Harriet's brother Ian in Tobermory. "Ian and Rupert get along so well as it is—" she continued, stopping suddenly when Allan took her by the shoulders.

"It's not them I want to talk about," he said, his voice sounding rusty until he cleared his throat with unaccustomed nervousness. "It's you… and me. I've just been working up the courage to say it."

Harriet's heart fluttered so she felt almost breathless, even dizzy with both trepidation and excitement. "You've no need of courage with me, Allan MacDougall," she said, but her voice sounded strange to her own ears. She could hardly believe that Allan was only finding the courage now—now, when he was to sail with the dawn—to speak his mind, and perhaps his heart. "We've always had plain words between us." She met his gaze squarely.

"I know." Allan grasped her hands in his own. "And it's plain words I'll use. I love you, Harriet Campbell, and I always have, since the day I found you here, hiding among the rocks. It was meant to be, between us. I've always known it."

"Oh, you have?" The note of cold skepticism in her voice took them both by surprise. These words were ones she'd longed to hear, but not now. Not now, when it was surely too late.

Allan frowned. "Surely you've known it."

"If I did, it wasn't because of your many words on the subject!" Harriet retorted, and Allan smiled wryly.

"I didn't want to bind you…"

"Why not?" Her demand came out harsh, and she pulled away, her back to him. She couldn't face him, face the useless promises he was making now, when he left on the morrow.

She'd imagined this conversation so many times, had expected to feel joy, not pain. Not anger, and certainly not despair.

"Harriet…" Allan began. He sounded lost, as lost as she'd been all those years ago, curled up among the stones of Duart Castle. Her anger drained away and she closed her eyes, summoned a silent prayer for strength.

Straightening, she turned around. "What is it you want to say to me, Allan?"

He drew in a deep breath. "I know it's much to ask. I ask it anyway, for love of you and believing the love you have for me. Will you wait for me, Harriet? Wait for me to come back to this land when I've made my fortune and bring you home to the New Scotland with me?"

Harriet was silent. She struggled with the bitterness and resentment that surged up inside her at his presumption to ask such a thing of her, and so late! "You've known you were leaving for months," she finally said when she trusted her voice to be even. "Why ask me now? If you loved me…?"

"I told you, I didn't want to bind you…" Allan's gaze was steady upon her but Harriet still sensed he was not speaking the whole truth.

"Bind me?" She shook her head, her words nearly carried away on the wind that was now rising, ruffling the surface of the sea. "What are you doing now, Allan, but binding me? Binding me to an empty promise, for you're sailing on the morrow!" She felt tears sting her eyes and she blinked hard.

Anger flashed in his dark eyes. "My promises are not empty!"

Harriet was too furious, too raw with this new grief, to apologize. "If you'd asked me months ago, Allan MacDougall, we could have been married by now! I could've been sailing on *The Economy* with you, looking forward to our new life together, perhaps a bairn in my arms already!" Her heart raced at her own audacity, but now she couldn't keep back the flood of regret and confusion. "Why?" she whispered.

Allan looked away, his expression wretched. "I… couldn't. Perhaps I shouldn't even ask you now, with my prospects so uncertain."

"And leave me here, thinking you didn't care? Have you any heart at all?"

Allan drew himself up. "Aye, I do, and more honor."

"I'm not seeing that from here."

Allan turned away, raking a hand through his dark hair. His whole body seemed to quiver with tension. "Ah, Harriet, don't make me do this!"

"What am I forcing you to do?" Harriet cried. "You're the one asking for promises!"

Allan sat on a mossy rock, his fists in his hair, an expression of such ferocity on his face that Harriet nearly quelled her tide of angry questions. She'd never seen him look so frustrated, so angry. When he spoke, however, his voice was calm and even. "When I tell you that I love you, do you believe me?"

Harriet swallowed. Despite the raw grief that threatened to tear her in two, of that she was sure. "Yes."

"When I tell you I'll come back as soon as I can, do you believe me?"

She scrubbed at her now-wet cheeks with her fists. "Yes."

"Will you wait for me, then, Harriet? Can I take that promise with me? I wouldn't ask if I didn't intend to honor it with my very life, my own soul." He stood up, his expression fierce in its sincerity. He touched her cheek with his fingers, brushing away the damp tracks of her tears. "I know you don't understand, and if I could explain, I would. It's my own honor that keeps me from doing so."

"I don't understand why you cannot explain," she cried and Allan smiled sadly.

"I know."

"So," Harriet said slowly as she searched his face, "I am supposed to understand something kept you from declaring yourself to me months ago? And you cannot tell me what it was?"

"I would rather not."

She held up one hand. Her fingers trembled with the force of her own emotion. "Answer me this. If you could have asked me to marry you, would you have done so? When you first learned you were emigrating?"

Allan rubbed a hand over his face, the answer drawn from him reluctantly. "Yes."

Harriet stared at the strewn stones of Duart Castle, once a mighty fortress, now little more than mossy rock. It didn't take much to ruin lives, she thought, only time. She raised her gaze to meet his own troubled one. He looked so tired—and so worried. She was used to seeing those dark eyes glinting with humor, not shadowed with concern and sorrow. And as she looked at him, as if to memorize every line of his dear face, she realized. "You did ask," she said slowly. "Didn't you?"

Allan pressed his lips together. "Harriet—"

"Tell me," she implored. "Please, Allan. Surely it would not tarnish your honor to do so. How am I to go on not knowing? Not understanding?"

Allan managed a small, rueful smile, although his eyes were still dark with pain. "You seem to have grasped the nettle already."

Harriet nodded. The new knowledge weighed heavily inside her, like a stone in her stomach. "You asked my father," she said flatly, "and he said no."

"I'm a man of little prospects at the moment, Harriet. Crossing the sea is a dangerous voyage, and who knows what waits on the other side? I must appreciate his position."

"You're the tacksman's son! You're richer than we are!" She spun away, her temper rising to the fore once more. She'd always been too given to high emotions, and no more so than now when it looked as if everything she'd ever wanted was to be denied her—and all because of her own father and his contrary nature.

"We don't own our land," Allan said quietly, "the way your father does."

"But you will in the New Scotland. Five hundred acres—"

"It's an uncertain proposition, though. Life will be hard there. I don't even know how hard, but I've heard tales of how harsh the land is. Snow three feet deep all winter long, storms like nothing we've seen here."

She closed her eyes, her hands curled into fists at her sides, and willed her temper to recede. Anger achieved nothing now. "What did he say to you, then?"

Allan was silent for a moment. "He told me to wait till I'd established myself, had my own land. Actually…" There was a wry thread of humor in Allan's voice now as he continued. "He told me that when I was no longer hanging on my father's coattails, he might consider my suit for you."

"How dare he say such a thing!"

"He is your father, *cridhe*. You must respect him, as I did." Allan reached for her wrist, stroking the soft skin on the inside with a movement so tender it made Harriet's insides seem to dissolve and everything in her turn to yearning. "Besides, he's right in this matter, as much as it pains me to admit it. You deserve more than what I can offer you now. And in any case, you can't leave Eleanor and Ian while they're still so young, nor can you leave Achlic. Not yet. Could you? If you had to choose?"

Harriet closed her eyes. She could still feel Allan's fingers on her wrist, the gentlest and most thrilling touch she'd ever experienced. "I wasn't given the choice."

"I had to respect your father's wishes."

"He didn't want you to speak to me at all," Harriet guessed, and turned to see the flicker of acknowledgment on Allan's face. "Then why," she asked, her voice an ache, "are you now asking me to wait?"

"Because I'm weak." Allan's voice was rough with emotion. "Because I love you, and though honor bid me not speak, I couldn't bear you not knowing. I couldn't bear the thought of losing you."

He cupped her cheek in his hand, and Harriet leaned into his palm. "I don't know what brand of honor it is, that keeps men from speaking from their hearts."

"Harriet." He lifted her chin with his fingers, their lips a breath apart. "I love you. Do you love me?"

"Yes." She could say nothing else; the truth was too strong in her heart. "There was never any question of that, not all these years. Not for a moment."

Allan drew her to him, and Harriet closed her eyes, savoring the feel of his roughened cheek against hers.

"I'll come back," he said in a hoarse whisper. "I promise you. As soon as I can. If you'll wait for me—"

Harriet nodded in mute acceptance. So much could change, in both their lives. Who even knew what waited for him, on that distant shore? Or even what waited for her? Illness, misfortune, perhaps even death. There were so many terrible possibilities.

And yet...

Providence would see them through. She had to believe that, longed to cling to it. By God's grace they would, in time, be reunited. All she had to do was wait... and keep the faith. She lifted one hand to touch his cheek, the gesture one of farewell.

"Yes," she said, "I'll wait."

CHAPTER TWO

Allan returned to Tobermory with a lighter heart, although worry and sorrow still picked at him. He hated seeing Harriet look so despondent. He wanted to remember her with laughing eyes, her red hair glinting in the sunlight as she teased or talked with him. He wished he had told her his intentions earlier, even though David Campbell had asked him not to, claiming his silence on the matter was fairer to Harriet. Yet David Campbell was a hard man, and Allan didn't think he understood the strength of the bond he and Harriet had always shared.

Even so, guilt and regret added their weight to his heart's burden. Should he have said anything to Harriet at all? If her father had had his way, Allan would have sailed without a word or even whisper of his intentions. And yet surely such silence would have been far greater a grief for Harriet to bear than waiting. At least now she knew how he felt, and that his promise was his word and his honor. He would do whatever it took to make his way back to her, a man of prospects and possibility.

Allan made his way along the harbor, seagulls wheeling over the choppy gray waters, their cries lost on the wind. Tobermory's one inn was heaving with people on the eve of sailing, for over two hundred Scots would be descending into the dark hold of *The Economy* tomorrow morning. Allan was grateful his father had, with his influence as local tacksman, been able to secure two rooms at the inn for his family's comfort. Many families would be sleeping in back rooms or barns that chilly night, if not out on the heath with nothing to shelter them.

Despite the cheerful fire blazing in the hearth of one of the rooms, and the rich mutton stew that Betty had brought from home and heated over the flames, the mood was somber. They all had their own thoughts and cares, Allan knew. He wasn't the only one with a fond farewell to make.

His mother had said goodbye that morning to her sister, Ann Rankin, an aging widow who would stay at Mingarry after they'd left, at least until James Riddell appointed a new tacksman. After that Ann would have to board with Rankin relatives, either in Kilchoan or further afield. Considering their age, Allan knew it was doubtful the sisters would ever see each other again.

And what of Margaret and Rupert, staying behind? Allan glanced at his younger sister and brother, a sudden, fierce pang of sorrow assailing him. He had a special affection for sixteen-year-old Margaret, with her black eyes and hair, and her quick, sharp wit. And who could fail to love Rupert, scampish and lovable in his puppyish way?

He might never see them again. Sandy planned to bring them over in two years, when Rupert's education was complete, but Allan knew there were no certainties in this life. Two years was a long time, and only God knew whether they would even survive this first journey. His stomach clenched at the thought of all that lay ahead—and all he couldn't know.

Allan glanced at his father, sitting at the head of the table with a benevolent and satisfied look on his face. Of all the family, Alexander MacDougall was the most eager to leave. Allan could still remember when he'd first broached the topic of emigration, five years ago.

"There's space in New Scotland," he told Allan one evening after the others had gone to bed. "Space to be your own man."

"There's space here," Allan protested. "You're one of the most respected men in the county, Father, with one of the most prosperous farms."

"Bah!" Sandy shook his head in disgusted dismissal. "Respected only because of James Riddell, and the power of his fist."

James Miles Riddell was the second Baronet of Ardnamurchan; he'd come into his title when he was only a boy of ten. Now a man of some forty years, he was taking a greater interest in the profits of his rents and the lucrative possibility of grazing sheep rather than sowing crops. As tacksman Sandy was the one who had to deliver the news to the crofters who were being displaced.

"There's a debt I owe to James Riddell," Sandy said quietly, "that I mean to owe to no man. In the New World, Allan, we'll be free. Our house may not be as grand, or our farm so large, but it'll be a better place for all of us."

At nineteen years old, Allan had felt a kindred longing in his own heart. He had dreams and ambitions of his own, just like his father did. Over the years he'd become increasingly aware of the hold the Riddell family had over them. It was a prison of some luxury, but Allan had come to realize that a prison was still a prison, no matter how comfortable the cell.

From that day, he found himself dreaming about Canada, a place where he too could be his own man, make his own way, wherever that path took him.

Looking at Sandy now, Allan knew that his father would miss no one here. He was respected, but because of his position he had few true friends. For Sandy, leaving Scotland would hold few regrets. He wasn't, Allan thought with a lurch of feeling, leaving behind someone he loved.

After supper Allan and Archie went to the docks to check on their baggage, piled high in the shed and watched over by two dozy stable lads. Betty had insisted on taking all their linens and china, and her own rocking chair as well. Satisfied all their belongings were well in hand, they turned back to their lodgings. Dusk was falling softly, the breeze rolling in from the murky water cool and damp, smelling of home.

"You've got a knowing smile," Archie said with a sly, laughing glance. "Been to Achlic this morn, have you?"

"So I have," Allan confirmed, his knowing smile turning to a full-fledged grin. Just the memory of Harriet's promise eased the worry in his heart. She would be faithful; he knew that absolutely. Beginning their life together was just a matter of time. He shoved his hands in the pockets of his trousers and whistled a merry tune. "And a good visit it was, too."

Archie raised his eyebrows. "You haven't asked Harriet to marry you now, have you?"

Allan shrugged. "I could hardly ask that, what with us sailing on the morrow. You know what her father said."

"Aye, he sent you packing!"

Allan suppressed the spark of irritation Archie so often kindled in him, just because he could. "For the meantime, perhaps, but I've prospects, and David Campbell knows that. So does Harriet."

Archie stopped in the street, the cobbles slick with mist, his hands on his hips, a mocking smile curving his mouth. "Does she, indeed? I thought Campbell wanted your interest kept quiet. Said it was only fair to Harriet, not to bind her that way."

"He wants her at his bidding," Allan retorted, then turned away, struggling for a calm tone. Picking a fight with his brother would serve no one, although Archie often enjoyed their spats. "I couldn't leave without her knowing, Archie. It wouldn't be fair to her. That kind of freedom to Harriet—it would be the worst sort of prison."

"There never was a pair to hold a candle to the two of you," Archie acknowledged. He fell into step with Allan, as easy as before, his quick words forgotten. That was Archie for you, Allan knew, light one moment, darkness the next, and then back again. Allan had always been steadier, but he also held onto his anger for longer. He knew he needed to let go of it, yet his brother always managed to bring out the worst in him, to his own shame. Archie clapped him on the shoulder, giving him an easy smile. "Everyone always hoped you'd be together."

Allan gave a small smile. "There's a long road ahead of us yet. Although it will be as short as I can make it, I'll grant you that!"

Ahead of them Allan could see the inn, the sign over the door swinging and creaking in the wind. The damp mist had turned to drizzle, needling his face.

"Have you told Father about it?" Archie asked. "He's not likely to be pleased, you know."

Allan hesitated, for although he had obeyed the letter of David Campbell's law and not asked Harriet to marry him, he had surely flaunted its spirit, and, as Archie had said, his own father might not be best pleased by his seeming disobedience. The thought made him uneasy, even as he felt a bone-deep certainty that to say nothing to Harriet would truly have been cruel. Now he stopped a few yards from the inn door and turned to face Archie. "Why shouldn't Father be pleased?" he asked, keeping his own voice as light as he could. "Harriet's as fine a woman as there can be, and Father's always been fond of her. He would approve the match, I've no doubt."

Archie shrugged. "You know him. He doesn't like anything happening without his knowing about it, or even doing it himself."

"He can hardly ask Harriet for me," Allan said, deciding to make a joke of it. "And I'm a grown man, not a boy. I'll live my own life, as I see fit."

"Will you now?" Archie cocked his head, his considering gaze sweeping over Allan in a way he didn't like. "And here was I, thinking you the loyal son."

"I am loyal," Allan replied sharply. He knew Archie was playing with him, as he often did. Allan never failed to rise to the light-hearted taunts, even though he'd long known better. Even as boys Archie had got the better of him with his mischief, his well-aimed taunts, those sly, pointed thrusts.

"Father would still want you to heed Campbell," Archie continued, that familiar, taunting note entering his voice. "If he said not to speak to her, then that's what you should have done."

"I'm my own man." Allan turned to enter the inn, his hand on the old weathered door. From inside he heard the laughter and chatter of travellers around the fire, the clink of mugs of ale and the irritable shout of the innkeeper towards a kitchen maid.

"And when we get to Canada?" Archie asked. "What will happen then? Father expects us all to work together on the land. There can be no other way, not in that wild country. We'll need every hand as it is."

"I'm willing to work." Allan's hand rested on the door, but he did not turn the handle. Archie's sly words were stirring up a ferment of doubt inside him, and he did not thank his brother for it.

"Will that satisfy Harriet's father?" Archie pressed. "A son working his father's land like a hired hand, never anything more?"

"It's not like that," Allan said shortly. "And you know it. The farm will belong to all of us. When Father dies—"

"You're going to wait that long?"

"No, of course not. I won't have to. Campbell knows—"

"Aye, he knows too well how Father is. The farm won't belong to us, Allan. Not till he's cold in the grave, God rest his sorry soul. And until then you'll be just what I said, and David Campbell knows it."

Allan stared at his brother for a long, hard moment. He knew his father could be autocratic, but he was kind and fair as well. In their work together, he'd never had cause to believe his father thought so little of his own judgment. Sandy often asked his advice on farming matters, and left Allan in charge of their fields when he had to be about his tacksman's business. There was no real reason to believe it would be as grim a picture as Archie painted.

"He won't be tacksman in Canada," Archie continued. "No one to order about but his own sons, and instead of coin, the price will be blood."

Allan's gaze flickered to the lighted window upstairs, where he knew his family waited. For the first time he felt a true sliver of doubt needle his soul. His father didn't like taking orders from Riddell, but Allan suspected he did enjoy the authority and prestige that came with his position as the baronet's representative—prestige that he would not enjoy in this new land. "If you think like that," he asked his brother slowly, "what do you intend to do about it?"

"I have plans." Archie's smile was pleasant, but Allan saw a flinty determination in his brother's eyes that both surprised and chilled him.

"You can't leave the farm," he said after a moment. He could not even imagine where his brother would go; as far as he knew, there was little to recommend the New Scotland except for the endless expanse of untamed land to cultivate. "Like you said, it's a wild country. Father expects it."

"Aye, he does."

"It's the way of it," Allan continued, though he realized he was speaking as much to himself as to his brother. "We all need to help. If we acted differently…"

"What would happen?" Archie issued the challenge in a dangerously soft voice.

Allan could not imagine turning his back on his own father, the expectations of the life they'd lead in the new world, working the land together. He wanted to be his own man, yes, and till his own land, but not at the expense of his father, his family. "It would break him," he said simply. "And Mother, too."

Archie laughed shortly. "I don't think there's anything to break that old bastard."

"Archie!" Allan glanced again at the lighted window. He'd never heard Archie speak with such cold contempt; it filled him with a sudden fear. "He's our father," he said, and Archie just shrugged, his eyes dark with defiance.

"What I say is true, Allan, and the sooner you realize the kind of pleasant cage you live in, the better. Father's spoken all sorts of claptrap about being your own man, working your own land, but you should realize the only man he's talking about is himself." He let out an abrupt laugh and shook his head. "You always did believe the best in everybody, fool that you are." In one fluid movement, he moved past Allan and opened the front door, disappearing among the heaving crowd within.

Allan stared after him, his mind and heart now splintered with sharp new doubts. First Harriet's father, now his own, demanding from Allan what honor insisted he fulfill. He wondered if it could lead him anywhere but to disappointment… or worse.

"Allan, there you are," Betty said when Allan finally entered their lodging rooms. The remnants of a game of spillikins lay on the rickety wood table, with Archie sprawled next to it, his booted feet stretched out to the small coal fire. The rest of the family was assembled in the small room: Rupert and Margaret, who would return to Achlic on the morrow, and Betty and Sandy in the most comfortable chairs.

"Shall we have a song?" Betty asked with a tremulous smile. "Margaret, you've always had a lovely voice. Give us a song, then, or a poem."

"Something lively, lass," Sandy added. "With all these long faces, you'd think it was someone's funeral!"

Margaret stood and cleared her throat, her dark eyes flashing once, compassionately, to Allan as she started to recite in a sweet, clear voice. "My luve is like a red, red rose, That's newly sprung in June…"

Allan leaned back in his chair as he listened to Margaret say the familiar poem by Robbie Burns. His thoughts drifted, and he found himself imagining his return to this room, a year or two hence, with Harriet as his bride. He pictured how the candlelight would shine on her auburn hair, her eyes warm and full of love, not dark and shadowed with pain as they had been this afternoon. She would reach her arms out to him…

"Allan's miles away!" Betty said affectionately, startling him from his bittersweet reverie. "No doubt thinking of your Harriet. I know you'll miss her." She smiled sadly. "She's a good woman, though, Allan. None of us can know what the future will bring. Perhaps she'll wait for you."

Still half in thrall to his daydream, Allan smiled and said with more confidence than wisdom, "I know she'll wait for me."

Silence descended on the room like a thunder clap, startling him out of the last sweet remnants of his fantasy. Allan caught Archie's knowing smile, and a chill of foreboding rippled through him. Why had he spoken with such reckless certainty? And yet, he acknowledged, how could he keep such a sacred thing from his family? It would be dishonest, as dishonest as saying nothing to Harriet would have been. He could keep the truth from no one, and he was proud of that fact.

"How would you be knowing something like that?" Sandy finally asked in a dangerously even tone.

"I asked her myself, this afternoon," Allan admitted, his voice as even as his father's. He would not apologize for doing what he believed—what he knew—was right. "I suppose I should've told you, but it's a happy secret I've been keeping."

"Oh, Allan!" Margaret's eyes shone as she clasped her hands to her chest, and Allan was glad at least one member of his family seemed pleased by his news. He managed a smile back before his father let forth with his rage.

"A secret?" Sandy's voice rose to a boom like thunder. "A dishonorable secret, that is!"

Allan flushed. "I have no intention of acting dishonorably towards anyone," he replied, "least of all Harriet."

"Then perhaps you can tell me why you'd ask a good, honest woman like that to wait for you," Sandy retorted. "She'll be an old maid upon your return, if Providence sees that you return at all." He shook his head. "No son of mine should treat a lady such, consigning her to misery and uncertainty for years."

Allan did not want to have this conversation in full view of his entire family, but he saw no other way. "I love her," he said quietly, "and she loves me. It would have been cruel to say nothing, Father—"

"I know the love you two have had," Sandy said, his voice softening slightly. "And if things had turned out differently with Campbell…" He shook his head. "But what has been said already must be left as such. You know the agreement made, and it was your duty to honor it."

"I know what he wanted," Allan corrected stiffly, "but I had myself—and Harriet—to consider. Leaving her in ignorance would have been cruel."

Sandy shook his head. "David Campbell is her father, Allan, and as such he must be respected. Besides, think of it, lad. Would you want to see Harriet old and withered, with no child or husband of her own?"

The image chilled him and he shook his head in vehement denial. "I'll be her husband!"

"You can't be sure of that." Sandy glanced somberly at each member of his family in turn, and each felt the weight of his gaze. "None of us can be sure of anything, even whether we'll all sit like this in one room again. It is for God alone to know such things, and for us to trust."

A solemn silence descended upon the room as they all glanced round at each other's faces, as if memorizing the familiar, beloved features, knowing they might never see each other again.

"We'll talk in private." Sandy stood abruptly and left Allan to follow him downstairs to the inn's taproom, and then out into the damp, chilly night.

The wind off the sea caused both men to turn up the collars of their coats and hunch their shoulders against its chill. Although it was midsummer, it had been a cold summer and was sure to be a bad harvest, and at that moment Allan felt a bone-deep iciness within him, as he felt his dreams of the future slipping beyond his reach yet again, leaving only despondency in their wake.

"I know what you and Harriet have is a thing apart," Sandy said after a moment. "Not everyone has it; not everyone gets to have a love like that." He turned to face his son, his expression sad but still firm. "I'm sorry it has to be like this. If David Campbell had said yes to your suit, you could have been married by now, Harriet with us. I would have liked that as much as you would have."

He doubted his father had felt the same disappointment he had at Campbell's refusal. Frustration bubbled inside him and Allan sought to keep his voice level. "I know that well, but it's not to be."

"Yes," Sandy agreed, "Providence saw otherwise. And we must trust all these things to the hand of God. And it is as well for it to be so, for Harriet has her own cares and responsibilities. She does not bear a light burden."

Guilt piled on top of his frustration and Allan turned away. "I've known that also, Father."

"Then why increase it for her? Her obligation to you is as sure a fetter as any—"

"I appreciate your view," Allan interrupted as calmly as he could, "but as you said, Harriet and I have a thing apart. If I'd gone without speaking to her, without declaring my own intentions, it would have been far worse a fetter."

Sandy was silent for a moment. "Perhaps, but one of her own making, not yours. Eventually she might have forgotten you…"

"And that is a better thing?" Allan said, incredulity lacing every word. "We love each other, Father. We want to marry! Neither of us have ever looked at another, not once, I know it. And when I'm established in the new world—"

"God willing, that won't be long," Sandy agreed, his calm tone making Allan feel like an unruly schoolboy who had to be disciplined. "Perhaps you will be able to send back for her, at the same time as I send for Rupert and Margaret. If Providence wills it, we'll all be together in two years' time, which is no time at all."

"Then why all this talk of not telling her, and setting her free?" Allan demanded. "I see no dishonor in my actions, Father, I swear to you that I don't."

Sandy shook his head. "Because her father asked it of you, Allan, and you must respect a man's word. And because there are no certainties in this life. We might not see through this winter, much less two years." He put a heavy hand on his son's shoulder. "Set her free, Allan," Sandy said softly. "If you love her, if you respect her, it's the only way. You know it is, for her sake, if not your own."

Allan took a deep, shuddering breath. "I thought long and hard before asking her, Father. It wasn't a whim, I promise you. And Harriet knows what it means. She was angry with me at first, I confess."

"Then perhaps she understands it more than you do, lad. You've no idea of the sacrifice you're asking her to make."

"And am I not making one as well?" Allan demanded. Desperation edged his voice. Sandy shrugged.

"Allan, you're a man. Harriet must be nearing five and twenty already. By the time you come back—if you come back…"

"She's twenty-three years old," Allan interjected.

"Still, most women have a bairn on their hip and one in their belly by this time," Sandy stated baldly. "If you'd married already—"

"And flown in the face of her father?"

"No, of course not. I feel for you, son, I do, for it's a hard thing to bear, but many have borne the same and lived to tell the tale. And it could be all for naught, and in a few years all your hopes shall come to pass." He sighed heavily, and in that sound Allan heard the death knell of his own dreams. "The only way is ahead, Allan." Sandy smiled, although the gesture seemed more one of resigned sorrow than any happiness or joy. "We'll create a holding together that no man, least of all Campbell, can sneer at. When you return, it will be with pride and honor. Don't sacrifice one for the other."

Allan looked away. He remembered the feel of Harriet's cheek against his own, the love and truth shining in her eyes when she gave her promise. Yet he also saw, with a sobering heaviness, that he'd bound her to a half-life of waiting and wondering, with, as his father had reminded him, no certainties to it.

He let out a sound halfway to a cry and turned away from his father, unwilling to let any man see him in such a state.

"Perhaps she'll wait. The way it is between you, I can't imagine her marrying another. But to bind her to you now—"

"Would be dishonorable," Allan finished for him flatly. His vision blurred and he blinked hard.

"In a few years, I'll have one of the best farms in the New World," Sandy reminded him. "And enough money to send you back to Mull on a ship I hired myself!"

Allan managed a smile, but something in his father's tone made him think of Archie's words. *I'll have one of the best farms,* he'd said. It made Allan feel like little more than a lackey. Now, however, was not the time to grasp that particular nettle.

"Yes, Father," he said at last, the words drawn from him with both resignation and regret. "I see the way of it."

"Good lad." Sandy clapped him on the shoulder, making Allan feel like a child who'd earned a pat on the head rather than the grown man he was, deciding his future and breaking his own heart, as well as Harriet's.

"I'll write her a letter," he said. "Margaret can give it to her tomorrow."

Sandy nodded and they both turned back to the inn. In their own rooms the rest of the family had gone to bed, and Allan listened to their sleepy sighs and snores as he gazed unseeingly into the dancing shadows created by a single candle. He thought of the conversation he'd had three months ago with David Campbell, when his hopes for a swift marriage to Harriet had been dashed.

He remembered the contemptuous curl of the older man's lip, his insistence that his daughter would not marry a man without land or prospects of his own.

"We'll have a farm in the New Scotland," Allan had insisted. He'd wanted to add, 'And bigger than yours by a sight!'

David, however, only shook his head. "That's dreams, for now. Show me the deed, the harvest, and then I'll think it over."

"Harriet wants to marry me," Allan said, a bit desperately, and David lifted his chin.

"She's needed here, and she knows it."

That was the crux of the matter, he realized now. His thoughts now edged with despair, he wondered if Campbell would entertain his suit even with the proof of his prosperity in his hand. He shook his head. Who knew when that would be. It seemed like a dim, distant dream at this moment, with the shadows of doubt and regret threatening to overwhelm him. A bone- deep weariness settled over him, and he sighed and rubbed his hands over his face, longing for things to be different. For Campbell to have agreed, for Harriet to be his, for his future to be as bright and unfettered as his father's. The candle had burned down to a waxy stub before Allan finally took parchment and ink and began to write.

CHAPTER THREE

The sky was streaked with the pale, pink fingers of dawn when Allan finally stirred. Every bone and muscle ached as he gazed blearily around the room at the inn where he'd fallen asleep over his letter to Harriet, his head pillowed on his arms, the stub and splattered wax of a burned-out candle by his elbow.

He heard the creak of floorboards, and then his sister Margaret's dark head appeared around the doorway. Allan smiled at the sight of her dark eyes full of hope and a bit of mischief, even though the ache in his heart felt as if it could cripple him.

"Allan!" Margaret hurried forward at the sight of him still in his clothes from last night, no doubt looking the worse for wear now. "Have you been here all night?"

"I suppose I have." Allan glanced down at the letter he'd been writing, each word drawn from his very soul. The ink on that precious page felt like his own blood.

"You've let the candle out," Margaret scolded gently. "You could've caught fire. The whole inn could've gone up in flames!"

"But it didn't." Allan covered the letter with his hand and smiled at his sister. "Out for one of your dawn walks?"

"I…" Margaret bit her lip. Clearly she hadn't realized that anyone had known about her secret jaunts. "I just wanted some fresh air."

"You can't fool me, Margaret," Allan said. "I suspect you'll be glad to have a little freedom, with us all out of the way."

Margaret blushed, and Allan guessed he had the truth of it. Boarding with the Campbells and keeping Harriet company would provide Margaret with some female companionship she'd missed living at Mingarry Farm with all of her brothers. "I expect you'd like to listen in to Rupert's lessons as well."

"And what if I would?" Margaret challenged, her dark eyes flashing.

Allan sat back, startled. He'd been teasing, even though he knew Margaret had always had a head for books. She'd had little learning, though, besides the reading, writing, and arithmetic they'd all done as children. Allan and Archie had both been tutored at Mingarry Farm until they were fifteen and started work on the farm. As a girl, Margaret had never had such access to education. Did she hope for it now, Allan wondered, away from the stern hand of her father? He decided not to ask.

"I expect you can accomplish whatever you set your hand to," he said lightly, and Margaret gave him a quick smile of gratitude.

"I'll miss you, Allan," she said, her expression turning serious. "And I shall make sure Harriet waits for you. She would never go back on her promise, no matter what Father says. I know she wouldn't."

"I pray not." Allan gazed down at the letter it had taken him most of the night to write. "But that's not Father's point. It's not right for me to bind her to me, when my future's so uncertain. I did it out of selfish reasons, because I love her so much. What if I took ill, or even died? I can't tie Harriet in that way, not when I have so few prospects of my own." He spoke the words by rote, for although he knew they were true, he didn't feel them. He felt as if he wanted to run all the way to Achlic Farm and sweep Harriet up in his arms and never let her go. Yet he needed to obey both Harriet's father and his own. Trust and obey. Allan sighed heavily. "She must be allowed to find her own way," he told Margaret, "and choose her husband if it comes to that."

"She won't—not unless it's you!"

"I pray not," Allan said again. He folded the letter and after relighting the candle, sealed the paper with a daub of wax from its stub. "Give this to her, Margaret, please. I think I've explained it all, as best as I could. And tell her…" He paused, for there were so many things he'd wanted to say to Harriet, declarations and avowals he no longer had any right to say. "Tell her I will think of her every day, and I will pray for her safekeeping."

Margaret took the letter with reluctance. "Very well, Allan, if it's your wish."

"It is." Allan reached into his coat pocket and took out a bundle of old letters, tied with a faded green ribbon. Over the years, he and Harriet had written to each other often, the letters going in the mail packet between Tobermory and Kilchoan. Although they'd been able to see each other with some regularity, those letters contained a precious sweetness, dreams and hopes shared on ink-splattered pages that could not be so easily confided in conversation. He'd kept the letters close to him, wanting to keep them safe on the long voyage, intending to while away the long hours reading them, and needing the hope and encouragement they would provide. He would have to do without.

"Give her these." His face and heart both hardening with resolve, Allan handed the bundle to Margaret.

She took it instinctively, then glanced down at the ribbon-wrapped parcel in surprise and dismay. "Allan! Her letters to you—why? Surely you should keep those! They're all you'll have of her."

"I give her my lines to show her she's free," Allan said simply. "Tell her she may keep mine."

Margaret shook her head, her face full of sorrow. "You might be giving her freedom, Allan, but I know that to Harriet, it won't feel that way."

*

"What's this?" Harriet took the bundle of letters from Margaret with a chill of foreboding. She knew only too well what they were. She recognized her own handwriting, as well as the hair ribbon she'd given Allan when he'd asked for it, years ago. She did not want to ask why Margaret was now handing this all back to her. She did not want to know.

Margaret said nothing, merely placed her hand on top of Harriet's. They'd arrived several hours ago, and most of the time since then had been spent in organising the bedrooms and unpacking cases. Rupert had gone off with Ian, two boys intent on a summer afternoon's pleasure. Harriet had watched them go with a worried frown, for she knew in summer her father expected Ian to help in the fields. He was fourteen, and certainly old enough to do his share, but he'd never been one for working with his hands, and he sloped off as often as he could. Then Margaret had given her this precious bundle and all thoughts of her brother flew from Harriet's mind.

Harriet led Margaret into the kitchen, with its wide hearth and scrubbed pine table. Her father would've been irritated to see a guest being entertained in the kitchen, but he was out checking on some ewes. Harriet knew she need not rest on formality with Margaret. Although they'd seen each other infrequently over the years, a close friendship had sprung up between them, so she felt more like a sister than the distant cousin she was.

She sat at the table, the letters in her lap. "Why are you giving me these?"

"Allan asked me to. He meant well, Harriet, I know he does. Writing to you near tore him apart. He was up all night…" Margaret trailed off, her eyes dark with compassion. "If you want some privacy, I understand. I can look after the noonday meal, if you like, with Eleanor."

"Thank you." From somewhere Harriet found her voice, although her throat was so tight and aching she felt as if it had closed up completely. She rose from the table, the letters clasped to her chest. "I'll be in the parlor. You're a true friend, Margaret."

Margaret gave her a fleeting, sorrowful look. "He told me to tell you he'd come back. He promised, Harriet."

Harriet, her throat so tight now she couldn't speak at all, only nodded.

Once in the quiet peace of the front parlor, Harriet allowed her grief to show, and tears trembled on her lids. She blinked them back, knowing they did her little good now. She still had too many responsibilities to give in to emotion now. Yet how she missed him! The wondrous new knowledge of his love for her made his absence much harder to bear.

Already she felt it painfully, and the fear of what his letter contained made her fight an urge to fling the precious parcel away from her. Last night she'd resolved to trust him, but only hours later she felt her heart tremble once more with fear and doubt, and she despised her own weakness. Whatever Allan had written, she could still trust him. That was a choice, and one she was determined to make.

The letter still clenched in her hand, she sank onto the bench by the pianoforte, her most treasured possession. It had come with her grandmother to this house as part of her dowry. Her grandmother had taught her to play until she died when Harriet was seven, and then Harriet had continued to teach herself. She loved the comfort of creating music, the wonder of hearing new sounds ripple from her fingertips.

Yet the instrument held no appeal for her now, and it was in the still silence of a summer's afternoon that she broke the seal on Allan's letter.

Dearest Harriet,

I acted a wrong part in taking any obligation from you, and others might say a dishonorable one. My honor bids me to set you at liberty, which I hereby do in releasing you from that promise which I hold dearer than my own life.

You may have an opportunity of getting yourself settled in life more suitable to your merits than I have a prospect of, but never with a man who will adore you half as much as I do. Whatever my fate, nothing could give me greater happiness than to hear of you being well settled. Providence is kind and may have something in store for us that we are not aware of. Until we meet again, adieu.

The letter fell from Harriet's fingers. *Well settled?* Fury and fear mingled within her, lodging in a burning lump in her chest. How could it possibly be his wish now for her to be married to another? A full day had not yet passed since his declaration of undying love, yet now she wondered if it was only so many cheap words.

Where had his hope, his faith in their future, gone? His promises? Why had he set her free, when he'd spoken only yesterday of binding her to him! Yesterday he'd wanted her to wait—and now? Harriet shook her head and tried to stem the tide of despair and confusion that threatened to overwhelm her. Allan was setting her free, but it felt like she'd been put in a prison—a jail of uncertainty and doubt.

She heard the front door open and close and then the heavy tread of her father's footsteps as he came in for his midday meal. Harriet swallowed down the resentment that lodged in her stomach like a hot coal. It was because of her father that she was not on *The Economy of Aberdeen* right now, on Allan's arm as his beloved wife.

Yet she knew she could not speak of any of it to her father. He would not countenance such a discussion, even if Harriet could work up the courage to say a word. Sighing, she folded Allan's letter back up and slipped it into the pocket of her apron. What was done, she knew, was done. Any anger or resentment she felt towards her father served no purpose now. Still, the ache in her heart did not ease as she rose from the pianoforte's bench. Work needed to be done; the midday meal, and her father's comfort, seen to. She did not have the luxury to dwell on her own sorrows.

David Campbell stood in the doorway of the kitchen, as haggard and surly as ever, his sparse gray hair damp with sweat from where it had been flattened underneath his knitted cap, now held twisted in his hands.

"Where's Harriet, then?" he demanded. "I need my tea."

"I'm here, Father." Harriet kissed her father's weathered cheek, shooting Margaret a calming glance at the same time. It wasn't easy getting used to David Campbell's unfriendly ways. She managed it only by grit and the grace of God.

"I suppose Ian's up to no good," he groused as he washed his hands in the basin by the pump. "It's time that boy was doing proper work. I was in the fields before fourteen, learning the land my father paid for with his very life."

"Which is why you always wanted Ian to have lessons," Harriet replied calmly. She had heard many times how her grandfather had worked in the fields he'd so proudly bought until the day before he died of a heart attack—undoubtedly from a life of hard labor. Harriet moved with quick, agile grace around the kitchen, taking a cloth and reaching for the fish pie that had been resting on the warming shelf over the hearth. "Ian is receiving the education you never had, Father."

"Much good it will do him," her father answered with a grunt. He glanced at Margaret, his expression turning shrewd. "Well, then. Sandy's finally done it, I suppose."

"They're on the ship, yes," Margaret answered, her eyes flashing although her tone was level enough.

"Never thought he would. Had a good position, though, didn't he, as tacksman? Still, there's nothing to being your own man." His chest puffed with familiar pride. "We've the largest landholding on the island. Free land—" His face darkened for a moment, and Harriet tensed for another diatribe. What had her father found fault with now? Then his expression cleared, and he said firmly, "The land's ours, always has been."

"And always will be," Harriet finished with a smile. She knew how proud her father was of being a landowner among so many tenants. "We all look forward to hearing of the MacDougalls' good fortune, I'm sure," she added, and her hand slipped inside her apron pocket to feel the weight of her letters. She wished Allan had kept them for the long ship journey, to remind him of her, to comfort him in the moments of doubt and discouragement he would face, as surely as she would.

"In due time." Her father shot her a coolly speculative glance, and Harriet thought she knew just what he was thinking—no doubt wondering if Allan had spoken to her.

Let him wonder, she thought with a sudden burst of savage satisfaction. Let her father feel just one slight flicker of the uncertainty and doubt she'd harbored over the last months, and even years. She knew the thought was unworthy of either her or Allan, and she forced the bitterness away. Surely now was a time for peace—if only she could find it.

"Let me get your dinner, Father. Margaret will call the others to the table."

As Margaret left the kitchen, Harriet bustled around, laying plates and cups. David watched her, a brooding expression on his face.

Harriet felt his heavy gaze upon her and she looked up from the table. "Is everything all right, Father?"

"As well as it can be." He rubbed a hand over his whiskered jaw. "I suppose you've said your farewells… to all the MacDougalls?"

"Allan was here," Eleanor piped up as she came into the kitchen, a mischievous grin lighting her elfin features. The others followed behind and took their places at the table. Grace was said and the meal served before Eleanor could continue, blithely ignoring Harriet's sharp warning glance. "Harriet and Allan took a stroll down to Duart, and when Harriet came back she was as flushed—"

"Eleanor!" Harriet cut in sharply. "Enough. You're gossiping like a fishwife."

Eleanor blushed in shame, and Harriet bit her lip. She'd no cause to shout at her little sister. Eleanor did not know the whole truth of the matter, and neither did Margaret by the confused look she was giving Harriet.

"But of course you've said, Harriet!" Margaret exclaimed.

"Said what?" David Campbell demanded.

A silence, tense and heavy, descended on the table. Even Ian and Rupert, their heads bent together over some boyish nonsense, looked up in perplexity. Margaret flushed and glanced at her plate, clearly realizing she'd spoken amiss.

Harriet sighed and decided honesty was the better course, even if such plain talking incurred her father's wrath. "Allan asked me to wait for him, Father. I'm sure you've guessed it already. When he returns, his fortune secure, he will ask me to marry him, and I will accept."

Her father fixed her with a gimlet stare. "And you're prepared to wait?"

Her heart fluttered—was it with excitement or fear? "I am."

"It's as likely he'll never return," he warned her grimly. "If he survives at all, he'll make his fortune and no doubt find his own bride in that new land."

Margaret opened her mouth in angry denial, but Harriet stayed her with one firm hand on her shoulder. "Perhaps, but I trust Allan, and I'm willing to take the risk."

"We're not a gambling family," her father snapped, and Harriet could have almost laughed at his sheer orneriness.

"This is not a wager, Father," she said, "but a trust in God and His hand upon both me and Allan."

They didn't speak of it again, and her father returned to the fields with a piece of cold mutton wrapped in muslin to see him to supper. Harriet turned back to a kitchen filled with dirty dishes, a garden outside that needed weeding, and the clean washing to take down. A woman from Craignure had been coming three days a week to help her with the heavy work, but she'd stopped a month ago, apparently on her father's orders, and Harriet felt the burden now.

Margaret returned to the kitchen, tucking an unruly tendril of hair behind one ear. "Shall we get on with it?" she said cheerfully, and Harriet, tired and overwhelmed by the happenings of the last day, suddenly felt near tears.

"Ah, Harriet." Margaret pulled her into a quick, fierce hug. "Dinna fash yourself. He'll return, you know he will."

"It's not that." Harriet let out an inelegant sniff and dabbed her eyes with the corner of her apron. "It's everything. I almost envy him, Margaret, and the grand adventure they'll all be having."

Margaret stepped back with a shiver. "I don't. Have you not heard how wild that land is, Harriet? Endless snow and cold, and the natives…"

"I'm sure there are tales to tell around a fire," Harriet said, "but they're just tales."

"It's a hard place, there's no denying," Margaret said, and then her face suddenly fell. "But you might be there in a year's time! I'm sorry, Harriet…"

"And you will be as well," Harriet reminded her with a small smile. "Your father intends to fetch both you and Rupert back within a year or two, doesn't he?"

"Yes," Margaret said, but she sounded hesitant, and Harriet wondered just what had made her friend and kinswoman so eager to stay behind.

*

The rest of the day went smoothly enough, with Margaret helping Harriet and Eleanor with the housework. David Campbell returned for the evening meal, but he was too weary to talk much, and the little group around the scrubbed pine table was mostly silent. It was only when Harriet was alone in the kitchen, wiping down the table, that her father finally spoke at all.

"You're a good daughter to me, Harriet," he said gruffly, and Harriet ducked her head in mute thanks. "But I wish you'd been a son."

Harriet smiled and said nothing. She'd heard this many times before. No matter how well she managed her father's house, having been housekeeper since she was Eleanor's age, beating rugs, churning butter, and baking bread, it would never be enough. She could never be the boy her father had wanted. She understood that, and the importance of a son, yet she still felt a helpless sense of loss at her father's words.

"A son to help me manage the farm," he continued heavily, his shoulders slumping. "I'm an old man now, and I can't do it alone."

"You can hire help," Harriet suggested, and her father scowled.

"It's time Ian gave up his lessons. He'll be a man soon. His place is with me. This farm will be his one day, and he needs to know how to run it."

Harriet strove to keep her tone reasonable. She knew arguing with her father when he was in this mood did no one any good. "He'll take time out for lambing and harvest. And he'll be learning with Rupert now. There's plenty of men to help from the village if you need them." David had hired two such men already, but clearly it was not enough, or at least not what he wanted.

"Why should I hire a man when I have a son?" David demanded.

Harriet couldn't answer. This argument had been going on for months. Ian was desperate to continue his lessons. He'd a far better head for books than sheep or crops. Harriet continued to stand between him and their father, in an attempt to keep him with the tutor in Tobermory for as long as possible. Now she wondered just how long that would be.

Her father looked like he wanted to argue, but then with a sigh he shook his head and retired to one of the front rooms of the house that he used as his study. Harriet sank tiredly into the rocking chair by the fire. She reached into her apron pocket as she had several times already that day to feel the bundle of letters Allan had returned. They were both a comfort and a wound.

Would it always be like this, she wondered as she gazed into the glowing orange embers of the fire. Would the rest of her life be spent waiting, smoothing over the ruffled waters of this family while dreaming of the day when she'd finally have her own?

Since the death of their mother, Harriet had always stood between David and her siblings. It wasn't easy. Ian and Eleanor were both sensitive children, and David had turned into a sour, embittered man when his beloved wife had been taken from him in childbirth.

It was only catching the glimpses of the loving father she remembered that kept Harriet strong, determined to bind her family together with the strong ties of love. Yet those glimpses had become rarer, and the recent knowledge of her father's refusal to consider Allan's suit made her wonder how she could continue to endure.

Eleanor came around the corner of the kitchen, her toes peeking out from underneath her nightgown, one tawny plait lying over her shoulder. "Will you read me a story, Harriet?"

"You can read them yourself," Harriet protested, but Eleanor simply held her hands out in mute appeal. Harriet knew it wasn't the stories, but rather the closeness, that both of them cherished. Smiling tiredly she rose from the rocking chair.

"All right, then."

Upstairs, with her knees drawn up to her chest, her nightgown tucked neatly around her ankles, Eleanor looked younger than her eleven years. Harriet felt a fierce pang of love for the little sister she'd raised like her own child. She'd been twelve when Eleanor was born, and her mother had died. In the course of a single night Harriet had left her childhood behind, and taken on the burdens of the household as well as a bairn. David's sister, her Aunt Morag and a widow, had helped for a few years until illness had claimed her as well. Then Harriet had truly taken on the running of Achlic Farm—and she'd never stopped.

"What shall we read, then?" she asked Eleanor as she sat on the edge of her bed. Eleanor smiled and held out the already worn copy of *The History of Little Henry and His Bearer*, an adventure story set in India written by the ever-popular Mary Martha Sherwood. "Again?" Harriet asked, amused. "You've read it a dozen times at least. She must write something new for you to read."

"New books hardly ever come this way," Eleanor said, and Harriet nodded her agreement. Any book besides the Bible was a precious thing indeed on the island, or even in all of Western Scotland.

"Well, it's a good story, at least," she said with a smile. "I suppose we could read it a few more times." She opened the book and began to read. "Henry L—was born at Dinapore in the East Indies…"

After half an hour or so Harriet saw Eleanor's eyelids start to flutter and she closed the book. "Sleep, I think," she said softly.

"Very well." Eleanor rested her chin on top of her knees, gazing at her sister with sleepy yet thoughtful eyes. "Are you very sad, now that Allan is gone?"

Harriet traced the embroidered design on the counterpane with one finger. She couldn't quite meet her little sister's eyes, for she did not want Eleanor to see the sorrow she knew must be shadowed there. "A bit."

"Is that all?" Eleanor wrinkled her nose. "I thought you loved him."

"I do." Harriet took a breath and managed a smile. "I hope to marry him one day."

"I heard you at dinner as well as anybody." Eleanor smiled in knowing delight before a frown wrinkled her brow and shadowed her eyes. "But then where will you live? Not in the New Scotland, surely?"

"Would that be so terrible?" Harriet asked lightly. "I know the Indians can be frightening, but—"

"Indians!" Eleanor waved one hand in contemptuous dismissal. "I'm not scared of them. But it's so far away." She paused, her hazel eyes as clear as a rain puddle. "I don't suppose you would take me with you?"

"Oh, Eleanor." Harriet's heart ached at the seriousness of her sister's question. She realized she couldn't envision leaving for the new world—a new life—without either Eleanor or Ian. Yet if she married Allan, she surely would, unless her father agreed to emigrate as well and she could hardly see that happening. The only way he would leave Achlic Farm was in a coffin. "You'd miss Father too much," she finally said with a smile, but Eleanor was not swayed.

"I'd miss you far more! Why won't you take me with you?" Eleanor's lip trembled, even though she gazed directly at Harriet with hazel eyes, making it impossible for her to dissemble.

"Ah, Ellie." Harriet gathered her sister in her arms and kissed the top of her head. "Allan may not even return, you know." The prospect brought a lump to her throat that she resolutely swallowed down.

"He only left yesterday. You can't be doubting him already!" Eleanor sounded so indignant, Harriet had to chuckle even though there was some painful truth to her words.

"I don't think we should worry about something so far away," she said softly. Her heart felt heavy as she released Eleanor, smoothing her hair back from her brow. "It will be years yet before he returns."

"I'll keep you company," Eleanor promised, "till then."

"I know you will." As Harriet left the room, she felt a pang of something akin to fear. How could she ever leave her sister, her family? They needed her more than anyone, perhaps more than Allan did. She'd been thinking so much of losing Allan, she had not considered what she might lose here. Troubled, she frowned as she left the warmth and comfort of her sister's bedroom for the dishes and darning downstairs.

It was only later, when Eleanor, Ian and Rupert were settled for the night, that Harriet once again allowed herself the luxury of private thoughts and dreams. She reached for her shawl as Margaret looked up from her embroidery, her eyebrows raised in question. "You're not going out at this hour?"

"It's still light." Harriet shrugged. "I like to walk on an evening."

Margaret smiled. "I prefer the morning. Go on, then. I'll keep the peace here."

Although it was ten o'clock, the sun had not yet set. A soft purple twilight was falling, and the air was cool and still, the sea spreading out to the horizon in a rippling sheet of blue-gray.

Harriet found herself following the path she and Allan had taken yesterday, to Duart Castle. Her mind roamed restlessly over the words in Allan's letter, as well as the words they'd spoken between them in this very place.

She thought of her father, yet her resentment was dulled by a sudden thought. If David Campbell had not stood in the way, would she even have gone? Could she have left all she'd known—Eleanor and Ian—for a life apart and so very strange?

Not yet, she realized painfully, not yet. She was not ready. Not with Eleanor still so young and tender, and her father seeming grimmer and dourer with each passing day. They needed her—all of them, even her father, although he would never admit it.

Harriet shivered in the gathering dusk. Would she be able to leave when the moment came? Could she go so far away to make a life apart with Allan? Even as her heart thrilled at the thought of being his bride, she felt herself quail with fear. Perhaps this was a choice she would never be asked to make.

She knew Allan might never come back. The new world was full of both opportunity and danger. She had heard tales of the harsh winters, the native people, and all manners of wild beasts. Then there was illness; anyone could be taken at a moment's notice, a life demanded this very day.

And even if he lives, a sly voice whispered inside her, the voice of fear and doubt, *what if he forgets you? There will surely be girls in this new land. Unmarried girls in need of young husbands. And he doesn't even have your letters to remind him of your love, your promise.*

The bundle of her own letters lay heavy in her pocket. It would have given her such comfort to imagine him reading them, far away in this new land. She'd wanted to picture him lying in bed, the snow drifting up the windows of their little log cabin, smiling as he read them and remembered their lively debates and laughter. What comfort were they to her here, her own lines?

He was setting her free, Harriet reminded herself, because he loved her. She'd never resented freedom so much, or thought it so useless. Tears stung her eyes as she gazed out at the bay, the point of Lady Rock visible in the low tide.

Legend had it that three hundred years ago Lachlan Maclean had abandoned his wife Catherine on the rock, to be submerged at the high tide. Harriet had often imagined how the poor woman must have felt, left to die by the man who'd promised to protect her. Fortunately her brother had rescued her, and Lachlan had later come to an untimely end.

Harriet shivered. She was not abandoned. Allan was trying to help her, not hurt her. A treacherous doubt whispered in her mind that he was only letting her down gently, escaping while he had the chance, but she pushed it away. How could she be so faithless, doubting Allan's love only hours after he'd sailed?

"He will come back," she whispered, and the growing wind whipped her words away. The sea had turned choppy, and Harriet knew *The Economy of Aberdeen* would be well on its way now. "He will return for me." She had to cling to that hope, for it was surely the only hope she had.

CHAPTER FOUR

"Land ahoy!"

Crowds surged to the decks of the ship. It had been nearly four weeks since *The Economy* had left Tobermory, and the last few days had been spent in an anxious fever, waiting for the first sighting of the New Scotland.

The salty wind stung his cheeks as Allan made his way to the deck with his family. In their comfortable private quarters, they'd experienced little of the harsh sufferings of the passengers in third class, who had had to bring their own food and cooking utensils, and sleep four to a bunk that was no more than a rough wood plank. They were only allowed out of the hold for an hour every day, to walk the decks and enjoy the sea air. In contrast, Allan and his family had two cabins to themselves and could come and go as they pleased. They dined with the captain and the other few private passengers every night, and all in all it had been a remarkably comfortable crossing, yet one that left Allan uneasy. Although Allan had not experienced those deprivations himself, he felt a keen discomfort at knowing that most of his fellow passengers—and future neighbors—had, and he wondered if such distinctions would exist in this harsh new land they were all travelling to.

"There it is." Sandy leaned on the ship railing, one stubby finger pointed west. "Land."

A faint gray-green smudge was all they could see of the new world, yet this time tomorrow they would be docked in the small town of Pictou, ready to make their way to Prince Edward Island, where the MacDougall holding lay while *The Economy of Aberdeen* made preparations to sail back to Tobermory. Throughout the journey Allan had written several letters to Harriet to send back with it.

Now he put his arm around Betty. "Land, Mother. Land that doesn't move!"

Betty smiled weakly. Her face was pale and drawn, her shoulders hunched. Despite the comfort of their quarters, she had suffered badly from seasickness, and had been confined to her bed for most of the journey. "It's been a long time coming, but I expect there will be hardships of a different kind once there."

"Nothing we won't be able to tackle with our own hands!" Sandy protested robustly, and Allan grinned in return. The doubts Archie had planted in his mind seemed to blow away on the sea breeze as he saw his father's determined smile, felt their shared camaraderie and excitement at the challenges that awaited them.

The sight of the land, fertile, wild, simply *there*, made Allan clench the rail of the ship, his blood surging with anticipation at the possibilities ahead.

He offered a silent prayer of thanksgiving for their safe passage, and prayed that Harriet and her family were safe as well. Perhaps a letter would arrive on the next packet ship, and he would have news of her within a week or two. The thought filled him with as much joy as that faint green smudge of land on the horizon.

The next day the earth seemed to heave under Allan's feet as he disembarked from the ship. All around him sailors shoved and shouted, hurrying to unload their cargo. Passengers streamed out, some hesitant at the sight of the wild, untamed land that seemed to stretch endlessly in every direction, others eager to meet their new homeland and embrace all of its opportunities.

Allan stood with his mother, his arm around her protectively as they stepped across the rough wooden boards that served as a landing dock, to the road thick with deep, dark mud. Sandy had gone to secure their trunks, and Archie loitered behind them, hands in his pockets as he took in the strange and unfamiliar sights.

Archie had kept to himself for most of the voyage, taking his dubious amusements with the sailors on deck. Allan had seen his father's narrow-eyed glance follow Archie on the ship, yet he remained tight-lipped, saying nothing, allowing his younger son to go his way, as he always had.

Archie had inspired that leniency, Allan knew, with his dancing eyes and roguish charm, and it made his own burden as the older, dutiful son so much harder to shoulder.

"Allan…" Betty's voice was little more than a whisper. "It's so… *dark*."

At first he didn't know what she meant. The sun was high in a brilliant blue sky, burning with a fiercer heat than any he'd known back in Scotland.

The docks were lined with wooden buildings, some mere shanties and others two or even three stories high. The people he saw exhibited a wide assortment of clothes and colors—Indians in beads and feathers, their faces expressionless and unfathomable, settlers in homespun, wide-brimmed hats jammed low on their heads, and the newest arrivals, the greenhorns, clutching bundles and gaping at this large, new world with a mixture of fear and anticipation.

Yet, he realized, everything was covered in mud and dirt, and looked as if it might last a season, no more than two. There was no stone, at least not by the dock, although he'd heard talk on ship that in the fifty years since the first settlers had arrived in Pictou, a church had been built, and a grammar school courthouse, and jail as well. The harbor boasted a battery, built five years ago, to prevent attacks from the sea.

As he raised his gaze, Allan saw that beyond the buildings there was only forest, thick, green, towering and impenetrable. Dark.

The trees seemed to go on forever, unyielding and unforgiving, rising high above the small settlement, like nothing he'd ever seen back home, where the sea was always in sight.

It was a world more likely to conquer than to be conquered. It amazed him that settlers had come here at all, thinking to tame this rugged land. It looked merciless, and he could imagine the settlers being absorbed by the woods, the winter, so that the next shipload never even knew they'd been here.

Allan quickly suppressed the thought. Fear would help no one.

"There's a packet ship to Charlottetown in three days," Sandy announced when he'd returned from his first foray into the town itself. "We can stay at a boarding house till it arrives."

"Three days." Betty stared at him in dismay.

"Never mind," Archie said cheerfully. "It could've been three weeks! Besides, we can get outfitted here. From what I've heard, supplies are scarce on the island. Even nails have to be shipped over."

The boarding house was on the main street, a respectable clapboard building across from the courthouse. Betty cheered a bit at the sight of the main road lined with buildings, half of them made of stone. The boarding house itself was crowded with recent arrivals, and the MacDougalls were all squeezed into one small room. Betty stood at the window, watching as the fur traders swaggered down the street towards the tap room, their faces covered in bushy beards, sacks of smelly pelts across their backs. They looked utterly savage, and yet seemed at home in this hostile world.

"I've never seen such things," she murmured, dropping the thin muslin curtain back in place, and Allan saw the fear plainly on her face. He knew this journey had been Sandy's dream, not hers; he placed his hand on her elbow.

"Never mind, Mother. In a few days we shall be in Charlotte-town. There are no fur traders there."

Betty shook off his elbow with a wan smile, but when she spoke her voice was strong. "I was the mistress of Mingarry Farm, Allan. A few crude fur traders will not defeat me."

Sandy returned to their little room, a thunderous look on his face. "I asked for another room, but the mistress of this place refused me," he said, as if still he could not believe such audacity. "It is unconscionable that we should be stuck in here like a haul of herrings."

Archie, who had followed behind his father, gave Allan a smirking look. Allan knew just what he was thinking. His father was not tacksman here, and he had yet to realize it.

"This will do nicely," Betty said, and Sandy pursed his lips into a thin line, looking as if he still wanted to argue.

"Archie and I can sleep in the barn," Allan offered, "to give Mother some privacy. Plenty of men are doing the same, and the weather's still warm."

Sandy nodded, satisfied, and behind his back Archie rolled his eyes. "Who said I wanted to sleep in a barn?" he muttered, but at least he went downstairs with Allan to bring up the rest of their trunks.

As Allan left the room, he heard his father say in a low voice, "This will be the last time you have to share a room, I promise you that."

Betty smiled slightly, her eyebrows raised. "Don't make promises we've no knowledge to keep. I'm not above sharing a room, Sandy, and nor should you be."

Sandy grunted, and Allan caught another of Archie's knowing looks. It would be hard for Sandy to let go of the privileges he'd become accustomed to, no matter how he chafed against the restrictions on his role as tacksman.

A sailor jostled Allan's arm hard as he passed and then gazed at him rudely, clearly spoiling for a fight. Allan passed by quickly, keeping his head down. There was no point involving himself in a useless brawl at this stage—not when he had so much to live for.

"Not quite the same, is it?" Archie said cheerfully as they settled into the hay to sleep that night. "A far cry from Mingarry Farm, or even our ship cabin."

"Lower your voice," Allan told him. Archie had been in the taproom with some of the sailors, and it was clear by his jolly manner and bright eyes. "We don't want to cause trouble."

"It won't come easy to Father," Archie said. "Nobody cares if he was tacksman of Ardnamurchan here, that I already know."

"He realizes that," Allan said with more conviction than he actually felt. "In any case, there were plenty of Scots aboard the ship. A tacksman will mean something to them."

Archie chuckled as he kicked off his boots and wriggled his toes. "As innocent as a dove, you are! And how do you suppose they'll be thinking about tacksmen, Allan MacDougall, in this world they've come to?"

Allan stared at his brother, unwelcome realization dawning far later than it should have. Archie had always grasped things more quickly than he did; it was one of the things about his brother that annoyed him. That, and the fact that Archie knew it.

"It's tacksmen they've come to escape, Allan," Archie said, as if explaining the alphabet to a slow-witted child. "If they realize Father was a tacksman, it won't be for his benefit, that much is certain."

"Aye, so you've said." Allan turned over in the hay, preparing to sleep.

"Here there's no one to answer to, and no one to do Father's bidding." He paused, and Allan waited, his back still turned. "No one but us."

"I seem to remember that we've already had this conversation," Allan said in a weary voice. "You can bait me all you like, Archie, for I know that for what it is. Father might need to adjust to this place, as do we all. I'm not yet thinking he's going to turn on us like a mad bull or an angry laird. He isn't Riddell, by any means."

Allan thought of their previous laird's cold, shrewd eyes, the little smile he gave before asking Sandy to do something unpleasant. Allan had often been at his father's side during those visits, had seen his father's clenched fists and tightened shoulders when he was instructed to turn another poor crofter out. Riddell's increasing demands had hastened the MacDougalls' departure, of that he had no doubt.

He had to believe his father was different than a man like Riddell, no matter what Archie thought.

"Sweet dreams," Archie whispered mockingly, and Allan gritted his teeth.

Closing his eyes, he tried to picture Harriet. Just the image of her, the very thought, calmed him. He liked to imagine her as he'd last seen her at Duart, her auburn hair blowing in curls about her face, her eyes shining with love and promise. *I'll come back.* As fanciful as the notion was, Allan imagined she could hear his thoughts, and be certain of his vow.

Tomorrow he'd bring his packet of letters back to *The Economy*, and pay the captain well to make sure they were delivered to the MacDougalls' shipping agent in Tobermory. He felt better just at the thought of knowing that Harriet would have his letters in little more than a month or two. Then she would be reminded of his constancy, and she'd have no cause to wonder or doubt.

*

"I've no head for learning, Maggie. You know that." Rupert gazed at her mournfully as they broke their fast in the kitchen. In less than an hour he and Ian were expected at Master Simon McIlvain's lodgings in Tobermory for their lessons.

Ian, tousle-headed and sleepy over his oatcakes, glanced at Rupert with two years' smug seniority. "Master McIlvain will know it as well," he replied with a grin. "Or he'll learn, no doubt!"

"Away with you, Ian," Harriet chided as she served more oatcakes to the children gathered around the table. "And enough with your idle chatter." She smoothed her hair back into the neat bun at the back of her neck, and caught Margaret's concerned gaze. She knew she'd been irritable lately; everything seemed to conspire against her. Even with Margaret's help the housework was never-ending, and over the last few weeks her father had become surlier and surlier.

Yet despite these cares Harriet knew that none of them were truly the cause of her discontent. The truth was a packet ship had arrived from the New Scotland three days ago, and as far as she knew it held no letters for anyone at Achlic.

Of course, there could be a dozen—a thousand—reasons why Allan hadn't written. *The Economy* had been delayed, he'd been too consumed with responsibilities to put ink to paper, he was ill. Or dead. Or he'd simply forgotten her.

Harriet shook her head impatiently, the thoughts buzzing inside like flies she could not simply swat away. Margaret laid a hand on her arm.

"What ails you, Harriet?" she asked, and Harriet bit her lip.

"Nothing. That is... I wonder if any letters have come on the ship that docked recently. I thought we would have heard by now."

"Letters!" Margaret brightened, her eyes snapping with excitement. "My father ordered them to be held with his shipping agent until they could be collected. I could call in, if you like..."

"Why don't we both go?" Harriet suggested. Her heart felt lighter as she considered the possibility. Perhaps Allan's letter had been simply waiting for her all this time, in Tobermory. Why should she have thought it would somehow make its way to the farm? "I could use an outing."

"So could I," Margaret said, and Harriet saw a flash of discontent in her friend's hazel eyes. She suspected Margaret was resentful of Rupert's opportunity to take lessons with Ian, especially when he had no head for learning—and she did. Yet what use would protesting do? Margaret was sixteen years old, far past the age when girls were educated. She was fortunate, Harriet thought, that Sandy had provided a governess for as long as he had. Harriet had not had such opportunity; her mother had taught her letters and numbers, and that was all.

"May I walk with you?"

Harriet jumped in surprise. She'd been so lost in her thoughts she hadn't even noticed Jane MacCready come alongside her and Margaret on the road to Tobermory.

"Of course," she murmured. Jane was known on this side of the island for her sharp tongue, even if her observations were often correct. Harriet was discomfited to see the spinster's shrewd eyes now turned appraisingly upon her.

"Harriet Campbell…" Jane mused, and Harriet imagined the woman was recalling everything she'd ever known or heard about her. "Although it should've been MacDougall, I warrant."

"Wh-what?" Harriet stammered in her appalled surprise. She'd not realized her friendship with Allan was so well known, even though she supposed it should have come as no surprise. Even Margaret looked startled by this pronouncement, although she smiled.

"I never understood why the pair of you didn't make a match of it," Jane continued. "Such friends as you were. It's rare, that."

"So it is." Harriet couldn't think of anything else to say. She glanced helplessly at Margaret, who smiled in sympathy. How could she admit that her father had refused him? Allan's promise of return, especially since he'd released her from her own vow, seemed too small a token to explain, and yet too precious to share.

"It won't be easy to find a husband on this island," Jane said in a warning tone, "especially since you must be nearing five and twenty."

"I'm twenty-three." Harriet realized she was blushing, and willed herself to stop. "And I'm not looking for a husband at present." The only husband she wanted was Allan.

They'd reached the edge of Tobermory, the harbor glinting in the autumn sunshine, the cries of gulls raucous in the morning air. Jane put a steadying hand on her arm. "I mean no harm, lass. You know I always speak my mind." Harriet nodded stiffly. "There was a man I could've married once. He loved me and I loved him, but he had to wait. I'd promised to care for my father first. He wasn't well."

Intrigued in spite of herself, Harriet turned to face the older woman. "What happened?"

"My father took five years to die," Jane replied, her usually sharp tone softened with more than a trace of sadness. "He didn't wait."

As they walked towards the harbor side and the shipping agent's office, Jane MacCready's words seemed to echo through her. *He didn't wait.* It wasn't the same, Harriet told herself. *She* was the one waiting. Yet the treacherous thought kept slipping in, reminding her that it had been his idea for her not to wait after all. What if life in the New Scotland held him in a way she, thousands of miles away, could not? Who knew what opportunities, what *women*, awaited him there?

"It's not the same, Harriet," Margaret said quietly, and she turned to her in surprise.

"What do you mean?"

"Mistress MacCready and you. It's different. Allan is different. He'll wait."

"He's not waiting," Harriet said with a tiny trace of resentment. "I am."

"My brother is faithful," Margaret insisted. "How can you doubt him?"

Harriet sighed. "I don't. At least, I don't mean to. But so much could happen, Margaret. So much could go wrong. I'm afraid." Her voice trembled and she blinked back tears. Margaret squeezed her hand.

"Just wait. We'll go to the shipping agent and find a nice fat packet of letters. I warrant he's written you every day while he's been on that ship! You'll be reading letters from now until Christmas. Just you wait and see."

*

There was frost on the ground. Allan stared at the thin white film of ice and felt as if were creeping into his soul. Frost on the ground in mid-September did not bode well. They'd barely laid the foundations for their cabin.

He glanced at the building site now, the rough-cut logs stripped of their branches and leaves, the deep notches in each made so they fit together neatly. The sun was just beginning to rise behind a stand of birch trees, their leaves already turning yellow. It was early morning, the time of day he liked best, the sky already deep blue, every leaf sparkling with dew. Now he could be alone with his thoughts and the peace of the countryside.

The beauty of this rough, wild country had taken him by surprise. At first it had seemed threatening, the towering trees and darkness a menace just as his mother had felt on that first day in Pictou.

Prince Edward Island, with its sandy beaches and rolling hills, its rich red soil and winding rivers, had a gentler wildness than Scotia, although it was still untamed—swathes of forest waiting to be turned into fields, its only town still in its infancy. Alone in the quiet of the dawn, Allan knew he was beginning to love this place if not as his homeland, then at least as a place he'd be content to live out his days. He loved the dazzling sky, the distinctive red soil, the brilliant green of the leaves, the freshness of the earth and the purity of it all—sea, earth, and sky. He respected the savagery that lurked underneath the beauty, the blue of the sky that would turn to slate or stormy gray boiling with violet clouds, the crumbly red soil which would soon be covered in snow.

This was a land that spared no mercy for weakness, error, or faintness of heart. Looking at the foundation of the cabin, those slender logs, the ice clutched at his soul once more. They would not be ready for winter.

And it was their own fault.

When they'd first arrived on the island, they'd had the fortune of befriending another family, the Dunmores.

The Dunmores had emigrated five years ago and possessed a solid, pleasing cabin as well as a cautiously prosperous farm. Their land bordered the MacDougalls' and they'd agreed to let Sandy and his family stay with them until their own cabin was built, as was the custom among all the Scots settlers.

In midsummer, with the sun shining and the air warm, the breezes soft, they'd all been confident the cabin would have walls and a roof before the leaves began to change color.

The leaves were red now, scarlet and crimson and gold. They were already beginning to fall, the air was crisp with a morning frost, and they'd barely started on the walls.

And all because of Sandy's stubbornness. Allan tasted resentment, like acid on the back of his throat, at his father's high-handed actions.

In July, when they'd arrived, he'd argued with his father for a smaller cabin. They'd stood in a clearing, a thicket of raspberry bushes dripping with ruby-colored fruit framing a view of the river, the water dazzled by sunlight.

"Why don't we build here?" Allan said. He breathed in the clean air, still cool in the morning light, and grinned at his father. "There's everything to hand, and we can start with something small. Four walls and a roof to see through the winter."

"That sounds like a barn," Sandy had replied shortly, his gaze narrowed as he surveyed the rich land. "I didn't come all this way to live like a crofter."

"A crofter doesn't own five hundred acres," Allan replied, slightly startled by his father's curt tone. Archie stood nearby, staring at his boots, a nonchalant grin still visible on his lowered face, as if none of this really concerned him, and he simply found it amusing.

Sandy strode away, leaving Allan no choice but to follow him like a lackey. Sandy strode through the raspberry thickets, pushing the brambles back with disregard for his son behind him, or the berries that fell to the ground.

Allan pushed a thorny branch from his face, and waited. Tension seemed to crackle in the air, tension that had not been there a moment ago, when every dew drop had sparkled like a diamond, bright with promise.

A bird chirped, one whose sound he'd never heard before, its tune lonely and mournful, and then fell silent.

Sandy stood on the other side of the thicket. It was a smaller clearing, closer to the river, bordered by a stand of birch trees.

"We'll build here," he announced, and his voice brooked no argument.

"Are you sure?" Allan pressed. "There was more sunlight in the other, and room for Mother's garden."

Sandy turned to look coolly at his son. "The garden doesn't need to be next to the house, and I want to be close to the river, especially in winter. We'll be chopping through the ice every morning, I warrant." He smiled as if to ease the finality of his words, but his eyes were still flinty. This was his decision, and no one else's.

Allan forced himself to shrug. This battle was not one worth fighting to the death, and one clearing was surely as good as another. Yet he could not shake the feeling that his father had changed locations simply because he wanted to be in charge, almost out of spite. Still he managed to keep his voice equable as he gave his assent. "All right, then."

Sandy began to pace out the foundations with his feet. "We'll need two good bedrooms, of course, and a great room with a fireplace. A loft above, and of course a root cellar…"

Allan stared in astonishment, words temporarily deserting him. Most settlers built one room cabins when they first arrived, ten feet by ten feet at the most. There was little time before the onset of winter to build anything else, and grand aspirations could be saved for later. They certainly wouldn't keep you warm.

"But it won't be finished before the snows," he said finally, his voice rising despite his attempt to sound reasonable. He saw Archie whistle and gaze up at the sky.

Sandy frowned. "We've got more men working than most do. We'll finish it," he said flatly. He strode away without looking back. Allan sighed in exasperation and began to follow.

"It's our farm, then?" Archie said. Allan kept walking.

Since that day, Sandy had become more and more consumed with building their cabin, and making sure it was the finest dwelling on this side of the island. The foundations now included a pantry and a third bedroom. No wonder they had yet to start on the walls.

Allan had stopped making suggestions weeks ago. He took orders numbly, keeping the smile on his face, hoping that once their cabin was built and the pressure on Sandy eased, things would be different.

He would feel like a son, not a servant.

Now, alone on this cool dawn, Allan breathed in the crisp air. With the sunlight dappling the river in silver, the dew as fine as cobwebs strewn in the yellow-gold leaves of the birches above him, he could almost recover his optimism. They were working hard, and it might not snow for months yet. Once the foundations were laid, the logs went up more easily.

"It won't be finished."

Allan was startled to see his mother standing near him. The walk from the Dunmores' farm was considerable, and he hadn't yet seen her venture far from the safety of the cabin, the warmth of its rooms. She was thinner now and paler, pulling her shawl tightly round her shoulders.

"It might be," he said.

"Come now, Allan. We can both see what's before our eyes." She swept a weary arm towards the unfinished cabin. "It's too big, isn't it? Too grand."

"It'll be a pleasing house," Allan said cautiously.

"A house of dreams. Perhaps we could've built such a place in a few years, when we knew the way of this land. But now…" Betty shook her head. "Winter's coming on. All we need is something small, to live in through the worst of it. I've heard about the snow here. It's like nothing you've ever seen, or so everyone says."

"Mother…"

"What shall we do?" She turned to him, and he was surprised to see strength and concern in her eyes, rather than the fear and worry he'd expected. "I understand what your father is trying to do, Allan. Don't mistake me on that. I know he wants a proper place, a place like we had before. He wants it for me, another Mingarry Farm in this wild land." She sighed, biting her lip. "We shall have to ask the Dunmores if we can stay with them through the winter. Perhaps if we help more with their own work… Lord knows, there's much to be done in this place. It won't be easy." She shook her head and smiled wearily at Allan. "I shouldn't be talking to you like this. Your father has such dreams, Allan, but they're good dreams. They've brought us here, and that's a good thing."

"Yes, it is." A voice clamored inside him. *What of my dreams? My place?* With an effort he suppressed that small cry of doubt. There would be time for his dreams later. He could be patient.

Allan put his arm around his mother's thin shoulders and pulled her close. "It will turn out well, you'll see," he said. "We'll have a grand place here for you and for all of us."

He could almost believe it.

*

"A letter from MacDougall?" The shipping agent, Douglas, squinted at Harriet in surprise while Margaret fidgeted next to her. "And who might you be?"

"Harriet Campbell." She stood in the cramped one-room office along the docks in Tobermory, twisting her gloves in her hands. So close now, she thought. On the walk into town Margaret had convinced her there would be a letter from Allan. Of course there would be! And now the thought of reading it, knowing what he'd been through, where he was now—all of it would bring her closer to him even as an ocean yawned between them.

The man glanced briefly through a packet of letters. "No… I don't see any here. There was a letter to Ann Rankin, which has been delivered, and I've one for Margaret and Rupert MacDougall."

"I'll take that," Margaret said, holding out one hand.

The man smiled at her. "I thought I recognized a MacDougall," he said, and handed it to her.

Harriet watched the exchange; the man didn't even look at her. "You mean…" Her throat was dry and scratchy. "There's nothing else? None for me… Harriet Campbell, from Allan MacDougall."

"I'm afraid not."

"Are you sure?" Harriet knew she sounded desperate. She felt desperate. But no letter from Allan, when others had written, when they must have arrived safely, to have the letters sent back? It was unthinkable, and yet…

"I'm certain," the man said firmly, and Harriet knew better than to harass him, even though she wanted to demand he check the floor, the sack of post, any crevice or cranny where a precious, precious letter may have slipped and lain forgotten.

"I see," she finally managed. "Thank you." She knew she was close to tears and forced them back. It would not do to cry here, in this stranger's quarters.

"Never mind, Harriet," Margaret said in a low voice. "There's bound to be a reason."

"Yes…" Blindly Harriet turned towards the door.

"There's another ship due in six weeks' time, the last before winter," the man called. "Perhaps then."

"Yes," Harriet agreed hollowly. Six weeks sounded like an age. "Perhaps."

She stood outside on the road, muddy from recent rains. The sky was the color of pewter and a cold, unforgiving wind buffeted her from the sea. She swallowed, her mind numb, as blank as the sky above her, or the flat horizon that stretched out to nothing, promised nothing.

No letters. Allan hadn't written. Hadn't bothered to write. Hadn't cared.

"Perhaps there is some news of him in this letter," Margaret said, and her forehead creased in a frown as a new realization assailed them both. If there was news, it surely couldn't be good.

Panic clutched at Harriet with icy fingers as she considered this new and unwelcome possibility. If Allan had become ill, or worse… "Open it," she whispered. "Open it, Margaret, right now."

Biting her lip, Margaret broke the seal. Harriet turned away, too fearful even to watch Margaret read the letter, see the expression on her face. What if Allan had taken ill? What if he'd *died*? Her stomach roiled and she paced the quayside, one hand to her mouth, while Margaret read the letter out loud.

"Dearest Margaret and Rupert," she began. "Thanks to the hand of Providence, we all of us arrived in this rough and wild country, the New Scotland, in August. It took five weeks and a day to sail, and God be praised not one soul was lost, but four new bairns joined us in the crossing!"

"All of us?" Harriet repeated. She turned back to Margaret, hiding her trembling hands in the heavy folds of her skirt. "Then he's well."

"Wait, there's more." Margaret continued reading, skimming through the lines. Her mouth tightened as she read the last few lines of the letter. "We are much blessed, all of us in good health and strong. I pray that you both are in good health and comfort. You are never out of mind. Your own most affectionate Mother."

Margaret looked up from the letter, her eyes bright with unshed tears. "They seem so far away now. 'Tis strange, to think of it."

Harriet nodded. A moment ago her stomach had been writhing like a nest of snakes, and yet now she felt strangely empty inside. "God be praised, they're well," she said, but it came out flat. Allan was well. Allan was healthy and strong, and had not written her.

"Harriet, there must be some reason…" Margaret folded up the letter and tucked it in her pocket. "Even though Mother didn't say. I know Allan and I know he loves you."

"You knew Allan," Harriet corrected in a low voice. "Three months ago, aye, he loved me. But much has happened since then, Margaret. Much could change."

"Three months is hardly a lifetime! Feelings don't change as quickly as that, and certainly not Allan's. He loves you, and he is not capricious." Margaret's eyes flashed angrily and Harriet almost laughed to think of them arguing over a man they both loved dearly.

"I know he is not." How could she doubt Allan's loyalty? She knew he was steadfast, as solid in his word as an oak. Yet the ocean that separated them seemed vast, a distance so great mere miles could not measure it. It was a lifetime away.

Margaret laid her hand on Harriet's shoulder. "There is a reason, Harriet, and you will discover it. I vow the next ship will bring a whole packet of letters from Allan to you."

Harriet smiled weakly. "I hope you are right."

"I know I am," Margaret declared. "Allan loves you, and he would not forsake you. He will write." Her voice softened. "He will come back."

"You could write back," Harriet said. She couldn't bear to talk about Allan any longer. "The ship sails again in a week's time."

Margaret's expression hardened. "Aye," she said after a moment, "I have some things to write."

"Don't scold Allan," Harriet said quickly. "I'll not have him write me on your account." Margaret looked as if she wanted to argue, but then she sighed and nodded. "Very well." Fighting a tide of despair, Harriet smiled her thanks and turned towards the road and the long walk back to Achlic Farm.

As Harriet and Margaret entered the house an hour later, they heard the low murmur of voices from the front parlor. Ted Carmichael, their farm manager, had been speaking with her father most of the day, and it sounded as if matters had become heated.

Unease rippled through Harriet, for she didn't know what business could take so long, but it was replaced quickly enough with the hollow ache of despondency that made her feel no more than a shell. She wished she could stop thinking of Allan, yet he remained persistently in her thoughts—even if she wasn't in his.

She spent the afternoon in mindless work, first helping Eleanor with her lessons, then rolling out pastry for a pie and kneading bread. At supper time Margaret paused in their work and turned to Harriet, anxiety creasing her brow.

"You will write him?"

Harriet hesitated. She had thought about whether she should send a letter to Allan all afternoon. "How can I?" she finally asked. "If he didn't write me…"

"This isn't the time for pride! There has to be a reason, and if he has cause to doubt you—"

Harriet felt her face flush and her chest heave. "He does not have cause to doubt me!"

"What is all this racket?" David Campbell stood in the doorway, his shoulders stooped, his face haggard, although his eyes were still sharp. "Ted Carmichael will surely think there's a pair of cats screeching in here!"

"I surely won't." Ted Carmichael, a balding man in his forties, stood behind David, twisting his hat in his hands.

"Hmmph." Her father stumped over to the kettle. "Not even hot. What are you about, lass?"

"I'm sorry, Father. I'll see to it." Harriet reached for the kettle. "I'll see to it now. Have you finished your business with Mr. Carmichael? Or shall he stay to supper?"

Ted had disappeared back into the parlor, and her father shrugged. "We're as finished as we'll ever be."

His tone was so weary that Harriet looked up in alarm. "Father…?"

His eyes were shrewd and he lifted a hand repressively. "I know what you've been about. In Tobermory, eh? Fishing for letters. Did the MacDougall boy write you, then?" The way he spoke, Harriet thought, you'd think the MacDougalls were wastrels and not prosperous farmers—and kin. "He didn't, did he? Not a single line. I doubt he'll ever return." He sounded almost gleeful as he cocked a knowing glance at Harriet, who suddenly found herself burning with a quiet, desperate rage.

"I don't doubt him," she said in a low, shaking voice. "Even if you have done your best to see it otherwise!"

Her father narrowed his eyes. "What are you on about?"

"I know you forbade Allan to marry me," Harriet said, and David's expression turned stony. "I could've been on that ship with him, far from here, with a family of my own and a husband at my side." She clenched her hands into fists as all of her anger and resentment spilled out.

"A landless fool for a husband," he snapped. "I chose well for you."

"It was not your choice to make!"

"Aye, but it was." David's voice came down flat and hard. "You're my daughter and ward, and I will choose as I see fit." He threw a quick glance at Margaret, who was standing, rooted in fury, her cheeks and eyes bright. "I've nothing against the MacDougalls, lass. We're blood kin, no matter how distant. But I won't have my daughter haring off across the world on a whim." He raised one crooked finger. "You'll see. They'll all come back, begging for scraps once again from the Riddell table. Or they won't come back at all."

"How can you say that!" Harriet shook her head, tears of temper spilling from her eyes. "You've turned into a spiteful old man, Father, and one day there will be no one here to make your bread and sit at your table! I vow I will not!"

Her words fell into a room turned eerily silent, save for the hiss of the kettle and crackle of wood from the fire. Her father's face was ashen. Harriet bit her lip, struggling to form an apology she couldn't even feel.

He opened his mouth, let out a strangled croak, then, while Harriet and Margaret both watched in stunned horror, he fell to the floor like a stone.

"Father!" Harriet's voice rose to a shriek as she flew to her father's side and knelt by him. "Margaret, get Mr. Carmichael! Someone must go for the doctor."

Margaret hurried out of the room, and Harriet stared at her father's pale face, a thready pulse beating at his throat. She'd as good as killed him, she realized in a sickening rush. Words could never be taken back. Why had she let herself get so angry?

Ted Carmichael came in, his own face pale, but his manner efficient. He took his pulse, then glanced at Harriet, worry shadowing his eyes. "I'll fetch the doctor from Craignure. We ought to get him comfortable first though."

Harriet nodded, unable to find her voice.

"Let's take him upstairs," Margaret urged.

A few minutes later Ted was on his way to the doctor's and Harriet sat by her father's bedside. His face was still pale and lifeless, his breathing shallow.

Margaret laid a hand on her shoulder. "It wasn't your fault."

Harriet closed her eyes briefly. Tears threatened, making her throat ache. She couldn't speak.

"I'll go downstairs. The children will be wanting their supper." Margaret left with a soft click of the door. Harriet pressed her hands to her eyes, willing the tears—the tide of emotion—to recede.

"Daughter?"

Harriet dropped her hands. Her father's eyes were open, though hazed with pain. "We've gone for the doctor. Don't tire yourself, Father. You'll be all right." She reached for his hand. "I'm sorry for what I said. I didn't mean it."

David turned his head away from her. "It's I who should be sorry," he said in a low voice.

"It doesn't matter…" Harriet began, even though it was far from the truth. Her father's decision mattered too much, but she couldn't let that stand between them now.

"Aye, but it does." David's face was still to the wall. "I'm not speaking of your beau, Harriet, much as you might care for him. There's something else. Something I've not told you. The farm…"

The bleak despair in his words alarmed her but she tried not to show it as she squeezed his hand. "We don't need to talk about farm matters now, Father. Let us get you well first."

David turned to her, the sudden, angry light burning in his eyes taking her by surprise. "There's no time for that," he exclaimed hoarsely. "If we don't do something quickly, the farm will be lost, Harriet, and all you know with it." The light faded from his eyes and he fell back against the pillow, looking pathetic and vulnerable, a broken old man. "God only knows what can be done." His trembling fingers grasped hers, his gaze pleading for understanding. "Forgive me, Harriet. Forgive me. I'm afraid I might've lost it all."

CHAPTER FIVE

Dearest Harriet,

I know too well that you, my dear girl, will be longing to hear from me again, as I long for word from you. This is not a rebuke, but an entreaty for you to break your long silence…

Allan lowered his quill and watched the flames dancing in the hearth. It was late, and everyone was abed except for him. He'd taken these snatched moments to compose another letter to Harriet, but now that he'd a chance to put ink to paper, he didn't know what to write, when she had chosen not to write to him all these long months.

Why hadn't she written? The last ship from Tobermory had arrived last week, and it was now nearly Christmas. Allan had feared that Harriet's letters might've somehow been lost, but deep inside he knew that couldn't be true. Already there had been letters from Ann Rankin, as well as ones from both Margaret and Rupert. His own brother and sister, who lodged with Harriet at Achlic Farm! How could a letter from Harriet have been lost, and not from them?

The more worrying question, he knew, was how could she have not written? He'd written her over a dozen letters since leaving Tobermory back in July. A dozen—and he'd not had a single one back.

Margaret had mentioned Harriet in her letter, as well as concerns over the Campbell farm. Harriet's father was not well, and she was working all the harder for it. There had been an implied rebuke in Margaret's letter: *Dear Harriet has little time for frivolity of any kind, with the work placed upon her. She would do to have her spirits lifted, Allan, and I know a letter from you would cheer her greatly.*

Well, he certainly hoped another letter from him would cheer and comfort her, as well as assure her of his own faithfulness. Yet perhaps that was not what she wanted… perhaps this silence was her way of grasping the freedom he'd given her with both hands, and finding her spirit lifted somewhere else… *by* someone else.

The fire crackled and a few sparks scattered across the stone hearth, quickly turning to cold ash. Had Harriet's love burned out as quickly? Had she taken the freedom Allan had honorably given her to find another? If so, Allan knew she'd every right to act thus.

Yet, surely she should tell him, then? Set him free, as he'd set her free? Not that he wanted such freedom, but he wanted to know. This awful wondering felt worse than knowing all was lost. Now, with the sheet blank before him, Allan wondered what to do. He couldn't bear to remind her of her own freedom, when he felt it so sorely himself. The only recourse left to him, he decided, was to assure her of his own constancy yet again.

He continued to write, dutifully telling her of their travails. What would she make of life here, the crude cabins, the piercing cold, the endless snow? The first snow had been over two months ago, and yesterday the blizzard had been so ferocious that Andrew Dunmore had tied a rope around his son's waist when he went outside to get the firewood, in case he became lost in the blinding whiteness. It had been known to happen before.

Allan shivered as a draught of icy air chilled him, and the howling wind outside rattled the waxed cloth covering the windows.

*I trust that with God's will and my industry I shall soon
be able to come and offer you a hand and heart which is
wholly devoted to you.*

He could state it no plainer than that, surely. Doubt crept
into his mind as he wondered if he was indeed playing Harriet
false. They'd been in Prince Edward Island for nearly five months
and they had not even finished building their own cabin. Its
foundations were covered with snow, useless till the spring thaw.

Even worse, Allan could see no way for him to be the man of
property and standing David Campbell wished for his daughter.
His father barked orders, and he took them from him like a lackey.
Even with winter setting in and little work to be done on their
own property, Allan felt the pressure of his father's heel. He was
beginning to wonder if it would ever change.

And if it didn't? He would never be able to return for Harriet.
Was he acting justly in hoping she would wait? Her best years
would be stolen from her, wasted on dreams turned to dust.

Allan turned back to his parchment.

*I beg you to keep up your spirits for if I deviate one part
from what I have said, may God pour down his vengeance
on me tenfold. May God bless and comfort you in the
sincerest wish of your heart. Your ever, ever faithful lover
until death, Allan.*

He sprinkled sand on the paper and put the writing materials
away. He wouldn't be able to send this latest letter till spring, when
sea travel was possible again. Yet he felt better for writing it, as if
Harriet were that much closer to him now. By the time the first
ship arrived in late March, he hoped to have a whole packet of
letters to send to her.

*

The next morning the family awoke to a fresh fall of snow. The drifts came halfway up the windows, making the cabin feel darker than usual, and it would be difficult to do much of anything in that kind of depth.

Over the winter, the MacDougalls had tried to make themselves useful to the Dunmore family by helping with the necessary work around the homestead as well as accompanying the Dunmore men out on the trap lines. Now, however, the snow would be too deep to venture out to check the traps and there would be little to keep them occupied. The debt they owed the Dunmores would be painfully obvious, and Allan knew it would make Sandy feel both restless and irritable.

In mid-morning Sandy and Allan stood on the porch now swept clear of snow, and looked out at the deep drifts, the small footprints of a rabbit crisscrossing the untouched whiteness.

They would not be able to walk to the clearing and check on the foundations of their cabin. Allan knew his father tried to walk there daily, to make sure all was well with the work they'd managed so far. He'd brush the snow from the half-built walls, pace the generous proportions of the rooms with his feet, smile and close his eyes as if he were imagining what it would one day look like.

"One day," he'd sometimes say to Allan, his voice ringing out through the frosty clearing, "I'll have the finest farm on Prince Edward Island, with my family reunited, and my sons by my side." Allan didn't answer his father then, because he didn't trust himself to say anything civil. His father clung to his own dream, but he wasn't allowing Allan to have his—a proper share in the farm, his own cabin to build for him and Harriet, a life apart even as they worked together.

This morning Betty joined Allan and Sandy on the porch, pulling her shawl more tightly across her shoulders. The world was still and silent save for the crackle of the tree branches, each tiny twig encased in ice as if preserved in crystal.

"I've never seen such snow," she said with a shake of her head. "There's a beauty to it, I suppose." She shivered and drew her shawl tighter around her thin shoulders. "I've stirred the fire up. There were quite a few embers this time."

Last week they'd let the fire die to ashes and had to run to a neighbor's for a live coal. Like much else, there were no matches on the island, and no shops to buy them in even if there were, and letting the fire go out was a terrible and potentially costly mistake.

Sandy grunted in response, still staring hard at the pearly sheen of ice on top of the drifts, making them almost glow. "There'll be no walking in that."

"The cabin will survive," Betty replied with a faint smile, but Sandy only looked even more grim.

"Aye, it will. It will." He turned away from both of them, shoulders hunched. "I'm tired of this. Living in someone else's cottage—we've nothing to call our own!"

"We do," Betty said firmly. "We've a holding of hundreds of acres, and the start to a bonny cabin. It's time we need, that's all. You must remember that. This spring, with your sons working beside you, the cabin will be built in no time at all."

Sandy nodded slowly. "I came to this land to be beholden to no man. That was my promise to myself."

"Perhaps there is a higher purpose than that," Betty countered softly. "To love and serve one another… and tend the earth God gave us, as we are instructed—"

"Don't preach to me, woman," Sandy said, suddenly irritable. "I'll take it on a Sunday, but not from you!" He strode away to get ready for the day, leaving Betty looking forlorn.

"Mother—" Allan began, starting forward, but Betty held up one hand to stop him.

"He's afraid, Allan, that's all. He doesn't mean anything by it." She smiled sadly. "Trust me on this, and don't worry on my account. I'm stronger than I seem, at least in these matters."

Allan nodded tersely, for he didn't like seeing his father speak to his mother in such a sharp tone. In truth, he'd never seen it before and it made him uneasy. His father must truly be frightened to take such a tone.

That night the MacDougalls and Dunmores gathered round the hearth as the wind blew and howled outside like a raging beast longing to get in. Agnes Dunmore and Betty worked on the large pile of mending and darning that needed to be done, while Neville Dunmore oiled a trap and Sandy, Allan and Archie watched, learning, as they'd never trapped before they'd come here, and it was an entirely new business to them.

"Come spring, there'll be a sight more to do here than now," Neville remarked conversationally. "Although I expect once your cabin is built, these young two will go their own ways."

The ensuing silence felt tense, as if everyone was holding their breath. Sandy glanced up sharply, his mouth thinned in disapproval. "I don't follow your meaning."

Neville raised his eyebrows, smiling. "No more than what I said. My own sons have gone to find their own adventure, come what may. One in Pictou, one in Upper Canada. Oh, they may come back here, but it's perhaps my own foolish dream. They want their own place, same as I did. That's what we all came for, isn't it? Each man needs to find his way."

Archie lounged back in his chair, a faint smile on his face. Allan felt the now-familiar burning of ambition that had so often been quenched. Why did Neville Dunmore understand something his own father refused to?

Sandy's expression hardened, and when he spoke, his voice was decidedly cool. "It's no foolish dream of mine, I can tell you that. My own sons will labor by me, that I am assured of. Our holding will be worked by all of us, together. That's the only way in this harsh land."

"Is that so?" Neville glanced thoughtfully at Allan and Archie. Allan could feel himself flushing. His father made it sound as if they all shared an equal weight of responsibility, but he knew the truth of it, and from the shrewd look on Neville Dunmore's face, he did as well.

Neville, however, seemed to have more sense than to prod the hornet's nest he plainly saw in front of him, for he merely smiled and said, "You're a fortunate man, then, Sandy MacDougall."

Archie snorted, the sound muffled by his hand, and set the legs of his chair abruptly on the floor.

Sitting by the warm fire, the comforts of home around him, Allan had never felt so suffocated—as trapped as one of the beavers they'd caught a few days ago, helpless and dying in the snow, unable to do anything but twitch in the iron death grip of the trap.

His father wouldn't change. Archie had known all along. Why had he remained so stubbornly blind, wanting to believe things would change? Once the cabin was built. Once they planted the first crop. Once the harvest came…but, no. As long as Sandy lived, Allan and Archie both would be no better than lackeys to do his bidding, never having any say in the MacDougall holding.

And if that were the case, David Campbell would not allow Harriet to marry him. Allan felt hollow, as if the earlier rage and ambition had leached right out of him.

Campbell had seen the truth of it, he realized. He didn't want Harriet under Sandy's thumb as neatly as her husband would be. He wanted more for his daughter, and so did Allan.

He rose suddenly, almost knocking his chair over and causing the quiet little group to look up in wary bewilderment.

"I'm going out."

"Allan, no!" Betty protested. "What can you be thinking of? It's nearly dusk and icy out there, you wouldn't last a minute."

"I just need a breath of fresh air. I've been inside for days… I'll just go for a minute."

Before any more protests could be made, Allan strode to the door, yanking on his coat and boots. He didn't look back as he opened the door, letting in a gust of freezing air, and walked out.

The sun was setting, sinking into the snow and turning the horizon to molten gold. Allan began to walk, sinking nearly up to his thighs in heavy, wet snow and not caring.

What could he do? If he returned to Harriet once the farm was established, she'd most likely still marry him, even if it meant flying in the face of her father's wishes. If she still even wanted him, of course. He didn't even know.

And yet if she did… could he even ask that of her? He wanted more for his own life than to be ruled by his father, and he wanted more for Harriet as well. How could he tie her to a life he didn't want to live himself?

Allan hunched his shoulders against the icy, howling wind. The only solution would be to strike out on his own, away from the MacDougall holding, perhaps even away from Prince Edward Island. Start his own farm, find his own place in this rough, new world. He knew he didn't have the resources to do that yet, and he didn't know when he might. Perhaps he would never find the means, as well as the will, to go his own way.

For it would surely dash Sandy MacDougall's hopes, if not break his heart.

*

The chill December winds caused Margaret to shiver and draw her shawl tighter around her. Tobermory harbor was flat and slate-colored, seeming as hard and cold as stone. The street was awash with slushy puddles, and an icy rain was beginning to needle her face.

It was not a good day to have gone to town, but Margaret could bear the narrow confines of Achlic Farm for only so long. She tried to help Harriet as much as she could, especially now that David Campbell had been confined to a sick bed. Yet once in a while she needed to escape the mundane routine of farm life, usually with one of Rupert's books hidden in her basket.

Most days Rupert came home from his lessons simply relieved to have them finished, and while Margaret did her best to smile and seem cheerful, inside she burned with a bitter resentment.

She would have changed places with Rupert in a heartbeat. To sit and learn and think all day, to discuss ideas and to *know* things… it sounded like heaven to Margaret, even if Rupert viewed it in quite the opposite way.

The fact that her father had denied her the same access to education as Rupert made bitterness spike inside her. She'd asked, when the arrangements were first being made, for her father to consider her being tutored as well. He'd looked completely shocked.

"How can you even think such a thing! It's unnatural."

"I could keep Rupert company…"

"Ian will see to that. And Harriet will need your help in the kitchen and farm. Those are a woman's duties." Margaret swallowed, knowing from the set expression on her father's face that there would be no moving him. Still she tried.

"Even just a few days a week…"

"Nonsense, lass. There's no sense in it. When you come to the New Scotland you'll marry and run your husband's farm with him. You'll learn far more useful things in the Campbell kitchen than in a dusty school room."

Margaret bit back the retort that she didn't want to learn how to make a pie crust or bottle fruit or tend a garden. Her father would not take kindly to such ideas.

So she'd let it go, and consoled herself that at least at Achlic, away from her father, she might have a bit more freedom. And while she was able to steal out for these walks and read some of Rupert's books, this little taste of freedom made her yearn for more. Far more.

Sighing, she eyed the descent of a murky sun in an iron-hard sky and knew she should head back to Achlic. She turned quickly, fired by her own resentment, and ran smack into the hard wall of a man's chest.

"Oof!"

"My goodness." A man's hands gripped her elbows to steady her as Margaret reeled in shock. "Are you hurt?"

She glanced up at the man's weather-beaten face, his hair a sandy brown, his eyes a friendly, faded blue. Although his skin was tanned and there were wrinkles around his eyes, she guessed him to be in his late twenties, no more.

"No, not at all, just surprised. I'm sorry I ran into you. I wasn't looking where I was going, I'm afraid." She stepped back, blushing at how close they'd been, and the man stooped to retrieve her book from the muddy street.

"*The Consolations of Philosophy*," he read out loud. "Boethius, if I'm not mistaken, sixth century. Could this fascinating tome be the reason why you missed your step?" His eyes crinkled with humor, but Margaret only felt wary.

"What do you mean?"

His smile was easy and open as he answered, "Not the usual reading material for a young lady."

"I suppose I should be reading some romantic nonsense," she said tartly before she could think better of it.

The man raised his eyebrows. "I have no such notion. Admittedly, most young ladies prefer such novels. Or at least the young ladies of my limited acquaintance. As for what you should be doing… that is hardly for me to say." He held the book out to her, and Margaret snatched it back. "Is there somewhere I may escort you to?" the man asked.

Margaret drew herself up. "That would hardly be proper, sir. I do not know you." It wasn't even proper for them to be standing in the street like this, talking, but Margaret found the conversation with this man was oddly stimulating. He might have been surprised by her reading choice, but he had not been scandalized or sternly disapproving.

"Then perhaps you will let me take the bold step of introducing myself." He bowed with mock flourish that caused Margaret's lips to twitch with suppressed laughter. "Captain Henry Moore, most pleased to make your acquaintance."

"I am Miss MacDougall," she said a bit reluctantly, for she was quite sure this wasn't a proper way to make a man's acquaintance. "Are you a sea captain, sir?"

He straightened, his eyes still full of humor. "Yes, I have a ship in port at the moment. *The Allegiance*. She runs between here and the Americas a couple of times a year. I've decided to stay in Scotland for the winter, though."

"But you're not Scottish." Margaret knew she should have drawn this conversation to a close long ago, and marched by this strange, forward man with a hint of gentle mockery in his eyes. Yet something about his forthright manner and the kindly laughter lacing his words compelled her to stay. This was, she realized, the most exciting thing that had happened to her.

"No, indeed I am not. I am American. My aunt is Scottish, and lives here in Tobermory." He grinned suddenly. "If I can't escort you somewhere, could she perhaps invite you to tea? Would that be more proper? I admit, as an American, I do not always adhere to the proper social niceties."

Margaret's eyes widened at his audacity—and her own ripple of pleasure that it brought. "I hardly think so, sir," she made herself say, even though she was tempted to recklessly accept. "As I don't even know the woman."

"Forgive me, but you hardly seem one to stand on stuffy propriety—or am I mistaken?" There was a thread of wistfulness in Captain Moore's voice, and she couldn't help but notice that his eyes were the color of the sea on a cloudy day. Margaret looked down, discomfited as much by her own thoughts as this man's impropriety.

"No, you're not mistaken in that, but even so such an invitation is unheard of."

"Until you hear of it," Captain Moore answered with a laugh. "And if my aunt, Mrs. Elizabeth Moore, a most respectable widow, were to send you an invitation, Miss MacDougall... to where should it be addressed?"

His eyes glinted with both challenge and humour, and before her courage failed her, Margaret blurted, "In the care of Achlic Farm, near Craignure."

Captain Moore bowed again. "Then I hope we will meet again, in more pleasant circumstances, Miss MacDougall. Adieu."

As he strode away, Margaret found herself gawping like a love-struck kitchen maid. She shook her head, and then turned smartly in the opposite direction. She could hardly believe the conversation had taken place, and yet it had. And she might receive an invitation from Mrs. Elizabeth Moore! A flicker of excitement licked through her at the thought. Who knew where such an acquaintance might lead? Or what would happen when she met Captain Moore again?

*

"I'm sorry there isn't better news, Mistress Campbell."

"Never mind, Ted." Harriet pushed the accounts book away from her and rubbed her eyes. She didn't bother to add that she was used to bad news by now, since that was all they'd had since September. Good news would come as a surprise, at this rate.

"Let me put the kettle on. The least I can offer you on a raw day like this is a cup of tea."

Ted murmured his thanks and Harriet went to the kitchen. She stood at the window while the kettle set to a boil, gazing distantly at the bleak midwinter landscape, the heather-covered hills turned a rusty orange under the darkening sky.

David Campbell had been bedridden for three months, and he was not an easy patient. Although his life was in no immediate danger, it was unlikely he would ever resume his full load of farm work again. The burden fell firmly onto Harriet's shoulders.

The piercing whistle of the kettle caused Harriet to yank it off the stove, burning her hand. Her father hated loud noises, and she didn't want to give him any more cause to complain, or voice his disappointment yet again that she'd not been a son.

Oh Allan, Harriet thought. *Why haven't you written? A letter from you would make this all so much more bearable…*

Another ship had docked in November, coming from Nova Scotia, and there had been more letters for Margaret and Rupert from their mother, as well as some terse greetings from their father. There had been nothing from Allan.

His silence, Harriet thought, not for the first time, was more damning than any words could have been. However constant he'd promised to be, it seemed that his mind—and his heart—had changed like the wind when an ocean separated them.

Yet as long as he was silent, what could she do? She'd not written back, and vowed that she would not bother Allan with her letters until he assured her of his own constancy.

The tea made, Harriet headed back into the parlor to speak with Ted Carmichael. There were more pressing problems to deal with than Allan's silence, painful as it was.

"It seems like the only solution is to sell some of our acreage," Harriet stated with blunt resignation as she handed Ted a cup of tea. "With the poor harvest return this year, we won't have enough money to hire the workers we'll need in the spring, as it is."

The corners of Ted's mouth pulled down in dismay. "Your father won't stand for that, Miss Campbell. This farm's been in your family for fifty years or more, and naught changed in all that time."

"Times have changed," Harriet replied, with a sigh. "Three years of bad harvests and dropping prices mean everyone's had to do without. If Father were well, if we'd some savings put by…" Harriet shook her head, trying not to give into the despair that always lapped at her. "In all truth, Ted, what else can we do?"

"There's always the sheep," Ted reminded her. "The price of wool is still steady, and there'll be new lambs this spring as well."

"Yes, but it won't be enough." Harriet knew they fetched a good price for their clip, but they'd always been primarily crop farmers, and the wool was used for the family, with a bit left over to sell. They could hardly pin all their hopes on that, even if they went without wool for themselves.

"It'll grieve your father mightily to sell any part of this farm," Ted said with a mournful shake of his head.

"Well, then he shouldn't have got us in this *moger*," Harriet retorted. As soon as the words were out, she regretted them. "Never mind what I said, Ted. I didn't mean it. I'm only tired."

"I know, Miss Campbell. Anna and I think you're a brave lass, if you want to know the truth. I don't *ken* how you put up with it all."

Neither do I, Harriet wanted to say, but she just smiled instead. "Thank you."

Later that evening, sitting by the fire, a piece of mending lying forgotten in her lap, Harriet's somber thoughts returned to circle uselessly in her mind. There seemed to be no solution but to sell the land, yet even that would only be a temporary answer at best. If next year's harvest turned out poorly again, they would be worse off than ever. They might sell another field, but the more land they sold, the less profit they could hope to make with what remaining land they had. It seemed a hopeless situation.

Eleanor came to stand in front of Harriet, a solemn look on her young face. With her fingers she gently stroked her older sister's forehead.

"What are you doing, Ellie?" Harriet asked, bemused.

"Don't worry, Harriet, please. I can tell you're worrying because you get that wrinkle in the middle of your forehead, like a dimple."

"Do I?" Harriet briefly touched her brow. "Gives me away, then, doesn't it? I'm sorry, love, I don't mean to trouble you with my worries."

"But you should," Eleanor protested seriously. "That's what we're here for."

"She speaks true," Margaret said, looking up from her game of chess with Rupert. "If we all pull together, perhaps we can think of a solution."

Eleanor sat on the stool by Harriet's knee. "It's money, isn't it? That we need, I mean."

Harriet put down her stitching with a sigh. "Yes, it is."

"Why didn't Father tell us things were going so badly?" Ian said suddenly, his voice full of frustrated anger. He gazed moodily into the fire. "It's as if he tricked us, all this while, making us think we were all right."

"Hush yourself, Ian Campbell," Harriet said sternly. "He was trying to keep us well out of it, and who knows what might've happened if the harvest had been better?" She closed her eyes briefly, the bleak numbers from the accounts book emblazoned on her mind. "As it is…"

"I wish we could forget it all," Ian said, sounding much younger than his just-turned fifteen years. "Who do we owe money to? They should forget it. If everyone's had a bad harvest, it's hardly fair to call in accounts."

"We owe money to just about everyone," Harriet said with a sigh. "Everything's been bought on credit lately. And I don't think it'll be forgotten, not in these hard times. We'll have to find the money somewhere." She smiled with poignant whimsy and quoted the old proverb, "Eaten meat is ill to pay."

"It is," Eleanor said feelingly. "Even if it tasted nice at the time."

"Surely we could do something," Margaret interjected. "I could write Father—"

"My father won't take charity, and neither will I," Harriet replied firmly.

"Harriet, we're as near as family."

Harriet just shook her head. Never mind that David would refuse such offers, she knew it would only be a temporary solution and a bad one at that. She patted Eleanor's thin shoulders. "Never mind, *cridhe*. We'll get by, somehow."

"Will we?" Eleanor's hazel eyes seemed to understand too much.

"I'll quit my studies," Ian spoke up suddenly. "We won't need money for a tutor then, and I can get a job, a proper one."

Harriet shook her head. "Ian, no. You love your studies. And no matter what Father has said in the past, he has always wanted an education for you."

"There are more important things now, aren't there?" Ian's eyes blazed with sudden, youthful determination. "I'm the man of the family now, at least while Father's abed. It's time I did things. Took decisions."

"But Ian," Harriet said, trying to be reasonable without hurting him, "what sort of job could you get? You're only fifteen."

"There are plenty of lads my age working already," Ian replied. "I could work at the docks in Tobermory, or even in Oban. Or do farm work on one of the bigger farms. They're probably doing well for themselves, the fat pigs!"

The bitterness in his voice was impossible to mistake. Harriet sat back with a sigh. How would Ian, with his slight build and fair skin, manage at a job that required the brawn and stamina of a full-grown man? He was used to reading and studying all day, nothing more arduous than putting pen to paper. Perhaps her father had been right, and Ian should have helped more with the farm before now. At least then his well-meant bravado wouldn't seem so ridiculous now.

Even so, Harriet knew the pennies Ian could bring to the household from a laborer's job would do little to cover the debt that threatened to drown them all. Desperate measures were required, and she only wished she knew what they were. Still, she turned to Ian and smiled.

"Thank you, Ian," she said softly, for she knew he had pride and she couldn't bear to hurt it. "You've become a man. I can see that now."

*

"Bring him in, bring him in, man!" Sandy's face was suffused with helpless anger and worry as Archie and Neville Dunmore stumbled in with an unconscious Allan lolling between them.

Agnes Dunmore gazed at Allan for a moment, her face stricken, before she turned briskly to the fire. "We'll need hot water… and whiskey. Lay him on the bed, Neville. But don't take his boots off, not yet. It needs a woman's touch, that."

Betty clutched at Agnes' arm, her face pale with shock and fear. "What can I do? Will he be all right?"

"Help me with the water," Agnes commanded. Her stern voice belied the gentleness in her eyes. "I know it's hard, but we all need clear heads now, Betty, if we want to do the best by him."

Allan lay on the bed, his face pale and speckled with frost, his eyes still closed, his breathing worryingly slight. Neville stood up. "It was a foolish notion he had, to go out after dark," he said with a shake of his head. "With the snow still falling, you could get lost going to the privy! Didn't he realize?"

Agnes shot him a quelling look. "Pay him no mind. Of course he didn't realize, Neville. They haven't seen a winter here yet. Now let's do the best for him we can. Pray God he doesn't lose any toes… or worse."

"Toes," Betty whispered, and half-staggered into Sandy's arms. "Oh, please, no…"

Sandy turned fiercely to Agnes. "What do you mean by worse?"

Neville put a hand on Sandy's shoulder. "Easy, man. There's no saying what it is. Wait and see how he thaws out."

Gently Agnes eased off Allan's boots and then began to cut away the frozen socks from his feet. Sandy stared at the lifeless, gray flesh in horror. "Fill the tub, Neville," Agnes commanded. "The water shouldn't be too hot, only warm. Let's bathe his feet gently, that's the way."

Neville and Sandy supported Allan, who stirred now with faint groans, as Agnes carefully bathed his frozen feet, pouring warm water over the frozen flesh. It seemed an eternity, but to everyone's relief after a little while his feet began to thaw and then to turn pink. With this, Allan began to moan, a piteous sound.

"It will pain him some now," Agnes said. "When the feeling comes back. That's the worst." Allan thrashed on the bed, his body bucking in pain. "You can see it's not pleasant," Agnes said with a nod. "Archie, bring him some whiskey."

"Why did he storm out of here like that?" Betty whispered, near tears. "So unlike Allan, to give into temper. He's always been my mildest child. And I don't even know why he was so angry."

"Don't you?" Agnes glanced at her, her expression shrewd. "It must have been something someone said."

Although he thankfully wouldn't lose any toes, Allan had to remain in bed for several days, for the spell in the freezing snow had thoroughly weakened him. Although he chafed at being bedridden, at least it gave him time to think, and realize the full extent of his moment of foolish bravado.

"It could've been the end of you," Archie said, his eyes sparkling with humour. Like everything else, Allan's brush with frostbite seemed like nothing more than a joke to him. "You must have tough skin, brother."

Allan grimaced in memory. "I suppose I must."

"Why did you do it?" Archie's voice was quiet, and serious for once. "Is it really that bad?"

Allan regarded him warily. Archie was always so cheerful and carefree, nothing seemed to bother him, not even their father's high-handed ways. How could his brother understand his own feelings of suffocation, of loss, that had to do as much with Harriet as with Sandy?

"You could get out, you know," Archie continued in a low voice. "Father's will isn't law. You can go your way, if you feel you must. Plenty of men do. They join regiments in Charlottetown, or trap out west. That's what we came here for—adventure, freedom. Not to work like a slave."

"Perhaps, but the cost is too high." Allan didn't even like to imagine the betrayal both his parents would feel at such an act. They'd come to this new world as a family, to work together. He just wished his father saw things a bit differently. "I'll stay here. I have to... for now."

As Allan rested, the rest of his family and the Dunmores made preparations for the Christmas season. Although the snow was deep and there was little to fashion presents out of, the islanders sought any reason to celebrate, and break up the long, dark days of winter. There would be supper parties and dancing at neighbors' houses, and a minister out of Charlottetown was coming to the community along the river to hold services.

Agnes and Betty set to making the traditional Christmas fare from the old country, raiding the precious winter stores. Soon the house was full of the delicious smells of black buns and sun cakes, and the hearty Christmas drink Atholl Brose, made from oatmeal and whiskey.

On Christmas Eve another foot of snow fell, so the drifts went as high as the rooftops, blanketing everything in white.

"*Is blianach Nollaig gun sneachd*," Agnes quoted with a wry smile. "Christmas without snow is poor fare."

"We've no need to worry about that," Sandy replied. "I've never seen such snow in my life!"

That evening they all sat around the fire, enjoying the warmth of the flames and each other's company.

"By this time next year, you'll be having us in your cabin," Neville said as he raised his glass. "Everyone who's built a cabin on this island has had help, so never fear about that."

"Thank you." Sandy was silent for a moment, as if struggling with himself. "You have been exceedingly generous to all my family," he said at last. "I trust we will have opportunity to do the same."

Betty smiled and clasped Sandy's hand. Allan thought he seemed more at peace this eve, and he wondered—and hoped— that he'd turned a corner. Perhaps they all had.

"No one could survive on their own here," Agnes said with a shake of her head. "The first Scots on the island had to wade in from the shallows to land, and then walk all the way to Charlottetown to beg for help! Thank heaven it's not like that any longer. We're all here for each other. We must be if anyone is going to survive. It's as simple as that."

Perhaps it wouldn't be so bad, Allan told himself as he raised his own glass. Here there was warmth, and love, and true friendship. Perhaps his father could change… and his dreams could wait a little while. Perhaps Harriet would have written, when the first ship returned in the spring.

The clock on the mantle, the Dunmores' pride and joy brought all the way from Inverness, struck its tinny chimes.

Neville smiled and glasses clinked. "Happy Christmas!"

*

The Campbells had a somber Christmas. David Campbell had never believed in all the heathen nonsense as he called it. Christmas was just like any other day, and should be treated as such. Since they'd little cause to celebrate anyway, Harriet was happy to keep the work and expense to a minimum.

Still, as Hogmanay approached, Margaret convinced her that they should at least celebrate that.

"Just a little something," she said. "It'll be our first Hogmanay without Mother and Father, as well as our brothers. Gladden our hearts, Harriet, you must!"

"Don't try that with me," Harriet said with a laugh. "I can hardly put on the kind of celebration you had at Mingarry, with all the parties and dancing."

"Just something quiet, then." Margaret's eyes glinted with mischief, and she looked more animated than she had in a long while. "A few games, a nice pudding… I'll make it, don't fear. A drop of whiskey, perhaps?"

"Margaret!" Harriet tried to look scandalized, but then laughter overcame her. "All right, then. We could all do with a little cheering. But we'll have to keep it quiet… if Father wakes up and hears us, he won't be pleased!"

Margaret held a finger to her lips. "As quiet as mice," she promised.

The party proved to be a success, with both the Campbell and MacDougall children as well as Ted and Anna Carmichael making a good crowd.

They all became a bit silly, playing parlor games that Harriet hadn't indulged in since she was a child. She grew weak with laughter at the sight of Ted Carmichael playing bullet pudding, where he poked his face in a dish full of flour to search for the hidden bullet which he'd had to retrieve with his teeth. Unfortunately, his laughter caused him to sneeze, the dish tipped, and soon everyone had a good dusting of flour.

They were still giggling when it came on midnight. As the clock struck twelve, Harriet joined in with the singing of "Auld Lang Syne", and for the first time in many months she felt something akin to peace. Even if Allan hadn't been true, she was a fortunate woman, blessed with family and home. The unease of their financial situation she pushed firmly away, to think about another day.

A sudden, loud knock at the door caused them all to start in surprise. "A first-footer!" Eleanor cried. "Let's hope he is a tall, dark stranger, to bring us good luck, as well as a *handsel*."

"You'd best give him a drop of whiskey," Ted warned her, "lest he go away unwelcome!"

Laughing, Harriet went to the door. It was custom for a friend to pretend to be the stranger at midnight; it meant good fortune for the coming year. Last year Andrew MacDuff had come upon them, dressed in a long cloak and funny hat, and brought a gift, or *handsel*, of a sack of apples.

She threw open the door, ready to greet Andrew or another neighbor, only to find the words die on her lips unspoken. The man on the doorstep was a stranger, tall and dark as well, just as any first-footer should be. Harriet had never seen him before.

"Excuse the lateness of the hour," the man said with a sweeping bow. He stepped into the circle of light cast by the lamp, and Harriet saw saturnine features, dark eyes full of amusement. "I thought I might bring you good luck as well as this."

He handed her a letter, and Harriet took it in blank surprise. "But who on earth…"

"Read and see, Miss Campbell."

She opened it with trembling hands.

Sir James Riddell requests an audience with Mistress Harriet Campbell at her earliest convenience.

"Sir James Riddell!" Harriet stared at the stranger in amazement. Of course she knew of the Riddells, since Allan's father had been their tacksman, but she had never had cause to meet the powerful family that owned half of Mull and all of Ardnamurchan, as well. "Why should he want to meet me?"

The man shrugged and smiled. "He asked that I take your reply. Can you meet him tomorrow?"

Wordlessly Harriet nodded. If Sir James had business with her, she wouldn't keep him waiting, yet she struggled to think what it could be.

"Good day then, Mistress Campbell. Till tomorrow."

Harriet watched the stranger disappear into the night, her mind spinning. The whole episode seemed like something out of a dream, or one of the Gothic novels that had been so popular. Margaret appeared at her elbow.

"You didn't invite him in! Why ever not, Harriet? Who was it, anyway? We're sure to have bad luck, now!"

The laughter in her eyes died as she saw Harriet's face. "What's the matter? You look almost ill. Who was it at the door?"

"I… I'm all right. It was just a man… someone I'd never met, deciding to honor the tradition, I suppose. Silly."

"Are you sure?" Margaret frowned. "You seem shaken."

"I'm all right, Margaret." Harriet took a deep breath and turned away from the door. Whatever good luck the stranger had meant to bestow, she knew he'd failed. Business with Sir James Riddell surely did not promise good fortune, not when she considered the state of Achlic Farm, of her family's affairs. Tomorrow she would discover just what that great man wanted with her.

CHAPTER SIX

Harriet shivered as an icy wind blew in from the sea. It had taken her most of the morning to walk to Lanymoor, Sir James's large manor house on the southern tip of Mull, and her fingers and toes were numb with cold. Now that she was here at the gate, she felt not relief, but dread.

What could Sir James want with her that was anything good?

His reputation among the farmers and crofters of the island was that of a spider. Cold, cruel, with an ever-expanding web. Some said he wouldn't rest until all of Mull's property was in his name, every last crofter under his boot.

Harriet vowed he would not have the Campbell holding, no matter what their debts. Some prices were too high to pay.

Squaring her shoulders, she marched up the sweeping drive. The house of mellowed stone had been built a century ago, and it retained the elegant lines and spaciousness of a gracious home. Harriet hesitated at the large front portico. Should she go around to the servants' entrance?

No, she decided with more courage than her stomach seemed to think she had. She was no one's servant, least of all this man's.

A parlor maid answered her knock, and after taking her plain woollen cloak, directed her into a small morning room. A fire blazed in the hearth, and Harriet stretched her hands out towards its warmth with relief.

"Sir James will be with you shortly." With a flounce of her skirts, the maid disappeared. Harriet looked round at her sumptuous surroundings in both amazement and trepidation. She was conscious that even her best dress that she'd worn for the occasion was well out of fashion, and the lace on the collar she'd added herself. Her best boots still needed to be re-soled, and her bonnet was in desperate need of some repair. She didn't fit into this world, not remotely.

"Miss Campbell."

Harriet whirled around at the voice. Sir James Riddell stood in the doorway, surveying her with shrewd, dark eyes. He was tall and spare, with short graying hair and a finely trimmed moustache. His breeches and morning coat were of the finest quality, his boots polished and gleaming. He looked to be no more than forty or forty-five.

"Good morning, sir." Harriet sketched a curtsey. "I believe you have business with me?"

"Ah, yes." Riddell smiled, and the sight made Harriet feel even more unsure of herself. It was the look of a man who knew he was in control, in power, and relished it. "Why don't you sit down?" he invited. "I've asked for a dish of tea."

Reluctantly Harriet sat on a striped silk divan. Sir James sat across from her.

"Ah, Miss Campbell." Sir James smiled at her in a way that made her skin prickle. "Things have not been easy for you and your family, have they?"

Harriet clenched her hands in her lap, and tried to cover the motion with her skirt. "Everyone has had their share of difficulties in these trying times, sir."

"Of course…" Sir James nodded in understanding, steepling his fingers under his chin. "But what with your father's illness, and of course the dire straits Achlic Farm is in at the moment…" he trailed off delicately, his dark eyes watching her.

Harriet forced herself to unclench her hands. Her gloves were damp with sweat. How did he know these things? Why had he taken care to learn them?

"And of course, your sweetheart... my dear cousin's son..." Sir James's smile turned knowing, even sly. "Leaving for Scotia like that. The whole family just upped and went. I lost a very good tacksman, I'm sad to say. I was sorry to see them go." His eyes were cold even as he asked pleasantly, "What was his name? Your beau?"

Harriet forced herself to speak calmly. She supposed Sir James knew about her through the MacDougalls, although it hardly seemed likely they would discuss her private affairs. The question was, *why* he knew—and cared? "His name is Allan."

"Yes, of course. I remember him. The oldest son. A pity you weren't able to marry before he emigrated. It would have made it all so much simpler."

Harriet felt her heart twist painfully inside her. With effort she lifted her chin and met Sir James's predatory gaze. "Yes, a pity."

His smile widened, looking falser than ever, making her want to shiver. "Forgive my rudeness. I only ask because I commiserate with you, my dear Miss Campbell. I loved someone once, you know."

"Did you indeed?" Harriet could not imagine it. Neither could she imagine the woman who would be the unfortunate object of this man's affections.

"Sadly, my guardian did not think it a good match. Understandable, of course, as I was an impressionable young man with a title and fortune since I was but ten years old." Harriet inclined her head in acknowledgement. She knew Sir James Riddell's history well enough.

He sat back in his chair, crossing one leg neatly over the other. "By the time I had gained my independence and was able to make an offer, the lady in question had changed her mind." For a moment, his expression hardened, the charming smile slipping out of place. "Fickle creatures that you ladies can be."

"I'm sorry that was the case." Harriet couldn't fathom why Sir James was offering such personal details, but she was still wary of his honeyed words and falsely compassionate tone. There was a sting hidden somewhere, she knew it. "Of course," she felt compelled to add, "Allan MacDougall need have no such fear of me."

"Ah, but we are all capricious, are we not?" His eyes glittered and he leaned forward. "Tell me, have you received any letters from your dear Allan?"

Harriet's mouth was dry and her mind raced even as her thoughts blurred with confusion. Sir James almost sounded as if he knew something. Had the MacDougalls written to him? Sandy might have, as tacksman, and yet... surely he would not parted with the private details of Harriet and Allan's intentions! But what could the wretched man possibly know? And why did he care so much? She did not like to consider the possible answers.

"His family has corresponded," she said in a small, tight voice.

"Ah, good." A maid brought in a tea tray and they were both silent until she'd left the room again. "Would you be so kind as to pour?"

Harriet nodded, and then willed her hands not to shake as she lifted the heavy pot. "Cream or sugar?" she asked in little more than a whisper.

"Both, thank you." Somehow Harriet managed to pour, and with another one of his unpleasant smiles Sir James took the delicate china cup and sipped. "I'm sure you're wondering why I've brought you here, Miss Campbell, and the answer is simple. You have something I want, and in return I have something you want. It all sounds very simple, does it not?"

Harriet stared at him in dumbfounded amazement. The teapot slipped slightly in her grasp, and quickly she set it down with an awkward clatter. She could not fathom what Sir James meant, and yet she could see well enough that he was toying with her, as clearly as a cat with a helpless, hapless mouse, and suddenly it made her angry. "What could you possibly have that I want?" she asked coldly.

Sir James chuckled, a dry, rasping sound. "I imagine," he said coolly, his gaze flicking around the room and all of its elegant objects, "that I have many things you want. However, I'm speaking in this instance of one particular item. Or really, several items, were I to count them." He reached into the pocket of his coat and withdrew a packet of letters, each one folded and sealed with wax.

Harriet felt the blood drain from her face and for a moment the room faded from her sight as she struggled to grasp what Sir James was so obviously showing her. *Letters…* letters that looked weathered and worn, as if they'd endured a long voyage, across a tempestuous sea. Letters that could only be from one person. Letters that Allan had written after all, and were in this awful man's possession. Her teacup rattled as she replaced it in its saucer.

"Where did you get those?" she asked faintly. She wanted to be angry but she felt too shocked.

"Shall we say I found them?" Sir James raised his eyebrows, but then his jocular expression hardened. "It would do well, Miss Campbell," he said, his voice dangerously soft, "to remember that I can get most anything I want on this island."

"Why did you want letters meant for me?" Harriet's voice came out in a thread of sound. She felt her heart thud hard in her chest and she thought she could be sick. She was near tears, yet the last thing she wanted to do was cry in front of this man.

"I told you, you have something I want. Something small… for now."

Harriet shook her head. "I don't know what it could be."

"I've heard it told that you are excellent on the pianoforte."

Her eyes widened in surprise. *The pianoforte?* It was the last thing she'd expected. She'd assumed he meant the farm, the Campbells' land as the largest smallholding on the island. "I play," she agreed cautiously.

"My niece, Miss Caroline Reid, is eight years old. I'd very much like her to learn how to play. I thought you could teach her. You'd be compensated, of course, for your time."

"You took those letters just so I'd teach the pianoforte?" Harriet's voice rose in disbelief. It didn't make any sense. If he'd asked her outright, she would have accepted. There was no need for subterfuge or trickery; the extra income would be welcome.

And with that realization came another unwelcome one—this couldn't be merely about some pianoforte lessons. Sir James Riddell had to have some other nefarious plan. Did he want her under his thumb, where he could watch her? Was he hoping she'd reveal something about their precarious financial situation?

Sir James clearly wasn't going to reveal his real motives. "Are you agreed, then?" he asked pleasantly, the packet of letters still in his hand.

Harriet knew she didn't really have much choice. Sir James Riddell was not a man to cross, not even in this small matter. She suspected then that he hadn't taken the letters so she would teach his niece. He'd taken them to show her his power.

She felt its weight with a sickening lurch of fear. There had to be something else Sir James wanted and she knew what it was. Her family's farm. Their whole livelihood. God help her, she would not be the one to give it to him.

"Yes," she said at last, her voice sounding far too thin and wavery. "I'd be… delighted to teach Miss Reid the pianoforte."

"Good." Sir James smiled. "Shall we see you here next Tuesday, at three o'clock?" He extended the letter to her. "Don't forget these."

Harriet took the letters with numb fingers. "Why," she asked, her voice little more than a croak, "did you ask me here, really?"

Sir James smiled. "I believe I gave you the reason, my dear."

"The real reason, then," Harriet said, her voice coming out stronger. She would not let herself be cowed by this man.

"Ah, Miss Campbell." He shook his head, his tone still pleasant. "Let us leave it at that, shall we? For now."

With those ominous words, Harriet knew he indeed had plans she was not aware of. Plans she realized she didn't want to consider too closely. Perhaps, they would never come to pass.

A few minutes later she was let out of the house, the letters still clutched in her hand. The sky was a pale, fragile blue, wispy clouds scudding across. Harriet closed her eyes briefly, enjoying the weak warmth of winter sunlight on her face.

Allan had written her. He had not forgotten her. He was not faithless.

She opened her eyes. Was he now wondering about her own lack of response, her faithless heart, since she hadn't written, not even once? Grief and guilt rushed through her in a scalding river. How many months had passed, with Allan doubting her? She was the faithless one, not him.

"We meet again."

Harriet looked up in surprise to see her Hogmanay visitor, dressed in the somewhat frayed coat of a gentleman. "You," she said dumbly. She'd almost completely forgotten about him, in her distress about Sir James and the letters he'd kept.

"Your first-footer," the gentleman said with a wry smile. "Please, let me introduce myself. I am Mr. Andrew Reid, nephew to Sir James." Although he resembled James Riddell in looks, his face was full of humor rather than shrewdness. He bowed low, with a flourish, and Harriet narrowed her eyes.

"You have a flair for the dramatic, Mr. Reid."

Andrew grinned. "It adds a bit of fun. I admit, coming to Achlic Farm on Hogmanay might have been a bit much. I didn't mean to frighten you off." He held out one hand in appeal. "You're not cross with me now, are you?"

There was a look of gentle whimsy in his eyes that made Harriet angry, though she could not fathom why. Perhaps it was because of her recent interview with Sir James; she was in no mood for banter, as if coming here had been some sort of lark. "Why should I be cross with a stranger?" she asked coldly, and inclined her head in farewell. "Good day to you, sir."

Harriet marched down the drive without looking back, her heart thudding in her chest. She couldn't bear to wait until she was home to read Allan's precious letters, and so despite the cold, she stood off to the side of the road and broke the seal on the first, her fingers trembling as she held the page and read his lines.

Dearest Harriet,

We have only just begun this voyage, and I am full of thoughts of you. How I long for you to be here with me, sharing in this adventure, daydreaming with me about what is yet to be. One day, I know, that will come to pass…

Harriet let out a little cry and opened another letter, and then another.

I miss you with all of my being… When I close my eyes, I picture you as I last saw you, at Duart… I had been hoping to receive a letter from you on the last sailing, but another ship is due next week…

Tears streamed down her face as she read of Allan's love and his constancy, even as she heard the sorrowful doubt creeping into his lines. She hadn't written to him, and of course he wondered why. There would have been time for him to receive at least one letter, and perhaps two or three, before winter had closed in, and there had been nothing.

Harriet closed her eyes in wordless remorse. Another ship wouldn't sail to the New Scotland for at least another two or three months, and all that while Allan would be wondering. Doubting. How could she have been so faithless?

*

"Now, Miss MacDougall, you must tell me all about yourself."

Seated in Elizabeth Moore's cosy parlor in Tobermory, with tea and scones and Henry Moore sitting across from her, his eyes twinkling with wry humor, Margaret felt a warm flush of pleasure. It was so very pleasant to be here, with people who found her interesting and worth talking to. It was certainly better than being trapped in a kitchen, slaving over a cooking pot or ironing endless sheets. Until she'd come to Achlic, she hadn't realized how cossetted she'd been at Mingarry, with servants at hand to do the heavy work, and her only light duties a bit of needlework.

"My family has emigrated to the New Scotland," Margaret explained. "And I've stayed behind with my younger brother, Rupert, so he can finish his lessons."

"And have some lessons of your own?" Henry added with a smile. "You do seem fond of learning."

"And why shouldn't I be?" Margaret flared before she could help herself. "In this modern age, I believe an educated woman should be considered an asset to any household."

"Oh, my!" Elizabeth clapped her hands together in delight. "You're not a milksop miss, are you now, my dear?" She turned to smile broadly at Henry. "I do enjoy a good debate. You've done well, Henry."

Henry laughed. "You won't get one with me, Aunt Elizabeth. I've nothing against educating women… or anyone who's interested, for that matter, slave or free." His face darkened for a moment before he turned to Margaret and smiled. "Everyone has a right to learning. And you enjoy your reading, do you, Miss MacDougall?"

"I do," Margaret said, and then felt compelled to confess, "but the books belong to my brother."

"Does it matter the owner?" Henry asked lightly. "I would have thought the reader was far more important."

"Perhaps." Margaret found herself blushing under Henry Moore's kindly gaze. There was compassion in his eyes, but there was also too much understanding. She felt as if he already knew her, when he didn't at all.

"Perhaps," he murmured, "your brother's tutor is not as enlightened as we are?" He spoke with easy humor, yet Margaret still stiffened.

"I beg your pardon?"

"Could you not have lessons with your brother?"

Her gaze skittered away. "I fear not." Not wanting to admit anything more about her father's restrictions, she broke off and stared into her teacup.

"You must miss your family terribly," Elizabeth said to break the sudden, awkward silence. "Will you and your brother be joining them in the New Scotland?"

"One day, perhaps in two years' time." It suddenly seemed so far away, and Margaret was seized with a fierce desire to see her family again, especially Mother and Allan, who understood her and made her laugh. How was it possible that a familiar world had become so strange, when the people she loved most were no longer in it?

"I'm sorry, my dear, I didn't mean to make you mournful by speaking of it."

"It's all right." Margaret looked up and smiled. "I shall see them soon, I know, and in the meantime your company is most pleasant, I assure you."

"It is lovely to have such young company," Elizabeth agreed. "I'm thankful I was able to lure Henry away from Boston for a season. Scotland in the winter is hardly a pleasing prospect to one as travelled as he."

"It is your company, Aunt Elizabeth," Henry replied with a gallant little bow, his eyes alight with self-deprecating laughter. He turned to Margaret. "My parents emigrated to America from Oban when I was but a bairn myself. Aunt Elizabeth stayed, and I have long promised to stay a winter with her. I am finally making good on it."

"That's very kind of you."

"And it was kind of me to take him in," Elizabeth teased.

Listening to their banter, Margaret realized that her own home had been sadly lacking in that kind of ease and companionship. She and Allan had always rubbed along well enough, and Archie was good for a laugh, although not much else, and of course there was Rupert... yet somehow when she remembered Mingarry Farm, it was as if a shadow had hung over it, a shadow of something akin to fear.

Fear, Margaret realized, of her father. Sandy was an honorable man, a careful father, but he had always been stern, and often quick to disapprove. The four children had always made sure to watch their words, and even their looks under his sharp eye. And Mother, dear Mother, saw it too, Margaret knew. She realized now the burden she must have borne, of always being caught between.

Could they escape those old shadows in the new world? Had they already? Perhaps in a country so new and untamed, people could change. Her father could change.

"There seems an obvious solution to your quandary," Henry said suddenly, jolting Margaret out of her reverie. She realized the hour was late and she would have to hurry to meet Rupert and Ian before walking home. "Don't you think so, Aunt Elizabeth?"

"Perhaps I would, if I knew what you were on about," Elizabeth replied, her expression as puzzled as Margaret's.

Henry leaned back in his chair. "Miss MacDougall would like instruction. A tutor, even. I need something to occupy this long winter, and you could do with some entertainment as well, I'd imagine."

Elizabeth's eyes twinkled with sudden understanding. "Indeed I could."

"I'm sorry, but I've no idea what any of this means," Margaret said, trying not to be cross or worse hurt that they were talking over her head. "And I'm afraid I must take my leave very shortly. My brother will be waiting for me, and I wouldn't wish him to worry."

Elizabeth smiled up at her. "I think, my dear Miss MacDougall, that Henry is suggesting he could be your tutor." Margaret's stunned gaze flew between the pair of them. "My *tutor*... but..."

"I assure you, he's quite educated," Helena continued, now smiling broadly. "He attended university in America—where was it again, Henry?"

"Harvard."

Margaret sat back down, her mind whirling. "But..."

"It would be all very proper," Henry added quickly, covering his mouth in a sudden, embarrassed cough. "Aunt Elizabeth could act as our chaperone."

Margaret glanced up at him. His eyes were warm, and still a bit too knowing. Still, there was honesty there, and genuine friendliness. "I couldn't pay you," she warned, compelled to the truth. "I'm afraid that would be out of the question. I have no means of my own at present."

"Money need not come into it," Henry replied with a dismissive wave of his hand. "Let us consider it a matter between friends?" The questioning lilt in his voice made Margaret blush. Her mind spun with new possibilities, doors she thought forever shut now thrown wide open. An education... a *friendship*...

"Yes... of course." Her words came out in a stutter, and she concentrated on finding her gloves, suddenly unable to meet Henry's gaze.

The silence lengthened, and Margaret caught Elizabeth's smile of obvious delight from the corner of her eye. Did she imagine she was seeing the beginnings of some sort of courtship? The thought was scandalous... and thrilling.

"It's settled then," Henry said. "You can come here in the mornings, while your brother is having his lessons. And at the end of winter, when I return to sea, you can decide which of you has received the better education!"

Margaret nodded, still unable to believe this turn of events. She fumbled once more with her gloves and they fell to the floor.

With a little smile Henry picked them up and handed them to her. "Who do you think shall have the better education, Miss MacDougall? I wonder."

Margaret wondered if he was talking about an education of an entirely different nature—a romance that she could barely imagine. "I just want to learn," she blurted, and then blushed scarlet. "Out of books."

Henry grinned, unabashed, while Margaret cringed with mortification. "Of course," he agreed. "Perhaps we should start with Boethius?"

*

The snows had remained deep on Prince Edward Island throughout the winter, the drifts piling halfway up the cabins, as the long days passed slowly, with all of the MacDougalls waiting for the first signs of the spring thaw which didn't come until late March.

At least it was warm enough for the MacDougalls to begin building again, although the wet snow and endless mud made it a dismal business indeed. The three men slogged from the Dunmores' to their own holding every morning, to attempt to construct their cabin while thigh-deep in snow and mud.

One afternoon in early April, Allan and Archie stood knee-deep in slushy mud, joining logs together for the south wall. The cabin was made of stripped logs with corner dovetail notches, to reduce the need for nails which could only be had on the mainland. It was a style of building common in the Americas for the last hundred years, but foreign to the Scots. It had been the Dunmores who had shown them the way of it, and it was still slow going.

"Give me a nail any day," Archie had said more than once, rolling his eyes, and Allan was inclined to agree with him.

In the distance they could hear the loud crack of the ice floes breaking apart on the Platte River, each one as loud as a gunshot and making Allan startle, although he know the older islanders were used to the sounds.

"It's looking bonny now, eh, boys?" Sandy called as he waded through the mud to inspect their work, his hands planted on his hips.

Allan nodded his agreement. Putting the walls together would take relatively little time, compared to digging out the foundations. He couldn't suppress a stirring of unease, however, that the cabin was twice as big as most others in the Scottish settlements. Besides the large common room with its stone fireplace, there were three bedrooms and a separate kitchen. What was his father trying to prove, and in such a place as this?

"We'll have it finished before planting time," Sandy said in satisfaction. "This summer we'll be as any other family on the island, living in our own home, enjoying the fruits of our own hands, a harvest ready."

Allan had seen the plans for their acreage, though he'd had no say in designing them. Fields for barley, wheat, potatoes, and hay, as well as a kitchen garden for the family's needs and an orchard for apples and cherries.

Although he'd no place in the decision making, Allan was looking forward to the new challenges. Once finished, the MacDougall farm would be a prosperous place indeed, or so they all hoped. The soil was good—rich and fertile, and the growing season was long and hot and mostly dry. They would do much better here than back on Ardnamurchan, where the summer had been unreliable, the weather often wet and cold.

"I've heard talk about going across to the mainland," Archie said after Sandy had left. "Heading to Pictou and seeing what's there. The ice is breaking up enough to take a boat. Douglas MacPherson said we could take his boat across the bigger ice floes and make it that way. He'll guide us."

Allan frowned. He'd only met the MacPhersons, another neighbor with a holding along the river, a few times, and Douglas seemed as sensible a man as any. But the Platte River was still thick with ice, and the crossing to the mainland wasn't much better, as far as he could see. "Isn't it too early?" he asked with a shake of his head. "The Dunmores said no one ever tried to cross till April." As if to underscore his words, another loud crack of breaking ice echoed through the cold, still air.

"Scared, brother?" Archie raised his eyebrows in light mockery. "I haven't seen naught but the walls of that cabin, and this mud hole, for months. I'd like a bit of adventure. There's a taproom in Pictou. Enough ale to see me through till spring."

"It's dangerous, Archie," Allan insisted in a low voice. "You've heard the tales. Men have been trapped in the ice floes for days… and then found frozen, weeks or even months later."

"Them, perhaps," he said with a shrug. "Not me."

Allan sighed. Archie had always had a daring side, but this was foolhardy in the extreme. He knew he couldn't let his brother be so reckless.

If anything happened to Archie, Allan would be the one to answer to his father. For all the responsibility he thought he wanted, he didn't want this one, but he knew it was his anyway. "What does Douglas MacPherson think of this plan?" he asked, and Archie shrugged.

"He'll go."

Allan suspected Douglas, three years younger than Archie, looked up to him, envied his charm and careless attitude. No doubt the lad wanted to show Archie how daring he could be, and risk his life in the process.

"You know it's not a good idea. We don't know this land well enough yet. And what I've already seen of frostbite is enough to last me."

"Then don't go with us."

Allan sighed. "You're determined to go?"

Archie gave him a measured look. "I am, with or without you."

It wouldn't be without, that much Allan knew. He would have to accompany them. If anything happened to Archie on his watch, Sandy and Betty would never forgive him. And Allan knew he would never forgive himself. Archie was known to be reckless, wild. Even as a grown man he needed Allan to keep him safe.

"All right, then," he said finally, his voice filled with reluctance. "I'll go."

Archie grinned. "I knew you would," he said, and Allan chose not to reply.

The sky was a dispiriting bone-white, an unfriendly blankness to it, when they set out the next day to cross the sea to the mainland. Allan stared at its churning surface, large, jagged ice floes strewn across it as if flung by a giant hand. The water rushing past them looked cold and angry, having finally escaped its winter entrapment.

Douglas MacPherson stood on the shore as he shook his head, nibbling at his lip in an anxious manner. "It looks too rough today. Perhaps we should wait. It's still early."

"I'm not waiting," Archie declared. "We've dragged the boat all this way already. We'd be fools to go back now. Look, we could almost walk across!" He stepped onto a chunk of ice and did a little jig as he grinned at them. "See?"

"You won't be dancing when we're in the middle of that," Douglas said, pointing to the ice-laden waters—large chunks of ice trapped in the rushing, freezing waters. "Too many men have died that way. Men who should have known better."

Archie rested his hands on his hips as he raised his eyebrows in eloquent and damning silence. Douglas frowned unhappily, clearly seeing the folly of the expedition, yet unwilling to be labelled a coward, if only by silence.

Allan had no such fears. If MacPherson, a seasoned islander, had his doubts, then so did he. "Leave off, Archie. If Douglas says it's dangerous, then I reckon it's true. He's lived here longer than we have, and he knows this land and this sea. We'd be fools not to heed him."

"Yesterday he told me he'd done it before!" Archie scoffed as he gave Douglas a contemptuous glance. "You were brave sitting by the fire, weren't you? What's changed then?"

Anger licked through Allan and he strove to keep his voice even. "We're all brave by the fire. Enough, now. We'll go later in the season, like sensible men, so we don't lose our lives or even a few toes. It's not worth the risk, Archie, or the trouble."

"Ah," Archie replied as he rocked back on his heels, "but I've never been a sensible man." There was a glitter in his brother's eyes that Allan had never seen before, a gleam of recklessness far beyond his usual insouciance that chilled Allan even more than the frozen waters by their feet.

"And if you take us with you to your icy grave, how will that be on your conscience?" he demanded in a low voice.

Archie shrugged. "I'm not whipping you into the boat, am I? I'll go by myself if I have to."

"You can hardly go alone, you don't even know the route! And you've never paddled through ice floes before. You'd be in the water before we'd even lost sight of you. Besides, it takes at least two men to carry the boat over the big floes."

"Such touching confidence!" Archie spread his arms wide as he tilted his head to the opaque sky. "Still, I think I'll place the wager." He turned to Douglas. "Coming, or are you as womanish as my brother?"

Allan clenched his fists and forced himself to ignore the unjust jibe. He knew Archie loved to stir things up simply for the pleasure of seeing the trouble he'd caused, yet this was farther than he usually dared to go, and the wager he talked of placing affected them all—perhaps to the death.

Douglas stared at his feet, looking as miserable a man as Allan had ever seen. He was only seventeen or so, little more than a boy. "Aye, I'll come." He stepped reluctantly into the iceboat.

Archie waved at Allan. "Keep the soup warm for us," he mocked, "we'll be hungry when we return, no doubt, with our stomachs full of ale and our heads full of stories. If I find there are letters in Pictou for you, shall I leave them there?"

Letters. It was the last straw. "I'm coming too," Allan replied, his voice little more than a growl. "I can hardly let you go alone, and you damned well know it."

"Can't you? Or did Father tell you to keep me on leading strings?" There was a ragged note of bitterness in Archie's voice that caused Allan to turn his head.

"He's never…"

"Who accompanied him on visits to the crofts all those years? To see Riddell?" Allan shook his head in instinctive denial, but Archie pressed on. "You may chafe at how he treats you, brother, but it's a sight more than what he has done for me."

Allan stared at his brother for a moment, saw the careless laughter in his dark eyes replaced by something cold and hard, a kernel of bitterness nursed for far longer than he knew. The wind, even by the shore, was cold and raw as it blew over them. Allan started towards the boat.

Archie gave a cold little smile. "I never asked you to be my keeper."

"I know you haven't. But whether you wish it or not, Father would want me to keep you in my sights."

"Ah, but that's where we differ, brother," Archie cut him off. "You care what Father thinks. I don't."

He turned away to speak to Douglas, and Allan was left feeling cast adrift in more ways than he cared to number. He didn't want to go on this wretched journey, especially with Archie acting so reckless and strange. Yet he knew he had no choice. He was a man of honor, and part of that was protecting his younger brother, fools that they both were.

They pushed off from the shore. Lightweight and little more than a canoe, the ice boat was made to be carried across the larger ice floes, but it did not inspire confidence—or stability—out in the more open waters.

The wind was biting and as the island grew smaller behind them, Allan could see why the Mi'kmaq, who had settled there thousands of years ago, had named it Abegweit, 'Cradled by the waves'. Prince Edward Island was truly no more than a small smudge of land surrounded by a vast and relentless ocean that pulsed all the way back to Scotland.

It was only twelve miles to the mainland, but progress was painstakingly slow. Douglas crouched in the stern, shouting directions while Archie and Allan paddled, their numb hands curled around the paddle handles as they navigated around the ice floes that surged through the waters, a minefield of frozen waters and icy danger.

They'd just cleared an open stretch of water and were navigating between two large ice floes when Douglas suddenly shouted, "Turn around! Turn around, quick as you can! We can't go through here!"

Allan began to paddle as fast as he could, trying to turn the boat even as the two large ice floes began to push on its sides. Within a matter of moments the boat was jammed between the two large floes, water rushing behind them.

With a heavy thud that sent them all to their knees, the front of the boat hit a wide fissure in an ice floe in front of them, trapping them on three sides.

They were all silent for a moment, the air surprisingly still, their breath coming in frosty puffs as they looked around them at all the ice.

"Can you shift it?" Archie finally asked.

Douglas shook his head. "Not enough, with the ice on either side, as well. It's jammed right in. Perhaps if we all try…" He glanced behind them, his face going even paler. Another outcropping of ice had broken off from a larger floe and was floating towards them, pushed by the surging water. It wedged itself in behind the boat, locking them in completely, encasing them in ice.

Ice blocked them on all four sides. In every direction there was only more ice-strewn water, cold, unforgiving, promising nothing but despair. They were at least five miles from shore.

"It's no good," Douglas said hoarsely. "There's no way out."

Allan stared at him in blank horror. "What do you mean?" he demanded. "You've done this before, haven't you? You said you did. There must be a way out. The ice will shift itself, or we will. We can't just lie down and—and *die*."

Douglas stared at him with wide, hopeless eyes for a moment before shaking his head. "Have you ever tried to move ice? You might as well empty the ocean with a spoon. It won't move, and we'll likely damage the boat if we try."

"To hell with the boat!"

"I'd rather freeze to death than drown," Douglas said flatly. "It's an easier going, or so I've heard."

"And who came back to tell the tale?" Archie said with a laugh. He shook his head, his eyes narrowed as he looked around at all the ice.

"Then we're to wait here till we freeze to death?" Allan asked in disbelief. Anger followed fast, crashing over him in a useless wave. He suppressed a violent shiver. Already he was becoming more aware of the cold, a damp chill that seeped through his coat and gloves, into his very bones.

"Another boat might come." Even as he said it, Douglas seemed to know what a feeble hope this was. "They know we've gone, after all…"

"They'll think we spent the night in Pictou," Allan said flatly. "We'd hardly set back in the dark." Sandy hadn't been best pleased with their plans, as it was. He would have been furious if he'd realized how dangerous it truly was.

"Still, someone might come," Douglas insisted. "If a boat came near us, we could cross that ice floe to it, but even that would be dangerous."

"I thought we were *meant* to cross the floes!"

"Big ones. These are all small. A man could fall through, or topple over. They're little more than boulders. It would be like playing hopscotch across the waters."

"Will the ice shift by itself?" Allan asked. His mind was racing as if through a maze, looking for any small chance of escape. "Surely it will break up on its own."

"Perhaps… in time." Douglas shrugged.

"Then we can wait for that," Allan said with a firmness borne from desperation. "We have some food, and there's water." He gestured to the sea all around them. "We'll manage."

Douglas gave him an almost pitying look. "When the sun sets it will be below freezing, and we're out here in the open. How long do you suppose we'll last?"

The helpless rage inside him spilled over. "If it was so dangerous, why did you agree to go?"

Archie had been listening to their conversation, a faint smile on his face. Now he spoke quietly. "You know as well as I do it was my idea, Allan. Douglas wouldn't have gone if I hadn't suggested he was a coward." Douglas stared at his feet. "Truth is, he told me we should wait till after the syruping."

"A fine time to mention that," Allan snapped.

"And," Archie continued, ignoring Allan, "you wouldn't have gone at all, if you didn't have this ridiculous notion that you need to keep watch over me."

"You knew I'd come," Allan said in a choked voice. "You must have known."

Archie shrugged. "I suppose I did."

"Then perhaps," Allan said, struggling to keep his voice even, "you can find a way to get us out of this wretched *fankle*." He paused, the fury and despair hardening inside himself so he felt like a different person. A stranger, even to himself. "Because if you don't, you've killed us, Archie. You've killed us all."

Archie merely smiled, and Allan realized he was most angry with himself, for agreeing to Archie's foolish plan. For letting his brother have his way, as he always did. He could have persuaded him otherwise, surely, and prevented this disaster. The fault was his, for being led by his brother yet again.

"I'm not willing to give up quite that easily," Archie replied with a jaunty grin, although Allan saw that his face was pale, his eyes darker than usual. He was afraid, as well. How could he not be? "Douglas, what chance is there of another boat coming out in this cold, and finding us, truly?"

Douglas swallowed audibly. "None," he admitted. "No one goes out this early."

"Well, then," Archie replied easily, "I'll just have to go get one."

"You can't!" Douglas grabbed his sleeve as Archie stood up. "The ice is too dangerous, Archie. It may look solid, but see how it's black underneath? You'll go right through, and you won't last more than two minutes in the water, if that."

"We haven't another chance," Archie stated calmly. "And I'm deft on my feet, remember?" He glanced out at the water. "There are ice floes as far as I can see, and surely that's a good sign. I'll play that game of hopscotch."

"It's madness!" Douglas shook his head vehemently. "We must be six miles from the mainland."

And six miles from the island as well, Allan realized. Trapped right in the middle. "Douglas is right, Archie," he said. "There must be another way."

"And what way would that be?" Archie asked.

"Someone will realize. When we don't come back. We can manage one night out here, surely, if we huddle together in the bottom of the boat…"

Archie shook his head. "Douglas already said how cold it gets. And in any case… Douglas, did you even tell anyone you were coming out?"

Douglas shook his head. "They would've thought me mad."

Archie turned to Allan. "Father doesn't even realize the danger, he's that ignorant of the ways here. He wouldn't have let us go if he did. No one is coming to look for us," he finished flatly, and with a lurch of pure fear Allan knew it was true.

"Going out there alone is as good as a death warrant," he said in a low voice. "Archie, let me go. I'll do it—"

Archie laughed, the sound echoing like a gunshot across the sea, ricocheting off the ice. "I won't let you play the hero that easily. Can you imagine what my life would be like, hearing how dear Allan saved me from my own recklessness? No, I'll do it."

"I can't let you—"

"I'm not asking your permission," Archie said coolly. "As I recall, it was my fault we're in this *fankle*, you said so yourself.

Now let me take the responsibility off your stooped shoulders, brother. There's far too much placed there as it is."

Or not enough, Allan thought. He'd craved more responsibility at the farm, but he didn't want this. Never this.

"All right," he said at last, the words torn from him. "God be with you."

"He always is." With a mocking salute Archie stepped out of the boat onto the ice.

Both Douglas and Allan held their breath as they watched Archie navigate those first ice floes. He leaped nimbly from frozen boulder to boulder, yet at times it looked as if he would topple right into the rushing water. Several times he reached a dead end, with no further ice to reach, and had to carefully retrace his steps back.

The mist was already closing in, shrouding everything in ghostly vapor, and after a short while they could see him no longer, although they could still hear him as he called out his progress in a cheerful voice, as if it were all indeed a game of hopscotch. Then his voice grew fainter, until after a while it faded completely and they could not hear him at all.

Without the sound of Archie's calls, it seemed ominously quiet. The silence of the sea was broken only by the sudden, loud cracks of the ice breaking up, each one an unsettling reminder of their grim situation.

Allan realized he was shivering. The air was heavy and wet, and sharp with cold. He pulled his scarf up around his face and clenched his fingers together in his fur-lined gloves to restore the feeling in them. He'd no desire to get frostbite again. He'd no desire to die.

Would he die out here, Allan wondered. It seemed likely. How on earth would Archie navigate six miles of open sea, especially with the mist closing in? His brother had been brave, but foolish. So foolish.

And he, Allan, had been just as foolish, and not even brave at that. Just a fool. A hopeless, reckless fool. He closed his eyes, his face contorted with regret.

He would never make his fortune. He would never see Harriet again.

He tried to imagine her dear face. If only he'd ignored her father's refusal, begged Harriet to come with him. They could have defied everyone, run away together. Somehow it didn't seem as shocking now, with death staring him in the face. Why not grab what happiness while they could? They could have had a married life together already.

And now you would make her a widow?

The quiet voice inside him made him bow his head in shame. He could not have ignored David Campbell's request, if only because he believed in it himself. Harriet deserved more than what he had to offer now.

Perhaps she deserved more than him.

Would she hear word of his death? Would she marry someone else? The thought brought him both pain and a sense of relief, that she might be provided for and happy, that she might forget him in time, and so ease her own sorrow. That was something, at least.

The hours passed in numbing, agonising slowness, as the sky slowly darkened and the wind grew more frigid. The only sound was the lonely sweep of it across the open water, and the occasional crack of the ice, a reminder of its dangers. After an hour or so, he and Douglas lay down together in the bottom of the boat to keep warm, although it meant they would be less likely to be seen by any passers by, slim a hope as that was. Even then, lying pressed together out of the shelter of the wind, they shivered from the cold, the ice pressing in on both sides making the boat even colder.

"Do you think he'll make it through?" Douglas asked, his voice small in the vastness of the ice strewn wasteland. "It's madness."

"I know it is." Allan kept clenching and unclenching his fingers in the hope of keeping the feeling into them. The cold was seeping into his very bones, making it hard for him to move or even think. Already his feet were terrifyingly numb. "That's Archie, though. He's always been one for risks."

"Even if he does make it, he won't be long for this world," Douglas said, with both admiration and warning. "Not when he insists on these schemes."

"If he does make it," Allan acknowledged, "he'll have saved our lives." But he could not imagine that happening now. Archie would die out there among the waves, and they would perish here, huddled in the bottom of the boat.

"There's small hope of that," Douglas said without bitterness. He had either accepted his fate or become too numb and dazed with cold to rail against it. "In this weather, at least. He's been gone three hours already. He's probably dead, and we might as well be."

"Don't say it. Not yet." Allan's voice was harsh, and took more effort than he realized. His breath caught in his chest painfully, as a searing sensation burned through him. Already it felt harder to breathe. Was Archie dead, lost forever in the icy seas? As they would be, most likely, in a few hours…

The faces of his family drifted before his closed eyes, as he imagined their grief and their silent reproach. Even in his cold-induced daze, he couldn't shake the feeling that all of this was his responsibility, his fault. He never should have agreed. He should have prevented Archie from going…

They both drifted into something close to a sleep, their bodies too cold to keep conscious. "I've heard it's like falling asleep," Douglas said, the words slurring together. "Not painful at all…"

Yes, just like a sleep. Allan's eyes fluttered close. At least when he slept, he could dream of Harriet.

CHAPTER SEVEN

"Don't want to!" The little girl slammed her hands onto the keys of the pianoforte, creating a jangling disharmony as she subjected Harriet to a devilish stare.

"Please, Caroline, one more time through your scales, and then today's lesson will be over."

Harriet sighed inwardly as Caroline jutted her lip out in mutinous denial. She'd been teaching Caroline Reid the pianoforte for the last three months, but little progress had been made. Although the girl possessed a certain innate ability, her spoiled manners and fierce opposition to instruction of any kind was proving difficult indeed. Harriet suspected she resisted simply for the pleasure of thwarting her instructor. Considering the difficulties she faced, Harriet had thought more than once that Sir James had been asking far more of her than she'd ever realized.

"Try again," she said firmly as she gave Caroline a quelling look. Resentfully Caroline began to plunk out the scales, and Harriet knew she was doing a poor job of it on purpose. "That will do for today, Caroline." The girl sat back and Harriet closed the lid of the pianoforte. "Perhaps you could practice your scales a bit more before next week."

Caroline gave her a knowing smile before she scampered off, delighted with her freedom. Harriet sighed as she stared out the music room window at the rolling lawns of Lanymoor House. In the three months since she'd been coming there, she'd rarely seen Sir James, making her wonder uneasily at the true nature of his manipulations. She couldn't shake off the fear that Riddell had something in store for her—and her family—that had precious little to do with the pianoforte, and far more to do with the farmland she knew he craved.

"Will you join us for tea, Miss Campbell?" Andrew Reid entered the music room with a small bow. "Caroline requested scones especially today."

Harriet hesitated. Every week Mr. Reid invited her to take tea with them after Caroline's lesson, and every week she politely but firmly refused. She'd no desire to get even further entangled with the Riddell family, and she didn't like Andrew Reid's slightly mocking smile, the small liberties he took, perhaps because he was a gentleman and she was nothing more than a farmer's daughter. His manner had often bordered on flirtation, a flirtation that shamefully appealed to her femininity, even if she knew her heart was spoken for, even now.

Yet Caroline's particularly mulish behaviour today made Harriet reconsider for the first time. Perhaps if she tried to get to know the girl outside of lessons, she'd have more success actually teaching her something of the pianoforte. She suspected Caroline was so spoiled because she was lonely, without anyone her own age. Her older brother as well as her uncle both seemed to tolerate her rather than like her, and paid her scant attention.

"Very well," she said rather stiffly, and then amended, "thank you for your kind invitation."

Andrew's eyes glinted wickedly as if he had surmised her thought process exactly. "We're honored, of course, to have you join us."

Harriet pursed her lips. She'd no need of Riddell charm, even if it was from a Reid relation.

"What's she doing here?" Caroline demanded with a sulky pout as Harriet entered the drawing room a short while later.

"Caroline, you're a little savage," Andrew said mildly. "The proper thing to say is 'how do you do, Miss Campbell'."

Harriet smothered a laugh. Caroline's malevolent glare was a far cry from such niceties. "Never mind," she said brightly. "I'm happy to see you, Caroline. At least now we won't have the dreadful noise of the pianoforte to distract us."

Caroline looked at her suspiciously, clearly wondering whether Harriet was poking fun, but her innocent, demure expression gave nothing away.

Andrew Reid nodded. "That's the way of it, Miss Campbell. If you haven't already, you'll soon learn that Caroline dislikes anyone's attempt to be pleasant with her. She thinks they're toadying."

"What's toadying?" Caroline asked.

"Never mind, savage." Andrew tousled her head of blond curls with tolerant amusement. If only she could endeavour to be pleasant, Harriet thought, the little girl might be quite charming.

As Caroline retreated to a corner of the room with her scone, Harriet joked, "If I encounter more success through being honest rather than merely pleasant, it will be a relief. She certainly needs to learn some manners." Immediately she regretted her impulsive tongue. Andrew was Caroline's brother, and she was virtually a nobody.

Andrew chuckled. "Never fear, Miss Campbell," he said, seeming to read her thoughts once again. "I quite agree. Although I do feel sorry for the poor child. She's been motherless her whole life, and my uncle and I aren't much company."

It was as much as Harriet had guessed, yet she found now she was curious to know more. "What happened to your family, if it isn't too impertinent to ask?"

"Of course it isn't." He gave her a roguish smile that Harriet ignored. "Our mother, Amelia Riddell, died in childbirth. I was already sixteen at the time... Caroline was an unexpected blessing." His usually humorous expression clouded over briefly. "At least I have memories of her, but Caroline has none. And Uncle James, I'm afraid, has let her run wild."

"What of her… your father?" Harriet knew she was being far too curious, but she couldn't help herself.

"He was… dissolute." Andrew shook his head wryly, even as his eyes darkened in memory. "I'm afraid he preferred cards and loose living to family life, and I barely saw him. After Mother died, he disappeared completely. He'd gone through Mother's dowry in mere months… there wasn't anything left, and there still isn't." He shrugged. "Which is how we come to rely on the charity of our good Uncle James, poor relations as we are."

Did she detect a note of bitterness, Harriet wondered. She wouldn't blame him if he was. No one liked having to depend on charity, and through no fault of his own. Taking a sip of tea, she returned the conversation to safer ground… Caroline.

"She must have a nurse or governess."

"Yes, but her nurse is as indulgent as Uncle James. They both feel sorry for her, having no mother or father, but as you and I can see, they do Caroline no favors, and in truth they don't pay her much attention."

"That's no way to grow up." Harriet felt a certain sympathy for the little girl, yet she also thought of her own sister, Eleanor, with no mother, and how lovely and sweet she was. Surely anyone could overcome their circumstances? All Caroline needed was genuine love, rather than pity, and a firm hand.

"I think, Miss Campbell," Andrew Reid said, "you might be just what Caroline needs."

Harriet looked up sharply. "I'm only here to teach the pianoforte, Mr. Reid."

Andrew Reid's gaze held her own, and Harriet had trouble looking away. "Of course, Miss Campbell," he said, but laughter lurked in his voice and she could make no reply.

*

"Oh, please, that's enough discussion for today!"

Henry Moore chuckled. "I never thought I'd hear you say that."

Margaret smiled self-consciously as she held up both hands in mock surrender. "I didn't, either." For the last three months she'd been tutored by Henry Moore, and she truly felt she'd got a better bargain than Rupert. Henry didn't just instruct her, he opened her mind, encouraged her to question, debate, even argue. Margaret revelled in the kind of intellectual freedom she'd never known before, crossing intellectual swords with him again and again, all under his aunt's less and less watchful eye.

"Actually, Miss MacDougall, there's something I wished to discuss with you."

There was no reason whatsoever for Margaret's heart to skip suddenly, or her cheeks to flush, yet they did. She looked at Henry with as teasing a smile she could muster. "You sound rather serious, Captain Moore."

"I am."

Margaret swallowed. Although they'd only know each other for a few months, it felt much longer. At least once a week, sometimes more if she could get away from Achlic without causing too many questions, she made the journey to Tobermory and spent an hour or more in Elizabeth Moore's parlor where she and Henry conversed, joked, argued, and got to know each other in a way many married couples never did. After the first few weeks, Aunt Elizabeth had quietly withdrawn, looking in only periodically to check on them, a small smile playing about her lips.

The privacy—the intimacy—had been almost overwhelming, and something Margaret was utterly unused to. She found herself sometimes staring at Henry's bent head, the blond whiskers on his jaw, while they were meant to be studying a map. She watched his strong hand trace Magellan's sea journey across the Pacific, and every coherent thought flew from her head, unsettling her more than she'd ever expected to be.

Sometimes she would catch Henry looking at her, a half-smile playing on his lips, and she had to use all her determination to keep from flushing scarlet in acute knowledge of her own state.

She was falling in love.

Now she attempted a calm outward appearance even though her insides trembled with nervous expectation, desperate hope, and a little fear. She raised her eyebrows, managing to smile. "Pray, then, tell me what it is."

"Spring is here," Henry said. He glanced down at the map they'd been studying, the Atlantic Ocean a vast blue space between the continents. "The sea is fit for sailing again, and *The Allegiance* is almost ready to make way."

"You mean… you're leaving?" She'd known this would happen, yet somehow Margaret had managed to push the unwelcome thought to the far reaches of her mind, so now it came as a shock.

"Yes, for a while. I hope to be back here next winter, at least to visit."

Next winter! It was a lifetime away. Her father might have even sent for her and Rupert by then. She might never see Captain Henry Moore again. Margaret nodded, looking down, wanting to hide the naked desolation she was sure must be on her face. "I see."

"Aunt Elizabeth wanted me to assure you that when I'm gone, you may still come here and continue your studies. You'll have free use of any books and papers, and I'm certain I'll find you've learned more in my absence than in my presence."

"I would not fear on that account," Margaret said as she looked up with a small smile. "I am certain of no such thing."

There was an awkward pause as they gazed at each other, and Margaret longed to speak of a different kind of learning entirely—how she had learned of matters of the heart more than any found in books. She did not dare. Such matters were a foreign soil to her, as unknown as any of the distant lands on the map spread out between them. She could not speak of them, not to Captain Moore, not to anyone.

"Miss MacDougall..." Henry cleared his throat, a faint blush touching his cheeks as he spoke. "During my journeys back and forth I shall no doubt stop at Tobermory on occasion, and I would be honored to be allowed to leave a letter for you there, in care of my aunt. And... if you so wished... any letters you might write would reach me, if given to my aunt."

"Would they?" Margaret's mouth was dry as she managed a nod. "That is a sound idea, then."

"Yes." Henry nodded back, and they both smiled rather foolishly at each other before he leaned forward, his expression turning grave and earnest. "It would give me no end of pleasure to imagine that, upon my return next winter, you might still be unclaimed in your affections."

Margaret could not tear her gaze away from Henry's serious face as she considered the import of his words—and her own response. "I imagine that would be the case," she said, her voice little more than a croaky whisper. Although what her father might think of it, she had no idea. But Sandy MacDougall was half a world away, and she was here... with Captain Moore. Her affections were unclaimed by any except him.

"Then I am a fortunate man indeed," Henry answered. With a whimsical smile, he lifted her hand to his lips, the kiss feather-light, so Margaret wondered if she'd imagined it—or the tingling sensation that spread from her fingers through her whole body. "Then until next winter, Miss MacDougall."

*

"Give up, lad. They're gone."

Angus Pheeley's gruff voice barely registered in the icy twilight, the sea utterly still as the shreds of fog moved as silently as ghosts, obscuring their view. Archie shook his head and scanned the bleak seascape once more. "I told them I'd come back. I gave my word. I won't go back on it."

"If we stay out here much longer, we'll be trapped as well," Angus said. "Look—dusk is falling, and the ice will freeze right up as soon the sun sets."

"A little while longer." A fierce light of determination blazed in Archie's eyes. He was cold to the bone, and utterly weary, everything in him frozen and aching. It'd taken him four perilous hours to cross the treacherous, ice-strewn waters, wondering if every moment was to be his last as he danced across the floes in a deadly game of hopscotch, just as Douglas had described.

When he'd finally arrived on the mainland, nearly sobbing with relief, it had taken another hour to reach Pictou and then convince Angus Pheeley, the landlord of the town's taproom, to take his boat out. Most people shrank away, shaking their heads, claiming it was madness to attempt a crossing in this weather. Archie knew it was, but he refused to listen to their resigned assurances that Allan and Douglas were as good as dead, and there was nothing any of them could do.

Archie believed there was. He had to. If he didn't go back, they would surely die. He was their only hope of rescue, and he would rather die in the attempt than simply walk away. He appealed to Angus Pheeley's innate sense of adventure, coupled with a lingering guilt over a friend's death long ago on the ice. Finally, after precious minutes had been lost, he'd agreed to lend Archie his iceboat, and had even volunteered to go with him.

"Look, there!" Archie pointed to a sliver of broken ice lodged in a fissure in the ice, sticking straight up. "I left that there, as a marker, maybe an hour after I'd started. Turn here, quickly now, for they're bound to be close, I know it."

Reluctantly Angus steered the boat between two large ice floes as the sky darkened above them and the sun sank inexorably lower in the stormy sky. Archie knew full well the terrible folly of the mission, and his own questionable sense of honor which had made him agree to it, touched him sorely. It was his fault, and his alone, that they were in this predicament. Allan had said as much, and Archie already knew it. Douglas and Allan's deaths would be on his head, and no one else's. And now, in a mere matter of minutes, when darkness fell and the hope of survival dwindled even more, it could be the end for him and Angus as well.

They travelled on for another half hour, navigating the treacherous floes in grim silence as the ice bumped against the boat and the screech of its protest echoed through the freezing air. "There!" Archie shouted, and he heard the jubilant echo reverberate all around him. "I see the prow—stuck in there. It's them!" He raised his voice. "Allan! Allan MacDougall and Douglas MacPherson! Rouse yourselves, it's Archie, with Angus Pheeley. We've come back."

The ensuing, eerie silence which greeted his call chilled him far more than the icy wind cutting through his coat. He could see no movement in the boat, nothing. "They couldn't have gone."

"Archie…" Angus' voice was filled with gruff compassion. "It's likely they've—"

"No! No, I won't believe it. Draw closer."

"I can't, lad. Any closer and we'll be stuck as well, and that'll be the end of all of us."

Archie stood up. "Then I'll walk." With fearless determination he leaped from the boat and began yet another nimble dance across the ice. He reached Douglas MacPherson's ice boat in just a few minutes, and his stomach hollowed out when he saw them curled up in the bottom of the boat like a pair of bairns, their cheeks white with frost, their eyes closed. They looked peaceful… too peaceful. "They're here," he called hoarsely to Angus. "I don't ken whether…" He couldn't finish that terrible thought. Archie reached down to shake his brother's shoulder; it felt as hard as iron, nearly frozen solid, under his hand. "Allan, wake up! Wake up, man! It's me, Archie!"

*

Allan felt as if he were being roused from a deep and pleasant sleep. He'd been warm, and happy, and he'd been dreaming of Harriet, and now the cold and dark fell on him like a thunderclap. He couldn't feel his hands or feet. He couldn't feel his face. The whole world was black until he managed to blink his brother's anxious face into focus.

At the sight of Archie hovering above him, Allan tried to smile. The effort caused him a searing pain across his cheeks, and made him feel as if his face would crack in half.

"You… you came back." The words sounded garbled, forced through his frozen lips.

"I told you I would. Let me rouse Douglas. There's a boat there. You'll have to walk across the ice. Do you need help?"

Allan shook his head, then realized he could not command his limbs to move. They felt leaden, dead weights that did not belong to him. Terror clutched at his insides at the lack of sensation. Was he actually *frozen*? Would he lose his limbs? His life, even now, after rescue?

Archie put one arm around his shoulder, and another man Allan didn't know guided him in a stumbling, agonising climb towards the rescue boat. He couldn't walk properly, and he couldn't feel nearly enough, yet what he did feel hurt intensely. He bit his lip to keep from howling out loud as pain blazed through him.

"Not long now… we'll have you inside and warm, by God, I swear it." The other man's voice was rough with emotion. A frost-bitten man, Allan knew, was a terrible thing to see—blackened flesh that warmed up only to rot. Terror shook him once more.

Archie left Allan to scramble across the boat to shake Douglas. "He's not waking up." His voice was hoarse. "He's as cold as ice, Angus. Frozen right through."

Allan forced himself to turn to see Douglas' white face, flecked with frost, utterly lifeless, and he repressed a shudder. Angus deposited him in the iceboat, then returned to help Archie.

Allan slumped against the seat, exhausted and overwhelmed. He could barely lift his head to watch Archie and Angus half drag, half carry Douglas towards the boat.

"Let's lift him in," Angus commanded. "Between us we can manage it. He must have a bad case of frostbite, but he could be all right, even so."

But even in his exhausted state, Allan was able to see the two men exchange a single glance confirming their fears that it was much worse than that.

An Angus took his place in the boat he shook his head grimly. "For pity's sake, let's move, and quickly," he said in a low voice. "Or we'll all end up as him, or worse."

The next few hours passed in tense, terrified silence. It was easier to return to Pictou rather than back to the island, so they headed for the distant shore, the wind cutting, the last of the sun's murky rays disappearing behind a dense stand of evergreen.

Allan and Archie sat in the stern, Douglas cradled between them while Angus paddled. The pleasant numbness Allan had felt initially was fast turning into the worst pain he'd ever known, and both his feet and hands burned like fire. He gritted his teeth against the pain, his arms around the unconscious Douglas, as the boat slowly moved forward.

Darkness fell and Archie held a lantern high to light the way. The lantern was but a pinprick of light in the vast darkness, and it was a painstaking process to paddle by it, their progress slower than ever as the night grew colder still.

Finally, with an almost unbearable sense of relief, they sighted the shore and then reached it a few endless moments later. Angus jumped out first, and Archie and Allan carried Douglas between them, Allan stumbling on his throbbing feet. "He needs help, and quickly," he said. "Take him to the inn, it's the warmest place. I'll fetch the doctor."

"I'll fetch him," Archie said brusquely. "You need care yourself. Come to the inn with us, and warm yourself up."

Allan didn't object; he knew Archie would be faster, and in any case he wasn't sure he could walk much farther. A few moments later they all stumbled into the inn, and Allan had never been so glad to see a fire, or friendly faces, before in his life. In a matter of minutes Douglas was laid out on top of a table, and Archie went for the doctor.

Archie's face was white with tension as he watched the man examine Douglas MacPherson's lifeless body. The innkeeper brought hot water and towels to warm up Douglas' frozen flesh. The hours crept by slowly, as the doctor worked diligently to restore life to Douglas' limbs. At some point, Douglas gained consciousness, and his piteous moaning made Archie wince and flinch. Someone dribbled whiskey into his slack mouth and thankfully he fell asleep again.

Finally, the doctor turned to Allan and Archie. "He'll live… just. But he's going to lose some toes, if not his foot."

Allan could see Archie blanch. For a man to lose his feet in this country was a fate close to death. He would live life as a cripple, with no way to support himself. "Thanks be," Allan said in a low voice. "I feared the worst."

The doctor turned a critical eye on Allan. "You suffered as well. God willing you won't lose any toes, but let's have a look at you. You never know."

"I'm fine," Allan said, but Archie pushed him forward.

"Don't be a fool. You were out there as long as Douglas. It's a miracle you're still standing."

Reluctantly Allan let the doctor lead him away, and gritted his teeth against the pain as he took off his boots and cut away his socks.

"Can you feel this?" The doctor asked, and Allan stared at him blankly, for he could feel nothing. The man's expression tightened. "You'll as like lose your little toe. It's frozen through, which is why you can't feel it."

Allan swallowed. One toe. He didn't need it much, but he still hated the thought. At least it wasn't ten.

"I'll come back in the morning," the doctor said. "We'll know more then."

Allan nodded, and lifted his gaze from the doctor's bent head to meet Archie's anguished eyes. Then he looked away.

Later, numbed with several tumblers full of whiskey and a large bowl of venison stew,

Allan stretched out his throbbing and bandaged feet towards the fire.

They'd made arrangements to stay here at the inn for a while longer, as it wouldn't be wise to attempt another crossing for a week at least.

"Mother and Father will think we've died," Allan said in a low voice. He felt too tired to summon much emotion.

"I know it's my fault," Archie replied flatly. "You don't need to tell me. I know it full well."

"I wasn't," Allan protested. "I just..."

"No, don't." Archie's voice sounded savage. "Mother and Father giving us up for lost is the least of it, since we're safe as it is. Douglas may be losing his feet..." Archie shook his head. "What kind of life can there be for him now?"

"It might not be that bad. Perhaps he'll only lose a few toes. There's many a man, and woman as well, who've lost as much if not more." He thought of his own likely loss and said nothing more.

Archie shook his head. "By God, I won't risk anyone's life but my own again," he said in a low voice. "It was foolishness, stupid foolishness, all of it!" He stood up and strode away from the fire, tension evident in every taut line of his body. "I'm finished with all that. I'll be my own man, and that's all. No responsibility for anyone else."

Allan was silent. He was grateful that this experience had awakened Archie to his own foolish whims, yet he also felt a pang of unease. He'd wanted to be his own man for a long time now, yet it had been denied him. Looking at Archie's fierce expression, he'd a sudden apprehension that his brother would not be denied so easily—and once again Allan would be the one to pay the price.

*

Harriet gazed out at the steadily falling rain with a sinking heart. If it kept on like this, she'd be soaked to the skin before she made it down the sweeping drive. The long walk home along the rutted and muddy road from Lanymoor House to Craignure was a bleak prospect indeed.

"You can't go out in that."

Harriet turned in surprise at the sight of Andrew Reid. Although she'd joined him and Caroline for tea on occasion, she'd declined today as Caroline had gone off with her nurse and she had neither the intention nor the desire to take tea alone with the man. "I can't stay here," she replied, trying to sound light and failing.

Andrew smiled. "Let me take you in the carriage. It's the least I can do. I'm ashamed to admit I haven't thought of it earlier—you've been walking home all winter, haven't you? And it must be an hour or more."

"Of course I have," Harriet replied. The Campbells were hardly wealthy enough to afford a carriage for Harriet's personal use, and especially not with the current state of their financial affairs. They'd just about held on to the farm through the winter, but now that spring was here and it was time for planting again, Harriet knew something more would need to be done.

"Then surely it's my duty to escort you home," Andrew said lightly.

Harriet wanted to wave aside such gallantry. She was perfectly capable of walking, and she'd been doing so for months. Yet the prospect of getting soaked, especially when she already felt weary and worn down, was a depressing one. She didn't want to catch a chill, or worse.

"What's this about duty?" Sir James strode into the room, smiling in that predatory way Harriet didn't like. "What are you spouting off about this time, Andrew?"

"I was offering to escort Miss Campbell home in the carriage, sir."

"An excellent idea, and one I should've thought of sooner." Sir James turned to smile at Harriet. "The pianoforte lessons seem to be progressing excellently, according to my nephew's reports. And Caroline speaks highly of you, which is an achievement in any case."

"Thank you, sir." Harriet bobbed her head, hating herself for sounding servile but not daring to act in any other way with a man she sensed was dangerous.

"Very well." Sir James nodded in apparent dismissal. "Andrew, why don't you alert the groom? No doubt Miss Campbell wishes to return home as soon as possible."

Andrew excused himself to do so, and Harriet found herself alone with Sir James. He smiled at her with seeming benevolence, and Harriet forced herself to meet his gaze. She wouldn't be cowed, even if everything in her cringed in trepidation at his assessing look.

"You've given us all a great boon, you know," he said after moment. "I've no illusions about Caroline's behavior. She is utterly impossible, a complete termagant, and yet I can't help but pet and spoil her." He smiled ruefully. "The weakness of an old man, perhaps. Under your tutelage, however, she seems to have blossomed. She even, on occasion, obeys! A miracle."

Harriet smiled in spite of herself. For the first time, Sir James seemed human, even personable. She wondered if she'd been imagining the threat he presented to her and her family, because of her own fears. In this pleasant drawing room, the rain drumming outside, Sir James seeming so friendly, she could almost believe it was no more than a flight of fancy.

"There's the carriage. Let me get your cloak, Miss Campbell, and you can be away." Murmuring her thanks, Harriet followed him out of the drawing room.

The carriage was comfortable and sheltered from the rain and wind, and with the groom accompanying them, Harriet knew it was perfectly respectable. Yet she still felt a twinge of unease when she saw Andrew glance at her with a teasing grin that seemed too familiar and knowing.

"Don't scowl at me," he told her with a little laugh. "You're worse than Caroline's old nursemaid. I haven't done anything wrong, have I?"

"I wasn't scowling." Harriet glanced away. "At least, I didn't mean to."

"I know you disapprove of me," Andrew continued in good humor. "You needn't bother to hide it, although I suppose that would make things more pleasant for us, if you did."

"Why should I disapprove of you?" Harriet countered. "I barely know you, and you mean nothing to me."

"A direct hit." Andrew held one hand to his chest, pretending to be wounded. "I'd hoped, in the course of our brief acquaintance, we might've struck up a friendship of sorts." Harriet flushed. She hadn't meant to sound rude, but she was determined not to be friendly with this man, or with any of the Riddell family—at least not any more than she had to. Andrew glanced at her, eyebrows lifted. "Do you think that's possible, Miss Campbell?"

Harriet took a quick, steadying breath. "I think, in the current circumstances, that would be quite impossible," she said.

Andrew glanced at her thoughtfully. "Is it because of my uncle? I know you dislike him, and I can't say I blame you. He's a wily old fellow." He shook his head. "But he hasn't done any real harm, has he?"

"I suppose it depends upon whom you ask. The crofters whose land he cleared for sheep wouldn't say so."

"Assuredly," Andrew agreed. "But that's no more than what any laird in all of Scotland has done, or has to do, and I know Uncle James has done a great deal less than some."

Harriet paused. How could she explain her uneasiness when it came to the Riddells, and Sir James in particular? Despite his overture of friendliness, she still didn't trust him, or his nephew. Sir James had stolen Allan's letters to her, and that was not easily forgotten. She did not wish to divulge this to Andrew, however, and so instead she replied, "In normal circumstances, we wouldn't even be acquaintances. Surely you see that? We are from entirely different circles. It would hardly be seemly for us to strike up a friendship."

"What, with me the penniless relation?" Andrew's voice was teasing, but his expression was sober, even a bit bitter. "I hardly think there could be anything inappropriate about it. I am not Sir James' heir, after all. He has a son, some weedy fellow down in Berwick."

"I know." Although she'd never met him, she'd heard of the man.

"Yet you still object?" Harriet did not reply and Andrew inclined his head. "Very well, I shall acquiesce to my lady's wishes... for the moment."

Harriet decided to accept his words as agreement rather than the vague threat they felt like. The rest of the trip passed mostly in uncomfortable silence, until they came to Craignure.

"You may leave me here, if you please," Harriet told him. She'd no desire for her family to see her in the Riddells' carriage. "Many thanks for your generosity, Mr. Reid."

"I'm obliged for your company." Andrew gave a slight bow. "And I hope you may oblige me in such a way again, by allowing me to escort you."

Not wanting to make any such promises, Harriet simply bobbed her head and hurried from the carriage, helped by Andrew. She waited till the conveyance had rounded the bend in the road before turning for home.

The rain had slowed to a drizzle as she made for Achlic Farm. The road was empty of horse or human, and she was surprised when a voice called from behind. "Harriet Campbell! It's not fit for anyone to be out in this weather, but I'm coming to call on Achlic."

Harriet turned to see Jane MacCready hurrying towards her with a covered basket. "I should've come sooner, what with your father taken ill," she said by way of apology, "but I know how some folk like to be left alone."

"Father does," Harriet admitted with a wry smile. "He's not the most willing patient, I confess."

"I should imagine not." Mistress MacCready smiled, her weathered face creased into deep wrinkles. "You'll remember how I told you that I nursed my own father for some years, so I know what it's like."

Harriet nodded. She remembered that Jane had lost her suitor and her own chance of happiness, because of her duty to her father. With a chill, she wondered yet again if the same fate would befall her. Perhaps it already had. Although she'd written to Allan and sent the letter on the first ship over a few weeks ago, it was too early to have heard back. She hadn't wanted to explain that the letters had been stolen, and so she'd said they were simply mislaid. She hoped Allan believed—and forgave—her.

As if reading her thoughts, Jane lay a hand on her arm. "I know it's not easy, doing the nursing along with all the housework, and as I'm an old woman now with few duties, I'd be happy to help."

"Thank you kindly, Mistress MacCready, but…"

"Don't waste your youth, my girl," Jane advised. "Not in a sick room. There's plenty of time for sick rooms later, I promise you." The look in the older woman's eyes was one of both bleakness and compassion, and Harriet found herself suddenly blinking back tears as she realized the truth of Jane's words.

"Thank you," she whispered. "Thank you kindly."

CHAPTER EIGHT

By midsummer the MacDougalls had finished their cabin and planted their first crop of barley, wheat and potatoes. It had been hard but satisfying work, and Allan had been glad to see their once-distant dreams turned into pleasing reality. His father, he knew, was happy to be king of his domain once more.

They'd left the Dunmores' cabin as soon as they'd put a roof on theirs, and worked on all the finishing touches such as doors and windows while living in the dirt-floored rooms. Now, as Allan joined his father on the wide front porch, he knew there was no reason not to mention his own ambition, and yet still he stayed silent.

Although his father was pleased with their own holding, Allan had sensed an unease from him, and he suspected it was on account of their neighbors. The community along the Platte River was all Scots, and most of them were close knit. Most of the immigrants came from the western Highlands, and could, albeit distantly, be called their kinsmen. Yet Allan suspected his father felt little kinship with them at the moment.

At first, the other Scots had seemed to welcome the Mac-Dougalls unreservedly, and of course the Dunmores had shown unfailing hospitality. Yet in the last few months, since the MacDougalls had removed to their own property, Allan had noticed looks, particularly aimed at his father, that bordered on suspicion, if not downright hostility. He wondered at them, and if not for his mother's quiet comments, he would've dismissed them as products of his imagination or perhaps just his fear over his father's high-handed ways.

His first inkling that something deeper was going on had been when he'd listened to his father and mother discuss a meeting of menfolk in the community. Every few months the farmers all along the river gathered together to discuss community affairs, and although Sandy knew little about it, he told his wife that he intended to go.

"Should be a grand time," he said one evening, while Allan was at the table, writing another letter to Harriet. Perhaps this one would be answered. He had not yet been to the mainland to see if any letters had arrived yet with the spring, but he hoped to go soon. "Afterwards there's to be food, as well as music and dancing. We can all have a bit of fun."

"I'm looking forward to it," Betty replied. The long winter months, cooped up indoors for days on end with the Dunmores, had been hard on everyone.

"I imagine they'll appreciate a man of experience at these meetings," Sandy continued as he sat back in his chair, puffing out his chest a little. Allan looked up from his letter, frowning as he listened. "Some of these families were little more than crofters in the old country. It's time there was someone who could be a leader to them all, show them the way to go."

Betty's eyes widened and Allan knew she felt the same ripple of shock that he did at his father's superior tone. "It's true you've the experience," she agreed cautiously, "but is that what these men need—or want?"

"Of course it is. They surely know I've the largest landholding along the river. It's only natural that I'd be a leader among them. After all, I was tacksman."

"There are no tacksmen here," Betty said quietly, but Sandy shrugged her words aside. "Men need leaders. It is as simple as that."

Now, as he stood on the front porch with his father, Allan wondered if he should say something. The community meeting was that evening, and if Sandy broached the idea of being a veritable tacksman to the settlers, Allan knew it would go very badly for him—and all of the MacDougalls. He knew he hadn't been imagining the hostile looks he'd seen when he'd ventured into Charlottetown, or waved to people on the river. Had Sandy seen them? If he had, he hadn't admitted it to anyone.

"The meeting tonight," Allan said after a moment when the only sound had been the pleasant twittering of the birds, "it should be a pleasant occasion."

"Aye." Sandy nodded as he surveyed the green fields rolling down to those they'd just planted. "I'm looking forward to it, and that's a fact. These settlers—some of them are rough, uneducated men. They need to organize themselves. They need leadership. There's much that could be done, to unite these settlements along the river. I've thought long and hard about it."

Allan's heart sank at his father's determined tone. "And what have you been thinking?" he asked.

"They need someone to speak up for them in Charlottetown. Decisions are being made that might affect our settlements. I've heard about it. All these farms owned by absentee British landlords. The men with smaller holdings need someone to be their advocate."

"And you're thinking you're that man?" Allan had heard about the disputes; much of the island was owned by wealthy men back in Britain, and disputes often flared up between the colonial office, the landlords, and the tenants, sometimes to the detriment of those with smaller holdings. "They're not looking for a tacksman, Father," he said as gently as he could.

"And I wouldn't be a tacksman," Sandy replied irritably. "I'm Riddell's yes-man no longer. I'll be my own man here, Allan, and that's fact."

"But don't you think every man here wants the same for himself?"

Sandy threw him an angry look. "Of course they do. I'm not talking of taking anything away. I'm giving something to them."

Something Allan suspected no former crofter would want.

The meeting was held at a neighboring farm that evening. The barn had been cleared and rough wooden benches had been pulled up for the men who gathered from all along the river, some with small, crude farms that barely scraped a living, others more prosperous holdings owned by men of means. Sandy strode in confidently, followed by Allan and Archie. Allan hadn't spoken of his own concerns to his brother, but he suspected from Archie's half-smile and insouciant attitude that he already knew. Not much had changed in the two months since the March crossing; despite their brush with death, Archie seemed as devil-may-care as ever.

Robert MacPherson, Douglas' father, called the meeting to order and the men assembled themselves on the benches, work-roughened hands placed on homespun-clad thighs, faces lined and weary as they spoke of crops and harvests, droughts and floods, illness and accidents. Their main concern, Allan soon saw, was whether each family in the community was provided for. There was also talk of the road to Charlottetown, which was little more than a rutted track, and needed improvement that would have to be seen to by the community, rather than the colonial office. A wolf had been seen near the Campbells' farm, and some of their chickens taken.

Allan listened, interested in the way each man had his say, and everyone heard him out. There was a sense of equality and warmth which he had not encountered before, either back in Scotland or here on the island, isolated through the winter. Had he, he wondered, ever truly been anyone's equal, first the tacksman's son in his draughty castle, and now, separated from others through the winter, taking orders from his father?

He craved this—the community and the discussion, each man's voice heard equally, in the same way that a plant craved sunlight. He needed it, as much as he needed air.

Sandy did not speak throughout the meeting. Allan watched as he listened, his mouth pressed in a hard line as he seemed to take the measure of each man present. Afterwards, before Allan could say a word, his father got up from his bench and approached Robert MacPherson with what Allan suspected was meant to be a genial smile. He rose and followed at a distance, so he could hear what his father said.

"It's a fine group of men here," Sandy said with a nod.

Robert MacPherson nodded back, his expression wary. Allan knew he still remembered Archie's winter escapade, and did not thank any of the MacDougalls for it. Douglas had lost all of his toes on one foot, and three on the other. He needed crutches, and was of little use on the farm. Those who knew what happened blamed Archie, as well they should. If Sandy was aware of any of that, he had never said so.

"I've been thinking," Sandy continued in that same, easy voice, "this community needs a leader. Someone to speak to Charlottetown, tell the colonial office what's what. They only seem to care about the absentee landlords, not the smallholders like us. Why shouldn't they repair the road? It's that kind of thing I'm talking about. You've organized yourselves well enough, of course, but there's nothing like a man in charge to give people comfort, is there? Give them a sense of security as well as of belonging."

"Comfort?" Robert MacPherson's bark of laughter was hard and ugly. "That's not the kind of comfort we came here to seek, tacksman."

Allan saw Sandy flinch at the obvious derision in the man's voice, but still he persisted. "You've heard I was tacksman of Ardnamurchan, I see. I know well enough there are no tacksmen here, but I do know what it is to lead men, to give them their due and their say. In Scotland I obliged my uncle by marriage, Sir James Riddell, but here I'd do it for my fellow men."

MacPherson's face twisted in half grimace, half smile. "Riddell? I've heard of that scoundrel. I wouldn't think a relation to him is something to be proud of."

Sandy flushed. "He's my wife's kin, and while I've no ties to him, it was my duty, and one I was proud to—"

"Then you'll be relieved to know you're free of such duty here," MacPherson cut across him. "We don't need another tacksman, not in this country."

"Of course not." Sandy shrugged impatiently, as if MacPherson was too dimwitted to understand him. "A leader, though, someone to organize and speak to Charlottetown."

"I was warned you might do this." MacPherson shook his head. "I thought you had more sense, man, but I can see you're still full of foolish, old country pride. Well, it won't carry here, I can tell you. We're all our own men, and we make our own decisions our own way. Any say or due we have, we give ourselves. So you'd best remember that, tacksman, and realize no matter how grand your cabin or great your farm, it doesn't hold with us. Here we help each other, and we see eye to eye. We don't call anyone laird, and we never will."

Sandy held himself stiffly. "You've misunderstood me."

"Have I? I don't think so." MacPherson glared at him. "If you want authority, then lead your own sons. It's your Archie's foolishness that lost my Douglas the use of his feet, and for that I'm not likely to thank you."

Sandy jutted his chin. "You'd blame my son for what your own agreed to do, with him knowing the land and sea far more than mine? It was foolishness, no doubt, but they were compatriots in it, I know. Your son should have spoken up."

MacPherson's face hardened into a mask of blatant dislike. Allan took a step back at the sight of it. "See it as you like, old man. Just know, and know it full well, we don't all think as you do… about many things." Robert paused, and his expression thawed very slightly. "Take some advice, MacDougall."

Sandy drew himself up, his eyes flashing. Even now Allan saw he had his pride. "And what would that be?"

"This is a harsh country, and you're new to it. You might think you know all you need to now, but I can tell you surely you don't. And if you want help when the time comes that you need it, you'd better start seeing yourself as humble—or as grand—as Hamish McDermott there, who had a peat and turf croft on Skye and buried five children when the laird turfed him out. Here, we're all the same, and the island knows no different."

Sandy remained silent, his expression stony. After a long, tense moment he inclined his head and walked away. With not much other choice, Allan followed him.

Allan saw how his father was quiet throughout the dancing, although everyone caroused merrily around him. Archie took his turn dancing with the few eligible girls, and enjoyed himself thoroughly. Although he was reluctant to dance with any woman other than his own Harriet, Allan joined in a few of the country dances for the sake of the company; young, able-bodied men were scarce.

"That Fiona Campbell is a pretty lass," Archie remarked as they stood to one side of the swept-dirt dance floor, drinking ale. "I don't suppose she'd turn your head, though. Still pining for a different Campbell, I can see."

"I love her and plan to marry her, if that's what you mean," Allan said stiffly.

"Oh, Allan!" Archie laughed. "Always so serious. Have you heard from her, then? A mail packet came from Pictou last week."

And he'd been to Charlottetown as soon as he'd heard, to see if any letters had come from Harriet. Finally there had been one, and Allan had opened it with trembling hands. Harriet had explained how his own letters—all of them—had been mislaid, and only discovered over the winter, when no ships sailed. She'd sent her own letter on the first ship out, profuse in her apologies and assurances of her love.

To his own shame, Allan had had trouble believing her. *All* his letters lost, every single one? He'd written nearly a dozen. What if Harriet was only making an excuse, because she'd changed her mind—determined first not to wait, and then perhaps deciding to hedge her bets? The thought was unworthy of either of them, and yet Allan couldn't keep from thinking it, and that treacherous doubt had kept him from wanting to share the news of Harriet's letter with any of his family.

"Aye, I've had one letter," he told Archie. The realization that Harriet, believing he hadn't written, had chosen not to write herself, had shaken him. Did she suspect him of being untrue? If she thought he could forget after a few months only, how would their love fare through the years it would surely take before he could return? But perhaps she was the one who wasn't true.

"Just one letter?" Archie's voice was lightly mocking.

"One is enough," Allan said flatly. He did not want to talk of Harriet with Archie.

"Father's had a set down," Archie said after a moment. "Serves him right."

So Archie had heard MacPherson's reply, as well. Allan just shrugged, not wanting to debate or belabor the point, but Archie was determined to continue.

"No one wants a tacksman here! If he's not careful, we'll all be tarred with that brush."

"Surely not…" Allan glanced at his father, sitting apart, a stony expression on his face. Would all the Scots settlers see them in the same way? It was an unwelcome thought. "Father will see reason, in time."

"How much time?" Archie shrugged and then stretched, a little smile playing about his lips. "Ah, well, it won't matter much to me," he said in an offhand manner that Allan instinctively suspected.

"Why shouldn't it?" Allan stared at the insouciant grin on his brother's face and felt that old chill of foreboding. Archie was hiding something from him.

"Never you mind, brother. Let us just say I have some plans of my own."

*

"How bad is it, then?" Harriet had to steel herself for Ted Carmichael's response, for the look of regret on his lined face was bad enough. The farm manager shook his head sorrowfully.

"It's bad, miss. Worse than ever. I'm terribly sorry."

"It's not your fault, Ted." Harriet leaned back in her chair as weariness crashed over her.

Outside, the willow trees at the bottom of their garden were in full foliage, and lambs gambolled across fields that were purple with heather. The sky was a fresh, clean blue, the sea below the same bright color. Caught up in the lovely throes of spring, the island looked happy and at peace with itself. Inside the Campbell home, Harriet thought, there was nothing but turmoil.

Ian sat next to her, his face grim. As the self-proclaimed man of the family, Harriet knew he wanted to be involved, to do something to help, but he was woefully prepared for such a role. She appreciated his gesture, but knew it for all it was: a gesture. What could any of them do when the debt that engulfed them deepened with each passing day?

"You'll have to sell," Ted told her in a voice laden with sorrow. "I'm so sorry."

Harriet straightened, her eyes wide as she took in what he was saying. "Not… not everything, surely?"

"Oh no, miss." Ted gave her arm a clumsy but reassuring pat. "It surely isn't as bad as that, and never will be, God willing."

"God willing," Harriet echoed in a murmur. Nothing seemed certain at the moment, and only Providence knew what would become of them.

Ted cleared his throat. "There are about twenty acres of pasture that you could do without, if you had to. Of course, it would be better to keep the farm all together…" He trailed off apologetically.

"But it's past that, isn't it?" Harriet shook her head as the realization reverberated through her. The farm would have to be sold, at least some of it. "We must do what is necessary to keep the house and livestock, at any rate," she resolved. "If we can keep our souls together for a bit longer, perhaps the harvest will be a good one."

"Heaven knows we're due a good year," Ted remarked grimly.

Harriet sighed and rose from the table. "I'll speak to Father now."

Her heart beat faster in trepidation as she mounted the stairs to David Campbell's sick room. He had been bedridden for nine months, barely venturing out of his room in all that time, and there seemed little chance now of him ever regaining his full health.

Although he was able to walk for short stretches of time, he tired easily. Worse, Harriet knew, his spirit had been broken with the latest crop failure and round of debt, so he preferred not even to show his face to the rest of the family.

He was not an easy patient in any case, vacillating between bouts of rage and silent despondency. Harriet took it all in stoic meekness, for she still blamed herself at least in part for his collapse. If she hadn't lost her temper… but there were too many what-ifs to wonder about, and she knew none of them did any good.

She gently knocked on the door. "Father, may I come in?"

"Very well," her father called back in a croaky rasp.

Harriet entered the room and sat by his bed. "May I get you something to drink? There's tea brewed." She reached to adjust the pillow behind his head but David flinched away.

"Don't mollycoddle me. I don't want anything."

"As you wish, Father." Harriet sat back in the chair next to his bed and took a deep breath, steeling herself for what came ahead. "I've just been speaking to Ted Carmichael. He suggested that we sell the back pasture. Twenty acres of it. The money from the sale should tide us over till the autumn, and God willing, with a good harvest, we'll have a crop then to make good our debts."

"One year's good harvest won't do it," David answered bleakly, his face turned away from her. "It'll take more than five."

"It's a start," Harriet replied steadily, even as her heart sank at his observation. "And Ted thinks the creditors will wait a bit longer if we can give them something for now. After all, it isn't as if we're the only ones who have had a bad year. It's been bad for everyone."

David shook his head. "They'll be patient as long as it suits them, and not a moment longer."

Harriet stifled a useless pang of irritation. Her father's bleak outlook didn't help anyone, not when she was doing all she could to save their livelihood, their home. "I don't know what else to do, Father," she said quietly.

David was silent, his face still averted. Harriet could hear the skylarks twittering outside in the lilac bush, as well as the painful rasp of her father's labored breathing. All around the world was coming into bloom, but here in this room the mood was as bleak as winter.

"There's naught else to do," he said at last. "I only pray it is enough." He turned to face her, the lines of his face deep with regret and pain. "You should go with Ted to our man in Fort William. He'll know how to go about selling it. Women shouldn't…" He frowned and began to cough. Harriet waited. She didn't particularly welcome another speech about the limitations of her sex, but she'd learned to mask her emotions when dealing with her father.

"Never mind," he said when the coughing had finally stopped. Then, to her complete surprise, he laid his hand on top of hers. "You're a good lass, Harriet."

She felt a ripple of shock from the simple contact, the sad smile on her father's face. His words meant a great deal to her, gruff as they'd been. "Thank you, Father."

"If I pained you in refusing Allan's suit," David continued, "it was for your own good. You wouldn't be happy there, Harriet, in that rough land, with no place to call your own. You're just like your mam that way."

"I intend to sail for Scotia when Allan returns," she said. "You know that."

"Aye, but then he'll have his own stead, out from under his father's thumb." David managed a small smile. "If he didn't have the determination to do it before, I surely gave it to him by refusing."

Harriet didn't want to argue. She'd spent all her rage already, wasted tears and time wishing for what had not come to pass. At least she knew now her father had meant what he'd done for good, not ill. It was small comfort, but it was something. She patted his hand.

"Thank you, Father."

Later that evening, when Eleanor was in bed and all was quiet, Harriet retreated to the front parlor, and the pianoforte. She ran her hands lightly over the keys and let the rippling sounds soothe her. For a few moments only, in the quiet comfort of this room, she could forget the worries that lay heavily on her and lose herself in the world of music.

"Harriet?"

She stopped playing and turned to face Ian, who stood in the doorway, a mixture of timidity and determination on his young face. "Is something troubling you, Ian?"

"No. Yes. That is…" Ian came into the room and closed the door. "I want to go to Fort William."

Harriet stared at him blankly. "What for?"

"To talk to our man of business, of course," Ian replied, his young voice rising. "I'm the man of the family now, it's my duty to take care of you all. You know it is."

Harriet pursed her lips. At fifteen, Ian did very little taking care of anything. When he wasn't at his studies, he was often off with Rupert, on his own lark or pursuit of pleasure. Even when they'd needed help with planting or harvesting, he'd done his share with grudging reluctance. She didn't begrudge him his fleeting youth, yet his sense of duty now was more of a burden than a help. "Ian, you may come with Ted and me—"

"No." Ian shook his head, his fists clenched at his sides. "I want to do this alone. This is a family responsibility, a man's job, and Ted needn't be involved."

"The Carmichaels are like family to us, especially since Father took ill," Harriet reproved. "And I welcome his advice, as you should, man of the family as you are. Father has always relied on it, and you would do well to do the same."

"Please, Harriet." Ian gave her his most beseeching look, as if he were a boy wheedling for sweets instead of the man he insisted he was. "I need to do my share, Father expects me to. If I could tell him I'd managed it by myself…"

Harriet found herself relenting in spite of her every intention otherwise. She knew Ian needed to be given responsibility in order to become a man. She'd learned that much in her dealings with her father. If Ian succeeded in this, he would gain confidence, perhaps even take more of an interest in the doings of the farm. And it wasn't too onerous a task. She'd ask Ted to write a letter beforehand, explaining everything to their man of business. All Ian would do was shake hands on the deal. Even so, she hesitated.

"Don't you trust me?" Ian asked truculently, when she didn't reply.

"Of course I trust you." That didn't stop the twinge of fear that a boy like Ian would not be able to do the thing properly. But then, Harriet reasoned, what was there really to go wrong?

"Very well," she said. "But you must listen to Ted, and do exactly as he says. He knows what he's about."

"But I may go alone?"

Sighing, Harriet nodded. "You will have to bring written permission from Father for the transaction, of course, but yes, very well then."

Twilight was finally stealing upon the world when Harriet retired to her bedchamber. She stood by the window and braided her hair, watching as Margaret slipped into the house.

"Coming back from one of her midnight strolls," she murmured. Sometimes Margaret stole out in the morning for a private ramble, but now that the evenings were lighter she'd often taken to walking down to Duart Castle to enjoy the setting sun, just as Harriet and Allan once had. Harriet didn't begrudge her friend and cousin the time alone, or the mornings she'd spent in Tobermory, whenever an errand called her there. Life was taxing enough for them all to resent a few small pleasures.

As she turned from the window, a knock sounded on her door and she heard Margaret's voice.

"May I come in?"

"Margaret, of course. I just saw you outside. Did you have a pleasant walk?"

"Yes, I suppose."

Harriet could not mistake the rather grim look on Margaret's face. "What is it?" she asked, a sudden fear making her insides plunge icily. Had Margaret learned something? Had there been a letter from Prince Edward Island that Harriet didn't know about? "Margaret…"

"I saw you the other day, alighting from the Riddell carriage." Margaret gazed at her steadily, a coolness in her expression that shocked Harriet.

"Then you would've seen it was a downpour," she returned stiffly. "Mr. Reid kindly offered to escort me home."

"I didn't realize you were on such friendly terms with the man."

"He is *your* kin, isn't he?" Harriet strove to keep her tone mild. She did not want to argue with Margaret, and over Andrew Reid of all people. "And I'm not on friendly terms with him at all. Civil, perhaps, but that is all."

"We're distant kin, no more," Margaret flashed back. "You know there's no love lost between the Riddells and us—Sir James as good as drove my father to the new world!"

Harriet frowned. "You mean because he was Sir James' tacksman?"

"My father had to do Sir James's dirty work, turning crofters out of their own homes." Margaret shook her head, her expression setting in hard lines. "I don't even know all of it, Father would never tell me. It was just what I heard as gossip, but he always resented being beholden to that man."

"You know I teach pianoforte at Lanymoor House," Harriet answered. "I've been beholden to Sir James since the new year, and surely, since you know he kept Allan's letters from me, there can be no love lost between me and any of his family. Why are you so upset now?"

"You didn't have much choice about that, did you?" Margaret countered. "I remember how it was. But carriage rides with Mr. Reid…" Margaret stared at her earnestly. "Harriet, I know it's been a long time, and Allan hasn't written as much as he should, even with the letters that were kept back. But tell me, please… are you playing my brother false?"

"I should think not!" Harriet glared at her, shocked and hurt. "One carriage ride in the rain and it comes to this! For goodness' sake, Margaret…"

"You haven't written Allan though, have you?"

"I sent a letter with the first ship in the spring," Harriet retorted. "You know I did."

"And several ships since then with not a word for any of my family!"

"And not a word back to me," Harriet replied sharply. "Even though Allan has surely received my reply, and knows why I didn't write before. There's been time enough for him to have received my own, and written back several times over. But there's been nothing!"

"If those letters went astray," Margaret objected, "perhaps others have, as well."

"I don't think Sir James cares enough to keep any more letters from me," Harriet said after a moment. "He only took those to show his power, I'm almost certain of it. He's like a cat, and everyone under him a wee mouse. But he knows I know that already." She shivered at the thought and then turned to Margaret, her expression firm. "But never mind him. I'll wait for a letter from Allan, and then I'll write. I'll not be badgering him with letters he doesn't want. If there's anyone you should think is playing false—"

"Allan would never!" Margaret cried. "If you knew him at all, you'd never doubt him, not for a moment. His word is his honor."

"Margaret, please." Harriet touched her hand. "Let's not fight like this. Surely there's enough going on without harsh words between us. I'll write to Allan, I promise I will." Although she was reluctant to do so, without word from him first. What if he didn't want her lines anymore? He'd given them back once already.

"I don't want to quarrel." Margaret sighed and shook her head. "But don't write to Allan for my sake."

"No, I will not," Harriet agreed with a tired smile. Perhaps she should stop waiting for Allan to write, and simply tell him her heart. She might feel better then, no matter what Allan's response. "Never fear, Margaret. It will be for mine."

"Well done, Caroline!" Harriet clapped her hands as the little girl finished a simple piece with a flourish. "You've been practising, I see."

Caroline, for once, did not have a stinging retort. Instead, she ducked her head and blushed prettily.

Harriet marvelled at the steps the little girl had taken, both in musical ability and manners. As it'd turned out, Caroline responded to vinegar rather than honey—Harriet had won her through plain speaking and a no-nonsense approach rather than any cloying overtures of friendship that rang false.

"I think we're finished for today."

"Will you join us for tea, Miss Campbell?" Andrew Reid gave her his usual wry smile, touched with a knowing whimsy, that Harriet could no longer decide if she liked or not. Over the last few months Andrew Reid had been both patient and kind, offering her use of the carriage whenever it was wet, and usually accompanying her.

Harriet had become used to his presence, and while she still distrusted the entire Riddell family, she'd come to the reluctant conclusion that Andrew Reid was the best of the lot. She wouldn't call him her friend, but something close to it.

Now, however, she hesitated over accepting the invitation. Normally she would've agreed but Margaret's rebuke from a few weeks ago still rang in her ears. She didn't want to become too familiar with any of the Riddells, or give anyone cause to doubt her love for Allan.

"Please, Miss Campbell!" Caroline said. "It's honey cakes today." Caroline looked at her with big, puppyish eyes, and Harriet couldn't help but laugh. She suspected the girl knew just how to look so sweetly adoring.

"Very well." For Caroline's sake, she would make the effort. As for Mr. Reid... she hoped she'd made it clear she did not wish to further their acquaintance past the wary friendship they already had. And in any case, she was not in any hurry to return home, and all the cares that waited for her there. Ian had travelled all the way to Fort William that morning to complete the selling of their back pasture, and it had put David Campbell into a resentful and irritable mood. Even though he'd accepted the selling weeks ago, the reality of it still stung and festered. Harriet would happily put off returning for a little while, at least.

They passed a pleasant half hour in the drawing room, with Caroline amusing both her and Andrew with her girlish antics, capering around the room and then pretending to waltz.

"She loves a show," Andrew said wryly. "As long as she is the star performer."

"Perhaps it runs in the family," Harriet returned, and was rewarded with a shout of laughter.

"Too true, Miss Campbell, too true."

"I see you're all enjoying yourselves," Sir James said as he entered the drawing room. "Excellent. And tea as well. I'll have a cup, if Miss Campbell will be so good as to pour."

"Of course," Harriet murmured, trying as ever to quell the unease this man always roused in her.

Sir James took the cup and beamed at them all. His eyes were bright, his face flushed, and Harriet felt a deepening of her usual unease. He looked almost *too* happy. Smug, somehow.

"You look as if you've had some good news, Uncle," Andrew remarked mildly, eyebrows raised in expectation.

"Indeed, I have." Sir James turned to Harriet. "I met your brother in Fort William today, Miss Campbell. A fine lad. We did a bit of business together... I'm sure it will be to our mutual benefit." His thin lips curled in a smile Harriet didn't like at all, and her stomach dropped as she considered what Sir James could possibly mean.

"Business?" She swallowed her tea, and tasted the sharp tang of fear. Ian had gone to Fort William to see their man of business—not Sir James Riddell. "What business might that be, pray?" she asked.

"I assume you knew of the arrangements," Sir James replied. "Indeed, I would be shocked if you did not, considering the magnitude of the business."

"Sir James, I beseech you, please speak plainly." Harriet strove to moderate her tone as a buzzing started in her ears, an icy panic creeping through her veins. What on earth could this wretched man be talking about?

"As you wish. It happens that I've bought Achlic Farm." His smile widened, and his expression made Harriet think of a spider spinning its sticky web.

"You mean Ian sold the back pasture to you," she corrected faintly. "The twenty acres." She'd no idea why Ian would've sold to Sir James instead of through their man, but she couldn't argue that point now.

"No, my dear." Riddell's voice was almost gentle even though his gaze remained narrowed and shrewd, with more than a hint of triumph. "Not the twenty acres. I have the contract right here. I've bought the whole farm. Everything."

CHAPTER NINE

Harriet slammed the kitchen door of the farmhouse, not caring if dishes broke or her father woke up. Fury and fear stormed within her in a terrible gale, a rage that had blown her from Lanymoor House back home, reeling from the news Sir James had so gleefully given.

Margaret looked up in alarm from the pastry she was mixing. "What on earth is wrong?" She rose from the kitchen table, one hand on Eleanor's shoulder as they both looked at her in surprise and worry.

"Eleanor, please go fetch some potatoes for dinner." Harriet's voice shook, and she strove to control it. She'd had the long walk home to try to calm herself and think of a way out of this disaster, but it hadn't helped in the least. She was as furious now as she'd been when Sir James had first told her, perhaps even more so. How could Ian have been so reckless? So foolish?

When she'd stammered her objections to Sir James, he'd simply shaken his head and shown her the contract where she'd read it for herself in bold, black ink.

"But we would never…" she began, only to realize how fruitless her protests were.

"There must be some mistake, Uncle," Andrew had protested, but Sir James had insisted it had all been legal, witnessed by the Campbells' man of business.

"If you are accusing me of not going through the law," he'd said in a dangerously pleasant voice, "I would think again."

Harriet had no choice but to leave, too upset to make any farewells or apologies. Andrew had offered the carriage, but she'd refused, determined not to take anything from any of the Riddells again.

Now Eleanor, her face pale, slipped quietly from the kitchen. Her sister knew something was wrong, but Eleanor was too wise and kind-hearted to make a fuss.

"Harriet, what has happened?" Margaret stood in front of her, hands clasped. "You look like… like death! It isn't Allan?"

"No, not Allan." Harriet drew a shuddering breath. "But a terrible thing, Margaret. The worst." Tears pricked her eyes and she blinked them back. "We've lost Achlic."

"No! How?" Margaret's face was white with shock. "Ian hasn't even returned yet…"

"It seems Ian…" Harriet swallowed, hardly able to believe what Sir James had told her. "Ian sold the farm to Sir James Riddell, instead of through our man of business."

Margaret blinked, looking blank. "You mean the back pasture."

"I wish I did! Sir James showed me the contract himself. It was for everything—all the land, even this house and all its possessions. My pianoforte… this kitchen table. Every single thing!"

"I don't understand…" Margaret whispered.

"Neither do I. How he could do such a thing… I keep thinking he must have been forced somehow, but I saw the contract myself. It was all there, in black and white, signed by our man of business."

The door opened, and a merry voice called from the hall. "I'm back! Hello, Margaret. Harriet."

Harriet and Margaret exchanged uncertain looks as Ian came into the kitchen, smiling at them both, his eyes twinkling with boyish excitement. "I've done as you said, Harriet, and it all went wonderfully. I got an even better—"

"Done as I said?" Harriet cut across him, her voice sharp and cold. From what she could see, Ian hadn't been forced to sign anything. "If you'd done as I said, Ian Campbell, we'd have money in our pockets and a roof over our heads! Instead of… instead of…" She choked on a sob, and then forced it back. "What on earth possessed you to deal with Sir James Riddell, instead of through our man?"

"You know about that?" Ian looked surprised, but not particularly discomfited. "Today's your pianoforte lesson, isn't it? Well, then… yes, I did, but our man of business must be crooked, Harriet! The price he quoted for the field was much less than what Riddell was willing to pay, and I thought…"

"Our man isn't crooked! For heaven's sake, Ian, if anyone is, it's that scoundrel Sir James! How could you trust him? What did he tell you?"

Ian drew himself up, all wounded affront. "We did business together, Harriet. I sold him the back pasture, just as you instructed, and I got three times the amount for it, so I'd ask you kindly to thank me!"

"I'll do no such thing—"

"Wait." Margaret held out a hand, staying Harriet's temper for a moment. "Something's amiss. One of you hasn't got the right of it. Ian, tell us what happened exactly."

Still looking disgruntled by Harriet's ire, Ian briefly told them the story, how Sir James had met him in the street on the way to the offices, and asked him if he was intending to sell Achlic Farm. When Ian explained he was only planning to sell the back pasture, Riddell expressed an interest and offered a price higher than the man of business had.

"But you didn't even know what our man would offer," Harriet interjected. "He was going to tell you when you met him."

"I know, and I told Sir James that. He said to meet him in the Lantern Inn after I met with Mr. Franklin, and we could discuss it then. I needn't make a decision either way, he said, till I'd thought about it properly."

"Then why didn't you?" Harriet asked bitterly. "You should've discussed it with all of us, Ian, not gone haring off on your own! Or you should have at least asked Mr. Franklin what he thought about it, having wisdom in these matters that you don't."

Ian flushed guiltily, although his chin lifted. "I think I'm capable of making decisions as the man of the family. Mr. Franklin's price was so low, I couldn't help but wonder at it! And when I mentioned Sir James, he became all flustered and said I must do as I saw fit. He knew he'd been found out."

Or, Harriet thought, he'd known not to tangle with the likes of Sir James Riddell. "And so you went back to Sir James, and signed a contract to sell what you thought was the twenty acres."

"We did it in front of Mr. Franklin, so it was all right and proper. You needn't take that tone with me, Harriet!"

Harriet bit back the insult she wanted to fling at him. "Don't you realize what you've done?" she asked despairingly.

"Sir James offered a higher price," Ian insisted. "He told me he was interested in acquiring more land on Mull, and so he was willing to pay for it. While I was meeting with Mr. Franklin, he'd had his own man draw a contract up. He told me I could have the money in my hand, right then, if I signed it… and look, Harriet, I do!" Ian fumbled with his pockets to bring out a few wrinkled bank notes. "Mr. Franklin witnessed the whole thing, and I got the money right then. I've made a good job of it—" He paused as he registered the stricken look on both Harriet and Margaret's faces. "So what have I done wrong?" he asked slowly, his face paling as realization finally sunk in. "Something's happened. You look as if you've seen ghosts, the two of you. What is it?"

"Ian, did you read the contract Sir James put before you?" Harriet asked.

"I looked at it. Of course I did." Ian shifted uncomfortably. "He told me what it said and I read most of it…but, well, there

were a lot of words! I was in a hurry and I wanted the money…
why? What does it matter? Sir James is a man of his word, surely?"

"Surely not." The anger drained out of Harriet, leaving her
limp and utterly hopeless. She sank into a chair at the table, her
head in her hands. "The contract wasn't for the back pasture,
Ian," she said wearily. "It was for Achlic Farm… all of it. You sold
everything to Sir James Riddell, including the roof over our heads."

*

The sun shone brightly on the golden green fields and red soil
of Prince Edward Island as Allan strode along the road to Charlottetown. It was late summer, just turning to autumn, and the
maples and birches which lined the road were tinged with red.
The sun was warm on his head, but in the evening there would
be a nip in the air, and in a few weeks there would be a frost.

It'd been almost a year since the MacDougalls had landed
in Pictou, and six months since they'd finished their cabin and
begun farming their own land. Since then they'd prospered, and
their first harvest of wheat, potatoes, and barley looked to be a
good one. Yet despite all this Allan was troubled.

Only yesterday evening the family had sat together on the
porch, watching the sun set over the river, gilding it in gold.
Everything should have been peaceful and perfect, and instead a
pall of unhappiness hung over the MacDougall home like a shroud.

Allan had tried to speak of it with his mother. "We didn't come
to the new world for this, did we, Mother?" he'd asked, when
Sandy had gone inside. "All this trouble and sorrow."

Betty turned to him, her lined face full of worry, her eyes
clouded with disappointment. "I don't know what you mean,
Allan," she said, despite the concern she so obviously felt. "Surely
we've everything we want here."

Allan shook his head as he reached out to gently clasp her
hand. "You can't be that simple with me. I see the way you look…

and Father, as well. We're more isolated here than we ever were at Mingarry, with him as tacksman. Why won't he involve himself in the community? He's shut himself out completely and it's foolish to do that in a place like this. We all need each other."

Ever since the meeting at the MacPherson homestead, Sandy had withdrawn completely from the Scots community. He would give a civil nod to someone in passing, but that was all. The rest of the Scots on the island were close knit, sharing each other's joys and sorrows, helping each other in both practical and emotional ways. With the winters so hard, and homesteading such a struggle, they all needed each other, and the MacDougalls were a world apart.

"We're as good as pariahs," Allan said aloud. "And it's our own fault."

"You mustn't speak such," Betty exclaimed in a low voice, but Allan saw the truth of it in her face.

"You must feel the worst of it, Mother." Allan didn't know too much of a woman's world, but he guessed that Betty missed the camaraderie and shared chores the other women enjoyed; the cycle of birth, marriage and death in which the other Scots women supported each other, whether it was with a shared jar of preserves, a sack of potatoes, a knitted shawl or simply a hug. They took part in each other's lives in a way that Betty did not.

Sandy's footsteps could be heard, and Betty shook her head, lips pressed firmly together. "Let's not speak of it," she said, and with a nod Allan acquiesced to her wishes.

Now, with the sun shining on his bare head, Allan wished he could throw off such cares. Yet with the way things were, his future looked as bleak as ever, even with their first good harvest about to be gathered.

His father's isolation from the Scots community made his own burden much harder to bear, his father's orders harder to take. There was no relief, no one to talk to, not even any slender threads of hope upon which he could cling. As for Harriet... he'd had but one letter from her, a short missive that had given very little news. She'd seemed distracted while writing it, and it had made him feel worse for the reading of it, after all that waiting.

Driven by disappointment in that regard, he'd decided to try to speak to his father about his own ambitions. They'd been standing by a field of potatoes that were nearly ready for harvest, their bright green leaves stretching to a cloudless horizon. Sandy had been in a buoyant mood as he looked out on his domain, master of all he surveyed.

"It's good work, this, isn't it, lad?" he declared.

Allan shaded his eyes from the sun and watched as in the distance Archie strode to the shore of the river and sluiced himself with water. His brother had seemed more shifty and secretive than usual, and Allan hadn't forgotten that Archie had claimed to be making his own plans. "Aye, it is," he told his father.

"Another harvest like this, and you'll be sending back for Harriet soon enough. I thought the two of you could have the back bedroom, when the time comes. It's more private." Sandy winked, and Allan stared at his boots, the toes grimed in red dirt, as he considered how to respond.

"I thought we'd build our own cabin," he said after a moment. He'd dreamed about this at night, listening to the crickets chirp their happy chorus and watching the clouds shift across the moon. He knew he couldn't leave his father; they were bound together by ties of duty and honor, as well as of love. Neither could he abandon the holding they'd both worked so hard to achieve.

Still, the thought churned in his mind that there *had* to be a way to be his own man, a man of property and responsibility, so he could return to Mull with his head held high, and win both David Campbell's approval and Harriet's love. The idea of his own home—his own domain, without the MacDougall holding—seemed like the best solution, and yet he felt trepidation at mentioning it to his father now.

"Your own cabin," Sandy repeated, his voice dangerously neutral.

"You know Campbell wants a man of property for his daughter," Allan stated quietly. He could feel the thud of his own heart, and hated the way he had to present his ambitions to his father as if they were broken toys in need of mending. "I thought perhaps when Harriet and I marry, I could take some of the acreage on the other side of the river. The farm is MacDougall land, of course, all of it, but it would be good to have my own land, our own house."

Sandy stared at the fields before them, his expression unreadable. "Well, we'll see about that," he finally said in a tone that told Allan the discussion was over.

Archie came over the knoll, his hair and shirt soaked, a broad grin on his face. There had been a new, relaxed ease to his brother recently that only put Allan more on his guard. What was Archie planning? For once again his own plans looked to crumble to dust.

Now other troubles crowded in his mind as well. In the year since he'd left Scotland, he'd heard from Harriet only once. He'd written many times, yet still waited for another letter. Only this morning he'd sent yet another letter to her, on the mail packet to Pictou. He thought now of the words which had poured from his heart.

> *How can I express the consternation of my heart, or account for the long and cruel silence on your part? This is the fifteenth letter I have written you since, but I am afraid they never got your length, or you would not be so long in writing me. I know you too well to imagine you capable of any change or caprice towards me, and I hope you know me too well to expect any change on my side…*

Had his words been foolish? Perhaps she *had* changed. Perhaps she'd found someone else, someone closer who could provide for her there on Mull. Ewan Andrews had always had a fondness for Harriet. What if…

There was no point thinking such things. Allan had promised to be faithful, and he would be. It was Harriet who was free, not him. One day he would return for her, and he would discover then what she felt for him.

"Hello there, Allan MacDougall."

Allan turned in surprise as his step faltered. A pretty girl with blond curls and laughing, hazel eyes stood behind him, smiling. Allan knew her slightly; she was Fiona Campbell, the daughter of their neighbor, and the girl Archie had once fancied, back at the barn dance.

"Good afternoon. A fine day, isn't it?" In his surprise he spoke brusquely, and then wished he'd moderated his tone.

Fiona's eyes seemed to laugh at him, as if she knew his thoughts. "It is, indeed. I'm going down to the river, to the raspberry patch by the bend. Are you going that way? Will you walk with me a while?"

"If you like."

They walked in silence for a moment, Fiona swinging her basket, Allan beside her feeling stiff and awkward.

"You're not like your father, are you?"

He started in surprise. "What do you mean?"

"There's talk about your family." Fiona flushed before continuing a bit recklessly, "He was tacksman back in Scotland, wasn't he?"

"Yes. What of it?"

"I'm sorry, I don't mean anything by it. Only…" She bit her lip. "He isn't friendly. I thought you were." Her wry smile made Allan realize she was teasing him a bit, and he forced a smile.

"I'm sorry. I don't mean to be…" He shrugged. "Yes, Father was tacksman on Ardnamurchan. I don't think he's realized yet that the same system doesn't work here."

"It's like that for some. They come to the new world, but they cling to the old ways, in spite of themselves."

"What about your family?"

Fiona's friendly eyes shadowed briefly. "We were thrown off our land. It was the clearances. We hadn't a penny, either. The tacksman took the laird's share and his own, as well. So you see why my father, along with many others, has no love for a tacksman."

"My father was honest and fair," Allan replied with some heat. "He shouldn't think ill of him just because of his own experience."

"I know that. It's just the reminder, you see, of the injustice of it all." Fiona smiled sadly. "It runs deep. That's why we—and many others—came here. To get away from the old ways."

Allan sighed. Fiona was not telling him anything he hadn't already known or guessed. He only wished his father would see the sense of it, as well. "My father is slow to change his ways," he said after a moment. "But he can change them." Or so he hoped, for his own sake as much as anyone else's.

Fiona smiled, the laughter back in her eyes. "Good."

They'd almost reached the bend in the river, and Fiona turned to walk off the road to the raspberry patch. "You're not like your father, and you're not like your brother, either," she called over her shoulder.

Allan stilled at that. "What do you mean?"

"He's always ready for a laugh, or some kind of mischief." Fiona shrugged. "You're more serious. Steady."

It was a comparison that had been made all his life. Allan merely nodded his head.

"I don't mind," Fiona said, and then blushed. "Goodbye, then." She gave a last smile before walking off, and Allan found himself staring at the spot where she'd stood long after she'd left.

*

Ian was not at supper that night, but Harriet was too anxious and heartsick over the loss of the farm to worry overmuch.

"I suppose he's hiding," she said wearily as she and Margaret cleared the dishes after the evening meal.

"You must feel a little sorry for him, Harriet," Margaret suggested. "He's only a boy."

"He wanted to be a man." Harriet sighed. "I'm too angry and afraid now to feel anything for Ian, Margaret. Perhaps that's low of me. It probably is." She leaned against the table and closed her eyes briefly. "I feel as if I've been holding this family together for too long, and now we're breaking apart into pieces. I can't clutch at them all. I can't carry them."

"You don't need to. You're not alone, you know."

"I know." Harriet opened her eyes and managed a smile. "But you've your own family to think about, and one day soon you'll be in the new world…"

"Perhaps." Margaret turned away, busying herself with hanging a tea towel to dry. "Have you decided what you're going to do? Will you tell your father what's happened?"

Harriet shook her head. "Not yet." She dreaded that interview, whenever it came. Would her father rage, or worse, would he be overcome with despair? "Tomorrow I'll travel to Fort William myself to see Mr. Franklin and ask about the contract. If he was there when it was signed… I just don't understand how it could have come to pass. He must have looked at it, and seen it was for the entire property. And if he didn't…" She shook her head resolutely. "There must be some way out of this." It was the only hope she could cling to, and cling to it she did. The alternative was like staring into a great abyss, a despair and hopelessness she couldn't even begin to think of, questions clamouring that she couldn't bear to consider, much less answer. Where would they go? How would they live? No, she could not give up hope yet.

"I'm sure he'll think of something," Margaret said with more cheer than either of them truly felt. "After all, Ian's only fifteen. Surely his signature can't be binding, at that age."

"I pray not." Yet Harriet knew Ian had possessed a letter giving his father's permission to sign a contract in his name. David had been pleased at his son's interest, even if it was only to sell the land. Harriet couldn't bear telling him the truth of the matter now.

By bedtime, Ian still hadn't made an appearance in the house. Uneasy now, Harriet searched the barns, expecting to find him hiding in one of the haylofts, ashamed. There wasn't a trace of him anywhere.

"Rupert, do you know where he's gone?" Margaret asked when they were all standing in the kitchen, wondering where to look next.

A shadow of apprehension flitted across the young boy's face as his gaze skittered away. "No…"

"You know something," Margaret said definitively. "You spend every day with Ian. Come out with it, then. We must find him, Rupert, surely you can see that. It's getting dark, and it's started to rain."

"I don't know where he went." Rupert's face was set in stubborn lines, a younger version of their father. "I saw him head down the road, towards Craignure. But I didn't ask him where he was going, and he didn't tell me."

"Did he have anything with him?" Margaret asked. "A rucksack, or…" she glanced at Harriet. "Rupert, was he running away?"

Rupert looked down, unwilling to meet their gaze. "I don't know."

Margaret and Harriet exchanged worried glances. "He's gone, then," Harriet said heavily. "I was too hard on him. I know I was. I was just so angry!"

"Of course you were. You mustn't blame yourself. He'll come back. Where could he go?" Margaret tried for a smile. "He'll have walked to Tobermory, perhaps, and he'll get a soaking, but that's no bad thing. We'll find him, Harriet."

A sudden loud knocking had them both flying to the front door. Harriet jerked back in surprise when she opened it.

"What are *you* doing here?"

"Not a terribly friendly greeting, but I've had worse." Andrew Reid smiled ruefully. "May I come in? It's pouring out here, and I'm getting quite wet."

"This isn't Lanymoor, Mr. Reid," Harriet told him coldly. "Is there any reason I should let you inside my house—it will be yours soon enough, thanks to your uncle!"

"That's why I've come," Andrew said. "I'd nothing to do with that, and I'm truly sorry for what my uncle did. More than you could ever know."

"Let him come in, Harriet," Margaret said, although her glance for Andrew Reid bordered on unfriendly. "He might know something useful."

Reluctantly Harriet stood aside, and let Andrew into the front parlor. He seemed too big and lanky for the small space, and he stooped slightly even though there was no need.

"Do you have something to say?" Harriet asked. There was no call to be gracious to this man any longer. He'd have his due soon enough.

"Actually, I do. I didn't know anything about my uncle's plan until he announced it to you."

"So you've said."

You must've known something," Margaret protested. "How did Sir James know the Campbells were even considering selling the land? Who told him that?"

"I've no idea," Andrew replied calmly. "I've known Uncle James wanted to buy land on Mull, and if I'm honest, I'll tell you I knew he wanted your land in particular."

"Why?" Harriet cried. "What does he have against us?"

Andrew shrugged. "You're the largest landholders on Mull, the last of the freehold farmers. If he took your land, it would send a message to all the landholders between here and Fort William. When he learned you were having financial difficulties—"

"You certainly did know something," Harriet rejoined bitterly. "Who was it who told him all this?"

"This is an island, Miss Campbell," Andrew said gently, "and a small one at that. You are a prosperous family. How was he not to know?"

Although Harriet could see the sense of it, she refused to acknowledge the point, and looked away instead. "Why have you come?" she said after a long, tense moment, her voice low. "What does it matter if you knew or not, if I believe you or not? It doesn't change things."

"I rather hope that it might. I want to help you try and get the farm back, Harriet. If there's anything within my power…"

The use of her first name caused a strange sensation, half pleasure, half pain, to ripple through her. Who was this man and why was he saying he would help her? Harriet lifted her chin. "And what would be within your power, Mr. Reid? I wasn't under the impression that you'd much influence with your uncle at all."

Andrew flushed. "Perhaps not, but I could still try. If you don't want my help…"

"Stop being so proud, Harriet," Margaret admonished. "You could use all the help you're offered, especially now, with Ian."

"What has happened to Ian?"

"He's run away," Harriet said bluntly. "Shamed by your uncle's trickery, and how he fell afoul of it—a mere boy! You should be ashamed of yourself, even if your uncle isn't."

"Why don't you let me help you?" Andrew urged. "I've brought the carriage. We can look for him tonight. It's a foul night out, and the sooner he's back in his bed, the better we'll all rest."

"You included?" Harriet raised her eyebrows in mockery. "I didn't know you cared about my brother, Mr. Reid!"

"Pax, Miss Campbell," Andrew said tiredly. "Please? For one night? So I can help."

Grudgingly Harriet nodded. She felt, in a sudden rush, an immense weariness. Holding in this anger and bitterness took its toll. Perhaps for one evening she could let go of it, for Ian's sake.

The road to Craignure was thick with mud and the carriage ride was bumpy at best. Rain sluiced against the windows and hammered on the carriage's roof. Twice they got stuck, and Andrew leaped out to dig them out. Worry gnawed Harriet's stomach and her mind went in relentless circles. They checked all the likely haunts: the inn at Craignure, neighbors' houses, before they went all the way to Tobermory and down to the waterfront, but there was no sign of him anywhere.

It occurred to Harriet as they sat close together, elbows jostling while Andrew handled the reins, how inappropriate it was that she was here, consorting with the enemy—and a bachelor at that. If anyone saw, her reputation would be maligned, but in the moment she had little patience for that sort of nonsense. Ian had to be found.

"He's holed up somewhere for the night, no doubt," Andrew said when there was nothing to do but turn back towards home. "It's wretched out. I think I should take you home. We can look again tomorrow. I'll bring the carriage at first light."

Harriet shivered. She didn't like the thought of Ian out in the lashing rain by himself, miserable and alone. What could he possibly be thinking of, running away in such a fashion?

"He's fifteen," Andrew reminded her gently. "Man enough to run away, and man enough, I hope, to come back."

"It'll serve him right, bearing an uncomfortable night," Harriet said with a decided lack of conviction. "But if he's not back tomorrow, I shall have to tell Father… and everyone. There will be no avoiding it." Her stomach clenched at the thought and she bit her lip, too numb and weary for tears.

"He'll come back tomorrow like a wet puppy, I'm sure. In the meantime, though, it doesn't solve your other problem."

"I don't know what will solve that, except for your uncle's repentance," Harriet said with a return of spirit.

"I agree." Andrew's voice was dry. "However, knowing my uncle, I'm afraid that's hardly likely. Why don't you show the contract to your man of business? There may be a way out yet."

"I was already planning to do that very thing," she replied with asperity. "I hardly need you to suggest it."

"I'm glad you were." He paused. "I'll go with you, if you like."

Harriet was about to retort that it would be hardly necessary, but the stinging words died on her lips. She could use a friend, a protector even, but she did not want it to be Sir James Riddell's nephew. Andrew read her expression perfectly, and to Harriet's shock he took her chin in his hand. Her skin tingled where he touched it.

"Harriet, I'm your friend," Andrew said gently. "I want to be. Will you let me?"

Her mouth was dry and she wet her lips before whispering, "I don't know if I can trust you."

"Let me prove it to you."

With an alarming fluttering of her heart, Harriet realized he was going to take the appalling liberty of kissing her. What sort of woman did he think she was? She jerked her chin from his grasp just in time. "Take me home, Mr. Reid, please," she said in as cold a voice as she could manage. "It's very late."

Silently Andrew took the reins. Harriet leaned back against the seat and exhaled a shaky breath. She didn't know what frightened her more: that Andrew would have kissed her, or that a tiny, treacherous part of her had wanted him to.

*

"I have an announcement to make." Sandy smiled at his family gathered around the supper table one evening in early September. Betty smiled back with a touch of worry clouding her eyes, and Archie leaned back in his chair, quietly confident, that knowing smile Allan hated lurking about his lips.

Allan stilled, his fork halfway to his mouth. He glanced at Archie, and his brother averted his eyes. Allan laid down his fork.

"Archie is going into the army," Sandy said proudly. "I've bought him a commission in the Thirtieth Regiment. He'll be a lieutenant to start with, and I'm sure he'll make us proud, won't you, son?"

Archie, lounging in his chair, nodded. Allan placed his hands carefully on the table as his heart thudded with terrible realization. He looked hard at his father, who stared back with a bland determination.

"What about the farm?" Allan asked. "Without Archie's help…"

"I can afford to hire a few men. The harvest has been good this year, and there's been talk in Charlottetown of men who haven't their own land. They're willing to work, in exchange for board and a little pay. We'll manage."

"I see," Allan said evenly. "So, no different to what I do then, except they get paid."

"Allan!" Betty's voice came out in a low, desperate entreaty, and Allan stood up from the table.

Sandy stared at him, eyes narrowed. "This is about Archie now, Allan. Surely you can see that."

Allan nodded, waiting until he could trust his voice to be level. "I can't quite see how Archie's joining the Army fits in with our plans, Father. I thought we were all meant to work the farm and enjoy its success, live and die together. Wasn't that the way of it?"

"I think you and I can manage the farm, Allan," Sandy replied firmly. "And Archie never had his heart in the land, did you, lad?"

"No, Father." Archie still wouldn't look at Allan and his hands clenched into fists.

Looking at his father's bland face, his mother's troubled countenance, and worst of all, Archie's smug understanding, touched with pity, was more than he could bear. His brother knew. His brother knew just how much this was costing everyone in the family—and especially him.

"Allan," Sandy said with quiet menace, "you haven't congratulated your brother."

Bitterness welled up in him as he forced his lips to curl into a smile. "Congratulations, Archie. You'll do splendidly in the Army. You always did know how to fight for what you wanted." He stood up. He could take no more. "Excuse me."

Blindly he made his way out to the barn. The air was cold, with a promise of frost, and in the gathering dusk he could see the beauty of the turning foliage, a blaze of gold and crimson against this rugged land they'd claimed for their own.

Yet he was blind to it all, blind to everything but the towering rage building within him.

The animals sensed his anger and there was a rustling and fidgeting from the stalls as Allan placed his palms flat against the barn wall, his head bowed, his breaths deep and ragged.

Why had Sandy seen fit to buy Archie a commission in the Army, a future of his own, while at every opportunity he reminded Allan of his duty to the farm? It wasn't fair. It was the cry of a little boy, unused to the ways of the world, yet Allan couldn't help but feel the injustice of it to the depths of his soul. Why should Archie be treated differently than him?

He let out a howl of rage, of frustration, of *hurt*, and kicked at the dirt floor. Then he dropped his head into his hands, already defeated.

"Allan." Betty stood silhouetted in the doorway of the barn, clutching her shawl around her thin shoulders. "Allan, *cridhe*, what is it?"

"Did you know about this?"

"About Archie's commission?" Betty shrugged, her eyes shadowed with worry and confusion. "I suppose I did. I knew Archie spoke to your father about going into the Army months ago. He never was meant to be a farmer."

"And what about me?"

Betty looked surprised. "Allan, you were born to it. You've always loved the land."

"My own land," Allan shot back. "Or at least, some say in the land I work with my own two hands." He took a deep breath and steadied himself. It was true, he'd always had an affinity for working the land, feeling the sun on his back and the wind on his face, growing and tending things with his own hands. "Why wasn't I consulted… if not about Archie's future, then at least my own?"

"I don't understand." Betty moved closer to him. "Your dream has always been to farm. You've said it yourself. You wanted to come here as much as your father, for the land. Always the land. It makes him proud, that you share this. Surely you don't want to go into the Army?"

"No, of course not." Allan stared out into the night, the indigo sky now deepening to black, the first stars beginning to twinkle in that vast, empty space. "But surely you see how Father acts? I'm like a lackey to him. He's never once asked my opinion on any matter, from where to build to what we plant, to even what damned hoe we buy! I'm tired of it, Mother. I'm tired of being someone's servant—their slave—sweetened with empty promises that will never come to pass. I can't give Harriet this kind of life. I won't." The words poured out of him; years of bitterness and resentment now released to bruise and wound.

"A slave?" Betty repeated. "You see yourself as a slave?" She shook her head, one hand clutching her throat. "I was afraid you might be jealous of Archie, for heaven knows it was dear to purchase a commission. But you can be sure your father will settle a similar amount on you…"

"Money," Allan dismissed her with a shake of his head. "It's not about money. It's about respect. I'm twenty-six years old, and I should be my father's equal, and treated as such."

Betty was silent, and Allan could hear the rustling of the animals, the wind in the trees. Sounds he knew and loved, yet now they felt like the bars of a prison he could never escape from.

Betty gathered her shawl around her shoulders. "What is it you truly want then, Allan?" she asked quietly.

Allan closed his eyes. *Harriet.* He would trade away all his dreams save that most precious one. She seemed further away than ever now, with no word from her and no hope of becoming established himself. But he knew his mother wanted a practical answer. "A homestead of my own," he said after a moment, "a place I can bring Harriet to, where we can raise our children, live our lives. I won't bring her back to my father's house, I've told her that. I've even told Father, much as he listens. It's what her father wants, insists upon, even. And I insist upon it as well. She needs her own home, we need our own life."

"You can't have that here?"

"I asked Father if we could build across the river. The farm would still be MacDougall land, but he won't give me even this longer leash! The back bedroom is good enough for us, and taking orders until he—"

"Dies?" Betty finished softly. "Don't waste your years in bitterness, Allan. Your father at least should have taught you the folly of that."

"Then what am I to do? I can't stay here forever, not like this."

"I thought you were happy." Betty's voice was tired and sad.

Allan shook his head. He could not bring himself to lie, not now, when honesty was the only weapon he had. "I'm sorry, Mother. I don't mean to sound disloyal…"

"Disloyal?" Her eyes widened. "With every word you've spoken, you've betrayed us and what we've striven to build, everything we've sacrificed for! This farm, this land—the reason we moved to this forsaken country—do you think it was for us, Allan? For me? I'm forty-seven years old, and I would have happily seen my days out back on Ardnamurchan. Your father chafed against the Riddells, it's true, but he lived a comfortable life and he was a man of standing there. No, all of this, everything—it was for *you*. You and Archie and the others, to have the opportunities there never were or would be in Scotland!" Betty ran out of breath, and perhaps will, for her face was red with anger, her chest heaving, even as her expression seemed to collapse on itself with sadness.

Allan glanced down, feeling chastised but still unrepentant. "From here, all the opportunity seems to come only to Father," he said quietly.

Betty sank onto an upturned pail. She looked old and frail, and utterly bereft of hope. "I could speak to him, about a cabin," she said after a moment, her voice weary. "Across the river."

Allan knew this cost her, and he crouched down to touch her arm. "I'll fight my own battles, Mother. And I'll stay. I'm not meaning to betray you or Father, or throw what you've worked hard to give us in your faces. I promise you that. It's... it's more about freedom. To do as I choose, to make my own way. I sound selfish, don't I?" He sighed, unable to explain his thoughts, the desires of his heart, more easily. "It's as the Bible says... a man shall leave his mother and father and cleave to his wife. I want that. I want to find my way, with Harriet." Allan heard the vehemence in his voice, and wished he could moderate it. But he'd been feeling imprisoned for so long, he couldn't keep the emotion from rushing into his words, even for his mother's sake.

"Were you going to tell your father this?" Betty asked after a moment.

Allan felt a flash of guilt. "I've tried… perhaps not as plainly as I should have, but Father hears what he wants to hear. And now that Archie's leaving, it binds me all the more to this place."

"And that's so repugnant to you?" Betty's voice was quiet and sad. "To live in the bosom of your family, and work the land with your own father, building a future for your own sons?"

"If it was like that, then no. But this farm doesn't feel as if it's mine, and sometimes I wonder if it truly is. If it ever will be. I wonder if Father will ever change. He's a stubborn man." Allan stood up, his expression grave. "I won't be my father's tacksman."

"Many sons would consider it a privilege," Betty replied sharply. She sighed, and passed a hand over her eyes. They sat in tense silence, each lost in their own desolate thoughts. Finally, with a shuddering breath, she spoke. "I see you have your father's strength of will, as well as his independent spirit. For all the pain and sorrow it causes us, I wouldn't have you or your father any differently."

"I don't want to grieve you, Mother," Allan said. "I know what my duty is, and I'll stay here for as long as I'm needed. I was angry now… I'm sorry. You all took me by surprise." He put his arms around her, surprised by her frailty. Her bones were as light and thin as a bird's, yet he could still feel the strength in her, running through her center like a wire. "Forgive me for being an ungrateful son."

"No, *cridhe*," Betty lightly stroked his cheek. "Forgive me, for not understanding. No matter what our own desires, you must make your own way, wherever it takes you. Remember that."

She slipped quietly from his side to return to the house. Allan sat in the darkness for a long time, surprised to find a new, fragile peace stealing upon him like the twilight. His mother's words gave him hope. Now might not be the time, but it would come. He would find it.

He could almost picture his cabin, see the sunlight glinting on the water, Harriet by his side, a child in her arms. The land would be his, as well as his father's. Someday he would be his own man. Someday, God willing, soon.

CHAPTER TEN

"I'm sorry, Miss Campbell, but I can't give you good news."

Harriet's heart sank as Mr. Franklin placed the contract on his desk and removed his spectacles. "What news can you give me, then?" she asked.

"The contract is binding. I knew as much yesterday, when your brother came here, insisting that I witness his signature. There was little I could do."

"But if you knew it was for the whole farm, couldn't you have warned Ian? He didn't even realize…"

Franklin looked away. "I'm sorry, Miss Campbell," he said, and his tone sounded both final and full of regret. It took Harriet only a moment to realize what the man wasn't saying; Mr. Franklin must have somehow been an unwilling, or at least reluctant, party to Sir James' plan. Riddell owned all the land from here to Tobermory. Of course Mr. Franklin couldn't go against the wealthy baronet. Still, the realization stung. Was there no one she could trust? No one who could help her?

"If only Ian had read the contract properly," he said, shaking his head in mournful regret.

"If only he'd had good men to advise and warn him," Harriet returned sharply. Mr. Franklin made no response. "Ian's only fifteen," she said in a milder tone. "Surely the courts will take that into consideration. How can a contract be binding when signed by a mere boy?"

"Your father wrote a letter giving him legal right to sign in his name. If not for that, you might have a case. However…" Another shake of his head, and Harriet bit her lip in frustration. He wouldn't say it in so many words, but Mr. Franklin was warning her not to go against Sir James Riddell when it came to the courts, or any matter. "Since your father gave him authority, Ian was acting within his powers. There is nothing you can do."

"So the contract can't be rendered invalid." Harriet spoke mostly to herself. Her mind was racing, searching for answers. There seemed to be none, and yet still she resisted accepting as truth what Mr. Franklin said so plainly.

"I'm afraid not. You may console yourself that at least you received a respectable sum for the property. I could arrange for you to rent a cottage in town, perhaps. With careful management and some enterprise, you could do reasonably well for some years. Since your father's ill, perhaps the farm is a bit beyond him now, as it is?" Mr. Franklin raised his eyebrows in delicate query.

Harriet swallowed her anger. Live in town in a cramped cottage, counting pennies? They'd been one of the largest landholders on the island, reduced now to near penury! Her bitterness against the Riddells burned like a hot coal lodged inside her.

"Thank you for that suggestion." She smiled tightly and began to gather her gloves and reticule.

"I know it isn't easy, Miss Campbell," Mr. Franklin said gently. "In fact, it's a remarkable piece of ill fortune, and I trust you understand me when I say there would have been nothing you could have done, regardless. Sir James is a very powerful man, but he has not left you penniless. He paid you a fair price for Achlic—"

"We wouldn't have sold Achlic," Harriet choked out. "And especially not to him."

"But at least there's a bit of money…"

"Even after we pay our debts?" Harriet returned, acid in her tone. "You know what they are as well as I do, I should think."

Mr. Franklin sighed. "Admittedly, there will be much less. But still, with careful management, you could survive. If you became a governess, perhaps, or did some needlework to help matters?" He shrugged, spreading his hands. "Without the farm requiring your attention, I'm sure there's some useful employ both you and your brother could find."

Harriet's gloves slipped from her fingers as she looked carefully at Mr. Franklin. There was a slight flush to his cheeks, a resigned look in his eyes. "Are you saying, Mr. Franklin, that we won't have enough money to live, unless Ian and I both go out to work?"

The flush heightened, and Harriet knew she was right. The pain of losing Achlic was temporarily muted by this new problem. How could she and Ian both work, with Eleanor and their father to care for? What could they even do, that would bring in a decent wage?

"Your debts were considerable." Mr. Franklin's look now was one of unveiled pity. "As I said, there's enough to clear your debts and rent a modest dwelling. After that…" He shrugged, spreading his hands. "You will have to find some useful enterprise, I'm afraid. It is no more than what many people have had to in these hard times."

Outside in the street, Harriet felt despair wash over her in sickening, soul-crushing waves. It was all so much worse than she'd thought. Not only would they lose Achlic, but they'd be one step from destitution or worse. And Ian was still nowhere to be found.

"Well?" Andrew Reid appeared at her side, frowning. "By the expression on your face, it doesn't appear to be good news."

"No, it doesn't." She'd allowed Andrew to drive her into town, but she had drawn the line at his offer to accompany her to Franklin's office. The last thing she wanted was a member of the Riddell family hearing the whole sorry tale of her family's finances. "The contract is binding, and there's nothing we can do. The farm is yours." She gave a brittle smile, suddenly on the verge of tears.

"Harriet, please. Don't make me the enemy."

"You are the enemy! Who knows what you told your uncle, what he learned? The whole reason Sir James engaged me to teach pianoforte no doubt was to get his claws into my family, and learn of our affairs. I'm sure of it."

"I don't know all of my uncle's machinations, but I told him nothing, and you know that," Andrew stated calmly. He helped her into the carriage, where she sat, trembling as the reality of what Mr. Franklin had said rushed over her once more. What was she going to *do*? "If there was a way I could undo this, I would." He paused, allowing her a moment to compose herself. "I only want to help. I hope you realize that." Harriet did not reply. Andrew Reid could not help her. "What will you do?" he asked after a moment.

"I don't know." Her wave of tears had passed, and now she felt cold, lifeless. Her voice sounded distant, as if coming from outside of herself. "You must know, as much of the island seems to do, that we've debts, many of them. The creditors will be crawling all over us once they hear what's happened. We've enough to pay them off now, but little else. I'll have to find work, and Ian as well." Sudden fire flashed in her eyes. "Don't think you need worry about us. We'll manage."

Andrew nodded, his lips pursed, clearly not wishing to debate the point at this particular moment. "And who will look after your father while you work?"

Harriet thought briefly of Jane MacCready's offer, made months ago now. The older woman's suggestion had seemed sincere, yet it stung Harriet's pride to have to ask for help. Even worse was the thought of tying Eleanor to such a job at twelve years old. "We'll find something," she said.

They rode in silence almost all the way back to the farm, Andrew lost in thought, Harriet adrift in her own misery. When they'd finally arrived back at Achlic, he pulled the carriage up a little short of the farm, and turned to her, a sudden, serious look on his face. "Harriet… there is another way, if you'll listen. A way for you to save the farm, and your father, and your whole family. But only…" He swallowed, color staining his cheeks. "Only if you wanted it, at least part of you… if you felt you could… perhaps one day…"

Harriet stared at him in confusion. "What are you saying?"

Andrew clasped her hands in his. "I know I'm not doing a very good job of it, but I am asking you to marry me."

Harriet stared at him in wordless shock. "Marry you?" she finally repeated, her voice little more than a whisper. She could hardly believe she'd heard him right.

"I thought you might have realized I have feelings for you," Andrew said. "But I see now that I've surprised you."

Harriet stared down at her hands still in his. She pulled her hands from his, her fists clenched, her gloves damp. "Yes, you've surprised me."

Andrew reached for her hand once more, clasping hers lightly in his own. Even through her wrinkled glove she could feel the warm strength and gentle pressure of his own larger hand cradling hers. "Harriet, I love you. I love your strength and spirit, and your loyalty to your family… even if part of that is directed against me. I hold no love for my uncle. When you're not raging against the Riddell family, I think you realize that."

Harriet nodded. Although it was easy to blame Andrew along with his uncle, she knew the truth of his words. She could not blame him for Sir James' treachery. But marriage…? *Love*?

"I think we could make a good life together. I don't have prospects, you know that, but I think I could provide for you, with the farm…"

"Farm?" Harriet's head jerked up, her eyes narrowing. "You mean Achlic Farm? You want it for yourself?"

"Why must you blacken my motives at every opportunity?" Andrew asked tiredly, although he managed a wry smile. "No, not for myself. For us. For your father, and Ian and Eleanor. For you."

"How could that be?"

"If we were married, I'm sure I could convince Uncle James to allow us to live at Achlic, and work the land. Your family could stay there. I know he's cold-hearted, but he's not a complete scoundrel, despite what you might think. He wants the land, not to throw you to the wolves."

"Aren't they one and the same?" Harriet retorted bitterly. "He doesn't seem to be bothered."

"These are hard times."

Harriet stared at Andrew in disbelief. "Are you defending him?"

"No, of course not. I'm only trying to show you there is more than one side to it."

"Not as far as I'm concerned." Harriet jerked her hand which had been laying limply, forgotten, in his. "So, let me see if I understand you correctly, sir," she continued, her voice laced with anger. "If I marry you, you'll save my family from penury. And if I don't, then we all might as well starve. The farm won't be ours—it will be yours, and we will live there on your sufferance, beggars at our own table, and all because of your uncle's despicable treachery!"

Andrew's face darkened with anger, and Harriet realized she'd never truly seen his temper. He was usually so genial and easy-going, yet for a moment she saw a glimpse of the hardness underneath, and knew he was more like his uncle than perhaps either one of them had realized. "If you're accusing me of blackmail," Andrew said in a low voice thrumming with emotion, "then I think that is despicable. I've told you I love you. Anything I do for you or Achlic is because of my love for you, not for personal gain."

Harriet flushed and bit her lip. Still, she could not bring herself to apologize. "How can you expect me to think any differently? It's your family that has tricked mine… I don't want any more trickery!"

"Neither do I," Andrew stated. "I only want you to marry me if you want to, Harriet. If you have feelings for me. I don't expect you to love me, not yet, but if you felt you could one day…" He shrugged, and picked up the reins once more. "That would be something worth waiting for."

"You know I'm betrothed to Allan," Harriet told him. She was shocked to realize she'd not thought of Allan once since Andrew's proposal—a realization which shamed and pained her. How could she have forgotten him for an instant?

"As I understood it, he asked you to wait, not to marry him."

"Even so, I promised."

Andrew looked as if he were about to say something, but then shrugged and looked away instead. "Whatever is between you and Allan MacDougall is your own concern, Harriet. You must decide for yourself what you wish for out of this life. But remember, he is far away, and building his own life there, away from you." He paused. "Tell me, has he written you?"

For a moment Harriet wanted to slap him. She hated Andrew Reid for knowing that Allan hadn't written her save the first packet of letters Riddell had taken. She hated him for voicing her innermost doubts and fears and stating them as facts. "That, Mr. Reid," she said in a voice needled with ice, "is not your concern."

"What concerns you concerns me."

"Only because you make it so!"

Andrew glanced at her, and for a moment Harriet saw tenderness and even love in his gaze before his expression became unreadable. "You might at least think about it," he said. "While there's time."

How much time, Harriet wondered bleakly? According to the contract Ian had signed, they had to vacate Achlic Farm within the month. And then…? They could find lodgings in Tobermory, humble and temporary, or she could become Andrew Reid's bride. It felt like blackmail, but in truth, Harriet knew that was no fault of Andrew's. He didn't control his uncle's despicable actions, and the brief glimpse of love shining in his eyes had shaken her. Perhaps Andrew's offer was one she couldn't refuse.

*

Captain Henry Moore breathed in deeply, savoring the scent of salt on the wind, as well as the familiar peaty tang of earth. This was not his home, as Massachusetts would always be that, but something now infinitely more dear. Scotland, the land of his ancestors, and also of Margaret MacDougall.

Would she be glad to see him? It was a thought which had occupied Henry's mind for most of the spring and summer. When he'd left at the end of last winter, they hadn't known each other well enough for him to extract promises which he had no right to expect Margaret to keep. Yet the thought of her snapping black eyes, her sense of humor and her passion for learning had sustained him through many a tempestuous sea journey.

He'd asked her to wait for him before he left, but the request and answering agreement had been nebulous, hardly the stuff a romance—or a lifetime commitment—was built on.

He wondered if there would be any letters waiting for him with his aunt. He hoped Margaret had written him. He'd written her several missives, and had posted them from his travels over the summer. He'd taken great delight in describing the sights and sounds of the many places he'd been, knowing she would enjoy the descriptions. Even the most trivial anecdote became inspiration for his writing; a way to share his life with her, and bind them together.

There was no way of knowing whether they'd reached her by now or not, until he saw her and asked her himself.

Now he was back in Tobermory, for three days only, before he began another voyage to the Americas. He wouldn't be back in Scotland for a year, as he'd a lucrative offer to ship freight in the Caribbean during the winter.

He was hoping fervently to see Margaret during his leave. But what would his reception be? Henry cherished hopes of love, commitment, even marriage. Would Margaret be willing to wait a year, based on their slender acquaintance? Did he dare ask her while on such short leave?

He chuckled softly to himself—he was as lovesick as a schoolboy, yet still as determined as ever to woo and win his bride. If Margaret wanted him, they would be together, no matter how long either one of them had to wait.

Henry went to his aunt's house as soon as *The Allegiance* was in port. Unfortunately, the news was disappointing.

Elizabeth was in Edinburgh visiting relatives, but her housekeeper told him the news. "There haven't been any letters, sir, that I *ken* of."

Henry knew Elizabeth would have made sure he received any noteworthy news, and he suspected his aunt knew the force of his feelings for Margaret MacDougall. Forcing a smile, he thanked the woman and turned towards the public house.

With his legs stretched towards the fire and a mug of ale in his hand, a large wedge of cottage pie before him, he considered what to do next. Dare he be so bold as to pay a call on Margaret at Achlic Farm? He couldn't bear the thought of not seeing or hearing from her at all, yet he wondered if she would welcome a visit. For why else would she not have written?

"Excuse me, sir." A young boy, tall and awkward-looking, cap twisted in his hands, stood at the corner of his table. Henry raised his eyebrows. "Yes?"

"Are you the captain of *The Allegiance*?"

"I am."

"Have you space for a ship's boy?" the boy asked. "I can do almost anything I put my mind to, and I wouldn't be any trouble."

"Is that so?" Henry looked the boy over. He had a shock of red hair and a face full of freckles, and although his clothes were worn, they were of good quality. He looked to be from a good home, although he must've been living rough for the last few days. "Why don't you sit down and share my pie, and we'll discuss it."

The boy needed no second invitation. Henry called for another pie and ale. "How old are you, then?"

"Seventeen."

Not likely, Henry thought wryly. More like fourteen, fifteen perhaps, certainly not more. "Seventeen's a bit old for a ship's boy," he informed his companion mildly. "I'd be looking for a midshipman then, and I'm afraid you don't have the experience."

The boy's face fell, and Henry had to keep himself from smiling at the transparency of his feelings. The serving maid came with the food, and Henry watched as the boy fell onto it, mumbling his thanks between mouthfuls.

"It looks as if you've not had a good meal in a time," Henry remarked. "Tell me the truth, boy, how old are you now?"

Shamefaced, swallowing a large mouthful of pie, the boy mumbled, "Fifteen last winter."

"I thought so." Henry leaned back in his chair. "Life on a ship is hard work, you know. Ship boys get biscuit and salt beef twice a day, and you'd share a hammock with another boy. You'd be up at dawn, working hard till night, and even then you'd have to take your turn at the watch."

"Aren't you a merchant ship?" the boy asked uneasily.

"Yes, but like many others I abide by the rules of the Navy. Helps to have order on a ship, and that's a fact. Besides, there's always the danger of pirates. The Atlantic isn't an easy ocean to cross, even with the wars over."

"Really?" The boy looked decidedly uncomfortable now, and Henry wondered why he wanted to board a ship. Most ship's boys were orphans, or working-class children with few prospects on land. The gruelling labor, tough conditions and small pay were hardly incentives for a boy from this background.

He had to be a runaway. What had he done, Henry wondered, to want to flee so far and so fast? Was there a family, waiting, frantic for him? Or an angry father who had washed his hands of him? It wasn't his business to know, but he still wondered.

"I'm not afraid, sir," the boy said now, lifting his chin. "I'd be an asset to you, I swear it."

"An asset, hmm?" Educated, as well, which gave Henry further pause. "What of your parents?"

"Dead." The boy's face closed, his lips pressed tightly together.

"There must be someone looking out for you, wondering where you are."

A shadow of vulnerability passed over the boy's face, making him look like a child. Then his expression hardened, and Henry saw the man he might become. "No," he said. "Not anymore."

Henry leaned back in his chair, considering. Fifteen was certainly old enough for a boy to carve his own destiny. He wouldn't stand in his way. "Six shillings a month, to start."

There was no mistaking the disappointment that clouded the boy's eyes, but he nodded in determination. "Fair enough."

"I run a tight ship," Henry warned. "Any disobedience or laziness, and I'll have you whipped or worse, off at the next port, no matter where you are." If he was trying to scare the boy, Henry knew he was succeeding, but it had yet to deflect him.

"All right. Yes, sir."

Why was he going to take this scrap on? Henry shook his head in bemusement. He could do without another ship's boy, and if the boy's family were looking for him…

Something about the boy's desperation spoke to him. He recognized someone with nowhere to turn… someone willing to fight.

"Report back to *The Allegiance* in two days' time," he said. "We sail for Massachusetts on the evening tide. What's your name, boy?"

"Ian, sir. Ian… Cameron."

The next day Henry rode towards Craignure. He enjoyed the sun on his face, the rock-strewn fields and purple-tipped mountains of his ancestral land, even if he was used to the open spaces and raw newness of America. There was something ancient and even wise about this land, he mused, even if progress was finally coming to the Highlands as well.

Work had recently started on a canal between Fort William and Inverness, which would speed travel for both passenger and commercial goods. One day, perhaps, there would be cities here, cities as large as Boston, New York, or Glasgow. Right now, however, Henry enjoyed the peaceful solitude of the countryside.

He rode to the inn at Craignure, and then asked directions to Achlic Farm.

"They won't be there much longer," the innkeeper said with a shake of his head, his face darkening with disapproval. "Achlic Farm's been sold, you know, to Sir James Riddell, and a fair bit of trickery it was."

Henry glanced sharply at the man. "It was? What of the MacDougalls? They were relations staying there—will they be cast out?"

The innkeeper shrugged. "Who knows where the wind blows? Their father should be sending for them soon as it is. They'll be in Canada next winter, or close enough."

"Perhaps," Henry acknowledged, and resolved all the more to speak frankly with Margaret when he found her. The last thing he wanted was for her to slip through his fingers, all the way to Canada.

Achlic Farm was a pleasant dwelling; a stone farmhouse, mellow in the afternoon sun, with a few chickens scratching in the yard. An older woman with small eyes and a suspicious look answered his knock on the door.

"Miss MacDougall? She's out at the moment, but what would you be wanting with her?" Her look was so grim and forbidding that Henry would've laughed if he didn't feel crushed by disappointment.

"We have an acquaintance," he said, "and I am only in the region for a short while. I wished to send her my greetings. Will she be back soon?"

"Gone all the day to Fort William, hasn't she," the woman replied. "They'd business there. I suppose you know what's happening to the farm?"

"I've heard."

"No business of yours," the woman snapped, "or mine neither, come to that. No business at all."

Henry murmured something placatory. "May I leave a note for her, Mistress…?"

"MacCready. All right, then. I suppose I could give it to her."

"Thank you."

When he'd been given ink and paper, he began to write. He only hoped Margaret received his letter in time.

Having handed Mistress MacCready his note, and suspecting the old woman would read it herself, Henry had no choice but to head back to Tobermory, feeling as far from Margaret as he'd been while halfway across the world.

CHAPTER ELEVEN

"Doesn't he look smart?"

Allan listened to the admiring whisper of one of the town girls and wondered at the crowd which had gathered for Archie's send off. In his new finery—red wool tunic, white breeches and polished boots—he did indeed look smart. Ready, Allan thought dourly, to face his future. To *make* his future.

Archie had finally received his orders from the Army. Today he was to report to the barracks in Charlottetown, and from there he would receive further orders off island.

The whole family had come to accompany him, and a small crowd had gathered to watch the soldiers parade into the garrison, a splendid display.

Allan had not been to Charlottetown in many months, and now he looked around in curiosity. Although the town had been officially founded over fifty years ago, there was a spirit of youth and energy to it, like an adolescent desperate to grow into maturity.

The grand plans had been laid at the start, with Thomas Wright, a surveyor, allotting nearly three hundred building lots, as well as a large central square and four separate green squares. Most of that was still dreams, and many of the houses were mere wooden structures, some looking as if they wouldn't stand the winter.

Still, there was plenty of building going on. The Round Market House was being built for trade, and Allan had heard of plans for a grand governor's mansion. The first island school was meant to start in Charlottetown this autumn. Charlottetown, he thought, had dreams… just like he still did.

"Well, then." Sandy looked at his younger son, his chest swelling with obvious pride. "I know you'll do well for yourself, Archie, and well for the family. We're pleased you've come this far."

Archie shook his father's hand and then kissed his mother's cheek. "There's talk of our regiment marching to Three Rivers in a fortnight. I should have leave in April, though, and I'll come back then, if the ice has broken up."

"We'll miss you at Christmas," Betty said. "You must tell us all your news. Send letters if you can, on the mail packet from Pictou."

"I promise." Archie turned to bid farewell to Allan, and Allan saw the rare hesitation in his brother's eyes. He could feel the hostility emanating from his own soul, and he was ashamed of the selfish feelings he still harbored. "Go well, Archie," he said gruffly.

Archie clapped a hand on his shoulder. "I'm sorry," he said in a voice low enough that neither Sandy nor Betty could hear. Allan nodded. Even though he felt resentful, he knew he couldn't blame Archie for taking charge of his fate. If he were brave enough, Allan thought, he would do the same.

They stayed to watch the soldiers on parade, a motley crew of British nationals and Canadian loyalists, proud and flashing in their bright uniforms. When the soldiers had all filed into the garrison, the MacDougalls finally turned to head home.

Back at Mingarry Farm, Allan retired to the barn for some needed solitude. He mucked out the cow pens and put new straw down, hoping the physical activity would relieve him of some of his restless energy.

It was nearing twilight, and he could hear the soft call of the whippoorwill, the tell-tale sign of the coming of darkness during these autumn months. The air was cold with the promise of frost—early this year and a sure sign of a long, cold winter.

"Come inside." Allan stiffened at the sound of his father's voice. "It's cold enough for a fire tonight."

"Aye, so it is." Allan continued laying down the straw. He knew he should turn to face his father, but he did not want Sandy to see the anger he suspected was still in his eyes.

"You've missed your supper," Sandy said after a moment. He leaned against the cow's stall. "Your mother wanted you to come in, but I said it'd keep. The boy needs to be by himself for a while, is what I said."

Allan turned slowly to face Sandy. "You're right, Father. But how would you be knowing that?"

"I know you," Sandy said simply. "And I know myself. I may be stubborn, Allan, and stuck in my ways, but I'm honest and I'm not blind. I know it wasn't easy watching Allan march off like that, a spring in his step and a smile on his face."

"I'm glad for him," Allan said. "He'll do well in the Army. Our Archie was never cut out for the farming life, was he?"

"No, he wasn't at that. And there's more opportunity for him here in this new country, as well as for us. He wouldn't get on with the old ways and the notions they had about being a gentleman, but in this new Army he could go far. Not all regiments want to be shipped off to the cold North, you can be certain!"

"I'm glad for him," Allan repeated, and turned back to the stalls.

"Allan." Sandy put a heavy hand on his shoulder, and Allan stilled. "You were never meant for the Army. You and Archie are as different as can be. You know that."

"I do. I never wanted a commission, Father. If you're worried I'm jealous of Archie for that reason, you may rest easy."

"There's another reason, then."

Allan sighed and lay down his pitchfork. "You've thought about what Archie wants. What he needs. Have you considered what I need?"

"This is that nonsense about the cabin," Sandy said, a note of frustration entering his gruff voice. "Wanting your own place, your own acreage even. Your own farm."

"Is that such a sin?"

"Families stay together," Sandy objected. "Always have. It's safer, and there's a loyalty. When I die, this farm will be yours, Allan. Can't you wait till then?"

"I don't want to hasten your death, Father, and neither do I long for it. You're a hale, hearty man still. Why can't I have some freedom now?"

Sandy stiffened. "What do you mean?"

Allan sighed. "This farm is yours, Father. I don't feel I own one piece of it. I'm as much a hired man as the ones in town you're thinking to bring on."

Sandy's mouth opened and closed, his face reddening. He struggled between temper and reason and finally choked out, "Allan, you're my son."

"Then let me have some say! Let me build my own place. You're still tacksman here, Father, don't you see it? And I'm the crofter." Allan gazed at him in desperate appeal, and Sandy shrugged in dismissal.

"This is nonsense." His voice was brusque. "I'm building up your inheritance, what more do you want? Are you going to whine like a spoiled bairn who doesn't get its every whim?"

"These are not whims." By sheer force of will Allan kept his voice steady. "And I am not a bairn, or even a boy."

"You seem to be acting like one." Sandy's voice became louder. "Shall I set you in the corner, or take a strap to you?"

"By God, you'll do neither!" Allan's chest heaved, and he realized he was shaking, as close to coming to blows with his own father as he had with any man.

They stared at each other, fists raised, both their gazes wild and determined. Their breathing was a ragged sawing of the air.

Sandy dropped his hands first. "What has it come to, that we're at odds like this?" His voice was small and as bewildered as a boy's. "Allan, this farm, all of it, I've built it for you. *You.*"

Allan dropped his own fists. His heart was racing, and he felt slightly sick. "So you say."

"You don't believe me?"

He shrugged. "I believe what you do, rather than what you say. That tells another story."

Sandy narrowed his eyes. "And what story is that?"

"That you're still tacksman, in your heart and mind. But there's precious few willing to take your orders."

"You can't be your father's lackey."

"You can feel like it."

Sandy sighed heavily. "What of Harriet?"

"What of her?"

"Will you not send for her unless you have a cabin and land of your own? Is that how it is to be?"

"I don't know how else it could be, with her father's demands."

"I never took it as that…" Sandy trailed off, rubbing a hand over his face. He still looked winded, and Allan couldn't help but feel guilty at how he'd hurt him. "You can build on the other side of the river," he said at last. "I'll help you find a good site. I can't grant you your own fields, not yet. What with Archie leaving, I still need you by my side. But perhaps you can write her and tell her of these arrangements." He nodded, the decision made, even though it pained him. "Write her tonight, so the letter goes on the last ship before winter. She could be here by summer, as your bride, in this new cabin of yours."

Allan knew he should be savoring this victory, yet the taste of it was bitter in his mouth. He felt as if something had changed between them, and even now he feared that he would not be free from either his father's demands, or his own sense of obligation.

"All right," he said quietly. "Thank you, Father." He turned to go back to work, but Sandy's voice stilled him.

"Perhaps I've been wrong," his father said. Allan turned, and his father looked at him with a naked honesty. "I want you to stay. You're my son. I need you here. Betty could use Harriet's help, Lord knows. If it made a difference to you…"

"It does," Allan replied. "It does." Yet he wondered if it truly would. Could things between his father and himself ever truly change? Or was he grasping at frail straws because they were better than nothing? He might need to go farther than across the river to find what he was looking for.

"You'll write Harriet?" Sandy pressed, and Allan nodded.

Yet what if she did not want to come? There had been no letters, except for the one, in over a year. Her feelings might well have changed, and she did not think even to tell him.

"Come spring, things will be different," Sandy said with a tired smile. "We'll all make sure of that."

Allan prayed it would be true.

*

Margaret hurried along the seafront of Tobermory. A bitter, salty wind whipped her hair from its pins and her shawl tighter around her shoulders. It had been three days since Ian had gone missing, and Harriet was frantic with worry. She still hadn't told her father, hiding Ian's absence as best as she could, yet knowing the inevitable was coming. David Campbell would have to be informed of the dire state of his household.

Margaret had offered to go to Tobermory to collect any letters from the MacDougalls' shipping agent, as well as scour the docks for a sign of Ian, in case he'd thought to stowaway on a ship, or even sign up as a sailor. Winter was closing in and soon there would be no more ships from the Americas till spring, although travel might continue for emigrants to Australia.

Margaret had another, hidden reason for visiting Tobermory's harbor, one she dared not divulge yet to anyone at Achlic, despite Mistress MacCready's crafty, knowing looks. She wanted to find Captain Henry Moore.

It had been almost nine months since they'd parted at his aunt's, and her affections were still unclaimed. The note he'd left for her at Achlic had been prudently brief, stating only that he would be in port till tomorrow's sailing.

Margaret hoped she'd be able to find him... and find the right words to say. What were his expectations, she wondered. What were her own?

He'd told her she could write letters in care of his aunt, but Margaret had been loath to do so. She smiled wryly to herself. That wasn't true; she'd longed to write him letters, and had poured her heart out in several missives she knew were too intimate to share. He was still more of a stranger than not, and she couldn't bear the thought of him looking at her askance, because of the nature of her letters. In the end, she'd kept them to herself, waiting to see Henry again, to judge his feelings for her... and hers for him.

Margaret strode purposefully into the little harborside office, its shingle sign, *Angus Buchanan, Shipping Agent*, swinging in the wind.

"May I help you, miss?" The clerk at the counter, with his great bushy beard and red cheeks, already seemed to be laughing at her. Margaret raised her head haughtily.

"I wanted to inquire as to the whereabouts of Captain Henry Moore. He told me he is in port. He's... an acquaintance of mine and he'd mentioned that I might receive news of him through his agent. Are you that person?"

The clerk's eyes twinkled, and Margaret knew he was amused. "I certainly am, but if it's news of Captain Moore you want, you might as well ask him yourself. His ship *The Allegiance* is outside right now, getting ready to sail on tomorrow evening's tide. He's on board."

Margaret's heart skipped a beat as she turned and saw Henry's clipper docked right outside the office, rigged like a schooner but with sleek lines built for speed. "Thank you kindly, sir," she murmured, and hurried outside.

The ship was a hive of activity the day before sailing, with sailors scurrying about on deck, everyone looking busy and industrious, and paying Margaret no notice. She hurried to the gangplank, hesitating to go any farther as an unaccompanied woman. Even so, a sailor glared at her standing there so uncertainly.

"Now, where might you be going, missy?" he asked. "Don't you know women on board ship are bad luck?"

"I need to speak to Captain Moore," Margaret said with as much hauteur as she could muster. "It is a matter of utmost importance."

The sailor planted his grimy hands on his hips as he cocked his head. "Is that so?"

She bit back a furious retort at the man's rudeness. "Yes, it is."

"Well, I'm afraid he's not here at the moment. Away on business." The sailor seemed to take pity on her, for he added, "He'll be back tomorrow though. We're sailing on the evening tide."

Disappointment swamped Margaret as she returned to the quayside. So close to Henry... and yet as far away as ever! She couldn't stand about on the docks all day, waiting for his return, even if that was just what she wanted to do. It would be most unseemly, and in any case she was meant to be looking for Ian.

She was so lost in her thoughts she almost missed sight of the familiar, gangly figure ducking into the dark alley between two timber buildings. Hitching up her skirts, Margaret ran forward.

"Ian... *Ian!*"

Picking up her skirts, she ran towards the alley, darting over mud puddles as she raced after Ian. He was halfway down the alley, trying to run from her, when she grabbed his shirt collar and breathlessly hauled him around.

"Where have you been?" she demanded as she gave his shoulder an angry shake. "Have you any idea what your family has gone through these last three days? Poor Harriet has been terrified—"

Ian's face was pale and drawn, his clothes terribly dirt, but there was still a glimmer of defiance in his eyes. "There's no place for me at Achlic," he declared, his tone a childish mixture of self-pity and anger. "It's my fault there won't be any Achlic. Everyone blames me, and so they should. I'm not going back there."

"And where will you go?" Margaret asked him, trying to gentle her tone even though she longed to give him a good shake. "You are more a burden running around the island than staying safe at home! You must come back with me, Ian. Harriet's been beside herself with worry for you, and your father will start to wonder where you are—"

Ian squared his shoulders. "I'm not going. You can tell Harriet I'm all right. As it happens I've got myself a job."

"What!" Margaret stared at him in disbelief. "What are you doing? And where?" She could not imagine who would hire Ian, fifteen years old, scruffy and dirty and defiant.

Ian shrugged. "Never you mind. I'll come back when I've made some money—I'll buy Achlic myself one day…"

"Buy Achlic?" Margaret let out a harsh laugh. "Ian, that is a nonsense! You won't even buy your dinner with the few pennies you might make as a bootblack."

"I'm not a bootblack!"

"Then what are you?" Margaret demanded. "And where are you staying? Don't add to your sister's travails by grieving her thus."

Ian dashed his face against his grimy sleeve. "I'll get it back, I swear."

Margaret sighed, her sympathy finally getting the better of her. "One day perhaps," she answered gently. "No one doubts your regret, Ian. I promise you that." She laid her hand on his arm. "I know you want to work to regain the property," she added. "But you mustn't think of all that, not now. Harriet needs you at home. She can't manage by herself, not with your father ill." Ian looked uncertain, and Margaret pressed her advantage. "You wanted a man's responsibilities? Then don't run away like a boy. Come home, where your family needs you. Come home with me now. Please."

Ian ducked his head as he wiped his nose with his sleeve. "I'm no good to anyone," he said, his voice very low.

"You're good to us, Ian. You must come home." Margaret gently pulled his sleeve, helping him to walk alongside her. "Harriet will be so relieved to see you, you don't even know."

Unwillingly, silently, Ian let himself be led, and Margaret thanked Providence that she'd found him at last.

Back at home, both Harriet and Eleanor fell on Ian with tears and recriminations, which he bore with stoic grimness. Rupert eyed him askance, for the last few days had turned Ian into an adult stranger, far removed from the boyhood friend who engaged in meaningless pranks with him, avoiding schoolwork whenever they could.

"I don't know how to thank you, Margaret," Harriet said after the others were settled in bed. She stood in the doorway of Margaret's bedroom, her hair in long plaits, her dressing gown wrapped around her. Her face was pale and still lined with worry. "I was so afraid he wouldn't come back. I hadn't even told Father he was missing yet." She looked down at her hands. "I haven't told Father anything."

"He must know, or at least suspect," Margaret said with a sorrowful sigh. "I can only think it's why he's kept so to his bed.

He could not miss the whispers flying round this place—surely Mistress MacCready has told him?"

"She's said nothing," Harriet answered bleakly. "She can keep her mouth closed when she chooses, and she knows it's my responsibility." She sighed, rubbing a hand across her face. "I'm weary of it all, I truly am. Ian… Achlic… Allan…" Her voice broke, and before she could try to compose herself, Margaret was standing beside her, her arms around her as Harriet broke down and wept.

There had been so many times for tears, and she'd held back out of necessity. She'd had to be the strong one. Now she feared she couldn't do it anymore; she felt only weak and tired, lonely and afraid.

"There, there," Margaret said softly. "You look ready to faint, Harriet. You've taken too much on your own shoulders."

"I'm better now." Harriet stepped away from Margaret, wiping her cheeks with the palms of her hands. "I'm sorry. Here I am, acting like a bairn."

"I'd hardly say that." Margaret looked serious. "I know I've neglected the responsibilities here, Harriet, and I'm sorry for adding to your burden. I've been so…" She exhaled almost angrily. "Consumed by my own petty concerns! I can't believe how selfish I've been, slipping off to Tobermory whenever I could. And here you are, struggling to keep heart and soul together."

"It's not as bad as that, and Achlic Farm isn't your own, Margaret. You've a right to your freedom."

Margaret pressed her lips together. "Even so. I've been distracted…"

"So I've gathered." Harriet gave her a small smile. "I wonder what distracts you so?" She waited for Margaret to say something, for she'd had her own suspicions about her cousin's many forays over the winter to Tobermory. Had she met someone? An acquaintance had told Harriet of seeing Margaret calling on an older woman, a Miss Elizabeth Moore, but Harriet hadn't wanted to say anything of it to Margaret, since she seemed so secretive herself. Still, she wondered who else might be in residence at Miss Moore's cottage.

Margaret flushed at Harriet's considering look. "Never mind that. It's not important now. What can I do to help?"

"Find some money?" Harriet joked on a tired sigh. She leaned against the doorway, too weary to stand. "To speak truth," she said slowly, "I think I've found a way out of this *fankle*. I'm just not sure whether to act upon it."

"A way out? But what could that be?"

Harriet shook her head. She couldn't admit what she was thinking of to Margaret yet, not when she knew how angry and even betrayed she'd feel. Besides, she hadn't made her decision, although in her heart she feared she already had. "I won't speak of it yet. We'd best get some sleep. There will be plenty of time to discuss things tomorrow."

The next morning, Margaret set out for Tobermory once again, determined to find Captain Moore before he sailed. She left Achlic's household in an unsettled state, with nothing decided about their future, Ian sulky and David Campbell still in ignorance.

"I'll only be a short while," Margaret promised Harriet as she reached for her shawl and bonnet. "I promise. It's—it's important."

"I can see that it is," Harriet answered with a tired smile. "Whatever—or whoever—is compelling you to Tobermory, Margaret, I do hope you'll tell me one day."

"One day," Margaret promised, and hurried off.

Her heart thudded with both anticipation and anxiety as she made her way towards Tobermory. Would she seem terribly forward, coming all this way to find Henry alone? And yet he'd come looking for her. He had to want to see her, surely? Still, as she approached the busy harborside, her whole body was nearly vibrating with nervousness. What if he'd already gone, her only chance missed by the matter of a moment?

The harbor was bustling with activity as several ships made preparations to sail that evening, sailors shouting to each other over the raucous cries of the gulls. Margaret's heart hammered as she caught sight of *The Allegiance* and she searched its deck, looking for his tall, familiar form. What would he say when he saw her? Would he be glad? Would he even be there?

She had not even reached the gangplank when he was there before her, hurrying from the ship, his face full of joy whose answer Margaret felt in herself.

"Margaret!" Henry stood before her, his blue eyes bright with happiness, his hands outstretched towards her. "I can scarcely believe it! I've been looking for you for days, but you'd seemed to have disappeared! You received my note?"

"Yes, I've been searching for you, as well," she admitted shyly. "I was afraid I would be too late."

Henry clasped her hands. "I'm very glad to see you," he said, the happiness clear in his voice. "I'd been hoping you would have written me over the summer, but no matter now that you are here."

"I... I wanted to," Margaret stammered, feeling like the kind of silly miss'ish girl she usually despised. "But I didn't know what to write." She paused as Henry's hands warmed her own. "How much to write."

A new light came into his eyes at that admission and gently he squeezed her hands. "Can you spare a moment to come below quarters so we may speak in private? Only for a moment…"

"I…" Margaret hesitated, conscious of the sailors' curious stares, the people passing by on the quay. "I don't know if that's proper."

"Of course!" Henry had the grace to blush. "Forgive me, I'm just so delighted to see you. I was afraid I would sail without sight of your lovely face, and another year would pass before we might meet again, which would have truly been tragic."

"And you must sail tonight?" Margaret said, her disappointment audible. They had so little time.

"Yes, I'm afraid so, and I won't be back for another year. I've a commission in the Caribbean over the winter." Henry took a deep breath as he squared his shoulders. "In light of that, there's little time to waste. I apologize for my forwardness, but I can't wait a year to declare my intentions to you, Miss MacDougall. It's the thought of you which has sustained me all spring, and I dare not hope you might feel the same…"

"You may dare," Margaret said, feeling suddenly breathless. Was Henry saying what she thought he was, what she could scarcely hope he was?

"Do you truly mean that?"

Margaret nodded, unable to form words, barely able to form thoughts.

"Margaret, I love you. Will you wait for me, for this year… that I may return and claim you as my own one day, as my bride?"

"Yes," Margaret whispered. Her heart seemed to want to beat right out of her chest. "Yes, I'll wait. Of course I'll wait."

"You've made me the happiest man today." Henry's face radiated his joy. "May I… may I kiss you?"

Margaret could barely speak. She wasn't aware of the bitter wind or the plaintive cry of the seagulls, or even of the sailors who went about their business around them, still casting them sideways glances. All she think of was Henry, and that he loved her. He loved her!

"You may," she said, her voice unsteady, and she closed her eyes as Henry briefly brushed her lips with his. His arms encircled her, and Margaret knew that home was not Achlic, or Mingarry, or where her family was, far across the sea. It was where this man was, this man who loved her. She laid her cheek against the rough wool of his coat, her mind and heart both bursting within her.

"You really will wait for me, then?" Henry asked as they stepped apart. "I know a year is a long time, but I'll come back to you, I swear it on my life."

"I know you will." She trusted Henry with her heart and soul, and the thought made her giddy with joy and a little fear. What would her father say to her forming this attachment, making this promise? Yet he was far away, too far to matter now. "I must go," she said reluctantly. "They'll miss me back at home. I've been away too much as it is."

"Tell me where to find you, when I return. I've heard the farm where you board is to be sold."

"I'm not sure where I'll be yet," she admitted. "Perhaps here in Tobermory."

"You could always lodge with my aunt—"

"Thank you, but I couldn't leave Harriet or the others. We'll find somewhere, don't fear. And in the meantime you can leave letters with my father's shipping agent, Mr. Douglas, right here on the quay."

Henry grasped her hands, his expression turning urgent. "You'll be all right? You'll stay safe—and where I can find you? And what of your father? The innkeeper at Craignure said you might be sailing for that shore soon. What if I miss you?"

"There has been no word yet," Margaret replied, her heart thudding at the thought of the many changes that lay ahead. "Whatever happens, I'll leave word with the shipping agent. You will find me, Henry."

"I vow I will," Henry agreed, although his face was still anxious. "You can write me in Boston, in care of Moore Shipping. I'll get the letters at some point, between journeys."

"I shall do so." She tried for a smile. "I will write this time, I promise."

"I'm loath to let go of you," he admitted with a shaky laugh. "Now that I've found you once."

"You'll find me again," Margaret promised, and dared to stand on tiptoe and kiss his cheek.

"I'll write you often, and think of you more," Henry promised. "Goodbye... but only for a little while."

Margaret watched him walk away with longing in her heart. A year was not a long time, she told herself, and yet it seemed endless. Harriet and Allan had been separated for little more than a year, and their own wedding seemed no closer. Harriet still doubted her brother, Margaret knew, and she couldn't blame her, not when Allan had written so infrequently. All it seemed to take was time and space for doubts to begin to fester and grow. Would the same happen to her and Henry?

After leaving *The Allegiance*, Margaret decided to call at the office of her father's shipping agent. She had not been in for some weeks, and she hoped there might be letters waiting.

"There's another letter here for you," Mr. Douglas told her. "From your family. Came in this morning, as a matter of fact."

"Are there any letters for Miss Harriet Campbell?" Margaret asked hopefully and the agent shook his head.

"Not this time."

She wasn't even surprised, Margaret realized, as she took the letter from her family, but she knew Harriet would be disappointed yet again. Why hadn't Allan written? If letters from Sandy and Betty could get through, then so surely could her brother's.

Not wanting to wait, Margaret broke the seal of her father's letter right there on the harborside, surprised when two pieces of paper fell out, tucked inside the letter. She looked down and realized at once what they were... two second-class tickets for passage to Halifax and then on to Pictou, for her and Rupert, on *The Harmony* next spring.

Her mind went numb as she stared at the two tickets. Her father had not intended on sending for her and Rupert for another year. She'd thought she would have time... time to wait for Henry to return. Yet as she scanned the letter, she knew she would have to go. How could she not?

Would Henry be able to find her in Canada, she wondered, her stomach taking an icy plunge. Would he even bother to look? Even though she still wanted to believe in Allan's fidelity, she felt the distance of the ocean between him and Harriet, and the frailty of old promises lost on a seafaring wind.

She could tell Henry at least, Margaret decided, although she wasn't sure what good might come of it. She walked quickly back to *The Allegiance*, only to be stopped by one of Henry's men before she'd even approached the gangplank.

"The captain's gone out again," the sailor told her without much regret. "Won't be back till late. I suppose you could leave a message."

Yes, Margaret thought, *but what message?* She longed for Henry's dear face, his hands warm over hers as she explained her predicament. She didn't trust this sailor to relay a message, especially as she wasn't sure what message she could give. What if her plans changed yet again? The future remained so uncertain.

"No," she finally said, her voice little more than a scratchy whisper. "No message."

Margaret's mind seethed with uncertainty all afternoon. Should she have left a message for Henry? What was she to do in the spring? Questions surged through her mind with no possible answers. She hadn't even shared her father's letter with Rupert or the others yet, although she knew her brother at least would welcome the news. Finally, in the evening, she threw her needlework aside with restless hands.

Harriet stared at her, eyebrows raised. She'd been surprisingly placid all day, despite the loss of Achlic looming over them all.

"What is it, Margaret? You look as if you've a storm brewing inside you."

"How do you do it?" Margaret demanded. "Wait all this time—it's a patience I cannot fathom!"

"I cannot, either," Harriet replied quietly. "It comes when there is no other choice, by the grace of God." She snipped a thread and gave Margaret a look of frank curiosity. "What—or who—are you waiting for then, Margaret MacDougall? Because it's obviously someone, though you're not wanting to tell me."

Margaret blushed and looked away. "Nothing," she murmured. "At least nothing I can say right now."

Harriet eyed her skeptically. "There are too many secrets in this house, Lord knows," she said softly, and turned back to her sewing. Margaret wondered what secrets Harriet might hold, and decided not to ask. Truly she had enough herself.

The next morning, Margaret rose early, intent on helping Harriet shoulder the burden of their household. She'd been far too slack as it was, haring off to Tobermory at a moment's notice. Not that she'd have reason to, for many months—*The Allegiance* had sailed on last evening's tide. Henry was gone.

She stoked the kitchen fire and filled the kettle before pulling her shawl around her to slip out to the henhouse to gather the morning's eggs. She had her hand on the door latch when she saw the note on the kitchen table.

> *Dear Family, I cannot stay, and I hope you'll forgive me. I've signed on as a ship's boy on* The Allegiance, *sailing to the Caribbean and the Americas. I vow I will not return till I have the price of Achlic in my hand. Give my regards to Father. Tell him I'm sorry. Ian.*

The note was still in Margaret's hand when Harriet came into the kitchen a few moments later, hurriedly putting up her hair. "You're up early," she remarked in surprise, her eyes narrowing as she took in Margaret's pale face and the page she was holding. "What's happened? What is that?" Margaret struggled to find words, but Harriet already knew. "It's Ian, isn't it? He's gone again."

Margaret nodded. "He left this letter. He sailed yesterday evening, as ship's boy on *The Allegiance*."

CHAPTER TWELVE

"Ship's boy?" Harriet stared at Margaret in disbelief. "How did such a thing come to pass…?" She snatched the note from Margaret, reading it before throwing it down in weary disgust. "That boy! How can he do such an idiotic thing? Going halfway around the world without so much as a by-your-leave. He's more than wet behind the ears, I can tell you that."

Margaret smiled faintly, for she far preferred Harriet's temper to her tears. "That he is. It's a shame he's not here for us to tell him so."

"Indeed, I'd give him a tongue lashing he'd ne'er forget!" Harriet sank onto the rocking chair by the fire. "What will I tell Father? And are we even likely to see poor Ian again?" She shook her head, dashing away her tears with an impatient hand. "All the way to the Caribbean! Is everyone destined to fly this place?"

"He'll come back," Margaret said, aware that she'd made this vow before, and it was not hers to give. Her mind whirled, but she was beginning to realize that Ian's situation on *The Allegiance* could be to his benefit. "As a matter of fact," she said slowly, "I happen to know the sailing master of that ship. He's a good man. I could—I could write him about Ian. He gave me his address, in Boston. I don't know if it will bring him back, but it might help keep him safe."

"You know the master?" Harriet's eyes widened in surprise, but she was kept from asking further questions by a knock on the back door. Before she could even answer it, Jane MacCready poked her head through.

"Good morning. I've heard about Ian, and I thought you could use some help."

"Bad news certainly travels," Harriet replied with a touch of asperity. "It's barely past the crack of dawn, and we've only just found out ourselves."

"He was seen," Jane explained as she loosed the strings of her bonnet. "My nephew saw him going on board a ship bound for the Americas last night, and came at once to tell me."

"He must have snuck out right after dinner," Harriet acknowledged in a hollow voice. "And we didn't even know! And what of Rupert? They share a room. He was part of the conspiracy, no doubt."

"I'll speak to him," Margaret said.

Harriet sighed. "There's no reason in blaming him. Ian's desperate to prove he's a man, so we might as well treat him as one, capable of taking his own decisions. Ship's boy!" This last was said in both exasperation and more than a little fear, and with determined effort she turned to Jane. "I'm sorry for the confused state you find us in. Do sit down. I'll boil the kettle."

"I'm calling so early because I thought I might be some use," Jane said in her usual forthright manner. "Now that the situation with Ian is what it is, you must speak to your father. There can be no more putting it off."

"I know," Harriet said heavily.

"This morning."

Harriet's eyes flashed, and she pressed her lips together. She didn't like being ordered around, yet Jane had made herself quite useful in the last few months, and moreover, Harriet knew she was right. "Yes, very well."

Jane nodded, her face cracking into a rare smile. "I knew you'd see the way of it. You'd best tell him now," she continued briskly.

"I'll brew some tea, and bring it up in twenty minutes. That will give you enough time to talk. And then if you need a rescue…" There was the glimmer of sympathy in her eyes, and Harriet nodded stiffly. Normally she would've objected to another woman busying herself in her kitchen, yet the sight of Jane's competent form and brisk movements was strangely comforting. For a few moments, someone else was bearing the burden—although she had her own, upstairs.

"Thank you," she said quietly, and slipped from the kitchen.

Upstairs, she knocked on her father's door, and upon hearing his gruff bidding to enter, came into the bedroom. As always, the sight of his pale, drawn face and tired eyes pained her. After nearly a year in bed, he was far frailer, the strapping man he'd once been reduced to little more than skin and bone.

She stared at him, not knowing what to say or where to begin. Her father looked back at her, his face dropping into despairing lines. "Something's amiss," he said after a moment. "What is it?"

So much, Harriet thought. Far more than she could ever tell him, and yet she had to confess as much as he could… as much as he could bear. She stood at the foot of the bed, her hands clasped as she drew a breath, steeling herself. "I'm so sorry, Father. Things… haven't gone well. I didn't want to bring bad news, I was hoping to spare you. I thought perhaps we could find some way…"

"Enough of this," David said brusquely. "Out with it. We've lost the farm, haven't we?"

Harriet blinked in surprise. Although she'd known her father must have suspected something, the flat acceptance in his tone still came as a shock. "Yes." Her voice wavered as she continued, "I truly am sorry, Father. I know I could've done more. I should have…"

"Come here, lass." David's voice was both rough and gentle as he beckoned her to his side. The softening of his voice and manner was the last thing she'd expected; she'd been bracing herself for him to rail and rage, or worse, to fall into terrible despair. But she heard neither from him, merely sorrowful acceptance and something else, something both sweeter and deeper that she couldn't remember ever hearing from him before.

Harriet went, sitting on the stool by the head of the bed. He reached for her hand, his frail, bony fingers clasping hers. "There was nothing you could do, Harriet. Do you think I don't blame myself for the fankle we're in? It was I who ran Achlic into debt, not you or anyone else. We had bad harvests, there's not a doubt, but at the end of the day the blame rests with me." He sighed and closed his eyes briefly, his hand still on hers. "Aye, me." After a moment he turned to look at her. "What happened, then?"

"Ian went to sell the twenty acres," Harriet explained hesitantly, "and he sold—he sold everything instead."

"What!" Her father's jaw slackened as he stared at her in amazement. "Why would he do such a foolish thing?"

"It was an accident, Father. A terrible trick. He signed the contract without reading it all, after being assured of what it said."

"That brainless lad, for all his lessons!" This was said with more resignation than anger. "He should have read the whole thing, I've not a doubt, but who would play such a low trick? It wouldn't have been Mr. Franklin, I'm sure."

"No." Harriet took a breath, knowing how this would anger her father. "It was Sir James Riddell."

"That scoundrel," her father spat, his face suffused with rage. "I've seen how he's always wanted my land. Can't get enough of it, can he?" He shook his head. "He wants the whole island, I'm sure. But to lose Achlic that way… after holding onto it for so many years…" Her father shook his head, his face etched with new lines of grief.

"Ian feels terrible, Father," Harriet said in a low voice. "He ran away."

"Good, for he ought to be whipped. He'll come back soon enough, when the cold and hunger have got to him. That should teach him a lesson he'll naught forget."

"No… he's run away to sea," Harriet explained, as her father's anger drained away once more, to be replaced by grief and shock. "On a ship to the Americas, as ship's boy."

He lay back heavily against the pillows, looking drained. "Well," he said at last, "well." He shook his head, his eyes dark with regret and sorrow. "All that way… I wouldn't have ever wished for such a thing, but I can only hope it will bring some sense to him. It hasn't come otherwise." He coughed, the effort wracking his haggard frame, and Harriet hurried to pour a glass of water from the pitcher by the bed. After he'd drank, he turned to face her. "What shall we do, Harriet?" he asked. "And how long do we have in this place?"

"I'm not certain. A few weeks at best." Harriet realized her father had never asked her advice before, and she felt a strange sense of gratified pride, despite the terrible circumstances that had warranted it. She took a breath and made herself continue. "There is another way, Father. A way to stay here, at Achlic."

He shook his head, clearly bewildered by such a notion. "And what would that be?"

Harriet let her breath out slowly, willing herself to say the words. "Andrew Reid, Sir James's nephew, has asked me to marry him. If I say yes, he's promised we could live here as we are. The farm would still belong to Riddell, of course, but we wouldn't be turned out onto the street."

Her father's mouth twisted into something close to a sneer. "Paupers, on Riddell charity? I'd rather beg for my dinner on the docks."

"We'd be family, of a kind," Harriet protested weakly. "And we'd have a roof over our heads. We'd be safe…" Even if she wanted none of it.

David was silent for a moment, lost in thought. When he looked up at her, his eyes were clear and shrewd. "Do you love him?"

Harriet swallowed. "He loves me. He's told me so."

"I asked if *you* love *him*."

Did it matter, *Harriet* thought. "I'm fond of him," she said slowly, realizing with some surprise it was true. "Even though I'm not sure if I always trust him. Perhaps that's just because of his Riddell connection. There's no love lost with his uncle, I know that. I might... I might be able to love him in time..."

"And what of Allan?"

I love him. Harriet looked away. "He hasn't written in a year, even though I wrote to him. I know he's well, for his mother has written Margaret and Rupert, and shared the family news all this while. They've planted their first crops, and had their first harvest. Their cabin has three bedrooms, as well as a great fireplace and its own kitchen." Margaret had read the letters out whenever she'd received them, and each word had pained Harriet, although she'd tried not to show it.

"You think he's given up on you?"

She flinched before taking steadying breath. "I don't know what to think. I never would have thought it of him, but the journey was a long one and people do change." Another breath, for courage. "But the truth of it is, Father, that there isn't time to find out whether he's stayed true or not. He gave me my freedom. I wouldn't be betraying him by taking it." And yet her heart said otherwise.

David coughed again, and Harriet handed him the mug of water. "You mustn't marry the Riddell boy, lass, to save us." He looked at her with eyes that were both wise and sorrowful. "It's not a mistake worth making. At the end of the day, love is all. Your mother and I... well. I'd want the same for you. We'll survive somehow."

How? Harriet wanted to ask. How could a girl, a woman and a frail old man survive on the pittance that would remain after they'd cleared their debts?

There was a knock on the door, and Jane MacCready came in with the tea tray. "A nice cup of tea should make everything a wee bit better," she said with a smile. "Harriet, I forgot the jam for the scones. Would you fetch it, please?"

Feeling summarily dismissed, Harriet rose from the stool. Her father clasped her hand gently once more before she left, and the loving gesture had her near tears yet again. She had not expected her father to be so understanding, so tender. It was a silver lining to the disaster that had befallen them, and she was grateful for it. As she walked downstairs, she could hear Jane's bustle and chatter, and her father's few gruff replies. It would take much more than some tea to make things better, she thought, but father's kindness was an unexpected blessing.

The next day Harriet made her way to Lanymoor House for Caroline's pianoforte lesson. She knew she would see Andrew Reid, and had resolved to tell him of her decision. It was the right decision, she told herself… the only decision she could make, considering.

Last night she had stayed up late, reading Allan's letters by the light of her candle, treasuring his lines in a way she never had before. Every assurance of his loyalty, every declaration of his love, had felt both sweeter and more painful than ever before. How could she betray him like this?

And yet it had been a whole year since his last letter, after her own explanation of why she hadn't written, and her assurances of the steadfastness of her own feelings. Had he not believed her explanation? Or had he simply not cared? Or had his letters somehow gone astray, and she was the treacherous one, turning to another?

Yet she imagined, fancifully perhaps, that Allan would understand. She was not doing this for herself. She was doing it for Achlic. For her family. Allan certainly knew about loyalty to family, about the nature of duty. She hoped the news of her marriage, when it came, would not pain him too much.

Outside the winter sun shone brightly as Harriet did her best to concentrate on Caroline's lesson, even as her mind wandered hopelessly. Would Andrew ask her for her decision, or would she have to broach the subject herself? She winced as Caroline banged on the pianoforte with unnecessary force.

"Gently, Caroline, gently, remember our fingers are like feathers on the keys." Harriet lightly played a few notes, but Caroline only pouted.

"Don't like feathers!"

"Don't be a brat, brat," Andrew said with humorous languor. Harriet looked up, her heart skipping a nervous beat at the sight of him. He leaned against the door frame, his hands in the pockets of his morning coat, the picture of elegance and ease as his gaze moved from his sister to Harriet. "Are you finished for today?" he inquired. "If so, I thought we could take tea in the back parlor. It's smaller in there, and cozier. There's a fire."

"It sounds lovely," Harriet replied, forcing herself to meet Andrew's eyes and smile even though everything in her trembled.

"Run along, Caroline," Andrew commanded. "Cook has fresh biscuits for you in the kitchen."

"I want to come with you."

"Not today, poppet," Andrew said firmly. "Hurry for those biscuits now. I need to talk to Harriet alone." His gaze moved back to her again, and Harriet saw the intent in it as she followed him out of the room.

The back parlor was cosy indeed, and Harriet stood by the fire, stretching her hands out to the flames as she steeled herself for the conversation she knew would take place.

"You're like ice." Andrew took her hand in his own, and with his other hand lifted her chin so she had to look at him. It was a liberty he was comfortable to take, and Harriet swallowed audibly, knowing there was no point in protesting. Soon she would be his bride. "I didn't mean to make you afraid, when I asked you to marry me," he said quietly. "We can forget it now, if it is easier for you."

As tempting as that was, Harriet knew she had no choice any longer. "I'm sorry if I seem distracted. There's been so much going on…"

"You found Ian?"

"And lost him again." Briefly Harriet told him of Ian's defection and her father's response.

"Your father is likely to be right," Andrew said frankly. "The discipline of a ship might be just what Ian needs. Perhaps he'll be better for it."

"That may be so," Harriet answered sharply, "but it didn't mean it had to be like this, with him running away in shame."

"You're right." He caught her hands in his own and lifted them to his lips while Harriet struggled not to pull them away. "Don't be angry with me, please, Harriet. I'm agreeing with you."

"I know." She slipped her hands from his and turned slightly away, conscious of Andrew's considering gaze.

"Have you reached a decision, then?" he asked, his voice a bit cool. "I spoke to my uncle and he has agreed to the plan. We could live at Achlic. I don't mind if your father runs the place. I know he'll still feel it's his own, and that's only fair. Besides, I must confess I don't the first thing about running a farm. I'm sure he could teach me well."

"He's too ill to do much of anything at the moment," Harriet replied after a pause as she considered everything he'd said. If Sir James had refused Andrew's request, she could have done the same and rejected his proposal. But now she really had no choice but to acquiesce. "I'm certain he'll rule with an iron fist from his bedside, however, and teach you many things besides."

Harriet forced herself to turn towards him, and Andrew caught his breath. "Does that mean…?"

"Yes." Harriet nodded, her heart like lead inside her although she tried to smile. "I will marry you, Andrew."

A delighted smile broke over his face as he reached for her hands once more. Harriet let him clasp them in his. "You have made me the happiest man alive, Harriet. I know you don't love me now, don't bother to protest, I accept it as it is. But in time… I swear you'll love me in time. I'll do everything I can to make it so."

Harriet laughed, a shaky sound. "I'm sure you'll make me very happy, Andrew." What else could she say?

"I promise I will." He squeezed her hands, his face alight with joy. "May I kiss you?"

The only time she'd been kissed had been by Allan, at Duart. She could still remember the feel of his lips on hers, his arms around her. The promises he'd made echoed in her head, now with a hollow ring, and she fought a sudden, desperate urge to yank her hands from Andrew's and run from the room. Run and never stop, until she was far from Lanymoor, from Achlic, even from Mull.

She didn't, of course. Harriet remained where she stood as tears pricked her eyes and she nodded. Andrew leaned forward and brushed his lips across hers, and Harriet tried to feel something, anything other than dread. She rested one hand on the lapel of the coat as he deepened the kiss and she pulled away, blushing. She felt as faithless as an adulteress, even though she knew she was free. Allan had made it so.

"I'll make you happy," Andrew promised again, and Harriet forced a nod. She could almost believe he would. She knew he would certainly try. "Do you have a preference for a date for the wedding?" he asked. "I know women have all sorts of notions about these things, and I wish to oblige you as often as I can."

A wedding date! Of course there was no need to wait, and all the more reason to rush. Harriet tried to quash the wave of dread that rolled over her. Andrew was a good, caring man, and he loved her. She would be well provided for. Most women could not hope for nearly as much. "Would you mind if we waited till spring?" she asked. "Father should be a bit more able then, and I might even be able to get word to Ian... and Allan."

"Ah, yes, Allan." Andrew's face was grave. "I know you loved him, Harriet, but do you think you'll be able to forget?"

Forget? Harriet didn't even know if she wanted to try. Perhaps she would make herself forget, for her own sanity, for to torment herself with sweet memories would surely be a fate worse than death, and a betrayal of Andrew as well. "I chose you," she said quietly. "Let that be enough, for now."

"It is." Andrew embraced her once more. "I promise you, it is."

Later that evening, Harriet sat at the kitchen table, a candle flickering by her elbow, and stared down at the blank parchment in front of her. Would Allan even care about her news? She had a sudden, piercing realization that he would, very much indeed.

"Oh, faithless heart," she whispered, "to doubt him for so long and then marry another." She thought of him on the hillside by Duart, the day before he left. *I love you, Harriet Campbell, and I always have, since the day I found you here, hiding among the rocks. It was meant to be, between us. I've always known it.*

She'd felt the same, as fiercely as he had. They'd been stitched from the same cloth, and everyone around them had known it. How could she betray him this way? Betray herself? And yet she had no choice. She could not bear to see her father, her whole family, turned out of the only home they had known.

"I'm sorry, Allan," she whispered. "There's naught I can do. If I had a choice..." But the choices had been taken from her, along with her home and livelihood. She hoped Allan would be able to understand that at least… and forgive. Slowly, painfully, each word causing a fresh grief, Harriet began to write.

The candle was burning low when she finally lay the quill down, and sprinkled sand over the drying ink. After she'd folded the letter and sealed it, she allowed for the tears to come. She lay her head on her arms and cried bitterly, for all she had lost, and all that she had hoped to have. She imagined Allan's return, as she so often had, and then their sailing to the New Scotland. She pictured the cabin they would have lived in, and the bed they would have shared. The children that would have come, God willing. She pictured it all, savored every scene, and then she forced herself to shut that part of herself forever. She would think of it—of him—no more. For Andrew's sake, as well as for her own. She couldn't live with a divided heart.

The letter went on the last ship sailing for Canada before winter. The day was cold and windy, and Harriet handed the letter over along with the last of her hopes.

"You don't know what you're doing," Margaret told her in furious despair late that night, after Harriet had made her announcement and the others had gone to bed. "Allan loved you, and he will always love you. How can you throw that away?"

"What would you have me do, Margaret?" Harriet replied with just as much heat. "Do you think my father will survive a cold, draughty hovel in town? Do you think Eleanor will enjoy life as a scullery maid or laundress at her age, working her fingers to the bone for a few pennies a day? There aren't many choices open to us, and I have to protect my family."

Margaret's face crumpled, and she flew to wrap Harriet in her arms. "Oh, Harriet, I'm sorry. If only this burden was not upon you. Can't you write Allan? My father has money. He might provide passage for all of you. You could all start anew in Scotia."

"It would be too late, by the time the letter arrived," Harriet replied heavily. "And you know as well as I do that my father isn't well enough to travel such a distance as that. We could hardly begin as homesteaders in such a rugged land. It's done, anyway. I've accepted Andrew's proposal, and I've written to Allan." She let out a heavy sigh. "Besides, you know Allan hasn't written me in a year. You don't know what might have happened. People change."

"Yes, they do." Margaret was quiet for a moment. "I suppose I should tell you, my father has sent the ship fare for Rupert and me. We're to sail this spring."

Harriet studied her friend's face, and the sorrow that darkened her eyes. "That should be good news, I would think, or at least expected."

"I don't want to go," Margaret stated flatly. "You've as good as guessed already, I think, but I've met someone, someone here. Well, he *was* here."

"What?" Harriet's brows rose nearly to her hairline. "This is the sailing master, isn't it?"

Margaret smiled tremulously. "Yes…"

"How on earth did you meet him?"

"It's rather a long story."

"I'm listening."

Duly Margaret told of how she'd met Henry in the street; how he'd invited her to tea at his aunt's.

"Elizabeth Moore, I believe," Harriet said dryly, and it was Margaret's turn to look surprised. "People *will* gossip. And from one afternoon's tea…?"

And so Margaret told of Henry's offer of lessons, and then his claim to her affections and his request that she wait for him.

"So much to have happened… and you've kept this from me all this time?" Harriet asked, not without a little hurt. She hadn't realized Margaret had kept quite so many secrets.

"I'm sorry, Harriet. The truth is, I was embarrassed at first, and unsure. It seemed... forward, I suppose, if not downright improper. I didn't want you to disapprove. I supposed some might have seen scandal in it, or worse."

Harriet nodded her understanding. "Only those whose tongues never cease to wag. I wouldn't have, although it's true I might have advised caution. He's asked you to wait?"

"Yes, for a year. At least, I think he'll be back then." Margaret's eyes shone even as she bit her lip in uncertainty.

"But you're not sure?" Suddenly Harriet shook her head, chuckling. "Och, these men!" She threw up her hands, and they both started to laugh for the first time in weeks. "Why do they always ask us to wait?"

"He is a sailing master," Margaret reminded her.

"Of *The Allegiance*," Harriet recalled with a sigh. "If you love him, he must be a good man, and I pray he'll keep watch over Ian."

"He will, Harriet, I'm sure of it." She paused. "If he does return in a year's time, I want to be here, not far away on Prince Edward Island." She sighed and then said simply, "I love him."

"You've all winter to decide," Harriet reminded her. "Spring is a long way away, as yet, and there will be no letters between now and then."

"You've all winter as well," Margaret said quietly. "Like you said, spring is not for many months. Things can change, Harriet. Remember what you told me? People can change their minds. Everyone, including you."

*

Ian lay curled up in his hammock, his chin nearly touching his knees, his back against another of the ship's boys, sleeping soundly beside him. In the few weeks since he'd been on board *The Allegiance*, Ian had not yet become accustomed to the heave and roll of the ship. Now, in the middle of the night, his stomach still churned unpleasantly, although whether that was due to seasickness or his general misery, he did not know. His whole body ached, his hands were covered in raw blisters, and his face was caked with brine. He didn't think he'd ever been in such a sad or weary state.

Ian had not taken to ship life. He himself acknowledged it, in the self-pitying privacy of his own mind, and it only made him angrier with himself and how he'd come to be here. Everything about the ship and its crew was foreign, to him, even frightening. There were three other ship's boys, a ragtag bunch that were from an entirely different social sphere than he was, and they'd taken to ship life with cheer and ease, grateful for the regular meals and place to sleep.

The food, a rough diet of dry biscuits, salted beef or greasy stew, made him long for the homemade roasts and puddings at Achlic. And when he'd received his first daily ration of sailor's grog, or watered-down rum, he hadn't known what it was or what to do with it. Having never tasted proper spirits before, he'd taken a long, healthy swig before the fire hit his throat and he coughed and sputtered. All the sailors around him had laughed and jeered—it had been days before they let him forget what a lubber he was, and Ian had burned with resentment.

Although he had never thought he was afraid of hard work, the mind numbing labor of swabbing decks, coiling ropes and washing down the sails frustrated him, as did the galling fact that he had no choice but to take whatever came from the sailors aboard ship. There was a definite pecking order, and ship's boys were at the very bottom of it. His job, he soon realized, was to make himself either useful or scarce, often both at the same time.

He ached to return home, yet what could he do? He'd signed on for a year, and he knew he had to honor that. He admired the ship's master, Henry Moore, although he'd rarely seen him since they'd set sail. Perhaps Captain Moore would let him off when they reached their destination in America, but then what? The thought of being alone in a strange land was even worse than being aboard the ship, and yet neither did he wish to return to home and the shame that waited for him there.

Tears pricked his eyes, but Ian forced them back. He would not cry. He was a man now, even if only a ship's boy. He'd made himself one when he took on the responsibility for Achlic, and even in the dark privacy of his hammock, he would not give into tears. No matter how dismal his situation was now, he was still determined to find a way to return home with the money for Achlic in his hand.

The next morning was cold and clear, and the ship made good headway. They were only about six days off the coast of Massachusetts, according to the master, and the sea stretched out like an endless blue blanket, ruffled in white.

Ian stood apart from the other ship's boys, watching as the sailors trimmed the sails. Although the ship's boys were in theory encouraged to learn as much as they could about the rigging, in practice most sailors shouted at them to get out of their way when work was going on; they didn't need a lot of inexperienced boys messing about with the ropes. So they stood to the side, kicking their feet and gossiping and not paying much attention to the work going on all around them.

All of a sudden, the brisk, efficient movements of the crew were interrupted as a coil of rope jerked around a sailor's foot, yanking him off the ground, his leg twisting at a horribly awkward angle. Ian's stomach lurched as he watched the man writhe in agony before his mates cut him down and laid him out on the deck.

Someone shouted for the ship surgeon, and he could hear the low, urgent murmurs of the sailors around the wounded man. Ian shivered. He must have broken his leg… It would have to be set on this rocking ship, with little clean water and nothing to dull the pain but a tot of rum. The thought terrified him. What if *he* had an accident, and was forced to lie under the surgeon's bloody knife? What if he never returned to Achlic alive?

Lost in the unhappy haze of his thoughts, Ian didn't realize that the murmurs had turned angry and accusing, or that the sailors were casting dark looks at the motley group of ship's boys. Suddenly a voice rang out, the American twang of one of the more belligerent sailors.

"I tell you, that rope was coiled the wrong way. That's what caught Mahoney up, and it's the fault of one of those scamps there!"

The first mate, Mr. Tisbury, whom Ian suspected disliked him anyway, turned his cold, blue gaze on the cluster of ship's boys. "Which one of you was responsible for coiling the ropes on that sail?" he demanded in a hard voice.

They all remained silent, casting each other fearful looks—and then realization dawned, first in Ian, and then in the others. He'd coiled the rope. It has been his duty this morning, while the others had swabbed the deck. His heart bumped in his chest and his mind emptied of anything but terror. He could not speak.

One of the other ship's boys, however, lost no time in pointing the finger.

"It was 'im, I'm sure of it," he said, with a jerk of his thumb towards Ian. "'Alf the time he don't know what he does."

Mr. Tisbury turned to Ian. "Is that so, Mr. Cameron?"

Ian's mouth was dry as he felt the weight of everyone's hostile stares. "I think… I might've…" he stammered, but then trailed off at the look of furious contempt in the older sailor's eyes.

"Take him to the brig," Mr. Tisbury ordered. "He can spend the rest of the day there. The master will decide what to do with him."

Ian let out a yelp as one of the sailors grabbed him by the scruff of his shirt and dragged him towards the ladder that led to the ship's hold.

"Please…" he began, but the man ignored him as he marched him downstairs and then practically hurled him into the brig.

Ian lay huddled on the floor of the small, cheerless room located on the lower deck of the ship. There was only one small porthole, high up, for light, and the air was stale and dank. He wondered how long he would be kept in this terrible place, and then decided he didn't want to leave. All the sailors would be angry with him, along with the ship's boys. At least here he was safe.

He sat on the floor, his knees drawn to his chest as he considered his plight. He knew what the punishment for careless conduct was. Flogging for sailors, a whipping for a ship's boy. So far, by luck more than skill, he'd managed to avoid the whip, but now he feared there would be no respite. It was his fault that Mahoney had broken a leg, and his fault alone. A whipping was no more than he deserved, but he still shuddered at the thought of it.

The hours crept past, and he watched as the little light from the porthole faded to inky darkness and the stars came out one by one, looking cold and faraway. The brig was so dark he could not even see his fingers in front of his face, and Ian found it was easier to close his eyes. He tried to forget how hungry and thirsty he was, or the punishment that surely awaited him. As the hours continued to slide by, he wondered if they'd all forgotten him, if they'd leave him here to die of thirst, and then throw his rotting corpse into the sea. One of the sailors had told of how bodies were wrapped in a sailcloth and thrown overboard if anyone died while at sea. The prospect made Ian's stomach churn.

Finally, when he'd fallen into a restless and uncomfortable doze, the sound of a key rattling in the lock awoke him from his stupor, and he blinked at the sudden light of a lantern thrust near his face. A sailor he didn't recognize stood there, smirking.

"Well, now. Maybe a spell in here has put paid to your uppity ways, eh? The master wants to see you. And if I were you, I wouldn't be looking forward to that little visit."

CHAPTER THIRTEEN

It had been six months since Archie had gone soldiering, and he was due back for his furlough tomorrow. He'd been stationed in Three Rivers, and would arrive in Pictou tomorrow afternoon, the long-awaited son returned home for the fattened calf and the feast. Allan strove not to feel bitter, but after six months of hard work and little reward, it was difficult. Not much had changed since Archie had left, despite the conversation and the promise he'd had from his father.

Now spring had come to the island, and the crop was soon to be planted. Cherry trees were frothed with pink and white, and the rolling fields had turned to bright, verdant green. The world was waking up at last, and with it came a frail hope that the latest ship crossing might have brought news from Achlic—and Harrriet.

Eager for news, Allan offered to cross to the mainland to meet Archie in Pictou, and then together they would take the mail packet back to the island. He was looking forward to going. He'd not been to the mainland since last autumn, when he'd sent his letter to Harriet, asking her to come. He hoped a reply had come with the first ship into Pictou, although in truth he feared it would not. If she had not written after all his letters, why would she write now?

Allan knew that the transport of letters from the old world was unreliable, despite people's best intentions. A letter from Betty's sister Ann had come via a ship from Aberdeen, then languished for six months in New Brunswick until a traveller coming the

Pictou way had brought it. A letter, Allan knew, could take well over a year to reach its recipient. It was a surprisingly comforting thought when he considered Harriet's long silence. Perhaps her letters simply had not reached him. Perhaps she'd written many times, and they'd all simply gone astray.

But then he remembered the letters that had come from Margaret and Rupert, and how they would have all been in the same packet, on the same ship, and he knew such hope was false. Harriet had not written. He did not know the reason, but he knew in his leaden heart that there were no missing letters, no declarations of love that had gone astray. She'd stayed silent, and he did not know why.

"So your brother's coming back, then," Roddy Campbell, Fiona's brother, remarked on the boat journey to Pictou, the sea flat and shining before them, the sky bright and blue above. "The hero, isn't he?" This was said with a bit of a grimace, which Allan chose to ignore. That was how Archie affected people… they either loved or hated him. Allan didn't even know how he felt at times.

"Aye, he is. We've all missed him."

"Have you, now?"

"Aye." Allan spoke firmly. It was true, he'd missed Archie more than he had expected to. The long, frozen winter months had seemed even harder to bear without Archie's cheerful patter and jokes, as much as his brother had sometimes annoyed him.

Now that the spring planting would be soon upon them, Allan hoped to start his cabin, to begin laying the plans for Harriet to join him—if the desire still seized her own heart as it did his. He prayed a letter waited for him in Pictou, assuring him of her love, even telling him she would be sailing soon. What a joy that would be. Just the faint possibility of it lightened his heart.

"There it is," Roddy said in satisfaction. Pictou harbor came into view, and it always gave Allan a fierce sense of pride to see how the town was growing, stone replacing wood, the buildings standing proudly against the darkness of the endless forest that was both threat and promise. Pictou was holding its own against the elements, Allan thought, if only just.

Once on land, Allan stopped at the mercantile where most of the letters from ships ended up, till someone could take it on to their final destination.

The shop was full of people, including many islanders who had taken advantage of the fine weather to cross on the ferry and do business. There were fur traders as well, coming in by canoe from the far West and North, and soldiers on furlough, like Archie. A few native Indians, the Mi'kmaq, stood silently by the door, their faces grave as they watched the business all around them with dark, wary eyes. Allan knew they traded furs and other items in town, but he was still surprised and intrigued by their strange garb and stoic faces, so utterly unlike anything he'd known back in Scotland.

While waiting for his turn at the till, he spent a few moments examining the consignment of new tools and listening to the local gossip, glad for the diversion. He hadn't had any news from off island since before the winter.

"Ship's coming in, I hear," someone remarked. "Full of settlers for a new colony out west. All Scots, every last one of 'em, and they've been kicked off their land."

"That's that Selkirk fellow's idea, isn't it?" another farmer said, and spat neatly on the floor. "Bought up a big parcel of land from Hudson's Bay Company to give to all those people. There's plenty who ain't happy about it, though."

"And why should they be? That land don't belong to no Scots. There are already people there who've been trying to homestead, and you've got the fur, as well."

"Well, the Company shouldn't have sold it, should they? It's a big parcel out by Red River. Good land, I hear. Soil nice and rich."

Allan had never heard of Red River, but the name alone sounded intriguing. A colony of Scots, all sent out to farm the land… His interest sharpened, and he wondered just where it was, and if any other settlers could join in forming the new colony, even as he recognised it for a false hope. He would never leave Prince Edward Island, or his father's farm. And if there was a letter from Harriet…

"The Company's finally joined with the North West Company," another man, a fur trader, wearing the distinctive red toque and fur cap of the Hudson Bay Company, commented. "Not that it should make any difference to me, but at least there's less competition."

Allan knew vaguely of the two trading companies which had dominated the fur trade for the last one hundred and fifty years. Hudson's Bay Company, founded in England, was the larger and older of the two, and had only that year finally swallowed its competition, the smaller North West Company based out of Montreal.

"The Company's getting too big for its britches," a farmer groused. "It controls all the land from Upper Canada to the Pacific, I hear. That's too much power for anybody. That's the sort of thing we were trying to get away from."

"I heard George Simpson is travelling round, organising the trading posts and even recruiting some new men," someone else volunteered. "Now that the companies have joined, he's going to close many of the outposts."

"And put good men out of jobs."

"He wants new men. Some of these traders are stuck in their ways. They like to work alone."

One the traders grunted in response, and Allan stepped out of the way in case it turned into a fight. More than once tempers had run high and fists had started flying while he'd waited for his mail.

In any case, he'd heard enough. He didn't care about the politics of the Hudson's Bay Company. They had no holding on the island, and the farmers there had other politics to worry about, such as with the colonial office and the English landlords. He approached John MacDonald, the shopkeeper.

"Any letters for Mingarry Farm, on the island?" he asked, the hope audible in his voice. "The name's MacDougall."

"I remember you." John Douglas nodded. "Your brother came across the ice last year when your boat was trapped. We still talk about that over here."

"He was a hero," Allan agreed with a small smile. "I would've died without him."

"Either a hero or a fool," the shopkeeper agreed a bit sourly. "There's a letter for Mingarry, I think. Been here since autumn, if I remember correctly. It came over on the last ship from Scotland before winter."

"Did it?" Allan's heart lurched at the realization that a letter had been waiting all this time. What if it was from Harriet? He watched, anxiety and hope both rising, as MacDonald rifled through a packet of letters before extracting one and handing it to him.

Allan nearly gasped out loud at the sight the neat, familiar writing. Harriet! He knew if the letter came in autumn, it could not be a reply to his own invitation, yet his heart still swelled with hope. She'd written him again, at last. Who knew what good news her lines might hold?

He longed to break the seal there and then, but he held onto his patience, if only just, waiting till he was settled at the public house with a pint of ale and a cold game pie before he opened it and began to read.

> *Dear Allan, Although I have observed a long silence on your part, and can only wonder at its cause, I remain assured in the memory of your promise, and the knowledge of your faithfulness…*

Allan breathed a sigh of relief. She trusted him. She would not change. He had been wrong to doubt her, even for a moment. Of course there was an explanation for the lack of letters, and one that had nothing to do with her constancy.

Therefore it grieves me all the more to relate to you the circumstances of the last year which have led my family to dire straits, and myself to a union which in time I hope I will come to appreciate, if not truly love.

In disbelief, Allan read of the loss of Achlic, and even worse, Harriet's betrothal to the nephew of Sir James Riddell, Andrew Reid.

We will marry in the spring, God willing, and I hope that some happiness may befall you, as well as me, even though we will live our lives apart. Dear Allan, know that I will always care for you, and should we not meet again, you will remain in my thoughts, if not my heart, as I will be wed to another and my loyalty is now to him. In Fond Memory, Harriet.

The letter fell from Allan's lifeless fingers as he stared blindly ahead, unable to believe the gross trick Providence had played on them all. That Harriet should be forced to marry another, and a Riddell at that! And to know she'd written months ago, and was most likely wed now…

His stomach churned at the thought and he pushed away his pie, his appetite utterly vanished. How could he have lost everything he'd hoped for, in a single blow? Harriet, wed to another. To never see her again…never hold her or talk to her or even to write her… to know she hadn't even found happiness or love, but had been forced into a union she didn't want.

And all because of the wily machinations of wretched Sir James Riddell. How much misery could one man cause? The realization was so bitter Allan raised his clenched fists, as if Riddell was right before him to fight.

Yet, Allan realized with a stirring of anger, what if she hadn't truly been forced? Surely, *surely* there must have been some other way. Any other way… she could've appealed to his father for help, or even to himself. The MacDougalls were relations, albeit somewhat distant, of the Campbells, and Allan knew his father would have willingly come to David Campbell's aid. If only she'd written! But she hadn't, and instead she'd been storing up all this trouble to bear alone.

Unless she really loved this fellow, and was trying to be kind to Allan, by pretending she didn't, to soften the bitter, bitter blow. A kindness, he thought, he could do without. A voice in his head mocked pitilessly. *You were the one who set her free. You returned her letters. You let her go.* This was no more than he'd said she was free to do, and what sort of freedom was it, if he was angry and bitter now? Yet he could not keep himself from it, not after everything he'd worked hard for, sacrificed and lost.

By now she would have read his own letter, asking her to come to him. Sending the money for the fare! Would she send it back? Would she ignore the letter, or laugh at it? What a fool he was, cherishing hopes that had long fallen to ash.

His head in his hands, Allan let the tide of regret wash over him. If only he had insisted on the betrothal, even asked that she sail with him. If only David Campbell had agreed. If only… if only…

Instead, he had given Harriet her freedom… and she had taken it, if not gladly, then with both hands.

*

It had been a damp and depressing spring on Mull. Harriet stood at the window of the music room in Lanymoor House overlooking the rain-shrouded lawns and shivered. She drew her shawl more tightly around her, as if it could ward off something more than the cold.

The cold, Harriet knew, was inside her, and had been there ever since she'd accepted Andrew Reid's proposal months ago now—long, lonely months that had still slipped by too fast. Her wedding day was fast approaching, and Harriet was filled with dread.

Sir James had been, to her surprise, delighted by their engagement. Shrewdly, Harriet realized he was relieved to have his nephew occupied with honorable labor, and also to not have the enmity of the Campbells, and therefore many of the islanders, because of his clever trick.

No one on the island liked Sir James, Harriet knew. The clearances, of course, accounted for much of that, although there had been fewer clearances here than in other parts of the Highlands. Islanders had never liked Sir James's high-handed manner, or the fact that he was from Berwick, and not a Highland man. They didn't like that the Riddells had bought their baronetcy, or the family's increasingly uppity ways.

And now she was to become a Riddell, or nearly. Harriet knew she wasn't imagining the looks of contempt from some of the neighbors who knew of her betrothal. She'd heard one sly whisper that Harriet Campbell was selling herself for a bit of gold. The cruel remark had made Harriet burn with shame. Was that what she was doing? Selling her body as well as her soul for merely a livelihood, a way of life she longed to keep?

"Nonsense," Margaret had told her when Harriet had quietly confessed her fears. "If it were just for you, perhaps then I'd wonder. But you're not doing this for yourself, Harriet! That's plain to see, if anyone takes a look at you. You're as pale and thin as a ghost. There's barely anything left of you."

Andrew had remarked the same, teasingly, before his eyes grew serious. "If you don't want to go ahead, Harriet…"

"I keep my promises," Harriet had replied stiffly. Then, in a softer voice, she'd added, "Please just give me time, Andrew."

Yet how much time did she need to get used to her situation? To learn to love the man she was pledged to? Time was running out… the wedding was a mere fortnight away. Harriet shivered again.

"Mistress Campbell?"

Harriet turned to Caroline, who sat hesitantly at the pianoforte, and realized the girl had stopped playing several minutes ago. "I'm sorry, Caroline. I'm having trouble concentrating today. The weather is so damp. Play that piece again, please?"

Caroline lifted her hands to the keys, then dropped them again. Harriet tried to stifle her impatience. The girl had matured a great deal in the last year, and rarely had tantrums anymore. Yet there was still a streak of stubborn impishness there, and Harriet continually came up against it. "Caroline?"

"I… I think I know something," Caroline blurted. "And I think, perhaps, I should tell you." She bit her lip, sudden indecision and even fear crossing her childish features. "But I'm afraid you will be angry, and I know Andrew will be."

Harriet stared at her in consternation and deepening dread. "Angry? Why?"

"I found something. I didn't mean to snoop… well, only a wee bit!" Caroline bit at her fingernails before she dropped her hands in her lap and gazed at Harriet anxiously. "Promise you won't tell, Miss Campbell? I don't want to get into trouble, not with Andrew! He might be ever so cross, but it doesn't seem fair."

"Caroline, I have no idea what you are talking about." Harriet took a deep breath and strove to keep her voice even. "But why should you get in trouble?" Trying to smile, she sat next to Caroline on the pianoforte bench. "Have you done something naughty?"

"I was only looking for a pack of cards," Caroline confessed. "I know Andrew has some in his room, and one of the stable lads promised to show me a card trick. He's a card sharp, he is, even better than Andrew!"

"A young lady should not be concerning herself with cards," Harriet said with what she hoped was an appropriate amount of severity. Her father did not even allow cards in his house, but she wasn't really surprised that Andrew possessed a pack. The Riddells were not God-fearing Presbyterians as the Campbells were, although it still gave her a moment's pause to think that Andrew most likely gambled. What would her father say if he knew? "And you shouldn't have gone in Andrew's chamber without permission," she told Caroline.

"I know. But it wasn't the cards I found… it was something else."

Harriet stilled, and the coldness within her lodged into an icy ball that made it hard for her to breathe or even think. She had no idea what Caroline was going to say, and yet she knew it couldn't be anything good. What did Andrew have in his bedroom that he didn't want to be found? She shuddered to think of the possibilities. "And you think you should tell me what you found?" she asked after a moment.

Caroline nodded. "I think… I heard you and Andrew talking once. And I've heard the maids and such talking. I know more than anyone thinks," she added with a proud toss of her head.

"About what?" Harriet asked. It was harder and harder to keep her voice even when she longed to know what Caroline had discovered.

"About you." Her moment of pride forgotten, Caroline now looked miserable. "You were going to marry someone else, weren't you? Before Andrew."

Harriet's lips trembled before she pressed them together. "I was, but he… it ended. What has this to do with anything, Caroline?"

"I found some letters," the girl whispered. "In the box where Andrew keeps his cufflinks and his pocket watch. He got it from father, it's ever so shiny—"

"*Caroline.*" Harriet laid a shaking hand on the little girl's sleeve. "Tell me about these letters."

Caroline nibbled her lip. "There were ever so many. I thought they were love letters, and so I took a peek. I was going to tease Andrew about the silly things he wrote! But I daren't say anything, now."

"Love letters," Harriet repeated faintly. "To Andrew?" But already she feared what the little girl was going to say. She *knew*.

"No, that was the funny thing." Caroline frowned, her childish face filled with uncertainty. "That's what made me wonder. They were addressed to you, Harriet."

Harriet swallowed, trying to ease the sudden dryness in her throat. "Who were they from?"

"I don't know. Not from Andrew, though. I know his writing. It's ever so messy."

Harriet felt dizzy as she pressed her cold hands to her cheeks. Caroline could not be saying what she thought… she couldn't be! The possibility was too awful, too horrifying, to consider. And yet… if there was any prospect, any chance at all, that Andrew had letters meant for her… "Caroline," she commanded, her voice strong now, "show me the letters."

"I daren't! They're still in Andrew's room!"

"He's not in right now, is he?" He had business in Tobermory this afternoon, and had promised to be back in time for them all to have tea together. "Show me now, before he comes back. We only have a few moments."

"But he'll be so angry—"

"Please, Caroline. This is so important. More than you could ever know."

Caroline eyed her uncertainly before finally giving a reluctant nod. She slipped off the bench and ran from the room, and Harriet followed. Her heart thumped loudly against her ribs as she followed Caroline quickly up the stairs, glancing behind her to make sure no one saw. She'd never been upstairs in the house, and yet she could not take in any of the luxurious furnishings or artwork. She walked as if in a dream, her mind buzzing and yet blank.

After passing a few rooms, Caroline pushed open a heavy oak door and darted inside. Harriet followed. Her panicked gaze took in a few details of Andrew's private chamber: a morning coat thrown carelessly over a chair, the rumpled covers of a wide bed that a maid had not seen to yet. A crystal decanter of whiskey on the dressing table.

Caroline went to the chest of drawers and rifled through one before she took a small wooden box, inlaid with ivory, and thrust it at Harriet. She took it with trembling hands. Inside it there was a pocket watch and some cufflinks… and a packet of letters. They'd all been opened, read. Harriet recognized the bold handwriting on the outside, and the broken seal. They were from Allan.

She sifted through them in numb amazement. There were at least a dozen. He must have sent more than one letter with each ship, she realized. She unfolded one of the letters and scanned the lines, everything in her quaking.

My dearest Harriet, How can I express the consternation of my heart, or account for the long and cruel silence on your part? I know you too well to imagine you capable of any change or caprice towards me, and I hope you know me too well to expect any change on my side…

With a cry she clutched the letters to her, unable to believe and yet somehow having known deep down all along that Allan had written, that he had cared… that he loved her as always. She had been the faithless one. Only she.

At that moment they both heard Andrew's cheerful, tuneless whistling in the corridor, and then he opened the door of his bedroom.

"What in heaven's name—" he began, then stopped, the blood draining from his face, at the sight of Harriet and the bundle of letters in her hands.

"Yes, what in heaven's name, Andrew Reid," Harriet replied in a voice of restrained fury. "What in heaven's name are you doing with all of Allan MacDougall's letters, written to me?"

Andrew's face was pale and his hand shook as he held it out in supplication. "I beg you, Harriet, give me a moment to explain."

"I'd like to see you try!" Harriet stared down at the bundle of letters, Allan's dear, familiar scrawl on each one. "He's written to me all this time," she whispered. "He's been faithful all this time." She looked up at Andrew, her eyes full of both fury and despair. "How could you deceive me so?"

"I thought… I thought it was kinder…"

"Kinder! To steal something that isn't yours? To lie to the person you claim to love?" The words came out on a broken cry. Even now she could hardly take in the full extent of his treachery. She'd been going to *marry* him. He would have said his vows with this deceit between them.

"I do love you." Andrew took a steadying breath. "This is not the place for such a conversation. Harriet, please come down to the drawing room where we can talk in a civilised manner. You shouldn't be here. If you were discovered…"

"You, Andrew Reid, are the one who has been discovered. But I'd like to hear your explanation, however unlikely it may be!" No reason, Harriet knew, would be good enough.

Clutching the letters to her, she followed Andrew downstairs. Once in the drawing room, Andrew dismissed Caroline to find Cook, which the pale-faced little girl was more than eager to do.

Alone, the silence between them was taut with betrayal and pain. Andrew rested his hands on the fireplace mantel, his back towards Harriet. Harriet knew he was troubled, she could see it in the set of his shoulders, but she felt no sympathy whatsoever—only a deep, unrelenting pain for the double loss she had experienced. She felt as if she were losing Allan all over again, only it hurt far worse this time because it was her own fault, for not trusting him. If she'd received Allan's letters all along, Harriet realized, she never would have agreed to marry Andrew Reid, no matter what the cost.

"Whatever I did, Harriet," Andrew said in a low voice, "I did for you. For us."

"All right, then." Harriet deliberately kept her voice even although she wanted to fly at him, to scream and punch like the worst of fishwives. "Tell me just what you did. I want to hear it from your own lips, the truth of your treachery. Tell me yourself, Andrew."

He turned to face her, his shoulders sagging. "All you suspect, and worse," he admitted heavily. "But only out of love for you. I knew if you received MacDougall's letters you'd hold on to the slim hope that he'd return for you. You wouldn't even consider my suit, not with that forsaken promise you made him. I knew you wouldn't."

"And you intercepted the letters so I'd think he'd forgotten me," Harriet whispered. "How? Mr. Douglas, the shipping agent wouldn't betray our family in that way."

"I paid a boy on the docks to steal them when the ships came in. The sacks of letters always just sat on the docks. It was easy enough."

She shook her head, hardly able to believe that he was capable of such terrible deception. "How could you do such a wicked thing?"

"What were the chances that he'd come back for you?" Andrew demanded. "He's made a new life for himself there, Harriet. If you read his letters, you'll see that for yourself. A prosperous farm…"

"Don't you dare talk to me of what he wrote!" Harriet's voice shook. "Don't you *dare*."

"I was sparing you," Andrew insisted. "It could've been years before he returned… maybe never, and you would have waited… and withered."

"How are you to know such things? And shouldn't it be me who decides my own fate?" Harriet cried. "You'd no right to take such matters into your own hands! You only did so I'd be more inclined to marry you, since you knew full well I didn't love you, and now I never will!"

"I do know full well." Andrew's face was full of sorrow as he reached for her hands, but Harriet jerked them out of his reach. Allan's letters fell from her grasp, fluttering to the ground. "Harriet, please. I was wrong to take them, I know that and I am sorry. I did it out of desperation—and yes, out of love. I love you. We can be happy together, I know it. I took the letters so you could have peace in your mind about our marriage—so you wouldn't feel you'd deserted MacDougall. I wanted you to feel at peace."

"But I have deserted him." Tears sprang to her eyes. "You've made me faithless, Andrew. How do you think I can live with that?"

He shook his head, his eyes dark with pain. "You were never to know."

"You would have kept such a secret for all the days of our married life?" she said incredulously. "You're despicable, Andrew Reid." Harriet's voice was choked. "I will never trust you again."

"Harriet, please. This need not ruin us. I only meant it for the best, if you can forgive me…" He stepped over the fallen letters to clasp her cold hands in his. "We can still have a happy marriage, my love. A good one. Don't turn away from me, not now, just over this. I am sorry, and I am desperate for you to forgive me."

Harriet saw the sincerity in his face, and suppressed a shudder. How could she possibly marry someone who had deceived her in such a fashion? She would never trust him… never even come to love him. Every time she so much as looked at him, she would think of his deception… and of Allan. *Allan…*

And yet, Harriet realized numbly, did she really have the liberty to refuse? Could she turn her family out of Achlic simply for the sake of her own fine feelings? Despair swamped her and she shook her head.

Slipping her hands from his, she bent to gather the letters to herself, each one unbearably precious. "Please give me some time to think, Andrew. This has given me such a shock. I don't know if I…" She swallowed down the bile that rose at the thought of going through with her vows now. "I must reconsider."

"Of course," Andrew agreed quickly. "Of course you need time. Just remember that I love you… and that I'm here, waiting. I still love you, Harriet."

She did not reply. With the letters clutched to her chest, she hurried from the room.

Back at Achlic Farm, Harriet retired to her bed chamber without a word to anyone. She'd hurried home in a numb daze, everything in her still reeling from all that she'd learned. Up in her room she spread Allan's letters on her counterpane, staring at the many pages and feeling the terrible treachery of her own soul. How could she have doubted him!

She picked up one letter and began to read.

Dearest Harriet, How I miss you, and think of you often. The land here is wild, but I know with strength and love we can tame it. I look forward to the not too distant day when we are here together, building our home and our life…

She let out a choked cry and closed her eyes, the letter falling back to the bed. Then, resolutely, she opened them again and picked up the page.

She read every single letter, torturing herself with every loving word and gentle reproof of her own cold silence. Her throat ached with the effort of holding back tears she felt she had no right to shed as she read of his plans to have her join him.

If your heart has not changed, as you know mine has remained steadfast, you could travel next summer with Margaret and Rupert. I have plans for our own cabin, on the other side of the river. It would be a humble place, but we could call it our own. My father has agreed…

The letter slipped from her fingers as tears finally spilled from her eyes. She could take no more of the agony of reading all of the hopes he'd had, and all those she'd lost. "Oh, Allan," Harriet whispered. She missed him now, more than ever, with a swamping sense of sorrow and grief. "Allan, Allan, forgive me."

CHAPTER FOURTEEN

Ian had to keep his legs from shaking as he left the dark brig, blinking in the sunlight. The sailor led him down a narrow hallway and knocked on the ship master's door.

"Enter."

"Here he is, sir." With more of a leer than a smile, the sailor pushed Ian into Henry Moore's private chamber.

Henry sat at a desk in front of him, ink and parchment on its surface. He wore spectacles, which gave him a bookish air and eased Ian's fear slightly, although his knees were still knocking together.

The room they were in was small but comfortable, with a sleeping berth and desk, a shelf of books with leather straps buckled over them to keep the tomes from falling out during rough weather. Maps were tacked to the walls, with even more scattered across the one table.

"Well, Mr. Cameron." Henry slipped off his spectacles and stared at Ian sternly. "How are you to account for yourself?"

"I'm sorry, sir. It was an accident."

"An accident? Or simple carelessness?"

Ian flushed. "Carelessness, sir," he whispered. "I know I should've taken more care with the ropes. I wasn't thinking…"

"Have you been down to the surgeon's quarters, Mr. Douglas?"

"No, sir."

"The sailor who was tangled in your carelessly coiled rope is there presently, with a broken leg. Fortunately it was a clean break and I believe the leg will mend. If it hadn't been, the man would've lost his limb, and perhaps you can imagine the suffering he would have endured as a result. Perhaps you've seen the soldiers back from the wars, with similar injuries."

Ian blanched. "I'm sorry, sir."

"I expect you are." Henry leaned back in his chair. "As a result, I've lost a fine sailor for the rest of this voyage. Do you think his wages should come out of your pocket?"

Ian knew a sailor earned much more than a mere ship's boy. "I… couldn't…" he began.

"No, Mr. Cameron, you couldn't. Never fear, I'm not about to take all your wages, and then some. But I do think it is important you realize the gravity of your carelessness. None of us, not the master nor the bosun nor the merest ship's boy, can afford a moment's carelessness on board. As you've seen, lives depend on it. We must all work together, trust each other. I'm afraid the other men's trust in you has been sorely tested this day."

"I realize that, sir." Ian swallowed painfully. "I know I should be punished, and if you want to let me off at Boston…"

Henry chuckled, a strange, dry sound amid the present circumstances. "Ah, now there's a thought. I'm afraid, Mr. Cameron, that you aren't to get off so easily."

Ian's face was the color of skimmed milk. "Am I to be whipped?"

"I considered it, and I know it is what many of the men want. In truth, I should whip you, but I'm loath to do it when I can see plainly that you are not used to such treatment. You're the son of a gentleman, if I'm not mistaken."

"A farmer, sir, yes."

"But you have an education."

Ian thought of his lessons in Tobermory with a longing he'd never expected to feel. "Yes."

Henry nodded. "I'm not a cruel man, though I believe in discipline. You're not happy, Mr. Cameron, are you?"

Ian stared down at his bare feet. "No, sir."

"Ship's life not to your liking, then?"

"It's passing strange, sir. I'll get used to it, I know."

"Perhaps your particular skills are wasted coiling ropes and such, Mr. Cameron," Henry mused. "I'm a merchant first, and I like to see a profit. I've hired you for this voyage, and if you're causing me a loss as a ship's boy then I need to rethink your responsibilities."

Ian shook his head, confused. "I don't understand."

"I've a fair guess that you're not a true orphan, Mr. Douglas. You've a family back in Scotland, haven't you?"

"Yes, but…"

"Never mind what's happened between you and them. That's not for me to know. But you said you've had some learning?"

"I… I had a tutor," Ian ventured. "He taught me history, and maths and Latin. A bit of Greek too. I liked it."

"Liked it well?"

"Well enough, sir. If I could've continued…"

"Something happened to your family's fortunes?"

Ian flushed and looked away. He'd no desire to explain about that to Captain Moore, kindly as he seemed. "Yes, sir."

Henry nodded slowly. "We're missing a surgeon's mate on this voyage," he told Ian. "Someone to assist him in his duties, organize the medicines, take inventory, and such. There'd be a bit of learning in it as well. My surgeon, Mr. Fingal, is a fine, learned man. Educated in America, at Harvard. You probably haven't heard of it, but it's a fine institution. He's a good friend of mine." Henry smiled wryly. "Do you think you'd be interested in such a position?"

Ian could hardly believe his good fortune. Was he really to be spared a punishment, and instead receive this unimaginable boon? "Oh, yes, sir," he stammered, "that would suit me very well, I should think. Very well indeed."

"So do I." Henry smiled. "I shall speak with Mr. Fingal today. Now…" He paused, and a flicker of sympathy showed in his eyes. "There is the matter of a punishment."

"I'm still to be punished?" Ian said, his hopes sinking. He was afraid to be whipped, but he knew he would take whatever discipline he was given. He would have to.

"I'm afraid that it would not be good for the crew's morale if they saw you going scot free," Henry explained almost gently. "And not only free, but given a better position. No, they must see that carelessness is punished, whether it is caused by a ship's boy or the first mate. You see that, don't you?"

Miserably Ian nodded. Yes, he could understand why he must be punished. It was only fair, considering what he'd done. He quaked at the thought of the whip. He'd never been beaten in his life.

"Yes, I think it's the tops for you, Mr. Douglas."

"The tops?"

"You will spend three hours this afternoon on the top masts. It's fine weather, so you might even enjoy it, once you get used to the height."

Ian stared at him, appalled. So far, he'd no reason to climb any of the ship's tall masts, and the thought of having to perch precariously on the highest point of all filled him with numbing terror. "But I could fall!" he exclaimed, almost gabbling in his shock and fear. "I could fall right into the sea!"

"You'll find that's unlikely," Henry replied with a smile. "And we can secure you with a rope, of course. I've no desire to send you to your death. You might be scared, lad, in fact I'm sure of it. But you won't be hurt."

Ian nodded and squared his shoulders. He would do his best to face this with courage, although privately he wondered if he preferred the whip. "Thank you, sir."

"You're welcome, Mr. Cameron. Dismissed."

*

Henry watched the young ship's boy leave with a half-smile. He hoped that the hours spent in the tops would give the boy some much needed spine. And with a job that used his skill, perhaps he could be of some use to the ship… and to himself. Henry hoped he would not regret taking the young boy on, although he half-did already.

He turned back to his letter, smiling slightly as the words on the page conjured his beloved's face. *Dearest Margaret, he wrote. We are six days off the shores of America, and yet you are constantly in my mind…*

*

"You can't, Harriet!" Margaret stared at her, appalled. "You can't marry him now, not when he's done this to you." She glanced at the letters, scattered across the kitchen table, evidence of her brother's faithfulness. "I knew Allan would stay true."

"I wish I'd had as much faith," Harriet replied in a low voice. "I feel I've betrayed him as much as Andrew has me."

"Now is not the time for self-pity," Margaret replied robustly. "You'd no choice, and how were you to know that Allan had written, when you had received no letters? This isn't your fault."

"I shouldn't have doubted. You told me as much."

Margaret held up a hand. "Enough! Regrets are useless now. You must think of your future." She leaned forward, eyes anxious, her lower lip caught between her teeth. "What are you going to *do?*"

Harriet shrugged helplessly, as uncertain now as she'd been before, when she'd spoken to Andrew. "What can I do? I was fortunate when I thought I was marrying a good, honest man. The fact that it has changed…"

"Changes everything!"

Harriet shook her head. "No, it does not, Margaret. We'd still lose Achlic Farm if I don't marry him. I don't have the luxury of choice—"

"Or of principles?" Margaret's brows rose as her eyes snapped with challenge.

"My principles are making me save my family and sacrifice myself," Harriet replied heatedly. "So I'll thank you to you cease with your high-minded lectures!" She pushed away from the table, near tears yet again.

Ever since learning of Andrew's betrayal, and far more painful, Allan's faithfulness, Harriet's mind and heart had been in utter torment. Her betrayal of Allan—the letter already sent and most likely received—was like a knife wound to the heart, to any last dreams she'd cherished, plunged in again every time she thought of it.

She *couldn't* marry Andrew, and yet what choice did she truly have? Allan wouldn't have her now, and there was her family to think about, in as dire straits as ever.

Her shoulders slumped and Margaret came to give her a quick hug.

"Och, Harriet, I don't mean to be scolding you." Margaret rested her head briefly on Harriet's shoulder, her arms around her. "It is only that I cannot stand to see you as a martyr, throwing your life away for that conniving scoundrel."

"Who is a conniving scoundrel?" Harriet's father appeared in the kitchen doorway, leaning heavily on a cane. In the last few weeks he'd been able to leave his bed, and Harriet was relieved to see the color in his cheeks return a little, in thanks, perhaps, to Jane MacCready's constant nagging at him to get on his feet. "And who might be throwing her life away?" He glanced at Harriet, his expression shrewd.

"It need not concern you, Father," Harriet said quickly. "Margaret was speaking out of turn."

"Was I?" Margaret's dark eyes sparkled with sudden, wry humor. "Very well. I'll leave you to tell your father about your decision." With a swish of her skirts, she left the room.

Harriet bit her lip, wishing Margaret had not left with so provocative a statement. David sat at the table with her, one eyebrow raised. "Well, lass? Are you going to tell me about it?"

"It's nothing."

"Your wedding is in three weeks, daughter," David reminded her. "If something needs knowing, now's the time. There isn't much time left to change your mind, if that's what you're thinking."

"I won't change my mind." Harriet began to gather up Allan's letters, but David took one before she could sweep them out of view.

"What's this?" He looked at the address at the top of the page: *A. MacDougall, Mingarry Farm, Platte River, Prince Edward Island.* "I don't know much about affairs of the heart, but should a woman betrothed to one man be reading the letters of another, just weeks before her wedding?"

"I didn't know about them." Harriet's voice broke on the words and David gazed at her, his frown deepening.

"Harriet…"

"He kept them from me, Father." In a tearful rush, the story came out. Harriet was relieved to tell her father, someone whose advice in the last few months she'd come to see and respect as sound.

David listened quietly, without interrupting, and Harriet was relieved to have told him. She was amazed to be speaking so candidly to him. Their relationship had grown more since his illness than in all the years before, and yet she did not know what he would counsel now.

After she'd finished, he was quiet for a long time, his expression distant and shuttered. When he finally spoke, his voice was low and even sad. "I had my doubts about you marrying Andrew Reid from the beginning. I certainly didn't want you to marry someone you didn't love, and a Riddel at that. But I hoped in time you might have come to have some affection for him, the same kind of love your mother had for me, and I for her." The corners of his mouth quirked upwards in a small, sad smile. "You know as well as I do that I haven't been the same since she died all those years ago."

"Yes, I know." Harriet remembered her mother as a quiet, efficient woman whose smile had been rare yet precious. She'd loved her, had been only Eleanor's age when she died. But the following years of hard work and toil had dulled the memory, made her mother like a ghost who haunted the far reaches of her memory, and nothing more. As for her father… she could only just remember a man who had laughed, and swung her mother up and around, and patted his children's heads. Only just.

"We had a partnership," her father continued quietly, "and that's rare. I'd like the same for all my children."

"So would I," Harriet whispered.

Her father covered her hand with his own. "Then you needn't marry him, lass. Not for my sake, at any rate. I wouldn't have that for the world. Besides, what of Allan? He's written you, I see. When I told him to wait, I did so always thinking he'd come back to you."

Harriet managed a wry smile even though her heart was aching. "You had an odd way of showing it."

"Perhaps I shouldn't have been so hard, but it was out of wanting more for you. I've told you as much. Still, perhaps you would have been happier then, to have gone? And none of this misunderstanding would have happened." He sighed heavily. "How were any of us to know?"

"I don't know anything anymore," Harriet admitted tiredly. "And I cannot bear to think of the what ifs."

Her father spread his hands wide. "If he's stayed true all this time…"

"But I haven't!" Harriet cried, angry desperation edging her voice. "Would he even have me now? I wrote to him last autumn and told him of my decision. He's known for months. No doubt he believes me to already be wed."

"Write him again, then, and explain."

Harriet shook her head. "What of the farm? And of us? If I don't marry Andrew Reid, we'll lose Achlic."

"There are other ways to manage." A slight flush bloomed on David's cheeks. "I'll admit I'm sorely grieved to lose this farm. It's been in our family for over a century, and I've poured my life blood into it. But times are changing and I've seen worse things happen. I've seen men torn from their homes without a shilling in their pocket, and all for the sake of sheep." He shook his head sadly. "We're fortunate in that we may have a place to go, and a comfortable one at that."

Harriet frowned in confusion. "What place do you mean?"

Her father's blush deepened as he stared at the floor. "The truth of it is, is Jane MacCready has offered to share her farm with us. She has a good size house and some acreage, and she's been hiring men to sow it since her husband died. I wouldn't take an offer of charity, of course, but…" He looked up, smiling slightly. "The fact is, since Mistress MacCready has come visiting, we've become fond of one another and I'm thinking of asking her to marry me."

Harriet stared at her father, open mouthed. She could hardly believe this unlikely turn of events. Had she been so lost in her own thoughts and worries that she'd not even noticed the romance blooming under their roof?

"So you see, lass," he continued, "you needn't think we'll be turned out on the street. Eleanor can live with us, and enjoy the last of her childhood. Even Ian, should he return home, God willing, is welcome. Our lives will be modest, of course, for the MacCready place is no Achlic, but we'll have enough. And we'll be happy." He smiled, and it was like a crack spreading across his face.

"I don't know what to say," Harriet said at last. She didn't want to admit to a faint resentment that her father had not thought to mention these plans earlier, or even that they might be brewing. "It seems as if you've solved everything in one stroke. And yet…"

"You shouldn't feel you have to honor your promise to that Riddell scruff," he said darkly. "Not after he's tricked you in such a fashion. When I thought you might come to love him, I was willing to have it all come to pass. But now? No one would look askance if you were to walk away. No one at all."

Harriet nodded slowly, unable to voice the new fear that stole over her. If she did not marry Andrew Reid, what would she do? Live with her father and Mistress MacCready, a spinster beholden to another's charity? She knew Jane MacCready's good will would most likely extend to all of the Campbells, but it still made Harriet uneasy. She was nearly twenty-five years old, and she had no place, no role.

She saw her life slipping away, lost in service to others. Harriet closed her eyes. Her father placed his large, rough hand over hers, seeming to understand a small portion of the uncertainty and confusion within her.

"Think it over, lass. There's still time."

"May I come in?"

Harriet's eyes flew open. Margaret stood in the doorway, her cheeks flushed, her hands twisting her apron. "If you'll pardon my intrusion into family matters, I think I have an idea that might be the solution we are all wishing for."

"You know you're as good as family," Harriet protested. "And," she added with a smile, "I've never known you to keep your ideas to yourself. But what answer can you possibly have?"

Margaret laughed in acknowledgment before pursuing her theme. "You know *The Harmony* sails in a month's time. Rupert and I are meant to be on it." She took a deep breath. "I've made up my mind, though, and I shan't be going. I intend to stay here. Mrs. MacCready has said I can stay with her while I wait for Henry."

"It seems everyone is staying with Mistress MacCready," Harriet said a bit tartly. "But Margaret, what will your father say?"

Margaret raised her chin. "I'll write him a letter, of course, but I don't see how what he says should affect me. I'm seventeen, eighteen come winter, and I've met a man I want to marry. Should I travel to the New Scotland, settle there, and hope Henry finds me, simply because my father says I should? He lost that right when he travelled on without me. I love him, but I won't be beholden to him. I want to live my life *now*, not simply stand about waiting and waiting like…" She stopped suddenly, biting her lip.

"Like me?" Harriet finished softly. She couldn't be angry for she knew Margaret was only speaking the truth. She'd waited so long already… and for what? For nothing, it seemed. Nothing at all.

"I'm sorry, Harriet," Margaret whispered.

"I don't blame you. If you know you want to marry Henry, and he's asked—"

"He's asked me to wait," Margaret said, and though her voice was firm, doubt lingered in the shadows in her eyes. "He told me we might marry next spring, when he returns." She bit her lip. "If he returns."

"I'm sure he will." Harriet said. "Heaven knows someone needs to come back!" She tried for a smile and tremulously Margaret matched it. "I don't begrudge you your happiness, Margaret."

"But I didn't mean to talk about me!" Margaret exclaimed impatiently. "It's you we must discuss. If I stay here, there's still no reason to waste a ship's passage. Rupert needs to be taken to my family, and my father wouldn't want him to go alone. He's only thirteen, after all. So here is my solution—Harriet, why don't you go in my place? Accompany Rupert and find Allan. You can send a letter ahead if you like, or explain everything when you see him face to face. I know Allan, and I know he will love you still. He'll understand why you felt you had to marry Mr. Reid… and why you didn't. You cannot throw away what you have with him, not for pride or for fear." Margaret let out a breath after this long speech, looking eagerly between Harriet and her father.

Harriet gazed at her in astonishment. The idea had never occurred to her... to go all the way to Canada, on her own, and see Allan! Even as a thrill came over her, she nearly shuddered with fear. Go all that way... uninvited? Unexpected? To have Allan reject her face to face, leave her no choice but to slink all the way back to Mull?

"I couldn't," she said after a moment. "Not as quickly as that. I'd have to write first, explain..." And even then, who knew if Allan would understand... and forgive? If she were in his place, Harriet didn't know how she would feel, or what she would be willing to accept.

"And if you write a letter, and wait for a response, it could be another year! Another year of waiting or more. And goodness knows if either of you will get the letters, since they do seem to go missing!"

Harriet let out an unwilling laugh before she pressed her hands to her cheeks, overcome. "And what if he rejects me utterly?" she whispered. "I wouldn't blame him. And then what would I do?"

"Come back here, or make your way in the new world," Margaret returned stoutly.

"As a woman alone? That's hardly possible."

"Anything is possible—"

"You're talking dreams!" Harriet turned away, suddenly angry. "No gently-bred woman would ever do such a thing. Nonsense. It can't be done."

There was a moment of silence, and Harriet could feel her father and Margaret's gazes on her, their silent reproach. Her shoulders shook with the misery of it all and she wrapped her arms around herself.

"Are dreams nonsense, *cridhe*?" Her father laid a hand on her shoulder. "Believe, Harriet. Believe and go."

CHAPTER FIFTEEN

"Is this seat taken?"

Allan looked up from his pint of ale to see a small, wiry man smiling at him. He shrugged indifferently and gestured to the empty chair across from him. "No, I'm alone."

The man sat down and held out a hand. "George Simpson."

Allan shook his hand, a bit taken aback at the man's forthrightness. Most people were friendly enough in these parts, but he was still surprised to meet a stranger who'd go out of his way to befriend him—especially when Allan knew he didn't look as if he wanted company. He wanted to be alone with his thoughts, and the grief that was reverberating through him, over Harriet's letter. "Allan MacDougall." He paused, frowning. "George Simpson... that name sounds familiar. Do I know you?"

Simpson had a friendly smile, but Allan saw that his eyes remained shrewd and even a bit cold. This was a man to be reckoned with, but what could he possibly want with him?

"You might've heard of me," he said. "I'm head of Hudson's Bay Company, and I'm looking for good men."

Allan sat back as he eyed Simpson with new consideration. So this was the man who'd taken over the Americas' largest business empire, a company started by adventurers that now stretched to the Pacific. He was known as the Little Emperor, and for a good reason.

"What is an important man like you doing here in Pictou?" Allan asked skeptically. He'd heard in the general store how

Simpson travelled with some fanfare, going from outpost to outpost simply in a birch bark canoe, yet greeted in each place with trumpets, flags, and parades.

"I'm travelling incognito," Simpson replied with a small smile. "I find it's easier when I'm recruiting."

"Recruiting? From what I've heard, you've been letting men go."

Simpson's smile widened. "You keep your ear to the ground, I see."

Allan shrugged. "Storefront gossip."

"Yes, you're right in that I am letting men go, all the lazy, shiftless ones who weren't earning their wage. I'm looking now for strong men, capable men. Men without ties. Men who are fearless. Do you think you might be one of them?"

Allan paused, his mug halfway to his lips. "Why would you think that?"

"I don't, not yet. I'm merely asking."

Allan looked away. Was it that obvious that he was all alone in the world? He certainly felt it at that moment, with Harriet's letter right there before him. "I'm a farmer," he said at last. "I always have been."

"Most men are, till they become something else. Fur traders, explorers… adventurers."

Simpson spread his hands wide. "But I'm not here to pressure you. There are plenty of men to be had. I just thought you looked the sort."

"The sort? For what?"

"For adventure. You look like someone who is willing to take a risk, but not a foolish one. Someone who wants to live, and not just eke out a living. Someone who wants to see the world, and do it alone." He stared at Allan steadily.

"And what if I am?" he asked after a moment, his tone not precisely friendly.

"Then you might be someone I want to hire. I'm staying at the boarding house by the harbor tonight. If you want to talk more, I'll be there till dawn tomorrow. I rise early. I've got other places to be." With one last fleeting smile, his manner friendly but his eyes sharp, Simpson left the table.

It was late afternoon and Allan knew Archie would be arriving any moment. In his last letter, he'd arranged to meet at the public house, yet Allan suddenly was loath to meet his brother in that smoky room, with him hunched over his ale, Harriet's letter still fresh in his mind. He needed some air.

He left the house and walked along the harbor, breathing in the cold, fresh air, spring still holding a hint of winter, and looking for his brother. Dark clouds loomed ominously on the horizon, and Allan hoped Archie would make an appearance soon. The crossing back to PEI looked to be choppy. Even though the ice had broken up weeks ago, it was still a bit early for a safe crossing. He saw one of the smaller vessels was making to leave soon, well before the later mail packet. If Archie arrived, they could get on board.

He stood on the wooden planks that made for a road and scanned the road for Archie's rangy figure and red tunic, trying not to think about Harriet or her letter. Not to think about his future, or lack of it. Nothing awaited him, nothing but more of the same.

"Allan!'

Allan turned to see Archie striding towards him, smart as ever in his uniform. His eyes were bright, his cheeks red with cold, and he was smiling widely. He looked healthy and happy, and Allan felt tired and old in his worn homespun, the brim of his farmer's hat pulled lower over his eyes. Archie clapped Allan on the shoulder before enveloping him in a quick, surprising hug. "Here you are! Ah, but I've missed you! How is Mother? And Father? To think we'll all be together again soon, and Margaret and Rupert as well, if I read Father's last letter aright."

"Mother and Father are well." Allan gazed at his brother. Army life clearly suited him. "You seem well also."

"I am! I've found my calling at last. Of course, we haven't seen much action in Three Rivers. Mostly patrols, a few skirmishes with Indians. The soldiers get restless, and go looking for a fight." Archie shrugged. "I won't talk of army affairs. It's dull work to a farmer, eh?"

"Not at all."

"You haven't been suffering on the farm, have you?" Archie suddenly turned serious. "You know, I never meant to thwart your ambitions with my own. I know that's how it seemed at the time, but…" He trailed off apologetically.

Allan stared at him, unsure how to reply. He thought he knew what Archie was feeling. Full of his own happiness, unwilling for it be tainted by past sins or regrets. He wanted a clean slate, and why shouldn't he give it to him? Archie's ambitions didn't change the lack of his own, now that Harriet was gone. He shrugged. "How could they?" he replied, doing his best to keep his tone light. "Our ambitions have always been separate, as are we. I do well enough on the farm, and I know I could never make a soldier." He nodded towards the clouds boiling up on the horizon. "But we'd best hurry if we don't want to be caught out in that. There's a small boat leaving shortly. I think we should be on it."

The clouds continued to darken and spread over the sky, becoming darker and more menacing as a brisk, biting wind began to blow. Allan gestured to the small boat making ready in the harbour.

"That looks a small craft indeed," Archie said with a frown. "This wind could blow it right over. It reminds me…" He paused, his throat working. "I put you in jeopardy once before, Allan, because of my own foolhardiness. I won't do it again. The mail packet leaves in a few hours. Let's share a meal together, and take it on the evening tide. We'll get back a bit later, but we'll be safe."

"I see you've changed, what with your soldiering," Allan said after a moment.

Archie nodded. "Aye, I have. There's enough risk involved in the Army. I won't take needless ones here."

Allan shrugged. He was in no hurry to get back; he was in no hurry to get anywhere, now. "Very well, then. The public house does a good game pie. I've had one already, but I'll join you in a cup of ale."

It was only after they'd eaten, and were returning to the harbor to take the mail packet, that Allan's thoughts became suddenly, painfully clear.

He'd listened to Archie natter on about Army life for over an hour, had seen the new enthusiasm and zeal glowing in his eyes, and realized he no longer felt any bitterness or resentment at all. How could he blame Archie for his own shortcomings? No one had forced him to stay at his father's farm, taking orders, waiting for things to get better. No one had tied him to the plow, except perhaps himself.

He'd been angry for so long, blaming Sandy, Archie, even Harriet, for the disappointments he'd faced. Now Allan realized with a sudden, piercing clarity that the only person to blame was, and had always been, himself. He should have stood up to his father long ago, or he should have left. He'd hid behind honor and duty, had let himself be led, and be miserable, waiting for a time when things might change.

Now there was nothing and no one left to wait for.

"Ah, here it is." Archie stopped in front of the mail packet, just being loaded, and turned back to Allan. Whatever he'd been planning to say died on his lips as he saw the expression on his face—Allan could imagine how grim it looked. He'd made his decision, right here on the harborside. "Allan?" Archie asked uncertainly.

"Go on, Archie." Allan spoke roughly, his voice clogged with sudden, unshed tears as he realized all he was turning away from. "Give Mother and Father my love, and tell them I'll be back one day. But for now… I have to go on my own, at last." He clasped Archie briefly before stepping away. Archie stared at him in confusion.

"What are you talking about? Where are you going?"

Allan smiled. It was easy, now the decision was made. He felt a lightness in himself that he hadn't experienced in years, if ever. "I'm not going with you. I'm not going back."

"But…" Archie looked dumbfounded. "What will you do? Where will you go?"

Allan shrugged. "I'm not sure yet. But there's a man I need to see in town."

*

Harriet stood on the deck of *The Harmony* and watched as her homeland became a faint green smudge. Rupert stood next to her, his expression unexpectedly solemn as they watched Tobermory edge towards the horizon.

He'd been full of boyish excitement for this journey, yet now Harriet suspected the enormity of their departure was finally taking its toll on him… and her. She really was going to find Allan.

The last few weeks had been a blur of activity as she prepared for departure, packing only two small trunks of clothes and a few sentimental items. It broke her heart to leave her pianoforte behind, but she could hardly haul it all the way to the new world, especially when she didn't even know what her reception was likely to be. Allan might not even want to see her, a prospect that made everything in her shrink with fear.

Two days earlier, her father had wed Jane MacCready in a small but joyous ceremony. Harriet had stood in the kirk at Craignure and realized with a little pang that her father had found love again. She was happy for him, and thankful he'd had a second chance at love and life, and yet seeing him with Jane made her realize all the more that there was no place for her there any longer.

There had been other farewells too. Harriet did not like to remember the look of hurt on Andrew's face when she told him she was breaking their betrothal. Even though he'd betrayed her, she still had felt a small stirring of pity for the man.

"You can't do this, Harriet," he said desperately as they stood in the drawing room of Lanymoor House. "It's such a fleeting thing, too small to matter! I'd make you a good husband, I know I would, if only you'd forgive me…"

"I do forgive you," Harriet said, although that wasn't quite true. She still harboured a resentment in her heart for how he'd deceived her, although she was trying not to. "But I cannot trust you, Andrew, and I know I will never love you." She took a steadying breath before continuing, "The truth of the matter is I love Allan, and I mean to find him. Now that my father is planning to marry, the need to keep Achlic is not as great, and I can leave with a clear conscience."

"A clear conscience? You really were only marrying me to keep that wretched farm," Andrew sneered, his face twisting with bitterness. "You never loved me."

"You knew that," Harriet reminded him as gently as she could. "I never said any different."

"I thought you would come to care for me, in time. You still could—"

Harriet shook her head. Her mind and heart were both decided. "No, Andrew," she said. "This is goodbye."

"I hope you find him," Andrew told her bitterly. "Then you'll realize what you've thrown away here, with me."

Harriet did not reply.

The other farewells had been far both more pleasant and more poignant. Harriet had embraced Margaret, wishing her well in her wait for her sailing master.

Eleanor, who at nearly thirteen was fast turning into a young woman, had thrown her arms around Harriet and clung to her, though she stoically refused to shed any tears.

"When Allan and I are set up, I'll send for you," Harriet had promised. Even though Eleanor had not said anything, she knew that the young girl felt adrift in this new order of things, moving to Jane MacCready's house and learning to love her new stepmother. "You'll like the new world, *cridhe*, I'm sure of it."

"How would you know," Eleanor had replied with a little smile, "when you've never seen it yourself!"

True enough, Harriet thought now. There were so many uncertainties. As she gazed out at the horizon, she could understand how sailors of old thought they would fall off the edge if they sailed too far. That was a bit how she felt… as if she was falling off the edge of her known, comfortable world, and into one entirely unknown.

The Harmony was a cargo ship, and Harriet and Rupert were among only a handful of passengers. When they'd boarded, the ship's captain had greeted them, politely expressing only faint surprise at a young woman and boy travelling alone together.

"Are you meeting someone in the new world, Miss Campbell?"

"Yes, my betrothed." Allan *was* her betrothed, or the closest she had to one now, even if he didn't realize it at the moment. She held the captain's gaze and told herself it was no lie.

"A brave man, to allow his beloved to travel so far and so long alone," the captain had commented.

Harriet lifted her chin. "He is working hard to prepare for my arrival, Captain, and I assure you I am quite capable of taking care of myself."

"Besides," Rupert had added, "I can look after her as well."

The Captain had glanced at thirteen-year-old Rupert, still scrawny, and smiled. "Yes, I can see Miss Campbell has quite the protector," he said, a gentle amusement taking any sting out of his words.

How different it would have—should have—been, Harriet could not help but think sadly. She'd imagined this voyage many times, but it had always been with Allan at her side, the two of them newly married and full of hope. Instead, she travelled alone, save Rupert, going towards an unknown country… and an unknown welcome.

Rupert must have felt some of her worry, for he now put his hand on her arm. "We ought to get ready for supper, Harriet. We're dining with the captain tonight."

Harriet smiled and ruffled his hair. "Right you are, then. Let's return below."

Since the ship was not really equipped for passengers, they were required to share one small cabin. Rupert had gallantly rigged up a blanket between the berths to provide a modicum of privacy. Still, as Harriet changed her dress and washed her face and hands, she wondered how they would manage like this for five or six weeks. She knew they were fortunate, far more so than most of the immigrants who journeyed to new lands and hopes in the crowded, disease-ridden hold, with no privacy at all. Still, she looked forward to when their journey would reach an end, even as she dreaded that day and what it might bring.

As the ship travelled on, the days seemed to blur into one another. Harriet spent most of her time walking the deck when the air was fresh, or else in their cabin reading one of the few books she'd brought. She'd also brought Allan's letters, the ones Andrew had kept from her as well as the ones he'd written to her back on Ardnamurchan. She treasured his words of love and fidelity, and reading them once more helped to buoy her hope that Allan would forgive her and love her once again when she arrived in Pictou.

Rupert soon grew restless with the smallness of their cabin and company, and befriended a few of the sailors who taught him how to make knots and other seafaring tricks. Although a bit rough, they were friendly enough, and Harriet allowed him to roam free while he could. Watching Rupert, Harriet couldn't help but miss her own brother. It was nearly six months since he'd left on *The Allegiance*, and she had no idea where he had travelled or if he was well. She only hoped Margaret's sailing master really would keep an eye on him.

After nearly six weeks of sailing, they finally came in sight of land. Harriet and Rupert both stood on the deck to watch as the coast of Nova Scotia came closer, even though there was a steady drizzle, and the smudge of land on the horizon was half-obscured by mist. Harriet didn't mind the rain which dampened her face as if with tears, and turned her hair into a mass of unruly curls beneath her bonnet. Finally—finally! They were in sight of the new world, and in reach of Allan.

Instinctively Rupert reached for Harriet's hand, and Harriet smiled down at him. Taking a deep breath, she nodded towards the rugged coastline. "Here we are, Rupert. This shall be home now, for both of us."

They landed in Halifax, only to have to take another, much smaller boat onto Pictou, with several of the other passengers. Everyone was tired and weary of travel, and Harriet felt as if she were holding onto her patience by only a thread.

Finally they reached Pictou, a small, rougher-looking town compared to Halifax, the forest towering above it. It seemed to take an age for the ship to be steered into the harbor and for their trunks to be unloaded. At last they stood on solid ground, amidst a stream of varied humanity, trunks piled at their feet and the strange, forbidding landscape rising up all around them.

Even though Harriet was used to the formidable mountains and glens of her homeland, the dense, impenetrable forest of this new world gave her pause. How, she wondered, could anyone think they could tame this wild land? Take control of it?

"What should we do now, Harriet?" Rupert's voice wavered slightly, and Harriet knew he was feeling the same trepidation as she was. It was easy enough to be full of cheerful excitement on board ship, she thought wryly, when there was a bed to sleep in and food on the table. Standing alone, strangers in a strange land, was something else altogether.

"Your father said he would meet the ship," she told him. "He must have had word of *The Harmony* landing, and known we'd take the packet onto Pictou. If we don't see him in a little while, I expect we can find an inn or some respectable place to wait. He shouldn't be too long." Although Harriet didn't even know if they would be able to find such a place. Pictou didn't look to offer too much in that direction, and she had no idea how long they might be expected to wait. If Sandy MacDougall hadn't heard about *The Harmony's* landing, he might take hours or even days.

"What about our trunks?" Rupert asked.

What about them, Harriet wondered. They were in a disorderly pile on the muddy planks that served as a road, quite in the way of the people passing by—travellers like herself, strange, savage-looking men all decked out in fur, and even stranger folk she supposed were the native people, wearing breeches made of animal hide, with paint on their faces. She felt helpless and ill equipped to handle any of it. "Perhaps we could hire—"

"Rupert!" A familiar, strident voice relieved her of finishing the thought. Sandy strode towards them, and quickly enveloped Rupert in a tight hug.

Harriet was shocked by the older man's appearance. His hair was far whiter than when he'd left two years ago, and there were deep lines etched in his face, lines of suffering and pain. The years in this new country must have been hard, she realized. Harder than perhaps any of them knew.

"It's good to see you, lad." Sandy turned to Harriet, and his mouth dropped open in surprise, and, Harriet feared, dismay. "You've come! We all hoped before, of course, but where... where's Margaret?"

His voice was hoarse with fear and Harriet hastened to reassure him. "She's well and hale, but there were reasons for her to stay in Scotland, at least for the while." Hesitantly, Harriet held out the letter Margaret had written her parents to explain. "She wanted me to give you this, to explain why she didn't come."

Sandy took the letter, unfolded it and scanned its contents quickly. When he looked up, tears glinted in his eyes and his voice was quiet with both acceptance and sorrow. "It's as much as any of us can ask for, to grasp what happiness we find. We've had precious little happiness for ourselves, these last few months, I'm sorry to say."

Harriet felt a sudden chill of foreboding at Sandy's words, as well as the despairing look on his face. What had happened? What was he not telling her? "And how is Betty?" she asked when she found her voice. "And Archie? And... and Allan, of course. No one knows I'm coming. I know I should have written, but the time was too short..."

"We're pleased to have you here, lass, of course we are. It was I who urged Allan to write in the first place. But..." He faltered, his expression so troubled that Harriet's stomach swooped with fear.

"What? What is it?" Her fists were tightly clenched, her nails biting into her palms. Had Allan married another since she'd released him? She couldn't blame him for it, and yet...

"There's been news, terrible news," Sandy said, his voice choking, and he reached out to clasp Harriet's shoulder in a gesture of comfort. "Nearly two months ago now, it was."

Harriet felt a buzzing in her ears, even as a curious numbness came over to her. "What... what happened two months ago?"

"There was a storm... the mail packet went down halfway between here and Charlottetown. It was a terrible thing, so many people lost, and not one survivor." Sandy shook his head, his eyes now bright with unshed tears, and Harriet felt dizziness sweep over her in a sickening wave as she realized the implication of Sandy's words. Still, she had to hear him say it.

"What are you saying?" she asked, her voice seeming to come from far away.

"They're gone, Harriet, Rupert. My two boys are gone. Allan and Archie both drowned when the mail packet sank."

The dizziness swept over her again, stronger this time, and the buzzing turned to a roaring in Harriet's ears. Then the world went dark.

CHAPTER SIXTEEN

It had taken Allan two months by pony and then by birch bark canoe to reach York Factory on the lower end of Hudson's Bay. It was hard work, paddling twelve hours a day, eating little more than pemmican, a form of dried deer or buffalo, and what berries, nuts and other fruits of the forest he could scavenge, and sleeping rough every night. It was how all the voyageurs travelled and ate, and he forced himself to become used to it.

After he'd left Archie, Allan had met George Simpson at the boarding house and signed up as a fur trader, or voyageur as the French traders of the old North West Company called themselves—men who travelled and worked alone, journeying through Canada's wild upper reaches, trapping for fur.

He enjoyed the work, being alone in God's creation, seeing the landscape change from the rolling hills and forests of the coast to the dense and uninhabited forests of Upper Canada and then Rupert's Land where the mink, bear, and beaver all still roamed free and wild—and easy to be trapped.

There was plenty of time to be alone with his thoughts, and he often found himself thinking of Harriet. Was she happy in her new life? Did she love her husband? Perhaps she was already expecting a child.

He thought of Archie, back in Three Rivers living the life of a soldier, happy in his ways, and then of his parents at Mingarry Farm. Had Rupert and Margaret joined them already? He wondered if they had been disappointed when Archie told them he was not coming back. He hoped, somehow, that they'd understood.

In his darker moments, alone in the night, the sounds of the forest around him, he wondered what future he could have. There could be no more dreams of Harriet, of the life they would build together and the family they would have. There seemed little point in returning to Prince Edward Island, toiling by his father's side—and for what?

Sometimes, he entertained thoughts of going home, marrying a girl like Fiona Campbell, rebuilding his life from the ashes. Yet he could not face the bleak prospect, not yet, and maybe not ever.

Perhaps he would stay a fur trader, a lone traveller going from outpost to outpost. Yet, despite the adventure, it too was a bleak thought, the life of a nomad, destined only to roam.

He was relieved to arrive at the bustling York Factory, trade in his furs, and be among other people for a while, to distract him from the restless, lonely circling of his own thoughts.

York Factory was one of the Company's larger outposts, and many of the traders gathered there to load up with supplies before heading west or north to the more distant outposts where the animals were still plentiful.

When Allan arrived, it was deep summer, and the outpost was hot, humid, and thick with mosquitoes. York Factory was built on little more than a bog, and Allan couldn't help but think it a rather unpleasant place to stay, although he'd been looking forward to some company.

Many other voyageurs must have agreed, for tempers were running high and more than one fist fight broke out between traders gathered around their campfires in the evening.

"There's going to be trouble," one trader, a French-speaking Nor'wester, growled ominously after there had been a bust-up that Allan had steered well clear of. "And I'll be the one to start it."

A group of voyageurs were sitting around a fire one evening, chewing tobacco and talking in a way that Allan didn't like. He knew there was much dissension between the Hudson's Bay Company and its recently acquired North West Company, comprised mostly of French and Métis, or half Indian, half French traders.

"What can you do, alone?" someone else scoffed. "There are hundreds at Fort Douglas, and I've heard that more are coming. They're like rats! Besides, the governor stands behind all they do at the Red River settlement, and that's a fact."

The first trader spat on the ground. "Yes, he makes new laws to help them, and never mind the Métis and the voyageurs who were here long before, trying to make a living. What does he expect? For us to bow and scrape and say 'oh, yes, thank you, sir'? He's asking for trouble. It's happened before, it can happen again." There was a murmur, almost a growl, of agreement, and Allan felt the back of his neck prickle with alarm.

He turned to a trader next to him, a Frenchman from Lower Canada whom he knew slightly. "Pierre, what are they talking about over there?"

"Haven't you heard?" Pierre smiled wryly, but his eyes were dark and serious. "The governor of Rupert's Land had passed a new law. No one can take food out of the colony, not even pemmican."

"But why would he do that?" Allan asked in bewilderment.

"He says to help the settlers at Red River. Food's been short, and they need the food more than we do, I suppose. They haven't yet learned how to live off the land as we do."

"Is that why there is this talk of trouble?"

Pierre shrugged. "It was a foolish idea, building a settlement this far out west. This land isn't meant for farmers, it's for the voyageurs. These farmers don't even know what they're doing. In the first year alone they had to leave the settlement and chase the buffalo to keep from starving." He paused meaningfully. "Our buffalo."

"But it's only one settlement, surely the traders can't expect the west to remain wild forever? The more settlers that come…"

"There's plenty of land for them in the east! They've scared most of the game away from Rupert's Land. They're saying you must travel another week by canoe to get anything decent now. And when more settlers arrive…" Pierre shrugged again. "Why shouldn't there be trouble? All we want is what is fair. This land was ours first."

Allan gripped Pierre's arm. "What kind of trouble?"

"I don't know, my friend. The Métis have burned Fort Douglas once already. The settlers fled, but they came back and rebuilt. They're worse than the mosquitoes! Who says it won't happen again?"

Allan was chilled. Fort Douglas was the center of the Red River settlement, bought by Lord Selkirk from the Company several years ago. He knew it was meant to be a settlement for displaced Scottish immigrants, families who'd lost their homes in the clearances, like many on Ardnamurchan and Mull had. He felt sick at the thought of all those people who had lost their livelihoods once already being turned out yet again, this time with perhaps even worse violence.

"Surely an agreement can be reached. If the voyageurs can be made to see sense…"

"See sense? Why are they the ones who must see? What about the settlers seeing sense?" Pierre shook his head. He was smiling, but Allan heard the warning in his voice. "Don't get involved, my friend. This does not concern you. You are new, you are from the old world, the old order, even if you do all right as a voyageur. Still, you don't know about these things. If there is going to be trouble, then there simply is, and there is nothing you can do about it. If you know what's good for you, stay away."

The murmur of voices around the campfire had turned even surlier, and Allan saw the anger and restlessness plainly visible on many of the voyageurs' faces. He knew this was their land; they had possessed it in the name of the Company, they roamed it, and for all intents and purposes they felt they owned it as well.

Yet he could not help but fear for the settlers who were trying to carve a life for themselves in this harsh land, just as his family had, and who might yet again be torn cruelly from their homes and families, or worse.

Pierre was right, what could he, one man, one lone voice of peace among the angry tide of traders, do? Yet Allan knew if it came to the trouble the murmuring voices talked about now, he would have to do something. He would have to try. He had nothing left to lose, after all.

*

Harriet felt a cool cloth on her forehead and cheeks, and her eyes fluttered open. She was lying down on some sort of bed, in an unfamiliar room. A woman hovered above her anxiously. "There, dear, you're coming round now. You've had a shock."

Shock…? Then it all came back to her. Allan was dead. Harriet closed her eyes again, trying to block out the memory of Sandy's words, his grief-stricken face, the whole world as it was now, with no Allan in it.

"It'll be all right now," the woman continued soothingly. "Let me get Mr. MacDougall for you."

"It will never be all right," Harriet whispered. She heard the door open and close, and she struggled to a sitting position. She still felt dizzy, and there was a strange, metallic taste in her mouth. She realized it was blood. She must have knocked her mouth or bitten her tongue when she'd fallen.

"Harriet, thank heaven." Sandy came in and looked down at her, his eyes shadowed with concern. "I shouldn't have told you in such a fashion, and I'm sorry for it. It's still a shock to us, and what with you travelling all this way…"

"How else were you to tell me?" Harriet took a deep breath. "It is better that I know. But please… will you tell me what happened, exactly?"

Somberly Sandy nodded and sat on a stool next to the bed, his work-roughened hands resting flat on his thighs. "Archie was on leave from the Army. He'd just received his commission a few months before, but I expect Allan told you that in his letters. Allan met him in Pictou and they were to travel across together, to us. They took the mail packet, it was meant to be safer, God help us. There was a storm… often there is in April, the weather can turn foul in an instant and the ice had only just broken up." Sandy spread his hands helplessly. "The boat went down just a mile offshore. There was nothing anyone could do, and not one survivor, not in that icy water. They haven't even been able to recover the bodies, so we're denied the right to bury our dead."

Harriet grasped his hand, her fingers curling around his. "I'm so sorry."

Sandy nodded in acceptance. "Their mother and I have been fair torn apart by the grief. To lose both! Good sons, each in their own way, like my own right hand, and my left as well." Sandy shook his head. "And now you, coming all this way, thinking yourself a bride…"

Had Allan not told his parents about her betrothal to Andrew Reid? Harriet closed her eyes briefly. In all her imaginings of her reception in the new world, she'd never envisioned this, or the horror and grief which now swamped her soul. "Let's not talk of it. Not now." It was too fresh, too painful, and Harriet wanted to be alone when she finally gave vent to the wild grief inside her. "We must find Rupert."

"He's being taken care of by the innkeeper's wife. Lord help him, poor boy, to lose half his family in one blow! And having not seen them close on two years." Sandy held out his hand to help Harriet from the bed. "Can you travel, lass? Betty's waiting for us back at Mingarry Farm. We can talk more then."

Harriet barely remembered the journey to Prince Edward Island. Normally she would have been dazzled by the new sights and sounds, but her entire world seemed muted by grief. Rupert was also silent, and she could see the confusion on his face. Two years was a long time in a young boy's life, she knew, and the memory of Archie and Allan would've begun to grow faint. But there could be no denying the loss that they all felt as they travelled beneath a leaden sky, on a mail packet just like the one Archie and Allan had been on.

Mingarry Farm looked to be a prosperous place, and Harriet admired the spacious log cabin, so different from the stone and thatch homes back in Scotland. Betty met them on the porch, and Harriet saw the change in her as well. Her hair had gone white, and there were new lines on her forehead, lines made by grief and sorrow.

"Harriet! Lass!" Betty enveloped her in a hug even before the necessary questions were asked. "You've heard, then. I'm so sorry."

"I'm sorry, too." Harriet's voice came out choked.

They went inside, and Sandy and Harriet explained why Margaret had not come. Betty nodded, understanding yet clearly disappointed to not see her daughter as expected.

"Will she marry this sea captain, then?" Betty asked. "What do you think of it, Harriet?"

"I've never met him, but Margaret has every faith in him. She truly loves him, I believe."

"Well, I'm glad for that." Betty shook her head. "It's a strange world now, to be sure, what with families scattered across the earth. My own daughter alone across the sea, marrying a man I've never seen! I don't know what to think of any of it in the end."

"If she's happy, that's what lasts, in the end," Sandy said heavily. "God knows, I've learned that much when it comes to children. The lessons were hard learned, I can tell you." Harriet heard the regret in his voice, but did not want to question its root.

Sandy turned to her, and he must have seen the unspoken questions in her eyes, for he continued, "Allan wasn't happy here, lass, not like he should've been. How I hoped him to be. He came to this world with dreams of his own, and if I'd had any sense, I would've let him follow them, wherever they led."

"What kind of dreams?" Harriet thought of Allan's letters, the ones she'd read far too late. His description of life at Mingarry Farm had been full and yet, she realized, sometimes without his usual vigor and enthusiasm. Had there been some sorrow or worry he'd not wanted to share with her?

"I couldn't even tell you," Sandy said. "I wasn't really willing to listen." He smiled sadly. "He wanted to make his own way, out of my reach. To build a life for the two of you, here or elsewhere. Who knows? He had dreams he never shared with me, never mind bring them to pass."

Tears stung Harriet's eyes as she remembered the promise Allan had given her two years ago, before he'd left. It had been just that: to create a life and home for themselves. A simple cottage, a hearth they'd call their own. Now none of it was ever to be.

"We'll always have regrets," Betty said. She put her hand on Rupert's shoulder. "But we must look to the living now, to the future we can still have." She turned to Harriet, smiling in spite of her sadness. "You must stay with us, Harriet. You're like a daughter to us already, and you would have been one in truth had Allan lived. Your home is here, with us, as long as you want it."

The sincerity Harriet saw in the older woman's face brought tears of another kind to her eyes. The MacDougalls were being so generous to her, and she knew Allan must never have told them about her betrayal. "Thank you. You're both so kind." And yet, considering how she'd broken it off with Allan, did she really deserve their sympathy, their kindness?

Over the next few weeks Harriet tried her best to settle into this new, strange life. She helped Betty with the chores around the farm and in the house. It was high summer, the busiest time of year. She spent her days weeding the garden, picking berries, making jam, and churning butter. She was thankful for the work which emptied her mind and kept her from lingering on her sadness.

In her spare moments she often took walks along the river, enjoying the wild beauty of this young country, so different from home. Sometimes she sat alone on a wide rock jutting out over the river, dreaming of the life she could have had—the home across the river they would have built; Sandy had shown her the spot. She imagined them in that little cabin, sitting by the fire or at the table, lying in the bed in the sleeping loft above. After awhile she forced herself to stop such fantasies, for they hurt too much.

Occasionally on her walks, Rupert joined her, and they would stroll together in companionable silence, or remark on the red soil, the unusual trees, the wide blue sky. It was a beautiful land, but Harriet suspected Rupert felt as she did; it was not home. Not yet, and perhaps not ever. Not without Allan in it.

Like her, Harriet saw, Rupert felt adrift, a stranger in a place where he should've been at home. How different it could've been for everyone if his older brothers had lived. Now, all of Sandy's hopes were pinned on his young son, whom he barely knew anymore. Nothing was as any of them had hoped or wanted it.

Dusk was gathering one night in midsummer as Harriet sat on the porch, listening to the now familiar mournful call of the whippoorwill. A bowl of peas she'd been shelling was at her feet, and she'd left it for a moment, to enjoy the sweet stillness of the evening, the last of the lingering warmth before a chill stole through the air, even in July.

Yet despite the tranquil beauty of the evening, Harriet felt a now-familiar restlessness. She had been at Mingarry Farm for several weeks now, and as kind as the MacDougalls' offer of hospitality was, she did not feel at home here without Allan, and she could not imagine staying in this limbo forever. Once more she was anchorless again, without a role or home of her own.

Her future in Scotland had seemed bleak, yet this was almost worse. She'd come to the new world with dreams that could no longer be realized in any fashion, and she couldn't keep from feeling she was here under false pretenses, since the MacDougalls didn't know she'd been intending to marry another. How could she stay? What was she to do?

"Make new ones, I suppose," Harriet said softly to herself. She leaned her head against the back of the rocking chairs. New dreams… if only she knew how, or even where to begin.

*

Ian perched in the tops, the warm Caribbean breeze brushing his face, and closed his eyes in perfect contentment. It seemed hard to believe that a few months ago he'd climbed to these topmost masts, his legs shaking with fear and his breakfast threatening to rise. Now he silently thanked Henry Moore for his so-called punishment, for the hours alone there had begun a transformation in him.

At first, the sheer terror of the experience had left his mind numb, unable to do anything but concentrate on not tumbling to the waves far below. Then gradually he had relaxed, and he'd begun to admire the view of endless ocean stretching in every direction, the limitless possibility they excited inside of him.

He'd also had time to think, to acknowledge honestly the many mistakes he'd made, both on the ship and before he'd boarded it.

He knew Captain Moore was giving him a second chance. Many ship masters would have turned him out in Boston, his back whipped and with little or no pay, and left him to fend for himself, alone in a strange country. Captain Moore had been kind, and instead of punishment, he'd given Ian an opportunity to better himself. Ian intended to prove to him that his trust was not misplaced.

Since then, he'd applied himself diligently to the task of surgeon's mate. William Fingal was at first meeting a taciturn man whose face seemed set in stern lines and whose approval was clearly not easily won. Ian had been cowed by him at first, but with steady work, he'd begun to impress the older man and with time, he'd come to appreciate Fingal's rare flashes of dry humor, as well as commitment to the task at hand.

Since *The Allegiance* was not a navy vessel, the job of surgeon was not always rigorous. Most merchant vessels didn't even have a surgeon on board, but Fingal was a personal friend of the captain's, and Ian got the sense there was more to the story behind his position as surgeon than he yet knew.

Between the odd broken limb, injuries from scuffles between sailors, and some bouts of typhus and influenza, there was still plenty of time for learning and discussion. Mr. Fingal seemed to take pleasure in teaching Ian from his small and precious collection of books, and Ian enjoyed learning, even more than he ever had at Tobermory, when he'd taken so much for granted.

Thinking of Tobermory—and of Achlic—brought him an old pain that still felt fresh and deep. What had happened to his family? Had they been turned out on the street, and all because of his foolish, yet costly, mistake? The thought, and the memory of his terrible foolhardiness, still could make his face burn with shame.

He'd sworn he would not return to Scotland till he could make good the money he had lost, and it was a vow he did not take lightly. Yet even as surgeon's mate, Ian knew he would never save enough to pay so much as a fraction for Achlic Farm, or any other property. The problem gnawed at him. He was nearly seventeen years old, yet with little more than pennies to his name, and no chance of bettering himself. How could he make his old wrongs right, and win back the dignity and livelihood of his family?

"What do you think to young Mr. Cameron, then?" Henry sipped his port, smiling over the rim of his glass. He and William Fingal were sharing a glass of port and a rare quiet moment in Henry's private quarters. Outside the porthole, Henry could see the Caribbean sun setting over a tranquil sea, turning the azure waters into a rainbow of flames.

"He's a good lad." William nodded briskly, his mouth twitching, which Henry knew was as close as the man usually got to smiling. If they hadn't met at Harvard, and grown as close as brothers during their years there, Henry often wondered if they would have ever become friends. William was a quiet man, but deep. It'd taken a long time to get to know him, but Henry would now trust him with his life.

"What do you think of his prospects?" he pressed.

William raised his eyebrows. "Prospects? You seem to take a keen interest in the boy. I wasn't the only person aboard ship surprised to see you keeping him on at Boston. He was useless as a ship's boy, you know. Half the sailors still don't have the time of day for him, but the others are coming round slowly. The ones who've been in sick bay, at any rate."

"It was a surprise to me, as well." Henry paused. "I've had an affection for the boy since I first met him, I confess, but it runs deeper than that."

"Oh?" William raised his eyebrows as he waited for more.

"There was a letter for me when we came into Boston," Henry admitted. "From someone... dear to me."

William's eyebrows rose higher. "A woman?" he guessed shrewdly, and Henry laughed in acknowledgement.

"Yes, a woman. A wonderful woman whom I hope to marry one day." He blew out a breath as he recalled the shocking letter he'd read from dear Margaret, explaining who Ian was. "Mr. Cameron is her relation, albeit distant, but she asked me to keep an eye on him, and I mean to do it."

"You already have, by promoting him to surgeon's mate."

"Yes, and I am very glad I did. But tell me honestly—do you think he's good at medicine?"

William shrugged. "He has a quick mind, no question. And he's always anticipating my every request. It's rare to find a mate who can hand me the herb or instrument I need before the words have left my lips." He smiled, a true smile that took Henry by surprise. "Yes, he's good at medicine. In time, perhaps, he'd make a fine doctor even, if he ever got the chance."

"Interesting." Henry swirled the liquid in his glass, lost in his thoughts.

"You've always liked the boy," William acknowledged. "Now that you know who he is, what do you plan to do for him?"

"I'm not quite sure yet." Henry smiled ruefully. "It went against my better judgment to hire him as ship's boy at all. I had a suspicion he'd be little more than useless. But…" He paused, reflecting. "There was something about him that made me think he was worth saving. An educated boy, obviously from a well-off family, out on his own? Why?" He shrugged, smiling. "And now I know who he is and where he comes from, although I haven't told him as much. Mr. Cameron wants to keep his affairs private, and I will respect that… for now."

"So what are you intending to do for the lad?"

"When we next return to Boston, I think I'll introduce Mr. Cameron to some mutual acquaintances—if you really do think he's as clever a lad as you say."

"Do you mean medical school?" William asked in surprise. "You really do feel a responsibility to him, then."

"I suppose I have, and in any case, the world could use more fine doctors like yourself."

William shook his head, smiling slightly. "Flattery, Henry, and nothing more. But yes, he is as clever as I say. I think Mr. Cameron will do very well at medical school, and he should thank the Fates or Providence, or both, for your hand in his welfare."

*

Pictou harbor sparkled in the late morning sunshine as Harriet and Rupert disembarked from the mail packet one morning in late July.

"A bit different since last time," Harriet remarked softly and Rupert nodded. The last month at Mingarry Farm had been pleasant in many ways, but also hard, as they'd both worked through their grief even as they learned to live in this new land.

When Sandy had mentioned wanting to go to the mainland for the mail and a few supplies, Harriet had leaped at the chance to do the errands herself. After several weeks at the farm, she longed for a bit of freedom, an escape from the pleasant drudgery of life of farm and kitchen duties. With Rupert acting as her chaperone—or her as his—it seemed perfectly respectable to make the short journey across by themselves.

The mercantile was busy with people trading and buying as Harriet browsed among the goods. She fingered a length of green muslin, thinking how pleasant it would be to have a new dress, and yet at the same time wondering what good a new dress would do her. Who would see her in it? Who would care?

She needed to stop thinking this way, she berated herself, not for the first time. For better or for worse, this was her life now, and wondering and wishing about the many what-ifs did her no good at all.

"Quite busy today," she commented to the shopkeeper as she handed him her list of supplies.

He nodded briskly. "A ship arrived yesterday, from Scotland. It's full of settlers heading for Selkirk, and they want to get their supplies for the trip. Isn't easy, going that far, especially come autumn."

"Selkirk? Is that a new settlement?"

"It surely is, out west. Lord Selkirk bought up land from Hudson's Bay Company for Scottish settlers. They've been there for a few years now, but as far as I can see it hasn't been an easy time. This new batch is heading out in another few days, hoping to make a go of it." The shopkeeper shook his head doubtfully. "God bless them, at any rate. Lord knows it's hard enough here."

"All Scottish settlers?" Harriet was intrigued in spite of herself. A community of people like her, new to this country, seeking their own place in this world. "And they're travelling together?"

"Yes, by boat first up the river to the bay, to York Factory. From there they can sail down the Red River to the settlement. Fort Douglas, I think it's called." The shopkeeper turned to her list. "I'll just fill this order for you, Miss."

Harriet glanced at a young woman and her husband standing next to her in the shop. They were looking around them with wide eyes, and she wondered if they were some of the newly arrived, and headed for Red River. Their conversation soon confirmed it, and even though Harriet suspected she was being inquisitive to the point of seeming forward or even rude, she approached them.

"Pardon me, are you part of the new Selkirk settlement?"

They turned to her with eager, friendly smiles. "Yes, we've just arrived. Are you joining the travelling party?"

"No… that is…" Flustered, Harriet found herself stumbling over her words. "Are others joining here in Pictou? Is it… is it possible for others to accompany the group from the ship, if… if they would like to?" She barely knew why she was asking, yet she eagerly waited for their answer.

The woman frowned in thought, but Harriet could see the man was now looking at her with some suspicion. "Naturally we'd welcome Scottish men and their families," he said. "Are you travelling with your husband, Miss?"

Harriet flushed. "No, I'm alone."

"Alone?" The man shook his head as he drew back. "I hardly think a woman alone would attempt such rough travel. Come, Emily." He drew his wife away, frowning, and Harriet's heart sank. The impossibility of her position as a single woman in the new world was heavy inside her. Where could she go on her own? What she could do but live at Mingarry Farm and help the family that would have been her in-laws?

"I have everything ready for you, Miss." The shopkeeper returned with her supplies. Harriet settled the bill, and with Rupert at her side walked out into the sunshine.

"Harriet, why did you ask about that Selkirk place?"

Harriet turned to Rupert, surprised to see him looking so distressed. "I was just curious, Rupert, nothing more."

"No, you weren't. It was more than that." He gave her a challenging, almost angry look. "You're thinking of leaving, aren't you?"

Harriet sighed, wishing the boy were not so astute. "Perhaps I was, for a brief moment, but I can see it's a foolish dream, Rupert. Madness, more like! I can hardly travel alone, unchaperoned, and without supplies or money. Besides, what would I do when I arrived, with nothing to my name, no home, no family?" Harriet shook her head, feeling more hopeless than ever. "My only choice is to stay here, with your family. I know that."

Allan had once spoken of the many opportunities of the new world, but there seemed few for a woman alone. Was she destined to spend her life with the MacDougalls, an unhappy spinster? It seemed so.

"Why don't you like it at Mingarry?" Rupert asked quietly. "I know you miss Allan, of course you do, but... don't you like us?"

"Oh, Rupert, of course I like you all." Impulsively Harriet put an arm around the younger boy's shoulders. "You are family to me, you know that. It's just…" She shrugged helplessly. "It's not really my place to be there, not without Allan. I feel a misfit." She paused and then made herself continue, "Especially since your parents don't even know that I was planning to marry another."

"That hardly matters now."

"Still…"

"You could marry someone else. Mother said one of the Dunmore lads was sweet on you."

"Rupert!" Harriet shot him an admonishing look. She'd only met the Dunmores once in her time on the island. "I know no such thing, and anyway, I'm certainly not looking to marry right now." Or ever. She doubted whether her heart could be rekindled from the ashes.

Still, she supposed Rupert had a point, in his own way. There was no real reason why she shouldn't settle on Prince Edward Island, marry and have a family and home of her own one day. Why then, she wondered, did she feel so displaced? Would the restlessness that plagued her ever go away? Would this feel like her home?

"I don't want you to go," Rupert said quietly. "So many have gone already."

Harriet gave him a smile of sympathy. She didn't want to make false promises of staying, yet she could hardly see an alternative. "It won't always be that way."

Rupert gazed up at her with a wisdom that belied his years. "Won't it?" he asked, and Harriet did not reply.

They had just turned towards the harbour when Harriet heard a woman's strident voice calling from behind them. "I say, you there! You lass, with the hair as red as carrots! Are you the young woman from the mercantile?"

Harriet turned in astonishment. Red as carrots, indeed! "Which woman do you mean?" she asked the older woman who was bustling up to them, sandy haired and business-like.

"The one asking about the Selkirk settlement. I overheard a bit, and it sounded as if you were thinking of joining the travelling party."

"I was only curious," Harriet hastened to explain. "It seems such a… an adventure." She knew her words sounded feeble, but she was disconcerted by this woman's forthright manner. When she'd asked about the Selkirk settlement, it had been little more than idle curiosity, a vague notion of something she knew would never come to pass.

"Curious, eh?" The woman gave her a very direct look. "Lord knows a woman can't travel alone, and I heard you were alone."

"If you mean I'm unmarried, that's true," Harriet replied stiffly.

"Don't get starchy with me," the woman said with a dry laugh. "I'm speaking plainly because I'm alone as well." She stuck out her hand, and after a second's startled pause Harriet shook it. "Katherine Donald. My husband died on the voyage across. Typhoid. I've got my supplies and a place in the settlement, but I can tell there are folks here who frown upon a woman travelling alone. Think she'll be trouble."

"I'm sorry for your loss," Harriet said uncertainly. She still had no idea what Katherine Donald was talking to her for.

Katherine Donald shook her head. "Never mind that. I have a proposition for you. You haven't supplies, or a place to go to, I'd warrant. I don't have a companion, that is, someone to accompany me all the way to Red River. I'll share my supplies and cabin with you if you'll agree to travel as my companion, make me respectable, as it were, although that's one thing I've always been, I can promise you!"

Harriet stared at her, her mind whirling. "You… you want me to go with you?" she asked, hardly daring to believe it. "All the way to Red River?"

Katharine Donald laughed again, although her face was serious. "You were wanting to go, weren't you? You're alone and so am I. Why shouldn't we band together?"

CHAPTER SEVENTEEN

Harriet slapped absently at a mosquito as she hung up her petticoat on the makeshift clothesline strung between two poles. It would take ages for the clothes to dry in this damp weather, she knew, but there was no help for it.

For the last week, ever since they'd arrived at York Factory, they'd been living in crowded conditions, in a veritable swamp. Although the land around Hudson's Bay was frozen for most of the year, now in early September it was surprisingly humid and hot. With diseases like typhoid and dysentery breeding, damp clothes were hardly of the greatest concern.

The last six weeks had been a blur of travel. When Katherine Donald had asked her to be her companion all the way to Red River, Harriet had been too shocked to give an answer.

"I...I need some time to think," she'd finally stammered in the face of Katherine's beady-eyed determination.

"I can give you five minutes. We're leaving tomorrow, and if you can't go, I'll have to try and find someone else. It won't be easy."

"Surely a widow travelling alone is respectable enough?" Harriet had protested, her mind whirling. "Many women have lost husbands on the sea journey, I'm sure. How can they fault you?"

"The Selkirk settlement is a close group," Katherine replied shortly. "And the journey is a difficult one. They have their reasons."

Harriet had a feeling the older woman was not telling all she needed to know, but she could hardly demand answers now, when she was little more than a stranger.

"Well?" Katherine demanded. "You were asking about going, and alone as a woman at that, weren't you?" She glanced at Rupert. "Is this your brother? Do you have ties here, is that it?"

Rupert was staring at her with wide eyes, and Harriet was dry mouthed. "He's not my brother," she said quietly, "but as close as." She put her hand on Rupert's shoulder, her heart suddenly heavy. She couldn't leave Rupert, not when he'd begged her to stay. No matter where she was, in Scotland or the new world, she had obligations. Betty and Sandy would miss her as well. She couldn't leave them all behind, and at a moment's notice, at that. "I thank you kindly for your offer, Mrs. Donald, but—"

"You should go." Rupert's voice came out croaky, and Harriet jerked around to stare at him in surprise.

"Rupert…. what are you saying?"

"Harriet, this is your chance, don't you see?" Rupert gazed at her sadly. "You're not happy here with us, so don't pretend that you are. You said it yourself, anyway. You sacrificed your own happiness once for your family. Don't do it again. Not for me, or any MacDougall."

Harriet remained silent, touched and amazed by Rupert's understanding, especially for a boy his age. The recent months had taken the last vestiges of his childhood from him, she saw afresh, with both admiration and a little sorrow.

"I'd do it, twice more, if need be," she assured him. "But Rupert… are you sure? Do you mean what you say?"

Wordlessly, he nodded.

Tears pricked her eyes. She could hardly believe she was thinking of going, and yet what compelled her to stay here, in this place where Allan wasn't? She would wither away at Mingarry Farm without him, unable to move on or start over. Perhaps this truly was what she needed to do. Her heart beat wildly at the thought. To start yet again, in a new place? To travel even further from her family back in Scotland? And yet… There really was no hope here, she realized, no hope to build a life for herself. All her dreams had turned to ashes. Ashes and dust. There would be no rekindling them.

She needed to move on, find her own place. Her own life... her own dreams—new ones. She turned to Katherine Donald. "Do you mean what you say?"

"I do."

Harriet took a deep breath. She glanced once more at Rupert, who gave her a small, encouraging nod. "All right then," she told Katherine Donald. "I'll go."

Harriet didn't like to recall Sandy and Betty's faces when she'd told them she was going. She knew that her arrival had somehow blunted the loss of Archie and Allan, and now her leaving felt like a betrayal.

"We won't ask you to stay," Sandy had said sadly. "I can see you've made up your mind already, and I'll respect that. That's one thing I've learned, even if it came too late for my own sons."

Harriet embraced them warmly. "I'll write from Fort Douglas. I don't know how long letters take, but surely there will be fur traders and merchants going east?"

"It's a wild place out there, Harriet," Betty said anxiously. "Even more wild and harsh than here, if that can be believed. I know you want to go, but do take care. You're like a daughter to us, and we couldn't bear to lose another child to this rugged land."

"I'll take care, I promise," Harriet had answered.

The ship's journey from Pictou to York Factory had been crowded and uncomfortable, although Harriet had enjoyed getting to know a few of her fellow travellers. There had been only a handful of young women, and the ones she met were all married, but still eager for friends of a similar age.

Yet, strangely, Harriet had felt as if she were far older than these girls who clung to dreams she'd already given up. Small enough dreams, of a husband and children, a cabin and small farm in this new land; yet Harriet knew the life she'd once imagined for herself was gone forever. She had no more dreams, none at all, although perhaps at Red River she'd find some again.

She discovered she liked Katherine Donald, with her frank, almost brusque way of speaking and her honest eyes. She had a kind heart, Harriet decided, although Katherine would most likely prefer that no one know it. They managed to rub along together during the journey, and Harriet had told the other woman something of her own travails, although not all of them. Still, their mutual grief—Harriet's of Allan, and Katherine's of her husband—had knit them together in a way no shared joy could.

"These cursed mosquitoes." Katherine stood before her, surveying the clothesline, her hands on her hips. "We've been here a week already, and no word about when we're to move out. I don't know what Fort Douglas will be like, but it has to be better than this."

Harriet silently agreed. York Factory was one of Hudson Bay Company's fur trading posts, and its importance in the region had helped it to grow into a strange city of sorts, with a blacksmith, mercantile, and even a church, as well as the barns for storing fur, the barracks, and the shanties and makeshift dwellings which had sprung up around the main buildings for the newly arrived settlers.

Still, it was not a settlement of any sorts, not the kind Harriet had envisioned when they'd sailed round the bay, at any rate. It was a trading post, a temporary holding place for both people and goods, and nothing more. With an additional shipload of immigrants staying at the fort, it was also crowded and unpleasant.

"There's ill feeling here," Katherine said quietly. "Have you sensed it?"

"I believe so." Harriet spoke quietly as well, for she didn't know who might be listening. The grubby voyageurs with their rough ways and strange patois, as well as the stony-faced Métis, made her uneasy. So much here was so very unfamiliar.

Indeed, York Factory housed a motley crew: English soldiers, French fur traders, Métis or half Indians, and now Scottish settlers. She supposed there was bound to be some tension between all the different groups vying for the limited food and space. "I expect the crowd and heat add to the tension," she said with a sigh, but Katherine shook her head.

"Perhaps, but I don't mean just that. Lord knows we've had enough of that since we left Scotland. No, I'm talking about something worse." She lowered her voice even more. "The fur traders, the Frenchmen and the Indians, have been rumbling about something. They're not happy with us, I can tell you that. Only this morning I saw one of them shove Mr. Ferry." David Ferry was one of the leaders of the group. "He made it out as an accident, but I daresay it wasn't."

"Are you sure?" Harriet looked at her anxiously. "Surely he wouldn't dare start a brawl, with all these soldiers around."

"Don't be naive," Katherine told her brusquely. "The traders want to start something, only I'm not sure what it is or why. You know the settlement was burned by them once before. I suppose it could happen again, God help us."

Harriet's hands rested on the damp apron she'd been hanging. A prickle of unease ran through her like a shiver. "But that was a long time ago," she said, "when the settlement had just started. Surely now that it's bigger and more fortified, they wouldn't dare. They must have come to accept that it's here to stay." Even though she'd been warned of the dangers of heading West, Harriet realized she hadn't fully believed them. She supposed she'd thought life had already given her its worst; her past tragedies had granted her some sort of invulnerability. Now she realized what a foolish notion that was.

"All the more reason to dare," Katherine said darkly. "Prosperity breeds resentment faster than these cursed mosquitoes." She slapped at one on her neck, and Harriet managed a small smile.

"Governor Semple assured us it was safe," she said, as much to herself as to Katherine. The new laws—"

"The new laws are what started this," Katherine cut her off. "Governor Semple thinks he can come down hard on these savages, and that will be the end of it. But they've shown they're made of something even tougher. I just hope we leave for Fort Douglas before long. At least there are no fur traders or Métis there, and the walls are thick and strong. Staying here, we might as well take up residence in a powder keg."

With a grimace, Katherine walked away, and Harriet returned to hanging clothes. A group of traders loitered near her, the brims of their hats pulled low over their faces, their chins covered by bushy beards.

Their clothes reeked of sweat and animal, and their expressions were surly. Harriet studiously avoided looking at them. She'd already heard warnings about some of the traders' rough behaviour, especially with women. Even if it was unfriendly hearsay, she didn't dare put it to the test.

The governor must have agreed with Katherine's assessment, for that evening an announcement was made that they would be heading for Fort Douglas in just two days. The journey would take a few weeks, in boats down the Red River.

"Finally we're to go," Moira Ferry, a young girl of eighteen who had made friends with Harriet, met with her over the washing up. "I'm tired of living like a gypsy. Father says that in Fort Douglas we'll have our own farm, and a cabin with two bedrooms and wood floors." She smiled almost dreamily, and Harriet smiled back.

"It's something to look forward to, isn't it," she agreed. She was certainly looking forward to laying her head in a more comfortable place, but beyond that she didn't know what to think or hope for. Sometimes she wondered what mad, desperate notion had compelled her out here, far from any comforts. If she'd had any inkling of how dangerous or rough the passage was, she wondered if she would have agreed to accompany Katherine Donald. And yet she could not wish herself back at Mingarry Farm, or even on Mull. Neither place held anything for her now.

"What about you?" Moira glanced at Harriet curiously. "I know you're companion to Mrs. Donald, but what about when we arrive at Fort Douglas? Will you go your separate ways?"

"We shall keep house together, for the time being." Katherine had offered Harriet space in her cabin, as long as she helped with the housekeeping and chores.

"What if you marry?" Moira asked. "You're young enough. Surely you want a husband and family of your own?"

Harriet shrugged. "I can't imagine it," she said slowly. "Not anymore."

"Can't imagine it! Why, you're daft! It's all I think about, truly." Moira smiled. "Father wanted me to marry back in Scotland, a boy from our village. But I didn't love him. I'd fancy marrying a soldier—they look so grand in their uniforms. But then, they're off fighting all the time, aren't they? I daresay I wouldn't like that." She paused, a little wrinkle appearing on her normally smooth forehead. "Not anymore, you said? Did something happen that made you think that way?"

"My betrothed died," Harriet explained quietly. She was glad she could talk about it in an even voice. "He was lost at sea."

Moira's eyes widened and her hand flew to her throat. "Oh, how tragic! But you can meet another, surely? There are so many men here, plenty of bachelors…"

Harriet couldn't help but laugh. "Thank you for the encouragement, Moira, but I'm not quite ready to look for a husband yet."

Moira's eyes sparkled with challenge and mischief. "Well, when you are…"

Harriet held up a hand. "Oh, very well!" But she couldn't imagine when that time would come.

The night air brought a cool breeze, and some relief from the humidity and mosquitoes. There was even a promise of autumn in the air, now that it was September. It was hard to believe in just two months or so, most of this would be a frozen wasteland. Harriet pulled her shawl around her shoulders. Tomorrow they would start for Red River. Tomorrow, her new life would begin… whatever it looked like.

*

Allan could feel the temperature rising among the fur traders, and it wasn't simply because of the unexpected heat wave that had hit the fort in early September. Ever since the settlers bound for Red River had arrived at York Factory, the surly grumblings among the Métis had grown louder and more threatening. Allan had been planning to leave the trading post himself over a week ago, but he found himself staying and waiting… although waiting for what, he could not say. What could he do to help the situation? The last thing he wanted was trouble.

"Still here, my friend?" Pierre's voice was amused, as he came up to Allan one sticky afternoon, although his eyes looked hard. "It's best for you to leave, perhaps."

"Why do you say that?" Allan asked.

"We don't want trouble," Pierre replied, his voice soft. "I see in your eyes that you think we do. You feel for these poor settlers, no? They are Scottish, like you. You understand their plight."

Allan shrugged defensively. "I'm on the side of justice," he said after a moment, although he knew that wasn't really an answer. If he were honest, he could see both sides of the conflict, although he empathized more with the new settlers who did not yet understand the rough ways of this world.

"Then tell me, where is the justice in this?" Pierre demanded. "The Métis have been trading pemmican for decades. There was a proclamation stating they could do so sixty years ago! And yet now your governor—"

"He's not my governor," Allan interjected.

"Fair enough. Now Governor Semple makes this law, saying no one can trade pemmican at all? Every bit of it go to your poor, pale-faced settlers, because they are too stupid to find food for themselves!"

"I know it's unjust," Allan replied steadily, "but what will fighting accomplish besides more bloodshed and violence?"

"It's Semple who wants to fight," Pierre replied. "And some of your settlers are itching for a fight as well. They want to drive us out. They're already going on missions to drive the buffalo farther away. They think that will get rid of us all, the Métis as well as the traders."

"Why are you still here, then?" Allan asked. "If there's to be no fighting, why haven't you and the other traders gone out for the fur? Leave well enough alone."

Pierre shrugged, his gaze sliding away from Allan's. "There's talk," he said evasively. "Grant says something may happen soon. I don't know what."

Allan had heard of Cuthbert Grant, a half-Métis trader and an unofficial leader of the discontented group. "Something may happen?" he repeated uneasily. "What do you mean?"

Pierre shrugged. "If we have to, we will take matters into our own hands." He gave Allan a warning look. "And that, my friend, is enough for you to know."

Allan shook his head as his unease deepened. "I pray it won't come to a fight, for the sake of the settlers, as well as yours and mine. It will do none of us any good."

Pierre's smile was cold. "Pray for them, Allan," he replied, "for the Métis are excellent marksmen."

Allan's thoughts were troubled as he shared his dinner with a few other traders. Should he go about his own business, he wondered, after what Pierre had told him? If it came to fighting, there was little he could do. He'd seen Semple, an assured and confident man who ran to swagger and bluster. Such a man wasn't likely to take advice from a ragtag trader like him, and none of the settlers would, either. He'd heard the latest group of settlers were leaving for Red River on the morrow, and he was glad, for their own sakes.

Eager to take his mind off these troublesome thoughts, Allan turned to a trader he didn't recognize, a young man with fair hair, still clean shaven. "You're new here, I think. Where do you hail from?"

"Prince Edward Island. Just arrived today," the young man replied.

"I'm from the island," Allan exclaimed. "Do you have any news from there?"

The man shook his head. "Nothing, really. Nothing good, at any rate. I signed up with the Company after my father was lost when the mail packet sank last spring."

"The mail packet?" Ships sinking were all too common, yet Allan felt a strange chill of foreboding. "Which packet? When?"

"Early April," the young trader replied. "It was the first packet out to the island that spring."

"And your father was lost?" Allan's voice was almost a whisper. "Was anyone else?"

The trader shook his head sorrowfully. "Terrible, it was. All souls lost, not one saved."

Allan grabbed the trader's arm. "Are you sure?" he asked, his voice sharp with fear. "The first packet in April? To Charlottetown?"

The man jerked his arm away, affronted. "Of course I'm sure. I told you, my own father was on that boat!"

Allan sank back, dazed. Archie was dead, lost to the sea months ago, and he'd never known.

"Did you know someone?" the man asked in a gentler tone. "You look as if it must have meant something you."

Allan nodded. When he spoke, his words came out hollow. "My brother. I left right before it sailed. I never knew." All these months, Archie had been dead, and he'd never realized. He'd picture him soldiering, cheerful as ever. All these months, his parents had been grieving… grieving, he realized with a jolt of shock, for him as well. There was no way to send letters back across this wild land, and Allan wouldn't have known what to write anyway.

As far as his parents knew, he'd been lost on that ship along with Archie.

*

Ian stared out the window at the stately houses of Beacon Hill, and shook his head slightly in disbelief at his surroundings. He could hardly believe he was here, in this elegant parlor, in one of the best houses in Boston, enjoying the very best of that city's society.

Henry Moore clapped him on the shoulder. "Have you enjoyed your stay then, Ian?"

"Have I!" Ian laughed. "You must know it's been like some kind of dream."

The Allegiance had remained in port for several weeks to be outfitted for another run to the Caribbean over the winter. During that time, Henry had offered Ian a place to stay at his parents' house. It was unexpected, for Ian hadn't realized he commanded a place in Henry's affections more than any other man on board ship, although he knew Henry had been kind in giving him the position of surgeon's mate.

Yet now he realized Henry had an almost fatherly affection for him, both tough and kind, and he was grateful for it. The last few weeks had been like pages from a fairy tale, with visits to museums and the opera, walks in the gardens, and afternoon tea in the parlor. Ian had felt like gentry, an honored guest rather than a poor farmer's son out of his depth. He'd loved every minute of it, had soaked up every new experience like sunlight after a long, dark winter.

"I've been to the ship, and it will be ready to sail in another two days," Henry said.

Ian nodded, pushing away the heaviness that news brought him. His place was on the ship, he knew that, and yet he would be sorry to leave Boston and all it had offered him. "I'll be sorry to leave, although of course it shall be good to be at work once more." He forced a smile that he didn't quite feel.

"Yes… I've been thinking about that. Why don't you sit down, Ian?"

Surprised, Ian sat in one of the wingback chairs by the fireplace, and Henry took the other across from him with a smile. "I've been talking to Mr. Fingal," he said, "and he thinks you show great promise as a medical man."

"Really?" A thrill ran through Ian at being praised. "I do enjoy it, sir."

"Mr. Fingal and I are old friends, you know," Henry said. "We were at Harvard together. Mr Fingal could have had a surgeon's position in any hospital, he was that talented." He was silent for a moment. "Then his wife died when she was very young. A carriage accident. They'd only been married a few months. It affected him very deeply… his hands began to shake."

Ian flinched, for he knew that shaky hands would be the death knell of any hopeful surgeon's career.

"I took him on as surgeon. Not many merchant ships have surgeons, as you most likely know, but I wanted to help my friend and I've seen too many ship accidents turn nasty to not want the precaution of a medical man on board. As you've seen, he can control the shaking most times." Henry sighed and ran his hands through his hair. "The reason I'm telling you this is because you can see now that Mr. Fingal isn't any old hack with a rusty blade, and if he thinks you have promise, then you must have."

Ian blushed with pleasure at the compliment. "Thank you, sir."

"And you enjoy the work, don't you? Helping him with the surgeries?"

"Yes, very much so." Ian had been surprised at how much he had. He'd wondered if he would be squeamish or timid, but he found he was neither. He might not have been able to coil a rope, but he could hold a man's leg steady.

"I thought you did." Henry paused, his gaze reflective. Ian watched him, uncertain what his employer intended with his questions, yet wanting to give the right answers. Finally Henry turned to him. "I wonder, do you think you might like to go to medical school?"

Ian stared at him, his mouth agape. This was the last thing he would have ever expected. "Would I…" he managed, and then found he could say no more. His mind was swimming.

Henry chuckled. "I can see it's never crossed your thoughts. Well, I look at it like this. You've promise, and you've no one to vouch for you at present. I know you must have family back in Scotland, and something must've happened to make you run so far and fast, but I won't pry into your affairs if you do not wish it. Mr. Fingal has offered to write you a letter of recommendation to Harvard Medical School, which I believe will give you very good credit there. Now, here is your choice. You can sail with me in two days, or you can stay here, in my parents' house, and prepare for medical school, if you're interested in pursuing that path, and of course Harvard accepts you. Clearly there will be things to work out—fees and so forth. My parents, however, have taken a liking to you, and they're perfectly agreeable to having you stay until you can find lodgings of your own."

"Stay… here?" Ian struggled to take in all that Henry was offering. He felt as if he'd just been given an entire world, a whole new life, on a plate, and he hardly knew what to do with such an offer.

"I know it's a lot to think about. There are many decisions to make, and they will affect you for some time. If you stayed on *The Allegiance*, you could be back in Tobermory by summer." He paused. "If you wish to return."

"I don't." Ian looked down at his shoes as Henry made no reply and the silence stretched on.

"Are you certain?" Henry finally asked, his tone gentle. "There must be people who care about you."

"No." Ian swallowed. "That is…" He felt guilty thinking about Harriet and the others, and how worried they had to be. "I don't think so." He glanced up and saw Henry looking at him with a compassion that made him feel as if the man knew every thought in his head.

"Very well," Henry said at last. "You have two days to think about your decision." He rose from his chair. "Now, I'm afraid I have work to do. Let me know when you've decided."

The next two days passed in a welter of confusion. Although Ian inwardly leaped at the chance to better himself, he had a strange feeling about starting such a new chapter in his life, here in America. He felt as if he would be alienating himself even more from his family, his roots… Yet, hadn't he already done that when he'd signed on as ship's boy months ago now? At least here was an opportunity to one day earn the money to buy back Achlic.

The afternoon before *The Allegiance* sailed, Ian walked slowly through the Moores' garden, his thoughts still in a ferment. As much as he longed to stay, part of him yearned to return to Mull and see his family again. Choosing this path felt as if he'd cut the final ties that had bound him to Scotland, to home.

"May I walk with you a bit?"

He looked up to see Isobel Moore, Henry's younger sister, smiling shyly at him. She was a pretty, dark-haired girl, a few years younger than he was, and she looked as fresh as a rose in her simple white dress.

"Of course, Miss Moore. I do apologize for my rudeness. My mind was elsewhere, and I didn't see you there."

Isobel smiled and ducked her head. "You did look lost in thought. Are you considering whether to stay or not? Papa says you might go to medical school here in Boston."

"Perhaps." Ian smiled awkwardly. "I'd like to, as it is such an opportunity, but I must confess I'm worried about my family back in Scotland. I… I left abruptly and it would be a long time to be away."

"You could write them, couldn't you? Henry could take it when he returns in the spring. He's going to marry, you know. He's met a Scottish girl he loves. He hasn't told Father yet, but he said as much to me. " Isobel smiled dreamily, clearly caught up in the romance of her brother's actions.

"I didn't know," Ian said, startled. Henry had certainly given no indication to him of such plans, not that they had ever spoken of such personal things.

"It would be a good opportunity for you, wouldn't it?" Isobel continued seriously. "You mustn't waste it. Henry says wasting opportunities is a worse sin than not creating them in the first place… although to be completely truthful I'm not always sure what he means."

"No," Ian agreed slowly, "I mustn't waste it." He smiled at Isobel, and then found himself blushing. She was so pretty and charming, he felt like a clumsy oaf next to her, with his rougher ways and uncertain manners. Still, he managed to find his tongue. "Thank you, Miss Moore. You've helped me, I think."

Isobel nodded, looking pleased. "I'm glad," she said simply.

*

Later that afternoon Ian told Henry his decision.

"Good." Henry nodded briskly. "I was hoping you'd stay. I've become fond of you, Ian, and I like to see you come to something more than a common sailor. You've a good head on your shoulders. With any luck, you'll gain entrance to Harvard and win a scholarship besides."

Ian swallowed nervously. Henry had mentioned fees, and then there was the question of lodgings. How much did medical school cost? He'd no idea, or where he would get the funds. His wages as surgeon's mate wouldn't go very far at all. Perhaps he could get a job in Boston, although doing what he'd no idea. Despite Henry's patronage, there had to be a thousand obstacles in his path to success, and he didn't even know what they were.

"Thank you," he said to Henry, "for giving me this opportunity. It's more than I ever dreamed of."

"I'm happy to do it." Henry shook his hand, looking as if he wanted to say something more, but then he smiled and finished, "Just make the most of it, that's all I ask."

"I will do my best, sir." Ian paused as he fumbled for the letter he'd written Harriet. "When you return to Mull, will you deliver this letter to my family?" he asked as held it out. "You were right when you asked if there were people back home who might care about me. I want them to know where I am."

"Good." Henry took the letter. "It's time you wrote them. No matter what happened back in Scotland, they'll be worried for you."

"I know," Ian agreed, even though he still wondered if his father would be angry. "It's for Harriet Campbell. I'd send it directly to Achlic, but that's gone by now. I don't know where any of them are." He smiled bleakly. "You can leave it in care of Margaret MacDougall, with the MacDougalls' shipping agent in Tobermory."

Henry nodded, and then slipped the letter into the pocket of his waistcoat. "I shall do so," he said simply.

*

The settlers had left York Factory a week ago, but the rumblings among the traders still did not cease. At times Allan could hardly blame them. He'd observed Governor Semple's from afar, and the man's attitude towards the traders was one of a patronizing parent thinking he could restrain and discipline an unruly child. It seemed less and less likely that a bloody conflict could be avoided.

"Have you heard?" Pierre's voice was grim. "Semple ordered Fort Gibraltar to be burned."

"Burned!" Allan stared at his friend in dismay. This would surely only make tempers worse, and increase the possibility of a conflict. "But why?"

Pierre shrugged. "Who knows? He thought he'd teach us a lesson, I suppose. But he hasn't heard the last of us, I can promise you that."

Anxiety churned in Allan's stomach. He didn't want a fight—not for his sake, or the traders', or the settlers'. "What are you going to do?" he asked.

"Never mind." Pierre's expression softened a little, and he laid a hand on Allan's am. "I know you are concerned, whether for yourself or others, I cannot tell, but it is best for you to stay out of this, Allan. I mean it for your own sake. I would not like to see you caught up in this and hurt, or worse."

"Thank you." Allan was grateful for the warning, but he had no intention of leaving things there. If there was any way he could help avoid the disaster he felt sure was coming for them all, then he would do it. At least it would make his life count for something more than this mere waiting through the days, which was all he'd felt since he'd received that letter from Harriet.

It didn't take long to find out what was going to happen. Cuthbert Grant was organising a party to take some pemmican to Fort Bas de la Rivière. It was an illegal act, since Semple had decreed no food leave the colony's lands. Even so, Allan suspected it was a pretext for the real agenda: a showdown with the governor, who had left York Factory for Fort Douglas. A showdown with guns and violence, since the traders believed that spoke louder than any words.

It was surprisingly easy to attach himself to Grant's party. Men were eager to fight, and all he needed was a gruff manner and a rifle. By keeping his head down and asking few questions, he found himself with a group of traders setting out for the fort, Pierre among them. Allan did his best to avoid his friend, whom he knew would be angry at seeing him there.

He wasn't even sure what he hoped to accomplish by accompanying the traders. What could one man do, after all? And in his heart, he didn't even know which side he was on. He sympathized with both, and yet he didn't want any more lives uselessly lost.

Something in him had hardened since he'd heard of Archie's death, something that made him feel both reckless and determined. There was too much hardship in this harsh land to add such useless bloodshed to it. Hadn't Archie himself vowed to risk no man's life again? Then neither would he.

If there was something—*anything*—he could do to prevent even one small part of the brewing calamity, Allan resolved, then he would do it. He only hoped when the time came he would know what it was.

They travelled for several days by canoe, skirting Fort Douglas on the way to Fort Bas de la Rivière. Allan heard from others that Grant had seized the pemmican they carried from a shipment belonging to the settlers. Even though he knew this was little more than thievery, Allan listened to the Métis at night and found he could understand their anger.

"What does the governor want?" one man demanded before spitting on the ground. "Does he think we can live on air?"

"He would starve us, happily, as would all the other settlers," another answered. "As far as they can see, it's their land now. We are but an annoyance, a fly to be swatted away, and so they make new laws to do their swatting."

"We'll see what happens to their new laws!"

Allan didn't participate in these conversations. He didn't know what he would say, or whose side he would take. The traders had been here before, it was true, but the settlers were looking for a new start. In this huge, wild land, surely there was enough space for everyone… and yet it seemed there wasn't. It was confusing, at the least, he knew, and at the worst it was very dangerous.

It was several days into the journey when Pierre caught sight of him, his face suffused with anger. "What are you doing here? You know you're not a part of this, and if you are thinking to sabotage our efforts, I would think again, my friend. Now."

"I would never do that," Allan insisted quietly. "As long as you're not planning any bloodshed."

"Who are you to make such demands? It is Semple who wants bloodshed," Pierre flashed back. "I mean it, Allan, stay out of this!" He stalked off angrily, and Allan was left with the uneasy feeling that he'd made an enemy out of his old friend. At a time like this, he surely had enough enemies already.

That evening Grant told all the men gathered the plan. "Governor Semple and his men are riding out from Fort Douglas," he announced with grim satisfaction. "We will meet tomorrow at Seven Oaks… he says he is willing to talk. We shall see whether talking is enough."

Allan barely slept that night. From his bed roll he heard low, muttering voices, and knew Grant and his closest men were discussing tomorrow's meeting at Seven Oaks, an area on the west bank of Red River distinguished by the large oak trees that spread their boughs over the water, a place for peace and beauty, not bloodshed.

He strained to make out their words, but could hear nothing beyond the ominous mutterings and rumblings, the mixture of English and French patois he didn't fully understand. He closed his eyes, wondering what tomorrow would bring and praying for safety for all… and for deliverance.

The air was cool, with a nip of frost, even though the sun shone on the hill where the meeting between Governor Semple and Grant was to take place. Allan saw that Semple and his men were huddled on one side, with Semple out front on his horse. Grant had gathered his men some yards away, also in a huddle.

Allan suppressed the sudden, wild urge to laugh. It almost looked as if they were two teams, lining up for sport, rather than this deadly game of negotiation that could end in a single bloody moment, and all over a shipment of pemmican—although, he knew, really, an entire country.

"What do you have to say for yourself, then, Semple?" Grant shouted. "Are you going to be fair, and give us what we deserve?"

"What you lot deserve," Semple replied clearly in his American twang, "is to be disciplined like the unruly children you are. I've made the law, and if you don't obey it, then the punishment will fall on your heads, and as far as I am concerned, so be it."

"The law is a punishment!" someone from Grant's side shouted. "You act like God, without any thought of justice for those who came before you."

Semple was coldly unruffled. "Be that as it may, the law stands. I know you have pemmican with you. I'll take it now, and we'll be done here."

"You will not," Grant said. Even though he had to shout, his voice sounded low and menacing. "It is ours. It has always been ours."

"It is illegal, and you know it," Semple answered, and his voice was as much of a menace.

"I don't abide by your law," Grant declared. "If it isn't changed, you and your settlers will be the ones to regret it. That I can assure you!"

"Haven't I already burned Fort Gibraltar?" Semple sounded sneeringly incredulous. "What more do you people need, to be kept in line? Shall I take you over my knee?"

This insult drew a rumble of angry protests from Grant's men that Semple ignored. There was a feeling in the air like the expectant crackle before a bolt of lightning hit, almost a sizzle that Allan could hear. He stood slightly apart from both groups, alert and ready—but for what? If it came to bloodshed, there was nothing he could do about it, and he felt a sickening certainty that he should not have come here. It had been his own desperation and restlessness that had brought him to the brink of disaster, and now there might be no way back.

He'd stopped listening to Semple and Grant's exchange, for other men were shouting as well, and no voice could be made out. Then, tensing, Allan saw the glint of sunlight on silver, the metal of a rifle. He realized with an icy horror that although this meeting had been meant to be peaceful, both sides were armed and willing to shoot—and that is exactly what they were going to do. He felt as if he were stuck in mud, unable to move or even think fast enough. He needed to stop someone from firing, but before he'd even had time to frame that thought, the sound of a rifle's shot echoed through the still air, and Semple fell from his horse.

CHAPTER EIGHTEEN

"Governor Semple's gone out to meet with the traders," Katherine told Harriet as she came into the cabin they shared at Fort Douglas. She took off her bonnet and laid her basket on the table. "People seem to think he'll deal with them quickly, but Lord knows they've burned the fort before. They might do it again, and then heaven help us both, two women alone, with no men to defend us."

"Surely not." A tremor of fear went through Harriet at the thought. How had she arrived at such a place? She'd had no true idea of the dangers they'd faced when she'd agreed to accompany Katherine to Red River. Now she couldn't help but wish to be back at Mingarry Farm, or even on Mull—anywhere but here.

She looked around at the crude cabin she and Katherine had inhabited since arriving at Fort Douglas a few days ago. When they had time and resources, they would build their own, as others had, more prosperous looking places, although nothing near to what Mingarry Farm was. For now they would spend the winter in this, which was cruder than the humblest croft back on Mull, one windowless room eight feet by ten with a hole in the roof for a chimney, rough log walls, and a dirt floor.

Still, the threat of its destruction and all that would mean chilled her to her core. She didn't want to be thrown out of another home, and this time she feared it would be far more ungentle. Perhaps the Métis would be violent, abusive, especially towards two women on their own. According to all she'd heard, they had been so before.

"There's no point pretending it won't happen," Katherine said brusquely, her lined face drawn with worry despite her tone of bravado. "I've seen it before, just in a different time and place. Different people, but it's all the same." Harriet knew she was talking about the clearances, and yet she feared this might be far worse.

"What should we do?" she asked, her voice wavering from the enormity of it all.

"Nothing, for now, I suppose. What can we do, but listen and wait? There's nowhere to go, and the fort is the safest place. When Governor Semple returns, perhaps then we'll know more. Perhaps we'll be safe." Katherine shook her head. "I don't know. Perhaps I'm worrying over nothing. It gets to me, this. It's so like before. I feel so helpless."

Harriet put her arms around the older woman as for the first time Katherine's courage faltered. "This is a new world, with new opportunities. Surely Governor Semple will deal with these revels, and if he doesn't, there are enough of us to fight back. It's not one poor crofter and his family against a laird, Katherine. Not this time."

Katherine drew a shuddering breath. "It might as well as be. If they burn the fort? What then?"

"We'll rebuild it," Harriet said, with more conviction than she felt. "The settlers here did it before, didn't they? Why not again? And we're not alone. We might be two women, but there are many other settlers here, good people who are willing to fight for what's theirs."

Katherine shook her head. "That may be, but I don't know if I have it in me, to start again. It took all my strength to make it this far, and then to lose Brian, only a week from landing…"

For the first time, Harriet saw beneath the strong lines of Katherine's face, to the worry and fatigue beneath. "Let me make you a cup of tea," she said. Tea, brought all the way from Pictou, was precious, yet now seemed as good a time as any to indulge in the small luxury. Who knew when they would be able to again?

She filled the kettle from the water pail and hung it over the fire. "You mustn't worry about what might happen, not yet. Wait until Governor Semple returns. This might be a tempest in a teapot, and nothing more."

But Governor Semple did not return. As dusk fell, a messenger, exhausted and grim, rode into the fort with news of the meeting at Seven Oaks.

"It was a massacre," he told the anxious settlers who had gathered at the entrance to the fort. "I saw it, I was there. The Métis fired on Governor Semple and his men… they're all dead except for me and one other."

The settlers who had crowded around the man gasped with fear and some women fell to crying, holding their aprons to their faces in their dismay. Harriet clutched her shawl tighter around her, a chill spreading within her that had nothing to do with the frosty air. She had not expected it to be as terrible as this. What now, she wondered dazedly, with the governor himself dead? What would become of them all?

"Worse than that," the man continued, still trying to catch his breath from the harrowing ride. "The Métis are on their way here, and they're angry. We'll have to leave the fort, and as quickly as we can. I don't know what they plan to do, or if the fort will be burned. But now that the governor is dead, and the scent of blood is in the air, I warrant anything can happen."

Harriet caught her breath and exchanged panicked glances with Katherine. The older woman's face was gray with fear.

"Flee now," the man urged. "Take what you can, but leave the rest. You must leave this place, for your own safety."

"Come." Harriet put her arm around Katherine as she guided her back to their cabin. They would have to pack provisions for the trip. She didn't even know where they would go, or how, but she could see Katherine was not capable of making plans or decisions. She looked terrified. This last blow, after so many others, had been too much for her, and she let Harriet lead her as if she were a frightened child.

Katherine sat huddled by the fire and watched as Harriet gathered their warmest clothes and what little food they'd managed to gather. "You know," she said softly, "when Brian died, some people were worried that I would be a drag on the settlement, an aging widow. They argued it was too harsh a land to take women, older women at that, without men to care for them. Perhaps they were right."

"Nonsense," Harriet said with a briskness she didn't remotely feel. "You're worth two of many of the people here, Katherine. You work harder than any other woman in this place, and many of the men. Now I've gathered what we'll need… for however long we're gone." Harriet swallowed the fear that threatened to rise and choke her. How long would they be gone, she wondered, and would there be anything to come back to? Was there even anything to *go* to? The colony was built on a huge, empty plain, and Harriet knew the next settlement was over fifteen miles away, an endless distance in the darkness and cold. "Come now," she said, with what she hoped was a smile. "We must make haste."

"I can't…"

"You can," Harriet said firmly. And then, more bleakly, "You must."

Many of the settlers had already gathered by the gates of the fort by the time she and Katherine arrived, armed only with blankets and baskets, the few horses they had pawing the ground as if they could smell the fear. Everyone looked silent and pale-faced under the light of a harvest moon, and the stars glittered coldly in an ebony sky as they all left the fort, led by Mr. Ferry. They were heading to the utter unknown—the next settlement? Farther? Harriet didn't know, but she prayed it would be to safety.

The worst had come to pass, she knew, and they stood to lose everything—even their lives.

No one spoke as they started out into the black night, but the fear was palpable, a crackling in the air as if before a storm. All around them the plains grass rustled in a dry, chill wind, and Harriet followed the lantern of the people in front of her, no more than a bobbing light in a sea of black. She kept her arm around Katherine, urging her forward, but after less than an hour of walking she knew the older woman was already flagging. The lantern ahead of them was growing smaller as they slowly but surely fell behind the other settlers.

"I can't go any further," Katherine gasped at last, and Harriet's breath caught in her throat as the older woman stumbled to her knees.

"You can, Katherine," she urged, desperation edging her voice as she tried to raise her to her feet once more. "You must. We can't stay here, out in the open!"

"It's too far…"

Harriet didn't know how far they'd travelled, but it couldn't be much more than a mile. It was still fourteen miles at least to the nearest settlement. It *was* too far.

"Please, Katherine," she said, her voice a terrified croak. "We can't stay here." Harriet had to force herself not to think of the terror coming up behind them. Was the messenger from Seven Oaks right, and the traders were now violent, ready for an even greater victory? Harriet didn't know. All she knew was they had to keep going, one foot in front of the other.

Katherine was still on her knees, her breathing labored, her voice choked. "I'm too tired. You'll have to go on without me."

"And leave you here? Nonsense. You can lean on me, Katherine. I'll help you. Come, now." She struggled to raise Katherine to her feet, as the voices of the settlers ahead of them began to grow fainter and panic iced Harriet's insides. They couldn't be just left here, to fend for themselves. It was unthinkable.

Fear roughened her voice as she half-dragged Katherine along. "We need to catch up with the others, Katherine, otherwise we'll be lost out here on the plain. I don't know the way to go by myself."

Ahead she could see the swinging pinpoint of light that was someone's lantern, and it was getting smaller by the second. "Come on!" Harriet nearly shouted, but any further rebuke died on her lips as she saw Katherine's gray face and heard her ragged breathing. The older woman was not just fatigued; she was ill, seriously so.

Katherine sagged back on the ground, her eyes closing, her face beaded with sweat.

"God help us," Harriet whispered. She dropped her basket and kneeled by Katherine, cradling her head. "Perhaps if we rest for a few minutes…" she said, although she knew inside that a few minutes wouldn't do Katherine much good. There was no point going on. She would never make it. And yet if they stared here, they would surely die—either from those coming up behind them, or the cold, or the wild animals. A cry escaped her and Harriet pressed her fists to her lips.

Katherine had fallen into unconsciousness, and Harriet had no idea what to do. The air was sharp with cold, and she watched with a strange sense of detachment as the last pinpoint of light faded to nothing. They'd been left behind, as simple as that. Left in the cold and the dark, in a foreign land, with who knew what on their trail.

Harriet took a deep breath to steady herself. Fear helped nothing. And, she resolved, she would not lie down and die here, not without a fight. After all she'd been through to come to this country, to find Allan, and now to start a new life… she wasn't willing to give up yet. She'd had too many dreams broken to allow fate to cruelly snatch her last few faded hopes, tattered as they were.

"Stay here," she whispered to Katherine, although the older woman was not likely to go anywhere in her condition. Harriet took off her shawl and laid it over Katherine, bundling some extra clothes for a pillow for her head. "I'm going to look around and see if there's any shelter. I'll be back soon, I promise."

The moon was a medallion of silver in the night sky, and Harriet was grateful for the light it provided, bathing the prairie in an eerie, ghostly light.

There wasn't much to see in the flat prairie besides endless grass, and Harriet wondered what they could possibly do for shelter. Hide in the tall grasses? It would be little protection against the cold, or other, far worse possibilities.

She squinted her eyes and saw the land roll gently downwards in a hill some yards away, and a sudden, fierce hope lit her soul. It might be nothing, but at least it was a change from the endless flatness. She hurried towards the hill, hope buoying inside her like a sail. *Please...*

"Thanks be!" There, huddled in a dried creek bottom, was an old trapper's cabin, now half-falling down, its door nearly off its hinges, but at least with a passable roof and walls.

Picking up her skirts, Harriet hurried back to Katherine, half-stumbling in her haste.

Katherine was still half-unconscious on the ground when Harriet returned. Gently Harriet touched her fingertips to the woman's cheek. Her face was cold, but there was a pulse, and Harriet could still hear her labored breathing.

"Katherine, can you hear me? I've found a place. If we can just make it a little while longer, we'll at least have somewhere to shelter."

Katherine stirred, and her eyes opened. "What... what did you say?"

"Can you walk for just a little bit, if I help?" Harriet asked, her tone urgent. "There's a trapper's cabin down the hill from here. It's not much, but at least it's shelter for the night. Perhaps tomorrow..." She trailed off, not wanting to think of tomorrow, or the troubles it would surely bring. Where would they find food?

How would they get to the fort, or even back to Fort Douglas, if there was anything left? The future seemed full of insurmountable obstacles, with so very little hope.

Katherine struggled to a half sitting position, a faint, familiar determination, like an echo of the woman she'd been, hardening her features. "I can do it."

The short walk was a blur, with the cold and the darkness, and Katherine's weight sagging against her own. Finally, they stumbled into the crude, one room dwelling. It smelled musty and old, but at least it provided some escape from the cold wind, and, please God, the dangers of the men on their trail.

Harriet positioned Katherine as comfortably as possible against the far wall. "I'd make you some tea, but I'm afraid to light a fire," she confessed. "The smoke will show anyone where we are."

"Never mind." Katherine smiled weakly. "You're good to me, to keep me like this. You could've left me, gone off with the others to safety. I wouldn't have blamed you."

"Never," Harriet exclaimed, horrified. "You were the one who made it possible for me to come west. I'd hardly abandon you now."

"And was it such a good idea, for you to come with me?" Katherine coughed, her shoulders racked by the movement. "We've had nothing but trouble it seems since we started. And who knows what has happened back at the settlement… there may be nothing left for us to return to."

"Let's not think of that. Besides, I don't regret coming with you, Katherine." Harriet gazed into the darkness, thinking of Sandy and Betty, of Rupert, back on Prince Edward Island, and then of her own father and sister and Margaret on Mull. She didn't even know where Ian was. She'd left so many people behind. Where did her future lie? "There was nothing for me back east," she said quietly.

"What about a young man?" Katherine's faint smile gleamed in the darkness. "You're a pretty lass. I'm sure the young gentlemen wanted to call on you."

Harriet shook her head. "There was one," she admitted, "but I betrayed him… and he died."

Katherine did not reply, but her hand found Harriet's in the darkness and clasped it. Harriet realized she was crying. She could feel the cold tears slip silently down her face. She held Katherine's hand, grateful for the comfort, and wondered what she was crying for—the past, or the future. One felt as equally tragic as the other.

The hours passed slowly. Katherine drifted in and out of unconsciousness. Harriet sat next to her on the dirt floor, cold and aching. She dozed, haunted by dreams of fire and gun shots, only to wake suddenly, tired and cramped. The night felt endless; outside it was silent, save for the sound of the wind in the grass. The first pale light of dawn was stealing across the earthen floor when Harriet heard a rustling from outside.

She tensed, waiting, her heart starting to thud with heavy, frightened beats. Surely it was just an animal, a deer or at worst, a bear. If it were the traders, they would be louder. They would say something…

Then she heard labored breathing, the tearing gasp of someone who had been running for a long while. Katherine stirred, and then her eyes opened suddenly, alert and watchful as the two women stared at each other in silent terror.

"The gun," Katherine said, her voice barely more than a breath. She gestured to the basket Harriet had left by the door. She'd forgotten that Katherine had brought her husband's old rifle. Now she crawled across the floor to it. "Do you know how to use it?" Katherine asked.

Harriet shook her head.

"Still, it's something."

The gasping had subsided, but Harriet knew there was someone outside the door, most likely leaning against it, catching his breath. A man, alone, but was he a settler or a trapper, friend or foe? What would he do when he saw them, for surely he planned to come inside and find shelter for himself?

With shaking hands she fumbled for the rifle. The sound, she feared, was audible, as was her own terrified breathing. The man was moving now, standing probably, having heard her. Then the door creaked open.

Everything in her trembled as Harriet stood and aimed the rifle at the door. She didn't think she could fire it, and she certainly couldn't load it again, and the kick might fell her, but God willing the stranger wouldn't know any of that.

The door opened, and a man stood there, limping slightly. His fur cap and bushy beard told her he was a fur trader, and he stank of animal and sweat and blood.

Harriet's voice came out strong as she kept the rifle aimed at his head. "Don't move," she said, the words ringing out. "Don't move, or I swear to you, I'll shoot."

CHAPTER NINETEEN

The man stared at her, his face barely visible from beneath his hat and behind his bushy beard. He had a rifle, but it was slack in his hand as he froze where he stood, his eyes on Harriet.

"I will shoot," she warned him, her voice starting to quaver. "Don't think I won't." Her hands shook, and the rifle pointed briefly to the floor.

In one quick, fluid movement the trapper lunged forward and grabbed the rifle's muzzle. Harriet's finger fell from the trigger and for a few terrible seconds they struggled with the weapon, their eyes locked. Desperately Harriet tried to wrench the gun away and she fell to the floor, the man falling heavily on top of her. She let out a cry as he yanked the gun from her slack hands and tossed it across the room.

"Please…" she whispered, her eyes shut. She could feel his body pressed against her and she trembled. "We're two women alone. Please, for the love of God, have mercy."

Her eyes were still squeezed shut, the man still lying on top of her, when he suddenly tensed, and Harriet dared to open her eyes. She could barely see him in the dawn's half-light, but he was staring at her hard, and she felt an odd tremor of… what? It was a strange stirring of hope, of joy even, and she did not understand it.

"*Harriet…?*"

She opened her mouth but in her shock she could make no sound.

The man's gaze roved over her hungrily. "I can't believe…
how do you come to be here?" He cradled her face in his rough
hands and Harriet let out a breathy scream of terror. "Where's
your husband?" he demanded. "Why are you here?"

"I don't have a husband," she said in a choked whisper.

"Andrew Reid? What about him? You wrote me you'd married
him!" He let go of her, pushing away as Harriet scrambled to her
feet. "Where is he? *Why are you here*?"

Harriet stared at him in disbelief as shocked realization finally
penetrated her dazed and terrified senses. Hesitantly, wonderingly,
she stepped forward and touched his beard and then his cheek.
She took off his fur cap and let it fall to the floor. The hazel
eyes were the same, the face, underneath the beard, so achingly
familiar, and yet…

"I can't believe… Allan?" she whispered, tears slipping down
her cheeks. "*Allan*. They told me you were dead. You died in the
sinking of the packet, with Archie. They *told* me."

"I didn't get on the mail packet." Allan's voice was ragged as
he clasped her hand, pressing it to his roughened cheek. "I told
Archie to tell the parents I wasn't coming back…. I was going
away, to make my own fortune. I joined Hudson's Bay Company
as a fur trader. I didn't even know the packet had sunk, till I came
to York Factory." He turned on her suddenly. "Did you marry
him? Why? Why did you never write me?"

Harriet shook her head slowly. "I never loved him. I had to
do it, to save Achlic after it was lost. It seemed like there was
no choice, after Ian lost it all. But in the end, I couldn't go
through with it. Not when I still loved you." Her voice broke.
"He kept your letters from me. I thought you hadn't written. I
never knew…"

"You never received my letters?" Allan's voice was hoarse with
pain and disbelief.

Harriet shook her head. "Not till later, and then I broke the betrothal. I thought you'd forgotten me, Allan... I convinced myself that you'd be glad to be released from your promise. I'm sorry."

"Why?" Allan asked, and there was so much yearning and regret in his voice, the same that Harriet felt herself. "I told you I would keep faith. I promised, Harriet."

"I know... I know!" Her voice broke into jagged splinters of pain. "It is I who broke faith, and it has tormented me ever since. I travelled across the sea with Rupert, hoping you could find it in you to forgive me."

Allan cupped her face in his hands. They were rough and dirty and so beloved. "I set you free, don't you remember? I gave you back your lines. You were not faithless, Harriet. If anything, I was, for being so angry with you when I learned of your betrothal. I knew you had the right, but I never wished you to take it."

"Nor did I," Harriet whispered. "I am sorry—"

"No, you must not be. Why did you come all this way, to Fort Douglas? Are you part of the Red River settlement?"

"Yes, with Katherine Donald, after I thought you'd died. I didn't know where else to go, what to do. There was nothing for me at Mingarry Farm, without you there." She nodded towards the older woman, who was still slumped against the wall. "She needs help, Allan. I fear for her..."

"We will get help." He stroked her cheek. "I cannot believe you are here, you're *real*. To find you, after all this time... it is a miracle, truly."

"I know." Harriet shook her head wonderingly. "Providence has brought us together, after all this time. But how did you come to be here? Why didn't you go on that mail packet, Allan?"

"The same as you, I suppose. There was nothing for me back home, without you. I was angry, and I had been blaming everyone for my misfortune... everyone but myself. And so I kept running."

"I don't want either of us to run anymore," Harriet whispered and Allan pulled her toward him. She came gladly, reveling in the feel of his arms around her at last.

"Nor I." He looked down at her seriously. "Harriet, do you still love me?"

She nodded, her throat too tight with tears to speak.

Allan pressed his cheek against hers, his tears mingling with her own. "*Cridhe*, I've never stopped loving you. You've been in my mind, my heart, always."

From behind them Katherine stirred and let out a dry, rasping chuckle. "My goodness, but this is a change of plan."

Harriet laughed through her tears. "Katherine, you would not believe… this man, this stranger, he's Allan, my…"

"Betrothed," Allan finished firmly. "I have always been your betrothed. We will marry as soon as possible."

"This is the man you were talking about, then." Katherine let out an incredulous laugh. "How you came to be here I surely don't know, or how we'll get out." She glanced at Allan in both hope and uncertainty. "You're a trader. Were you with the Métis at Seven Oaks?"

"I was, in the vain hope that I could prevent such a disaster."

"What will happen to us?" Harriet asked. "Are they burning Fort Douglas?"

"The Métis will take Fort Douglas," Allan confirmed. "But they don't wish for blood, only justice." He sighed as he gathered Harriet more closely to him. "Eventually, those who rule will have to find some way for the Métis and the settlers to live together peaceably. I can see no other way. As for us…" He looked into Harriet's eyes. "I must return to the island, and my parents. They believe me dead, and I cannot allow them to think such a thing. Will you come with me, Harriet? Are you settled here? Can you come with me and make a life back east, at Mingarry Farm?"

Harriet glanced at Katherine. "Of course I can, I should want nothing more. But… I have obligations here."

Allan nodded in understanding. "Your companion is naturally welcome to travel and stay with us, of course." He turned to Katherine with a nod of thanks. "Harriet has made her home with you, you must make your home with us… if you desire it."

Katherine let out another laugh. "Not much of a home, as it happened. Yes, I'll come with you, if you'll have me. Since my husband died, there's been no place for me here. And I'm looking forward to hearing the story of how you two know each other, and came to be in this forsaken place!"

"It's quite a tale," Allan replied soberly. "However, first we must find our way to safety. The Métis have taken Fort Douglas, as I said, but I don't believe they will continue to be violent. I think they will let us stay there, especially as we have injured. When you're recovered enough, we can make our way back to York Factory, and from there to Pictou. It won't be an easy journey and with winter closing in, we'll have to spend the cold months holed up, probably at York. Will you be able to manage?"

Harriet nodded. She knew it would be hard, perhaps even harder than she could imagine now, and yet for the first time in many months the future held a joy she'd thought forever lost. Whatever hardships she endured, she rejoiced in knowing she would share them with Allan.

*

It was a cold, bleak day when Henry Moore sailed *The Allegiance* into Tobermory's harbor, but his heart was singing with both hope and joy. He'd spent the winter hauling freight in the Caribbean, for a handsome profit, and now as spring touched the earth he was finally returning to the home of his ancestors, and to Margaret. He could hardly wait to see her. He only hoped that she would welcome him as she'd promised, and that they'd be married within the month. The letters he'd received in Boston before making the journey across gave him reason to have such hope.

His first stop was the shipping agent's office at the harbor side. After he'd explained who he was, the agent's clerk nodded and smiled.

"Yes, Mistress MacDougall mentioned back in the autumn that there might be some sort of inquiry into her whereabouts. I trust this is a happy occasion?"

Henry could not contain his broad smile. "Yes, indeed. God willing, we shall be married as soon as possible."

"Then I offer my felicitations along with this letter."

Henry took it, his heart thumping. He waited till he was seated in a public house, waiting for his dinner to be served, before he opened it.

> *Dearest Henry, If you are reading this you have landed safely in Tobermory, and I thank God for your health.*

Henry put the letter down as his meal was served. "Thank you," he murmured, his voice choked with emotion. And thank God that he was safe, and that Margaret still loved him. All would be well. He turned back to the letter.

> *I am currently lodging at the MacCready farm, near Craignure. My dearest friend and kinswoman Harriet Campbell has emigrated to Canada, and I am staying with her father, and his new wife. His young daughter, Eleanor, enjoys a few lessons from me as well, which helps to pass the time as I wait for you. I look forward to your return, when we can be together again—and for always, God willing. Yours, Margaret.*

Smiling softly, Henry folded the letter and laid it by his plate. As soon as he finished his meal, he would leave for Craignure, and find Margaret.

A young girl stood outside the small farmhouse, feeding chickens. With the sunlight on her auburn hair, she looked, Henry thought, like a pastoral painting. He smiled at her.

"Hello, little miss. Is this the Campbell holding?"

"Aye, David Campbell is my father." She was about thirteen years old, still slender and girlish, with freckles across her nose. "Are you looking for him?"

"No, I'm looking for Mistress Margaret MacDougall. You must be Eleanor."

Eleanor stared at him curiously. "How do you know my name?"

"I know Margaret."

"Eleanor, are you talking to someone…?" Margaret came to stand in the doorway, a flush rising to her cheeks as she caught sight of Henry. She looked as beautiful as ever, he thought, with her rosy cheeks, black eyes, and a mass of dark hair caught loosely in a bun. She wore a plain, homespun dress, and there was flour on her apron. He loved her utterly.

He took a step towards her, holding out his hands. "Margaret."

She placed one hand at her throat, looking dazed. "You've come back."

"Didn't you trust that I would?"

Margaret walked slowly towards him, her expression dazed, as if she were in a dream. Perhaps they both were. "I knew you wanted to, but I was afraid. We've learned all too well how dangerous the sea can be."

"I'm safe."

Margaret stood in front of him, and it felt the most natural thing to put his arms around her. She pressed her face against his shoulder as a shudder went through her.

"I've been so worried, all this time, never knowing how you fared. How will I live as a sailing master's wife?" she cried, then gasped, flushing. "That is... I didn't mean to be so presumptuous!"

"You weren't." Henry couldn't help but laugh out loud. How he loved his fiery, feisty Margaret. "But for formality's sake, I will ask you now myself. Margaret MacDougall, will you be my wife? I love you to distraction and I wish to marry you without delay."

"Yes, I will!"

"What is all this carrying on?" An elderly man with white hair and a cane appeared in the doorway—David Campbell, Henry imagined. "I knew Margaret had a young man who wanted to come courting—"

"A betrothed now, sir, with your permission."

"It isn't mine to give," David replied. "The MacDougalls are in Canada now, God bless them. It hasn't been an easy time."

"Father wrote in the autumn with his permission," Margaret explained quickly. "I'll show you the letter."

"Then we can travel to Prince Edward Island after our wedding." Henry grinned broadly. "And you can introduce me to your family."

"And I to yours." As sunlight filtered through the trees, lighting their faces, Henry took Margaret in his arms once more. As he released her, he caught Eleanor wistfully watching them. "I can tell the gentlemen will be lining up to court you, Miss Eleanor, in another three years or so," he said, chucking her under the chin.

Eleanor blushed and looked away. Henry turned back to Margaret.

"We are finally together, my love," he said softly, and she nodded, tears of joy sparkling in her eyes.

"Yes," she murmured as she put her arms around him again. "At last."

*

It was late summer, and the leaves were barely touched with the red of frost. Harriet and Allan stood by the clearing, gazing down at the foundation of their small cabin, across the river from Mingarry Farm.

"It'll be a year yet before it's finished," Allan said ruefully, "what with autumn and winter closing in."

Harriet smiled at him and reached for his hand. "I don't mind."

It had been a long, hard year, with many challenges as well as joys. After they'd found each other in the old trapper's cabin, Allan had guided them back to Fort Douglas. Harriet had been afraid of violence, as the Métis had taken the fort, but after the battle of Seven Oaks, everyone seemed to want peace, even the traders. When the chaos had finally died down, they'd booked passage on a boat to take them to York Factory.

As Allan had predicted, they'd had winter at the trading post. Harriet had never been so cold. York Factory was embedded in ice and snow for months on end, and it wasn't until May that they were able to find passage on a ship returning to Pictou.

Harriet would never forget their homecoming. The island was awash in cherry blossoms as they made their way from the river landing to Mingarry Farm. Betty was sitting on the porch when they came up the road, and she half rose from her chair, her face paling, as they rounded the bend.

"Sandy… *Sandy*!" she gasped, and Allan hurried towards her, half afraid she'd fall in her shock.

"It's me, Mother," he said softly, his arms around her. "It really is. I'm alive."

"But how? How did you survive? They said everyone drowned." Tears ran silently down Betty's face. "Where have you been all this time? And Archie…?"

"Archie was on the mail packet," Allan told her as he embraced her. "I never boarded the boat."

"But how…"

Sandy, hearing Betty's cry, came hurrying from the barn, along with Rupert. His face mirrored his wife's own shock.

Quickly and quietly, Allan had explained all the events that had led to them being there, while Sandy and Betty listened, open mouthed and incredulous, yet so grateful to have at least one of their sons back. He also introduced Katherine Donald, and she was welcomed warmly by both Sandy and Betty, and invited to stay for as long as she could.

Harriet had learned news of her family as well—Ian in Boston, studying to become a surgeon and under Captain Moore's care, who himself was soon to be wed to Margaret. Her father and Jane, along with Eleanor, were still all back in Craignure, safe and well.

"It's a miracle," Betty had said, shaking her head, her tears still flowing unchecked. "To live, and to find each other again. Harriet, Allan, you've both been granted a second chance, by the grace of God. You must take it with both hands, and with joy."

And Harriet knew they would.

*

That summer, the wreck of the mail packet was found, and Archie's body recovered and buried. Allan often visited and stared down at the grave, placed on the edge of Mingarry Farm, near a copse of birches. He remembered Archie's vitality and enthusiasm, his desire for safety after their near miss on the ice floes, and the cruel trick of fate which had caused his death. He mourned the brother he had loved and lost.

"It doesn't seem fair that he should die and I should live," he had told Harriet once as he held her hand. "But after all this, I've learned not to question God. Archie was reckless, and sometimes arrogant, but he was brave and honorable as well, and I loved him."

In June Harriet and Allan married at Mingarry Farm, sur-rounded by family and new friends. A wedding was an occasion for everyone to celebrate, and the entire Scots community on the Platte River had come together.

"I never thought I'd see this day," Sandy had confessed to Allan during a break in the dancing. They stood on the far side of the barn, the river sparkling in the distance, the day a gift.

"Nor did I." Allan smiled back. Any ill will he'd borne his father had vanished when he'd learned of the ship's sinking. He would not ruin any second chances with futile bitterness.

"You and Harriet wed, and Rupert here by my side. And Margaret in Boston, wed to an American!" He shook his head ruefully before his expression turned serious. "I've wanted to tell you, I've been wrong," Sandy said. "I was stubborn, and set in my own ways, and in the end, it drove both you and Archie away from me, and from the farm here. I will always regret that."

"You can't blame yourself for the way we were," Allan told him. "We were both young and proud and as stubborn as you. I should have spoken my mind earlier. I should have done so many things differently."

Sandy's face creased into a wry smile. "We can all say that, I suppose. It's as Betty said, we've been given second chances. All of us." He nodded his head towards the crowd of guests making merry. "I had it stuck in my thick head that I was better than all of those good folk, and I can tell you true now that I'm not. Every one of those men and women has helped us in some way, even with me and my foolish pride. I'd do the same for them now. I've learned my lesson—one of them, anyway."

The music had struck up again and Sandy clapped Allan on the shoulder. "I haven't danced with your lovely bride yet. It's a pleasure I'm greatly looking forward to."

*

And now here they were, looking at the foundations of their very own cabin. Their hope for the future was brighter than ever, and with a little life stirring inside her own womb. Harriet lay a hand on her middle, smiling at the thought of it.

"A year ago, I'd never have imagined this," she said with a soft sigh of happiness. "I thought it all lost to me, forever."

"And I thought you lost to me," Allan said. He touched her cheek gently. "I am the most fortunate man, to have his bride restored." He paused, his face grave. "Perhaps I shouldn't have asked you to wait for me, Harriet. It was wrong of me, but I couldn't help it, I loved you so much. Releasing you from the promise afterwards was no great freedom, was it? It would have been better not to have asked at all."

"No, it wouldn't have," Harriet replied simply. "You'd never even have needed to ask, Allan, for I was yours always." She turned to look once more at the beginnings of their own cabin, the foundation of their life together.

The last few years had been hard, more trying and frightening than anything she could've imagined when Allan had first sailed away. If she'd known all that had been in store, she would have trembled with terror. Yet somehow, she had weathered the storms, and so had Allan. It was as Betty had said, a miracle. A second chance at life, at love, and she was so very grateful for it.

The sun was setting, a glittering gold ball low in the sky. Around them the leaves rustled and a whippoorwill trilled its twilight song. In the violet stillness, Harriet felt all was at peace with the world.

"Come," Allan said, tugging gently at her hand, love shining from his eyes as he turned towards Mingarry Farm. "Let's go home."

A LETTER FROM KATE

I want to say a huge thank you for choosing to read *The Heart Goes On*. If you did enjoy it, and want to keep up to date with all my latest releases, just sign up at the following link. Your email address will never be shared and you can unsubscribe at any time.

www.bookouture.com/kate-hewitt

The Heart Goes On has a long history, as I wrote the first version of it many years ago, as a magazine serial. It is based on the travels—and travails—of my own ancestors, but much of it is, of course, fiction. However, the premise of the story is true: in 1819, on the eve of his sailing to Canada, my great-great-great-uncle Allan MacDougall asked Harriet Campbell to wait for him. His father considered this dishonorable and made him return her letters, but Allan told Harriet she could keep his own, as a sign of his own faithfulness.

The MacDougalls were distantly related to Sir James Riddell (known in history as a bit of a blackguard), and Alexander Mac-Dougall did live at Mingarry Castle and act as Riddell's tacksman, a position he resented.

Archie MacDougall had a Commission in the Army, and he did drown in the sinking of a mail packet, which he insisted on taking rather than a smaller boat because of the rough weather. Margaret MacDougall, my own great-great-great grandmother, was known to be feisty and educated, and married a sea captain named Henry Moore.

Most poignantly, perhaps, the letters between Allan and Harriet featured in *The Heart Goes On* are taken word for word from the originals which have been handed down through my family, except for the one in which Harriet breaks off their understanding and those she discovers in Andrew Reid's keeping. Allan did experience a long silence from Harriet, and it was my own imagining of why that would be, that started this story.

The rest, however, including Riddell's scheming, the characters and exploits of Rupert, Eleanor, and Ian, and Allan's adventures as a fur trader are, alas, all fiction.

The events at Red River and the Seven Oaks Massacre in what is modern-day Manitoba are based in fact, and the settlers did have to flee into the night as described. However, my ancestors never made it as far as Manitoba!

In reality, it took Allan seven years to return to Harriet and finally marry her before bringing her back to Prince Edward Island. I took pity on him, and her, and allowed them to reunite after only two years.

I hope you loved *The Heart Goes On* and if you did I would be very grateful if you could write a review. I'd love to hear what you think, and it makes such a difference helping new readers to discover one of my books for the first time.

I love hearing from my readers – you can get in touch on my Facebook page, through Goodreads or my website.

Thanks,
Kate

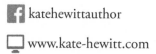

katehewittauthor

www.kate-hewitt.com

ACKNOWLEDGMENTS

The Heart Goes On has gone through many versions, and I'm grateful for the help I've had in bringing it to its current form. I'm especially grateful to my mother, Margot Berry, who first told me about the MacDougalls when I was a little girl, and even took our whole family on a trip to Ardnamurchan to visit Mingarry Castle, then a ruin, now, amazingly, a hotel. She also passed on typewritten copies of the original letters between Harriet and Allan, and gave me a love of our family history. Thanks, Mom! I love you!

I also want to thank the Bookouture team who are all so amazing and generous with their time and expertise. Firstly, my lovely editor Isobel, who has always been so encouraging. Also my copyeditor Natasha Hodgson, who really helped to shape this version of the manuscript. Thank you also to Kim, Noelle, and Sarah, who are all so unfailingly wonderful with their marketing efforts, as well as Alex H, Alex C, Leodora, Peta, Radhika, and many others whose time and talents invested in this book I'm not even aware of! I wouldn't want to be with any other publisher.

Lastly, thank you to all the readers who have loved the stories of the MacDougalls and Campbells over the years. I have written many, many books, and this series has always generated the most interest and affection, so I'm very grateful that readers have resonated with my ancestors' story almost as much as I have!

CPSIA information can be obtained
at www.ICGtesting.com
Printed in the USA
LVHW112247191021
700918LV00006B/188